Hat Dance

An Emilia Cruz Novel

Carmen Amato

Hat Dance is a work of fiction. Names, characters, places, and incidents are the products of the author's imagination or are used fictitiously. Any resemblance to actual events, locales, or persons, living or dead, is entirely coincidental.

Library of Congress Cataloging-in-Publication Data
Amato, Carmen
Hat Dance/Carmen Amato

ISBN
Ebook ISBN-13: 978-0-9853256-3-3
ISBN-13: 978-1492791775
ISBN-10: 1492791776

Also by Carmen Amato

Cliff Diver: A Detective Emilia Cruz Novel

Hat Dance: A Detective Emilia Cruz Novel

Diablo Nights: A Detective Emilia Cruz Novel

Made in Acapulco: The Detective Emilia Cruz Stories

The Hidden Light of Mexico City

The thief thinks that all men are thieves.

Mexican proverb

Chapter 1

"I never thought we'd be able to close down the casino," Emilia Cruz Encinos said. "Much less do it in only three months."

Kurt Rucker poured them both more wine from the bottle of Monte Xanic cabernet. "Three months isn't exactly fast, Em," he said.

"Maybe not in *El Norte*," Emilia observed. "But that's lightning fast in Mexico. Especially when we're talking about the El Pharaoh. It's an Acapulco institution."

"May it never regain its glory." Kurt raised his glass, and Emilia touched her own to it. The crystal chimed, Kurt drank, and the flame of the candle on their table flickered, sending shadows across the restaurant's brocade walls and creating a momentary halo over his yellow hair. Emilia drank her wine with a surge of incredulity that she was here in this elegant place, with a *gringo* man in a suit and tie, celebrating an event she was sure would never happen.

"Another toast," Kurt said. "To you, Em. The smartest detective in Acapulco. Rico would be proud."

"I hope so." Emilia smiled over the rim of her glass, but the mention of her dead partner brought a lump to her throat. Rico and another detective had been killed during an investigation into dirty cops and drug smuggling that had led to the money laundering case against the El Pharaoh casino. The squadroom was far lonelier now without Rico's good humor and the over-protective attitude that she'd once found so annoying. He hadn't been replaced and his empty desk was a constant reminder of her loss.

"How's Silvio holding up?" Kurt asked. "You obviously haven't strangled each other yet."

Emilia put her glass back on the table. "He came through," she admitted. "Walked into El Pharaoh yesterday morning as if he owned the place, showed the closure order, and got the files out before the manager really understood what was happening. You wouldn't believe all the stuff we took out of there. Spreadsheets, money orders, employee records. Boxes and boxes of dollars, pesos, euros, you name it. Most of it probably fake."

"I know you don't want to hear this," Kurt said. "But you and Silvio make a good team. Brains and brawn."

"Franco Silvio is not my partner," Emilia reminded him, waggling a finger for emphasis. "He's a *pendejo* who makes me nuts."

Kurt laughed.

"As soon as Lt. Rufino gets organized, we'll get some replacements," she went on. "After everything that's happened, they owe me a real partner."

"I know." Kurt slid his hand over hers, stilling it against the white linen tablecloth. He had a tan but her skin was still a deeper café tone than his. "Dessert?"

Emilia looked guiltily at her empty plate. The El Tigre was a fancy restaurant, a close rival to the restaurant at the Palacio Réal, Acapulco's most luxurious hotel, which Kurt managed. If she'd been to more places like this she might have known that "fancy" meant minute portions. Despite it being a Saturday, she'd been at work that morning, wrestling the boxes of evidence from the El Pharaoh into some sort of order, then spent the afternoon in a kickboxing training session with uniformed cops in the basement gym of the central police administration building. By the time she'd washed up, pulled her hair into its usual high ponytail, dressed in her one nice skinny black dress, and driven across Acapulco to the Palacio Réal to meet Kurt, her stomach was growling. Her elegant dinner of broiled *corvina* topped with caviar and accompanied by a dab of asparagus puree had hardly filled her up.

Kurt leaned forward. "Maybe we should just see what they've got."

Emilia raised her eyebrows at him. "You never eat dessert," she said. A marathon runner and triathlete, Kurt was always in training. Not only did he look different than any other man she'd ever been with, he didn't even eat like the men she knew.

"I just ate a piece of chicken the size of a peanut," he whispered and squeezed her hand. Emilia grinned. A moment later the waiter had cleared the table, wheeled over the dessert cart, complimented their choices, and served them coffee.

They traded bites of Emilia's chocolate cake and Kurt's *flan*. Kurt stirred cream into his coffee and put down his spoon, taking a moment to align it with the edge of the table as if needing time to gather his thoughts. "Now that the El Pharaoh is closed," he said. "How about a vacation?"

Emilia blinked as she stirred her own coffee. "A vacation? On Monday we start on all the crap we hauled out of there yesterday."

Kurt opened his mouth to reply, but his attention slid away from Emilia and towards the front of the dimly lit restaurant. Emilia half turned and followed his gaze.

"Local celebrity?" Kurt asked.

"It's the mayor's security detail," Emilia murmured.

Six burly men in dark suits and earpieces fanned out as the owner of the El Tigre stepped towards the door. Kurt had introduced Emilia to him, a dapper Spaniard named Jorge Serverio who had bowed over Emilia's hand and complimented Kurt on finding the most beautiful woman in Acapulco. Serverio owned two high-end restaurants in Acapulco. Kurt knew him from meetings of businesses supporting the local tourist industry.

Emilia watched as Carlota Montoya Perez walked into the restaurant, followed by a dark figure obscured by the security detail and Serverio's effusive gestures of welcome. Carlota gave a tinkling laugh, and everyone in the elegant restaurant pretended they weren't watching Acapulco's enormously popular and photogenic mayor.

Emilia swung around in her seat to again face Kurt across the table. There was a 100-peso piece of chocolate cake on her plate, a gorgeous man across from her, and every expectation that the night would end with a shower together in his apartment before she left the Palacio Réal and headed home. The mayor's choices of restaurant and dinner companion were none of Emilia's business even if her previous encounters with

Carlota had left Emilia torn, captivated by the woman's dynamism yet repulsed by her political machinations.

"Have you ever been to Belize?" Kurt asked.

Emilia pronged some cake. "No. Why do you ask?"

"I've been offered a job there," Kurt said.

"A job in Belize?" Emilia actually felt her heart stutter. The fork slid out of her hand, spraying cake crumbs and clattering over her dessert dish. It ended up in her lap. Emilia hastily plucked the fork off her dress and grabbed her napkin. She scrubbed at the fabric, glad of a reason not to say anything for a minute or two.

They'd only been dating seriously for a few weeks, the relationship paced by the time constraints imposed by competing work schedules as well as Emilia's innate caution. The ever-present feeling of unreality at finding herself dating— and sleeping with—a *gringo* meant that she'd told no one about him, not her mother or her cousins and certainly not any of the other detectives at work. Despite a strong mutual attraction, Emilia still wasn't sure she belonged with Kurt. He lived in a world of wealth and advantage she only touched when she was with him. Tonight, for example.

Kurt pushed aside his empty *flan* dish. "Em, this was all set in motion months ago, long before we ever connected. Some headhunter in London got in touch, asked if they could represent me. They're always trolling for good talent and tracking who's who in the hospitality industry."

Emilia stopped scrubbing her dress. It wasn't stained. She put her napkin on the table. "You want to leave Acapulco?" she asked.

"When they called, I'd been in Acapulco nearly two years, longer than I've stayed anywhere since high school," Kurt said. His tone was one of explanation, not apology. "So I said, sure, let's see what else is out there. They sent me a few proposals that weren't worth the effort, but this one is—" He paused. "Well, it's pretty good, and I think I need to look into it."

"Kurt Rucker! Looking both dashing and serious tonight!"

Kurt stood and Emilia realized that Carlota had stopped by their table. The mayor, whom many considered the most exciting and enigmatic politician in the entire state of Guerrero, was a striking woman whose age could be anything from 25 to 50 years old. Jet black hair brushed her shoulders and framed the well-known face. As before when she'd encountered Carlota, Emilia was struck by how she looked just like those famous billboards. Both in person and on a poster, Carlota projected a vibrancy that was at once amazingly attractive and disturbingly forceful. Tonight she wore a white silk pantsuit, her nails were blood-red, and her escort was Victor Obregon Sosa, head of the police union for the state.

"Jorge Serverio." Carlota fluttered her hand at the restaurant owner who'd obviously been leading Carlota and Obregon to their table. "You didn't tell me that Kurt Rucker was dining here this evening. I've been trying to get him for my Olympic Committee." She arched her perfect brows at Kurt. "You're a difficult man to pin down, Señor Rucker."

Kurt gave a tiny formal bow. "My apologies, señora." He spread his hands. "I'm sure my schedule will be opening up."

"Have you met Victor?" Carlota lowered one shoulder so that Kurt could connect with Obregon.

Emilia marveled at Kurt's cool composure as he shook hands with the man that Emilia was sure had been involved in the drug smuggling mess that had gotten Rico killed. She had no proof, just her gut instinct. And Obregon knew it. Their last encounter some months ago had staked out the distance between them.

She stood up, too, twitching the tight black dress as Kurt introduced her. Serverio gave her another warm smile. Obregon nodded. Carlota pretended to be pleased to see Emilia and gave her the mandatory ladies' cheek kiss as if they were peers or even friends.

"You're looking lovely tonight, Detective Cruz." Carlota's eyes flickered from Kurt to Emilia but otherwise hid her curiosity well. Neither did she give any indication that Emilia had once turned down an offer to work in her administration.

"Thank you, señora."

"And making quite another splash," Carlota said with that famous billboard smile. "I heard that you were the driver behind the El Pharaoh investigation. Keeping Acapulco honest. I'm pleased. My statement played very well in the international press this morning."

Which is the only thing that matters, isn't it? Emilia hushed her thoughts before they turned into words. She managed a tight smile in return. "That's good news, señora."

"Lt. Rufino has started his tenure as chief of detectives with a bang." Obregon had dark hair slicked back from a high forehead and angular cheekbones that spoke of a thick *indio* bloodline. Emilia had only ever seen him wear black, and tonight was no exception: black suit, black silk shirt, striated black linen tie. There was a slight bulge under his left arm, and he exuded an aura of power and entitlement that matched Carlota's own.

"I guess that depends whether you're a gambler or not," Emilia replied. Carlota in white and Obregon in black. The queen and king of opposing chess pieces.

Carlota laughed, tossing her head to see who was watching her. Serverio chuckled thinly and checked his watch.

"Chief Salazar really made a case for Rufino," Obregon said. "All the way from Mexico City. Now I see that he's hit the ground running."

It was on the tip of Emilia's tongue to say that the investigation into money laundering at the El Pharaoh had been under way for over two months before Lt. Nelson Rufino Herrera ever set foot inside the detective squadroom. But again she stopped herself. There was something insidious behind Obregon's words, something Emilia didn't quite understand, and it made her reluctant to be seen as either for or against her new lieutenant.

"Lt. Rufino is settling in," Emilia said neutrally.

"The squadroom must be taking bets," Obregon went on. "Silvio's probably offering ten to one that he won't last a year."

Emilia didn't react.

The corner of Obregon's mouth twitched upwards in a half-smile that let Emilia know that he understood her discomfort with his questions. "The union will be very interested to see what Rufino's got in his bag of tricks. No doubt he has a lot to teach us."

"Victor," Carlota broke in, now obviously bored. "Can't you see that Detective Cruz has other things on her mind tonight?"

"Of course," Obregon said smoothly.

Carlota said something to Kurt, he said something to bridge what might have become an awkward moment, and then Serverio said that the mayor's table was ready.

"Enjoy your dinner," Emilia heard herself say. The little group moved off. Carlota and Obregon made a striking couple and heads turned as Serverio seated them in a semi-private alcove. Carlota's security detail settled into a table at the back of the restaurant.

Kurt held her chair as Emilia sat back down. "*Madre de Dios*," she hissed as Kurt took his own seat. "Do you think they're dating?"

"The mayor has not confided in me, Em."

Emilia grinned. "Are you really going to be on Carlota's Olympic Committee?"

"God, no," Kurt said with a grimace. "A summer Olympics in Acapulco? I just find it easier to tell her no over the phone than in person."

Emilia shook her head and ate some cake.

"What was Victor Obregon up to?" Kurt asked. Although this was the first time the two men had met, Kurt was well versed in Emilia's experiences with the union boss. "Why is he so interested in your new lieutenant?"

"I'm not sure," Emilia said. In addition to Obregon's interest in Lt. Rufino, his reference to Acapulco Chief of Police Enrique Salazar Robelo had surprised her; she'd never been sure of the nature of the relationship between the two senior police officials. They could be friends or foes. "Maybe they don't like each other or Salazar didn't consult the union when he brought in Lt. Rufino," she speculated. "But whatever it is, I don't want to be caught in the middle of it."

The waiter glided by with fresh coffee. After Kurt added cream and stirred, he reached across the table again and caught up Emilia's hand. "I don't want you in the middle of their mess, either. So take a break. Come to Belize with me for a week. We can check out this hotel together. Help me decide whether I want to manage an eco-lodge or not."

"Is it a good job?" Emilia asked.

Kurt nodded. "They're offering me 25 percent above my current salary. An actual house on the property, not just an apartment. And a new car."

"*Madre de Dios*," Emilia said again, stunned. He was talking about a small fortune, plus a free house and car. Kurt already made a hundred times what she did, enough to travel anywhere he liked and buy the latest electronics. He didn't pay any rent or utilities for his small apartment on the fifth floor of the Palacio Réal and ate most of his meals at the hotel for free. The money he made paid for a nice car and expensive clothes like the perfectly tailored gray suit he had on right now. Emilia's entire outfit was worth less than his silk tie alone. Tonight's dinner would cost him more than she made in a month, and he probably wouldn't think twice about it. Spend that much tomorrow, too, if he felt like it.

Emilia swallowed hard. "That's a lot."

"It is if money's the most important thing," Kurt said with a shrug.

"Isn't it?" Emilia asked. She and her mother had been so poor that Emilia had spent much of her childhood selling guava candy to tourists, and she knew she carried the scars of too many days spent frightened and hungry in the hot sun.

Kurt leaned forward, his coffee forgotten and his ocean-colored eyes bright with intensity. "What should be the most important thing, Em? Let's talk about that."

The perfect evening was sliding away, and so was Kurt. She should have known it wouldn't last, that their time together, punctuated by the guilty pleasure of half a dozen episodes of phenomenal sex in his efficiency apartment at the Palacio Réal, was never going to be anything more than something to look back upon with wistful longing. Kurt was an athletic, exciting lover, but more importantly, he was a fully formed adult with a range of life experiences she'd never encountered before. He opened her mind to new ways of thinking about her job, leadership, and connecting with people.

He was confident about what he wanted from her and had pushed for a level of intimacy that was new and scary. Faced with the unknown coming at her hard and fast, Emilia had simply sidestepped, never staying the night or making promises. He knew what she was doing—she wasn't that clever—and so he would simply move on. Find a better life that didn't include a skittish girlfriend and having to speak Spanish all the time. He was from New York, a former Marine in his country's armed forces who had fought in wars and lived in a dozen other places before making hotel management his career. There was nothing holding him to Acapulco, and she'd jumped into his arms without thinking about that aspect of his life at all.

"I can't help you make a decision," Emilia said sadly. "If that's what you're asking."

"I'm asking you to come to Belize for a couple of days." Kurt's voice wasn't loud, but it had lost its usual ease.

"This isn't a good time." Emilia slumped back in her seat. "All this paperwork from the El Pharaoh bust. And there's my mother . . ." She let her voice trail off.

Kurt searched her face. Emilia looked away. She could just see Obregon's jacketed elbow. The rest of the union chief and all of the mayor were hidden by the curved wall of the alcove where they were sitting. In the far corner, the members of Carlota's security detail were engrossed in their own dinners.

"Right," Kurt said. He tossed down his napkin, caught the waiter's eye, and mimed writing a check.

When the financial transaction was over, Kurt stood and pulled out Emilia's chair for her. They made their way to the entrance, where Serverio again embraced Kurt and kissed Emilia's hand. "And how is it, Kurt, that you managed to have this beautiful woman consent to be seen in public with you?" Serverio asked.

He was charming, and Emilia couldn't help but smile even as she wondered if his attitude would have been different if Kurt had introduced her at the beginning of the evening as Detective Emilia Cruz. Many people had a bad reaction when they found out she was a police officer.

"One of my luckier days," Kurt said to Serverio.

"And your dinner was satisfactory?"

"Dinner was exceptional, Jorge," Kurt said. "Both the service and the food."

"Good, good," Serverio said. "So now you are in need of some entertainment, no? The Club Soledad has a very nice evening show. I know because they take business away from me." He checked his watch and smiled. "If you hurry, you can catch it now. Or join me at the Polo Lounge. I always split my evenings between my two restaurants."

"What do you say, Em?" Kurt asked. "A little music? Or drinks at the Polo Lounge?"

"Maybe just a stroll," Emilia said.

The two men shook hands again, and Kurt and Emilia walked out.

They were in the old part of Acapulco, a few streets south of the modern downtown area where a white ring of hotels and condos encircled the most picturesque bay in the world. The El Tigre restaurant fronted a small street near the famous Plaza las Glorietas, in which tourists gathered several times a day to watch the famous divers hurl themselves off the cliffs at La Quebrada and plunge into the rock-strewn water below. The building which housed El Tigre had been renovated to accommodate the restaurant. The result was a blend of traditional Spanish architecture and modern glass panels that allowed for a stunning view of the cliffs.

Emilia clutched her Sunday purse with both hands as they slowly walked through El Tigre's front courtyard. The space was set up as an outdoor bar, the décor leaning heavily on bamboo, fairy lights and palms in giant *talavera* pots. A soundtrack of popular guitar music was a pleasant accompaniment to the happy chatter of the dozen or so people sitting at the bar. It was November; the dry season had taken hold, and the air was comfortably cool.

They crossed the courtyard, but once down the stone steps that led to the street, Emilia could take the tension no longer. She stopped walking and stood her ground on the uneven sidewalk. "Are we over?" she asked.

"Over?" Kurt echoed. "What are you talking about?"

"You're restless. You want to get out of Acapulco," Emilia said. "You said so yourself."

"I said I've been in Acapulco longer than anyplace else."

The lights of El Tigre's courtyard were behind them, and Kurt's face was lost in shadow. The evening traffic was light. A car sped through the intersection half a block away. The growl of its engine faded quickly.

"You also told the manager that the food was excellent," Emilia said.

"It was excellent," Kurt said. The quiet confidence that always surrounded him, and which Emilia so admired, was accentuated by the deliberate way he said the three words. "There just wasn't enough of it. What are you getting at?"

"I live here," Emilia blurted, like an idiot who didn't have any experience waiting out witnesses or interrogating a suspect or tricking someone into an admission of guilt. "I'm not going anywhere. So if you're heading off to Belize, let me know now. I'm an adult, not some *estupida chica* who needs you to string her—"

A noise like a freight train crashed through her words and an invisible wave walloped the air. Emilia instinctively threw out her hands to break her fall as the sidewalk heaved beneath her feet. Suddenly Kurt's arm was across her shoulders, pushing her head down and curling her against the pavement. His body shielded hers as heat raged around them and debris rained down. Emilia choked as the air filled with smoke and dust. Bile surged into her throat, tasting unpleasantly of overpriced caviar.

Chapter 2

The silence was deafening.

Emilia put a hand to her nose; it came away bloody. "It's the restaurant," Emilia thought she heard Kurt say, but she couldn't be sure. She raised her head as the pressure of Kurt's arm slackened. As she sat up, she saw that Kurt was covered in dust and fine shards. Glass stuck to his hair and the woolen fabric of his suit.

A second explosion rocked the ground and again Kurt pressed Emilia down, protecting her with his body. His weight let up a few moments later as dust and ash swirled thickly around them. Emilia righted herself and looked around dizzily. Only yards away, the courtyard of El Tigre was full of smoke. People stumbled down the stone steps, drunk with panic. A window shattered and pieces of masonry fell into the courtyard bar area.

Kurt pulled her to her feet. Heat pulsed at them, roiling through the chute formed by the entrance to the courtyard. Emilia's ears weren't working properly. She knew that people were screaming all around them, but the sounds were muffled, as if they were coming at her through thick fabric. She saw Kurt mouth the words "You okay?" and she automatically mouthed back "Yes."

He pulled her a little farther away from the entrance to the courtyard, her high heels causing her to stumble a little. Kurt stripped off his suit jacket, glass sloughing off the fabric as he dropped it on the ground. "Call for help," he said.

Emilia nodded before she quite realized his intention, but she got it when he moved away from her. "Wait a minute," she exclaimed, but the air was full of smoke and the rest of her half-formed words were lost in a fit of coughing.

"Make the call, Em," Kurt yelled. He ran inside the courtyard of the El Tigre, his white shirt clean, his body tall and powerful in comparison to the people staggering away from the entrance to the restaurant. They were unsteady, bent and retching, sooty from smoke and ash.

Emilia realized she was still clutching her Sunday bag and scrambled inside for her cell phone, her fingers thick and clumsy with stress. The emergency dispatcher on duty was someone with half a brain who swiftly repeated Emilia's badge number and message and asked a few questions to get an estimate of the number of people who would need emergency medical care. As more people moved away from El Tigre and she saw flames on the roof lick the night sky, Emilia made a second call to Silvio's cell phone. Despite the late hour, the detective answered on the second ring. He listened to her brief explanation, muttered, "Fuck, I'm there," and hung up. It was as good a conversation as she'd had with him recently.

Emilia stowed her cell phone and slung her bag over her neck, messenger style. She threaded through the people congregated in front of the restaurant. At least 30 restaurant patrons had made it out and were still in the courtyard; some were sobbing, others talked jerkily about what they'd just been through, and still others looked as if they would soon be in a state of shock. Emilia waded into the bedlam, knowing that people had to be pushed further away. She immediately started pairing the able-bodied with those who needed assistance, directing people to the sidewalk past the El Tigre. Her voice rasped in the smoky air as she shouted to be heard over the crackling of the fire and the bedlam of frightened people and the sounds of braking traffic. The street quickly became clogged as drivers halted to look at the billows of smoke or avoid people stumbling into the street.

As Emilia ushered people away from the restaurant, desperately hoping to hear the siren of the *bomberos,* she strained in the semi-darkness to recognize faces. A burly man who'd been one of Carlota's security detail stumbled by. Emilia grabbed his lapel. "Where's the mayor?" she asked.

He looked at her, wide-eyed and bloody. She saw that his little plastic earpiece had melted, burning into his ear and down the side of his face. The man was in shock and she helped him to lie down. The bartender from the courtyard bar came over to them, and Emilia pointed out the security guard's wound before stepping away.

A movement by the door caught her eye. Taller than the others, Kurt had his arm around a soot-streaked Carlota, supporting her on one side while one of her security detail held her up on the other. Emilia met them, and they moved beyond the courtyard before easing Carlota to the ground. The mayor's head was bleeding and she was unconscious. Kurt coughed hard, hands on his knees, then straightened and grabbed Emilia's shoulder as she bent over the prostrate mayor. "There are more people in there," he croaked. "Where are the fucking *bomberos*?"

Before she could answer, he wheeled around and ran back through the courtyard and into the smoke-filled restaurant.

Assistance was coming from people who'd been in the square. Someone knelt by Carlota's side, and Emilia heard the word "doctor." An older man, unscathed by smoke, began examining the mayor with obvious professional confidence. Emilia backed away and ran after Kurt, pausing at the glass-strewn but still relatively intact outdoor bar. She found a wet cloth under some metal trays and pressed it against her face as she plunged into the El Tigre.

Inside, the smoke was thick and her eyes stung. The floor was a sea of broken dishes, glass, and more pieces of things that had once been part of her elegant evening. The effort to inhale and call "Kurt!" was like drinking liquid ash.

Emilia heard a cough and plowed on in that direction, her eyes watering so badly she could hardly see as she fumbled her way through a tangle of tables and chairs. She slipped on broken china and linen tablecloths and chunks of tattered brocade wallpaper. She met Kurt coming forward; with one arm he was holding up someone Emilia identified as another member of Carlota's security team. Kurt held a napkin over his face with his free hand. When he took it away to speak, his face was so dirty as to be almost unrecognizable. "Somebody else is back there," Kurt said.

The security man's head lolled; he was almost unconscious. "Get him out of here," Kurt said. He made to transfer the man to Emilia's grasp when an explosion rocked the place and Emilia fell heavily, crashing into a broken table. The decorative stonework remains of the alcove where Carlota and Obregon had been sitting crumbled down around her. As she fought to get to her feet, disoriented by the swirling smoke and dust, the back wall of the restaurant collapsed with a cascading thunder of falling concrete. A fist of murderous heat again sent Emilia sprawling. The cloth pressed against her face clogged with dust and she gasped painfully to find some oxygen.

She heard coughing nearby and reached out. Her hand touched glass and fabric and she realized that a man was buried in the rubble, caught awkwardly under a heavy wooden table. Small tongues of fire danced in the fissures where the tabletop had split, fueled by a burning tablecloth clinging to one end. Barely able to see, Emilia clawed at the jagged mess with her free hand, frantic Kurt was the man trapped under the table. Heat battered her and Emilia fought panic, but it was a losing battle.

But Kurt was next to her, on his knees. He'd lost the napkin and held his shirttail to his face. The security guard was still with him, now at least alert enough to be pulling a jacket lapel across his own face. "There's somebody stuck under the table," Emilia gasped.

The air sizzled. Fire leaped from the burning cloth and streaked across the cracked surface of the table. Kurt whipped off his shirt, wound it around his hands, and wrenched the table upwards. Emilia pulled the heavy body free, and together she and Kurt hauled the unconscious man upright. Kurt gasped, obviously finding it difficult to breathe without the protection of anything covering his mouth and nose. He pantomimed heading for the entrance and hefted the unconscious man over his shoulder.

With the bar napkin still pressed against her mouth, Emilia grabbed the security guard with her free arm and forced him through the smoke, blundering in the direction she hoped was the entrance. Kurt followed her trail, carrying the other man like a sack of onions while coughing with a guttural choking sound that was as terrifying as the fire.

It was a journey through the mouth of hell. The elegant restaurant had turned into a maze of blinding smoke, full of things that shifted and snapped in the scorching heat. Emilia's eyes streamed and she could hardly see as she stumbled forward, letting go of the security guard to shove aside the blurry remains of chairs, potted plants, and chunks of wall. Fire raced them across the restaurant, spreading forward from the rear of the place, hopping from table to table, feeding greedily on tablecloths, curtains, and wallpaper.

Someone pulled Emilia through the entrance and across the courtyard to fresher air. With difficulty, she recognized another member of the mayor's security team. Someone else helped Kurt, taking the unconscious man from him. Kurt doubled over, coughing. His undershirt was streaked gray, his hair was coated with dust and soot, and his bare arms were scratched and filthy. Emilia dropped her napkin and held him steady as he hacked up black phlegm and spat it out.

Kurt wiped his mouth with the back of his hand and stood up. "Are you okay?" he asked.

"I'm okay," Emilia said. She gulped lovely clean Pacific Ocean air. As her teeth started to chatter, she looked around at the people lying on the ground or huddled together on the side of the street.

Carlota was conscious, sitting by the side of the security officer whose earpiece had melted, flanked by two other guards who looked dazed but still ambulatory, including the man Emilia had just helped out. Six had come into El Tigre with the mayor.

The doctor who'd helped Carlota was now attending to the man Kurt had rescued from under the table. With a jolt, Emilia recognized the rescued man as Obregon.

Sirens sounded and suddenly the *bomberos* were there, creating their own orderly chaos as the fire trucks maneuvered in the narrow street. People were shepherded into the square as hoses uncoiled and streams of water attacked the smoking restaurant. Emilia saw Silvio stride through the crowd, leather jacket swinging open to reveal his shoulder holster and gun, his badge on a lanyard around his neck. The combination of size, badge, and gun got him noticed, as it always did. Emilia hugged herself as she watched him use his authority to good effect, getting the scene organized and the emergency vehicles up on the sidewalk.

As emergency personnel started examining people and leading burn victims into the ambulances, Emilia slumped to the curb. Her hands and legs were a mess of cuts and dirt, a burn across the heel of her left hand was an angry red weal that would soon be a painful blister, and blood dripped from her nose. The dress was a total loss, as were her shoes. Kurt looked worse, but at least he'd stopped coughing.

Thirty minutes later, Silvio caught up with her and Kurt as they sat in the back of an ambulance breathing through oxygen masks.

"Cruz." The senior detective was a dense, hardbodied man in his early forties with hooded eyes, a perpetual scowl, and a gray crew cut. A blunt nose and scar tissue around his eyes betrayed an earlier heavyweight boxing career. "What the fuck were you doing here?"

Emilia pulled off the oxygen mask. The burn on her hand was encased in salve and a thick bandage. Her teeth had stopped chattering, but exhaustion slid over her shaky body like a warm blanket, and she knew it was an aftereffect of shock. "I'm fine, thanks for asking." She touched Kurt's arm. "Detective Franco Silvio, meet Kurt Rucker. Kurt runs the Palacio Réal."

Kurt discarded his mask as well. The hand he put out was streaked with blood.

Silvio shook it anyway. "I heard about you," he said to Kurt. "They said you got the mayor out. And the union guy. Obregon."

"Is Carlota all right?" Kurt asked, his voice still raspy.

"Looked okay to me, but they were taking her up to Santa Lucia," Silvio said, naming the city's most modern hospital. "Obregon, too."

Emilia put the mask over her mouth again and sucked in oxygen in an effort to stay awake. Usually, Silvio's presence was enough to keep her alert and annoyed, but tonight the competence and authority that the big detective conveyed was almost comforting.

"How many dead?" Kurt asked.

"Eight," Silvio said. "Three officers detailed to the mayor's security. Five restaurant employees."

"*Madre de Dios.*" Guilt competed with the exhaustion encroaching on Emilia's ability to function. Could she have gotten someone else out alive?

Kurt coughed. "Do they know what started the fire?"

Silvio shook his head. "You were here," he said leadingly.

"Something exploded a minute or two after we walked out." Kurt stood up. His beautiful wool suit pants were ruined. "Something big. Maybe a big propane tank for the stove. Could be faulty wiring, bad gas connection. Something like that. Second explosion right after. A third a couple of minutes later. But smaller, not like the first two."

"Fire department will look into it," Silvio said. "Somebody will probably want to—"

"I need to get out of here," Emilia interrupted.

"You feel well enough?" Kurt asked. "Maybe we should let them take you to the hospital, get you checked out."

"I want to go home," Emilia said, knowing she was moving rapidly from exhaustion to simple survival mode.

"Okay." Kurt helped her out of the back of the ambulance, shouldering aside the attendant. "Let's go back to the hotel."

"No, I just want to go home," Emilia said.

"All right," Kurt said. He bent over and coughed, his chest rattling. "I'll take you home."

From the depths of utter fatigue, Emilia realized how exhausted Kurt must be as well. "Silvio can take me," she said. "You should go to the hospital."

"I'm okay."

Emilia struggled to stay upright. "Go home and get some rest."

"Her car's at the Palacio Réal," Kurt said to Silvio.

"I'll send a couple of uniforms to pick it up," Emilia heard Silvio say.

Kurt walked her to Silvio's unmarked police sedan as the

firefighters packed up and prepared to leave the burned husk that had once been the exclusive El Tigre restaurant. Silvio bleeped open the door and Kurt helped Emilia into the passenger seat. "I'm proud of you, Em. You're fearless," Kurt said. He kissed her forehead. "Get some rest. We'll talk later."

She nodded as he stepped back and closed the door.

"*Jesu Cristo*, Cruz," Silvio said as he got behind the wheel. "You smell like a cigar factory. You're going to stink up my vehicle."

"You didn't smell this good on your best day," Emilia mumbled. She was asleep before Silvio drove around the corner.

Chapter 3

Emilia filed out of the church of San Pedro de los Pinos with her mother Sophia. As usual, Ernesto Cruz trailed behind. Emilia's burned hand ached, it hurt to take a deep breath, and her hair still stank despite two showers and masses of shampoo. She would have felt better if she'd been hit by a car.

But Sophia had been upset when she saw the bandage on Emilia's hand and started to cry when Emilia made the mistake of saying she'd been in a building that had been on fire. Ernesto had helped to diffuse the situation, distracting Sophia with talk of church and the social hour that Padre Ricardo always hosted in the church's tiny garden after Mass. Although Emilia knew that Padre Ricardo would understand if she stayed home, she pulled her hair into a twist, dressed in a long skirt that hid most of the scratches on her legs, and pressed her sore muscles down the street to church.

The dark-haired priest always greeted his congregants in the tiny garden as they left the church. Padre Ricardo Suarez Solis was at least 50 years old and was the center around which the social life of the *barrio* revolved.

Emilia gave him the usual greeting of a kiss on the cheek and heard him sniff. "Don't say it," she murmured.

"You've been cleaning chimneys?" The priest gave her a questioning look.

"Restaurant fire last night." Emilia held up her bandaged hand. "I helped get some people out."

"Emilia!" Padre Ricardo's eyes widened and he clapped his hands to his chest over his vestments. The priest had been her confidant for years, ever since she was small and had told the school she was an orphan living in the rectory in an effort to avoid Sophia coming to school for Science Day. Although he constantly had some church activity to organize, he was always available to talk. She probably would not have been able to get through the horrible ordeal of Rico's death and the events surrounding it without him. "What happened?" he asked. "Were you working?"

"I actually was out for the evening." Emilia managed a smile. "Nothing ends a date like the restaurant burning down."

Her mother drifted to Padre Ricardo's side. Sophia had on one of her flowered dresses with her hair loose and trailing down her back. Mother and daughter shared the same generous mouth, high cheekbones, chocolate eyes, and arched brows but Sophia's guileless expression and floral clothing often made her look younger than Emilia. "Padre, this is Ernesto Cruz, my husband," she said, introducing Ernesto the way she did every Sunday. "He was gone for a time but he's back now."

Emilia felt Padre Ricardo's warning hand on her arm. "Yes, Sophia," the priest said, his face showing nothing except pleasure at the encounter. "We've met before. How nice to see you again, Ernesto."

Ernesto offered a work-roughened hand to the priest, and lines furrowed out from the corners of his eyes as he smiled in acknowledgment of the weekly introduction. His face was tanned from hours sitting in the sun, working his grinding wheel as he sharpened the neighborhood's knives and scissors for a few pesos apiece. He wore a simple shirt and trousers, but they were clean and neatly pressed.

"If you need anything sharpened, you just bring it by," Sophia went on. "Ernesto has his grinding wheel set up and he can sharpen anything."

The pressure of Padre Ricardo's hand against her arm reminded Emilia of the futility in telling her mother that everyone knew that Ernesto and his wheel were available in the courtyard of their house. The house that Emilia paid for and furnished. The house that she could not bring herself to deny him, a broken-spirited vagrant her mother had found wandering in the market a few months ago. His name was Ernesto Cruz, the same name as Sophia's late husband and Emilia's father. That Ernesto Cruz had died in a car accident when Emilia was small.

This Ernesto Cruz had left a wife in Mexico City after learning that his sons had died trying to illegally cross the border into El Norte. He'd wandered south, eventually fetching up at the market in Acapulco. Emilia had sent a letter to the wife but there had been no reply.

Either Sophia couldn't understand that Ernesto already had a wife or had just decided to ignore the fact. Emilia wasn't surprised at Sophia's behavior; her mother's inability to deal with hard decisions or complicated situations had forced Emilia to become the adult in their household at an early age. In this case, whenever Emilia brought up Ernesto's marriage, Sophia either cried inconsolably or got angry at Emilia's lack of respect for "her father." Meanwhile, Ernesto blunted all of Emilia's attempts with the simple phrase, "Sophia's been good to me."

Padre Ricardo smiled genially. "I hear Ernesto's business is becoming very successful." He gestured to the table on the other side of the garden that was laden with coffee and juice and pitchers of *agua de jamaica*. "Why don't you help Sophia to a *cafecita*, Ernesto?"

Ernesto dipped his head and led Sophia to the table.

"He's here to stay, Emilia," Padre Ricardo said quietly.

"I know," Emilia said. Her bandaged left hand was beginning to hurt and she cradled it in her right.

"Maybe this is a blessing in disguise," the priest said. "You're gone so much, maybe it's good there is someone with Sophia."

People milled about, waiting to have a few words with the priest. Emilia made to step away, but he held up thumb and forefinger pinched close together in the traditional *wait a moment* gesture. "Will you do me a favor, Emilia?" he asked.

"Of course," she said.

"Can you speak to Berta Campos Diaz?" Padre Ricardo asked. "She's the volunteer at the refreshments table this week."

Emilia sighed. "Sure, I'll do it next week."

"Thank you for the offer, but the parish ladies have that taken care of." Padre Ricardo shook his head. "No, this is about her granddaughter. The girl is missing."

"*Rayos.*" Emilia usually tried not to swear in front of the priest, but today she was too tired and the word was out of her mouth before she could swallow it down.

"Yes," Padre Ricardo said simply.

The priest was one of the few people who knew she maintained a binder of women who'd gone missing in Acapulco over the last few years, victims of Acapulco's soaring drug violence or encounters with the wrong man. They were *las perdidas*—the lost. The binder currently held 51 names, women from the area whose lives had been reduced to a grainy photo and a sketchy biography. Most of their stories were sadly similar; they were young women from the poorest *barrios*, prostitutes, low-wage earners with little education. No one knew what happened to them, only that they'd disappeared one day and their families never knew why.

Emilia found some of them listed in Missing Persons reports, but more often she came across newspaper advertisements featuring a picture of the women and asking for information. When she could, Emilia combed police reports and the official records that were available to her in the hopes of finding out what had happened to those disappeared women. But closure was rare. The last woman whose picture she'd been able to take out of the binder had been found beaten to death by a common-law husband who was still at large.

"I'll speak with her," Emilia said. "I'm glad you let me know."

She gave him a quick embrace and moved off as another parishioner greeted the priest. Emilia located Berta Campos Diaz behind the table. She was a dumpy woman like a hundred others in the *barrio*, with short permed hair streaked with a few strands of gray and a mouth set in a perpetual grim line that spoke of a lifetime of hard work, early widowhood, and family tragedy. Emilia steeled herself for the conversation to come.

"Emilia!" A deep voice called her name and she turned to see her cousin Alvaro. He was a few years older, but they'd grown up together and she'd followed his path into police work. She gave him a hug.

"New perfume?" he asked and sniffed at her hair. "Charcoal?"

"Burnt cork," Emilia said. The only way to avoid having to retell the story a dozen times was to shave her head. "I was downtown last night and the restaurant caught fire."

"That restaurant near the Plaza las Glorietas that burned?" Alvaro raised his eyebrows as he saw the bandage on her hand. "It was in the newspaper this morning. They said that the mayor was there."

"She was," Emilia said.

"That was a very fancy restaurant, *prima*," Alvaro said. "What were you doing there? Were you with the mayor?"

His expression was a mixture of curiosity and cool assessment.

Alvaro had been a cop longer than Emilia but was still in uniform as a sergeant. He'd never tried to climb the ladder by taking on dangerous assignments, but sought out jobs that kept him inside the central police administration building where he'd gathered an ever-widening network of those who knew all the right secrets. The strategy had paid off; he now ran the police department's evidence locker in the main police administration building and had two junior uniformed assistants.

He'd been married for half a dozen years and his wife Daysi, who didn't work, was pregnant again. They lived in a sizeable house not too far from what Emilia could afford on a detective's salary, which was roughly double that of a uniformed cop in Acapulco. Alvaro and Daysi had furnished it nicely, and Emilia knew they had a color television, a computer, and modern appliances. Even a microwave. Daysi had a smartphone, too. Their son went to a private Catholic preschool.

"No," Emilia replied. "I wasn't with the mayor." She glanced at the refreshments table. Berta Campos Diaz was still there, pouring coffee and keeping the table tidy.

"So you were just passing by?" Alvaro probed.

"The mayor was with Victor Obregon," Emilia said, knowing her cousin would be distracted by this juicy bit of insider police information.

Alvaro's eyebrows went up. "Business, you think?"

"I don't know. They looked pretty cozy together."

"Was anyone else with them?" Alvaro asked.

"Carlota had her security detail with her, but otherwise it was just the two of them."

"The newspaper said the fire started right near where her security detail was sitting."

Emilia nodded. "Three of her detail died." The memory of the fire made her shiver and she hugged herself. "The place was a mess."

"The names were in the paper," Alvaro said. "I didn't know any of them."

Alvaro looked down as his young son pulled on his pants leg. He scooped up the boy, who leaned out from his father's arms to give Emilia a slobbery kiss. He chattered at her, telling her some preschool adventure, and Emilia pretended to understand.

The little boy squirmed, apparently done telling Emilia about school. "I guess we need to find Mama," Alvaro said, referring to Daysi. He raised an eyebrow at Emilia. "You stay safe, *prima*." Alvaro gave Emilia a kiss, Emilia tickled his son's chin, and father and son moved off.

Sophia and Ernesto were across the garden, her mother holding forth to a group of elderly ladies, Ernesto by her side as if he'd been trained to heel. Emilia slowly walked over to the refreshments table and got a cup of coffee. She added sugar and granulated plastic creamer and stirred. The simple motions made the pain in her hand flare, and suddenly she didn't want to hear the story of the grim-faced woman on the other side of the coffee urn. All Emilia really wanted to do was to collect Sophia and Ernesto, walk home, and take a handful of the pain pills the ambulance attendant had given her last night. They'd let her nap, and when she woke up, she'd get a newspaper and read the report about the El Tigre fire. Make sure her name wasn't in it. The only real defense a cop had these days against the drug cartels and their street gang disciples was anonymity.

She'd talk to Kurt, too. Hear his voice, not just the texts they'd exchanged that morning, to know he was all right.

Talk about this job offer in Belize.

Or not.

She put the community spoon back on its coffee-stained napkin and summoned up a smile for the woman behind the table. "I'm Emilia Cruz Encinos," she introduced herself. "Sophia's daughter."

"I know who you are," the woman said. "Padre Ricardo said you could help me."

"Are you Berta?"

The woman nodded once. "I'm Berta Campos Diaz. I live on Calle Tulum. The *sastrería*."

Emilia knew the tailor shop; it was only a few blocks away. "Padre Ricardo told me about your granddaughter."

"Lila Jimenez Lata." Berta's face was stern. "She never came home."

"Yesterday?" Emilia asked. "She didn't come home yesterday?"

"Eight weeks," Berta said. "Eight weeks ago last Thursday."

Emilia's heart sank. The longer a person went missing, the more stale the trail became. Eight weeks might as well be eight years. She mentally pulled out her well-worn list of questions. "Did you report her missing?"

"I walked all over," Berta said with a sniff that implied Emilia should have known. "I knocked on every door in the neighborhood."

"Did you report Lila missing to the police?" She knew Berta would not have enough money to call a private security company instead of the police the way a wealthy family would.

"Yes. They gave me this." Berta had a battered vinyl satchel with her behind the drinks table. She pulled out a carbon copy of the standard police report form. Emilia put down her half-empty cup of coffee and took it.

The printing was so light as to be virtually unreadable. Squinting hard, Emilia made out the basics. The date on the form was 10 days ago. The signature at the bottom was an unrecognizable scrawl.

Emilia tried to remember if the name Lila Jimenez Lata had come up in the squadroom and was fairly certain it had not. She might have been busy with the El Pharaoh case, but the detectives reviewed cases every morning, and a missing girl would have gotten Emilia's attention. "Exactly when did you see her last?"

"That day," Berta said. "She went to school and dance class like always, but she didn't come home."

"How was she supposed to get home?" Emilia asked. "Walk?"

"The bus," Berta said. "The driver is Maria Ochoa's boy and Mercedes always waited with them, so it was all right."

Despite the assurance, Emilia knew that many women disappeared around bus stops, victims of random drive-by snatches or unscrupulous bus drivers. She'd definitely follow up with both the driver and the dance teacher.

"Is there some relative she might be with?" Emilia continued down the mental checklist she'd used so many times before.

Berta shook her head. "No," she said. "The *pobrecita* doesn't have anyone else. Her father was my son. He was a good man."

Emilia nodded. The aftereffects of the fire had sapped her and she didn't feel strong enough to hear another story of bad choices, violent acts, or a gory death. Padre Ricardo had created a tiny oasis in the *barrio*, but Emilia knew it was an oasis encircled by danger. Yes, the tourists were still coming, filling the luxury hotels and dancing in clubs and sunning themselves on the beaches. But behind Acapulco's sun-drenched façade, Emilia saw a tightening darkness. She found herself swaying with fatigue and thinking about Kurt. He was her light in that murk.

Emilia pulled herself back to see Berta still standing with her vinyl satchel held like a shield. The woman's son was dead and her granddaughter was missing. People lived with such pain. The least Emilia could do was keep asking questions and not dissolve into an exhausted lump.

"Did she have a phone? Did you call it?" Obvious, but something she always asked.

"No phone," Berta sniffed. "No calling boys."

"You said she went to school?" Emilia asked. It wasn't

uncommon for girls as young as 13 or 14 to go to work if their family needed the income. Many dropped out of school after the mandatory six years and worked as *muchachas* in the homes of the wealthy, earning a few thousand pesos each month.

"She goes to school," Berta said. "The Colegio Javier. She has a scholarship."

Emilia knew it. Colegio Javier was a private Catholic high school for girls. Not Acapulco's most well-regarded, but certainly nicer than the public school Emilia had fought her way through.

"Friends?" Emilia asked. "A boyfriend?"

"Only girlfriends from school," the older woman said. "No boys. I don't allow her to be no *puta*."

Emilia was surprised at Berta's use of the coarse word, but kept at the questions. "Does she belong to any clubs? Do things with a church group?"

Berta nodded again. "She goes to dance class. And the Rosarians."

"The Rosarians?" Emilia asked. She pressed her aching, bandaged hand into the warmth of the opposite armpit.

"A school club devoted to the Rosary and the Virgin," Berta explained. "The girls collect clothes for the poor and toys for the children at Christmas."

"And the dance class?"

"Mercedes Sandoval's studio," Berta supplied.

Emilia nodded. She knew who Mercedes Sandoval was, although they'd never spoken. Mercedes was from the same neighborhood and was a few years older than Emilia. When Emilia was young, Mercedes had been a successful ballroom dancer. Emilia and Sophia had lived with Alvaro and his brother and parents, and it was always an event when they all stayed up late to watch Mercedes and her late husband win ballroom dancing competitions on television. Sophia's eyes had sparkled at the swirling fabric of Mercedes's dresses and her handsome husband's powerful moves. Emilia had recognized Mercedes once in a neighborhood shop, and the dancer still had the grace and athleticism of those days.

Emilia wished she'd brought a pencil and paper with her, but the morning was supposed to have been just a brief walk to church and then home again. "I'll need to keep this," she said, indicating the copy of the police report. "I'll come by tomorrow after work to get a list of her friends' names, where they live, any phone numbers she kept. A recent photo would be good, too."

"So you'll find her?" Berta asked abruptly.

Emilia was struck by how little emotion the woman had shown during their conversation. Berta clearly was a woman for whom tears did not come easily. Maybe she'd cried enough when she was young. Now that she was older, she knew that tears did not mend broken things.

"I'll look for her, Berta," Emilia said.

"You'll need my cell phone number," the woman said with a sniff, as if she didn't think Emilia could really be useful, and dug out an old-model phone from the recesses of the big vinyl bag.

Emilia keyed in Berta's number, pressing buttons with a forefinger to avoid aggravating the burn. There was a touch on her shoulder and Emilia turned to see Sophia. Ernesto Cruz stood limply by her mother's side.

Sophia nodded congenially at Berta. "Berta, have you met my husband, Ernesto?"

"*Mucho gusto*," Berta said without changing expression.

Emilia wondered how many times Berta had met Ernesto. Padre Ricardo joined the group and gave Emilia a knowing look. "I see that you two have discussed Lila," he said. "Emilia, I know that if anyone can find Lila, you can."

"Do you need Emilia to find something?" Sophia asked Padre Ricardo. "I'm sure she can help."

"Mama, let's go home now," Emilia said.

"Ernesto, maybe you can see the ladies home," Padre Ricardo said. Emilia gave him a grateful smile.

"Emilia's very good at finding things," Sophia repeated brightly to no one in particular as Ernesto steered her toward the church gate and Emilia fell in behind. "Just like her father."

Chapter 4

"Nice that you could make it, Cruz," Lt. Rufino said. He pointed to Emilia's bandaged hand. "Serious?"

"A little stiff," Emilia admitted. "But I'll be fine."

"Make sure the clinic treats you right," he said. "Let me know if they give you any problems."

"Thank you, *teniente*," Emilia said. She'd stopped by the clinic in the central police building on her way to the smaller police station on the west side of town that housed the detective unit. Business was slow that Monday morning, and in just a few minutes the nurse had rebandaged her hand and sent Emilia on her way.

He jerked his chin at the squadroom door. "Take a seat. We'll be starting momentarily." Lt. Rufino walked off down the hallway, his ever-present travel mug in his hand.

Most of the conversations with Lt. Rufino were like the one she'd just had: brief, to the point, and no longer than they had to be. In the few months he'd been in charge of the detectives in Acapulco, Lt. Rufino had made minimal efforts to get to know his underlings and usually wore an air of slight distraction, as if he was concentrating on a thorny work problem and could only lend part of his attention to the immediate interaction. He was in his mid-fifties, Emilia guessed, older by at least 10 years than any of the detectives and definitely old enough to be her father. He had a narrow face, a small moustache, and short hair that was thinning on top. He normally wore a dark suit with a white shirt, a skinny black tie, and a small revolver in a belt holster.

Emilia wasn't sure yet if she liked him; Lt. Rufino's distance from the Acapulco detectives made him hard to read. His door stayed closed for much of the day, although he didn't seem annoyed if someone knocked. He sometimes popped out to confer on a case or to fill his ever-present steel travel mug from the community coffeemaker in the squadroom.

But Lt. Rufino was competent, keeping the paperwork moving and assigning cases according to the rota system that had started during Emilia's brief stint as acting lieutenant after Rufino's predecessor, Lt. Inocente, had been killed. Lt. Rufino chaired the daily morning meeting—another of her initiatives—and quietly made sensible decisions when they needed to be made. Most importantly, he had a good relationship with Chief Salazar, who'd made more appearances in the squadroom in the last two months than in the previous two years, something Emilia figured would have been of interest to Victor Obregon on Saturday night, but she wasn't going to be the person who made it any of the union *jefe's* business.

She continued into the squadroom and tossed her bag into her desk drawer. The front of Silvio's desk abutted the front of hers, so that the backs of their computer screens kissed. It was a different arrangement than when she'd been partners with Rico and his desk was across the aisle. It was still there, empty, waiting to be given to a new detective someday.

Silvio grunted a greeting and slid a folded newspaper across their conjoined desktops.

Emilia opened it and her jaw dropped.

It was that morning's edition. The bolded headline proclaimed *Special Edition! Mayor Survives Assassination Attempt!* Right below was a photo of Carlota leaving the hospital Sunday evening in a wheelchair with a bouquet of roses on her lap and waving to well-wishers crowded on either side.

Emilia hitched up her jaw and scanned the article, relieved to find that neither her name nor Kurt's was in it. The descriptions of the fire and Carlota's narrow escape were lurid and sensational, and by the time Emilia finished it, she felt a little sick. The newspaper's sources appeared to be Carlota's office and the fire department, with heavy emphasis on the deaths of the members of the mayor's security detail and how people at the scene had heard multiple explosions.

She put the paper down, folded her legs underneath herself in her desk chair, and logged onto her computer. Her email inbox showed 38 unread messages, but she quickly navigated to the dispatch database, using the login that had been granted to her as acting lieutenant and never revoked. The Lila Jimenez Lata dispatch had been forwarded to the detective unit last Friday. She could tell from the update log it had been bumped around the system several times, passed from one uniformed unit to another before landing in the detectives' queue.

But at least it was their case now. Emilia massaged her hand around the bandage as her typing caused the burn to sting again. The shabby, crowded squadroom with its metal desks and green filing cabinets, the place that she'd called her place of work for almost two years, felt like a good place to be today.

Macias, the best-looking man in the room, was rearranging the main bulletin board, making space to fit in some new pictures, which Emilia realized with a jolt were photos of the burned-out El Tigre restaurant. His partner Sandor was sucking down coffee by the machine and giving noisy directions. Beyond Silvio's desk, Loyola, the bespectacled and bookish former schoolteacher, and Ibarra, his chain-smoking partner, were both at their computers, tapping on their keyboards. Gomez and Castro, the two most raucous men, were seated at their desks nearest the door, talking their usual crap while tipping their rolling chairs in order to bounce off the back wall, which was dented by previous efforts.

Lt. Rufino returned and filled his travel mug from the coffee maker. He said something to Sandor and then walked to the front of the room and stood by the single community desk that had open Internet access. "Listen up," he said, which was the way he started all their meetings. The room quieted.

El teniente took a sip of coffee. "It's been about 30 hours since the El Tigre restaurant near the Plaza las Glorietas burned down." He gestured at the bulletin board and the big pictures of the charred building. "Eight people died, including three of the mayor's security detail." He read off names from a piece of paper. "No word on services yet, but we'll all be going, in uniform, to pay our respects."

There was a snapping sound behind her and Emilia knew that Castro or Gomez was shuffling cards again.

"In the meantime, we've got orders from Chief Salazar to put as much as we can on hold and focus on the fire," Lt. Rufino said. "We'll proceed on the basis that this was an attack on the life of the mayor of Acapulco and will rework priorities and assignments to catch whoever is behind it."

Silvio retrieved the newspaper he'd given to Emilia and held it up. "Is this the proof that the fire was an assassination attempt?"

Lt. Rufino raised a hand, palm out, before the buzz could start. "There may be some things we don't know yet, but the mayor's office and Chief Salazar think this is a legitimate threat. They're bringing in an arson investigator from the national school in Mexico City."

Emilia's stomach tightened. This was serious. There were always jokes—based on suspicion, distrust, and active dislike between local institutions and any *federale* counterparts—about what happened when the *federales* got involved. Asking for *federale* help was generally a last resort rather than a first step.

"Silvio and Cruz will head up our side of the case," Lt. Rufino went on. "Liaise with Fire Chief Furtado and the arson investigator. Cruz was at the fire so she has the best insights." He pointed the steel travel mug at Emilia and Silvio, the metal catching the light from the overhead fluorescents. "I want you two all over that site. Run down every lead the arson investigator comes up with. Shake the trees. There's a witness out there somewhere. Gomez and Castro will take over the El Pharaoh case."

If Emilia hadn't been sitting on her feet, she would have jumped up in protest. Maybe the fire had been an attack on Carlota and maybe it wasn't, but the El Pharaoh was a solid money laundering case. To prove the case against the casino's management, they would have to comb through the records, compare serial numbers of seized money against lists of known counterfeit bills, decode the money laundering process by tracking bank account deposits and withdrawals. Rico had died because of the players involved in that case and giving it to Castro and Gomez would be throwing away months of hard work. Castro and Gomez could barely count their own poker losses.

She shot a glance at Silvio, her eyebrows raised. He jerked his head in an abrupt shake of caution. Emilia hunkered down in her seat, knowing what he was telling her. She'd had run-ins with both of the other detectives. She and Castro had more or less made their peace with one another, but things were still bad with Gomez. A few months ago, he'd tried to force himself on her and she'd sent him to the hospital with a smashed nose and broken ribs. Gomez had been humiliated and received a reprimand from the union as well. Complaining that those two couldn't cope with the El Pharaoh case in front of the entire squadroom would not be good.

"Macias and Sandor, you'll be the liaison with the mayor's office," Emilia heard Lt. Rufino say. The meeting went on for another 30 minutes. Lt. Rufino went through the top cases the squadroom was currently handling, reassigning most of the other cases Emilia and Silvio and Macias and Sandor had open to Loyola and Ibarra. At any given time, each team of detectives worked at least a dozen open cases. Four or five new ones landed on their desks every week and an equal number were relegated to the file cabinet. It meant that they spent little time on extended investigations. The revolving case load was made more unmanageable by the fact that they were down in strength by two detectives and that most of the cases were drug cartel killings that were almost impossible to investigate or resolve.

When the meeting broke up, a wad of paper hit Emilia in the back of the head. She turned around to see Macias crumpling up another. "Just how many people do you think want the mayor dead?" he asked.

"Like I know," Emilia said.

"Heard you and Carlota were there together."

Emilia scooted back her chair. "Sure. We do dinner together all the time."

"She wasn't with the mayor," Silvio said, not bothering to look away from his computer screen. "Had a hot date with Rucker, the guy who manages the Palacio Réal."

Emilia was already out of her chair and headed for *el teniente*'s office before she fully realized that Silvio was shooting off his mouth about her love life. She got to Lt. Rufino's door just as he was closing it. "Can I see you for a moment, *teniente*?" she asked.

"Questions, Cruz?" He ushered her in, closed the door, and went around the side of his desk. Before sitting, he placed his mug carefully on a cleared space amid the clutter of file folders, scribbled notes, file cards, and forms.

"I'd really like to stay on the El Pharaoh case," Emilia said. He hadn't indicated that she should sit down, so she stayed standing. "I know the most about the money laundering, I traced all the links that got us the closure order, and I've been working with the state attorney general's office to build the case."

"So you can brief Gomez and Castro." Lt. Rufino shrugged. "Make sure they've got your contact list."

"We'll lose a lot of time," Emilia said, knowing she had to play this one carefully. She didn't want to seem like someone who shirked big cases, nor did she want the new lieutenant to brand her as someone willing to bad-mouth her colleagues. "It's a pretty high-profile case," she hedged. "I know the mayor wants to make sure it goes well."

Lt. Rufino raised his eyebrows and the moustache twitched. "The mayor doesn't want to get blown up, Cruz," he said. "You of all people should know the danger she's in."

"Pair up Silvio with Castro and Gomez," Emilia countered. "I can handle the El Pharaoh case alone."

Lt. Rufino put his hand on the travel mug but didn't raise it to drink. "Are you afraid to go back to the El Tigre, Cruz?" he asked.

Emilia didn't answer.

"You'll be all right," he said. Part of his mouth drooped in the start of a sad smile. It didn't last, however, and his bland, distant expression came back. "You have to get used to living with your fears in this business."

"It's not that, *teniente*," Emilia started to say, but Lt. Rufino cut her off with a wave.

"Chief Salazar recommended you as my best scene-of-crime expert," he said. "I'm sticking to his recommendation. You're not working on anything else as of now. Castro and Gomez will manage the best they can."

Emilia rocked up on the balls of her feet. "One other thing, *teniente*. There's an unassigned Missing Persons case. A 16-year-old girl. You didn't mention it this morning, but I'd like to be assigned to the case."

Lt. Rufino blinked. "Did you not hear me, Cruz? You need to find whoever tried to kill the mayor last Saturday night."

"It's not a big case, *teniente*," Emilia pleaded. "I'm sure—"

"No one is disputing that there are other urgent cases," Lt. Rufino interrupted her. "But right now I'm sending any Missing Persons cases to the federal Attorney General's new Missing Persons task force."

Emilia gave a start. He was sending a local Missing Persons case from Acapulco to some faceless federal unit in Mexico City? "*Teniente*, I really—"

"You've got work, Cruz," Lt. Rufino said pointedly. "Dismissed. Close the door behind you." He adjusted the travel mug's position amid the papers and started reading one of the forms on his desk.

Emilia waited, but he didn't look up. She opened the door and left, carefully shutting the door as she went.

Silvio was waiting for her by the coffee maker, leather jacket on, impatient scowl on his face, car keys dangling from one beefy hand. Everybody else was already gone except for Loyola, who was still at his desk. "Telling Rufino that he's fucking up, Cruz?" Silvio asked.

"Thanks for keeping your mouth shut about my personal life, Franco," Emilia snapped as got her bag out of her desk drawer, chagrined at Silvio for talking about Kurt and at the way the conversation with Lt. Rufino had gone. She was mortally tired again, her hand throbbed, and once again she'd let Silvio press her buttons. "Looking forward to returning the favor."

"Don't call me Franco." Silvio heaved himself off the wall.

"Don't call me Franco," Emilia mimicked.

As they left the squadroom, Emilia let her hand lightly brush Rico's empty desk.

Chapter 5

The entrance to the courtyard of the El Tigre was draped with yellow *PROHIBIDO EL PASO* tape. Emilia heard Silvio grunt behind her as he bent low to step underneath.

The fire department had set up a temporary plastic shelter in the courtyard where the debris had been shoved to one side, blocking off the bar area. Without the people and the lights and the music, the courtyard was nothing more than a chaotic way station, and it was hard to believe that it was the same place Emilia had been only two nights ago with a yellow-haired man and dressed like a real woman instead of in her usual work uniform of jeans, tee shirt, black cotton jacket, and gun in a shoulder holster.

A young fireman in a dark blue uniform with his badge around his neck on a lanyard, like the two detectives, came out of the temporary shelter. "You two the detectives?"

"I'm Silvio. This is Cruz." Silvio cocked his head in Emilia's direction. "We'll let you know if we've got any questions."

The young fireman looked appreciatively at Emilia. Silvio glowered at him, making the other man take refuge behind his shelter's transparent plastic walls. The two detectives walked into the restaurant.

Blackened tables and chairs lay tumbled about, strewn with chunks of glass and pottery. Everything was covered in ash and soot. The walls were streaked with black, burned shreds of fabric hung from the curtain rods, and every pane of window glass was gone. The stone sills oozed smoke stains. Only the restaurant's chandeliers were still intact, their graceful metal arms covered in soot, fragments of glass stuck in the sockets that had once held whole candle bulbs.

A light breeze from the empty window openings stirred up ash that swirled in the thick, scorched air. A panicky memory of her nightmarish passage to the door on Saturday night pulsed through Emilia.

"Guess you won't be eating here again anytime soon," Silvio observed.

The snarky tone of his voice cut through the vision in her head and Emilia pulled herself together.

The back wall of the restaurant's dining area was gone, revealing the blackened kitchen and beyond that, a truck-sized hole in the rear of the building. Piles of detritus were on display in the bright daylight. Nothing had been cleaned up.

Only the bar, a curved expanse of mahogany, was intact. Emilia recalled that an antique mirror had served as a backsplash. She peered behind the bar, careful not to touch anything, and saw a glittering wet heap of broken glass running its entire length. Thousands of pesos worth of alcohol, all gone.

Silvio crunched across the room. "They said the mayor's security detail were all in the back of the place," he said questioningly.

Emilia nodded. "The mayor had been sitting over there," she said. They kicked aside glass and china from around the torched remains of the table that Kurt had pulled off Obregon. There were wet and discolored lumps that might have been the remains of Kurt's shirt, or maybe the tablecloth. "Obregon got caught under the table and Kurt managed to move it off him."

"Hell of a favor." Silvio looked around, taking in everything. Emilia knew that later he'd be able to recall in detail what they'd seen. More than once he'd surprised her by quickly discerning patterns, recalling bits of evidence, and connecting facts and theories.

Emilia saw three red body outlines painted on the rubble of what had been the rear wall. "The entire detail was together back here."

"Hey!" Two men climbed over the rubble of the back wall, both wearing the heavy canvas pants and bulky boots of firefighters as well as the latex gloves used at crime scenes. "Who are you two?"

"I'm Silvio and this is Cruz," Silvio introduced them again and held out his badge, his voice as forceful as that of the other man.

Emilia recognized the taller of the two men from official bulletins that had appeared in her inbox. Rogelio Furtado Marcos had been chief of Acapulco's fire department for several years. His presence underscored the fact that they were investigating an assassination attempt; the fire chief would hardly be there in person for an ordinary fire.

Furtado gestured with a gloved hand. "I'm Chief Furtado. Don't touch anything."

"You mind if we look at the kitchen and the back of the building?" Silvio asked.

Furtado handed them latex gloves, and they followed the fire chief over the rubble and into what remained of the restaurant's kitchen. Darkened twists of metal looked like the ghosts of sinks, pans, and the legs of a prep table. The overhead lights were gone; chains and cords dangled from the smoke-blackened ceiling where they'd hung. A long stove was strewn with debris, the doors hung crazily from an industrial refrigerator as large as Emilia's bedroom, and a heap of metal could have been anything from shelving to worktables. The floor was ankle-deep in sharp-edged trash, although a path had been cleared along one side. As Emilia looked around, she counted five more spray-painted body outlines. The walls were dotted with neon orange paint.

The huge hole in the back wall exposed a rear courtyard that was probably used as a parking area. A transparent plastic shelter similar to the one in the front courtyard was set up there and two firefighters were bent over a makeshift table. Emilia couldn't tell what was on the table.

Chief Furtado led them into the shelter. "My guess is some sort of firebomb," he said, pointing to one of the larger twisted bits. "Exploded near the kitchen door and set off the propane tanks."

"There were three explosions," Emilia said.

Chief Furtado looked at Emilia. "You the cop who was here that night?"

Emilia held up her bandaged hand.

"She was with Rucker," Silvio said. "Guy who got the mayor and Victor Obregon out of here."

"I heard he's former military," Furtado said. "*Norteamericano* special forces or something. Runs the Palacio Réal now." He looked at Emilia inquiringly and she gave a nod. Later, she'd find a way to make Silvio die a slow, twisting death.

"Most of the dead were probably killed by concussion and falling debris rather than fire or smoke inhalation," Furtado said. "Nobody in the kitchen went out the back. The ones who survived went through the main dining area and out the front."

Silvio pulled on the latex gloves and picked up one of the fragments. Emilia did the same. The small bits of metal looked like what they were: tiny, twisted servants of death. She brought the metal to her nose and sniffed at it, and was rewarded with a sooty ferric smell. She put it back on the table.

"Let's look around," Silvio said.

The rear courtyard was basically a parking area. It was large enough to accommodate at least three cars. The metal doors were the kind that swung open wide enough for a delivery van or a large car. A narrow pedestrian gate was set into the wall as well. Emilia crossed the courtyard and tried the gate. It was unlocked, and she went out to look at the building from the rear.

A narrow alley ran behind the El Tigre. The fire chief's vehicle was parked to one side, all but blocking the narrow road, but Emilia guessed that not many cars came down the short street.

She walked to the far side of the alley and looked at the building from that angle, trying to fix the scene in her mind. There were only three buildings in the block, all of which backed to the alley. The El Tigre was the last building on the left as Emilia faced the rear. The alley curved away before emptying into a wider street that wound downhill.

The El Tigre and the middle house in the block were both built in the traditional Spanish architectural style, with pale yellow stucco and red roof tiles. Both buildings, which shared a common privacy wall, were encircled by walls punctuated by wide car doors and a pedestrian gate. The last building looked more modern, with a whitewashed finish and square rather than arched windows below a slate roof. The alley ended there and the cross street ran toward the plaza.

Emilia recrossed the alley to the El Tigre's pedestrian gate and realized there was no latch or knob, only a keyhole. The gate was solid corrugated metal, the same as the car doors. If she stood on her tiptoes and stretched, she could touch the top where it met the wall's overhang. She shoved at it, wondering if it was spring-loaded. It didn't budge.

She jammed her finger on the doorbell, and a moment later Silvio opened the gate from the inside. "*Rayos*, Cruz," he grumbled.

"Gate locks automatically when it closes," she said.

She waited for him to make a smart remark, but he just ran his hand over the edge of the gate, finding only the keyhole instead of the expected latch. "The garage doors are the same," he said. "Anybody can open from the inside to go out, but you need a key to get back in. The owner parked his car inside. Gates were closed Saturday night when the fire trucks came through."

"He'd already left," Emilia said. "Gone to check on the other restaurant he owns." She hauled out her notebook and a pen and started a timeline. "We'll need to find out what time the owner came in, what time the gates were closed."

"Who else had a set of keys," Silvio supplied.

"An inside job?"

"Either that or we're looking for somebody who is eight feet tall and voted for the other guy."

Emilia looked up at the wall surrounding the rear courtyard. It was topped with the usual coil of razor wire. "Could someone have climbed over the wall?" she asked doubtfully.

"Be a big risk," Silvio said. "You want to be climbing over that knowing a bomb is going off in a couple of seconds?"

Emilia's hand started hurting again as they crunched back through the restaurant, the midmorning sun invading the empty windows. A trick of light and soot danced over the naked chandeliers, causing them to cast swaying shadows like the noose of a hangman.

Chapter 6

"This is a law office," Ramón Cisneros said testily. He was a tall, thin man with a sparse moustache, as if he hadn't enough testosterone to grow a real one but wasn't going to admit it. "We don't keep the same sort of hours as a restaurant and until Saturday the arrangement worked out very well."

"We understand," Emilia said. The middle building that backed to the alley was the law office of this pompous ass. "We'd just like to walk through, see the layout, and talk to the security guard who would have been here that night.

"The chauffeur," Cisneros said.

"The chauffeur was there?" Emilia asked.

"His living quarters are here," Cisneros said. "We keep the town car here. The house is in the next block and only has room for my wife's vehicle."

It was common for a chauffeur to double as a night watchman. Emilia raised a shoulder at Silvio and he nodded in return. Silvio hadn't sat down in the lawyer's book-lined office but wandered around the office, making a show of looking at the diplomas and law books while Emilia sat primly in a chair near the desk. Emilia knew that the senior detective's restlessness made Cisneros uncomfortable. It was a good-cop, bad-cop trick Emilia and Silvio had used before. Agitated people often talked to Emilia just to get away from Silvio.

Cisneros led the way out of his office, down a hallway adorned with small oil paintings of Acapulco's better-known cliffs, and to a small room where two women sat clicking away at computers. The room was small, and they were hemmed in by rows of filing cabinets. "Please show the detectives to Santiago's spaces and tell him to show them the rear of the building." He turned to Emilia and Silvio. "Detectives, if you'll excuse me, I have an important case that needs my attention."

He walked out rapidly. One of the women rose from her seat, and the two detectives followed her down a hallway and out into the courtyard.

It was nearly a mirror image of the rear courtyard of the El Tigre building next door, with wide metal doors for a vehicle and a pedestrian gate, both made from metal pickets.

"Do the gates have to be unlocked from the outside with a key?" Emilia asked.

"Or the automatic opener in the car," the secretary explained.

Santiago was Cisneros's driver, a compact man in his mid-thirties with short hair and a pockmarked face. He was polishing the large black sedan parked in the middle of the courtyard, wearing jeans, a long brown apron, and rubber boots to keep his feet dry as water from the hose bubbled over the stone driveway.

The secretary's face pinched when she saw the water. "Turn off that hose," she snapped. "Señor Cisneros isn't going to want to hear that you waste so much water."

The chauffeur shuffled over to the spigot and turned it off.

"The police have some questions for you," the secretary said. "When they're done, you can go get your lunch at the shop."

"I'm Detective Silvio," Silvio said and flashed his badge. "This is Detective Cruz." He jerked his chin in Emilia's direction. "We want to ask you some questions about the fire at the El Tigre last Saturday night.

"I don't know anything about that," the chauffeur mumbled.

"Sure," Silvio agreed. He moved past Santiago to a small structure built up against the courtyard wall. "Do you live here?"

"Yes." Santiago watched Silvio.

"Were you here Saturday night?" Emilia asked.

The chauffeur spun around to look at Emilia. "Yes."

"Alone?" Silvio interjected.

"Yes, sure," Santiago said, turning back to Silvio before moving away to coil up the hose. The secretary folded her arms, face tight with disapproval.

Emilia exchanged glances with Silvio.

"So you were here when the fire started." Silvio let his

voice form it into a question.

Santiago shrugged, his back to both detectives. "I guess."

"What did you see?"

"Nothing. I was watching television in my room." Santiago wrestled a kink out of the hose.

"Nothing?" Emilia asked. "It was pretty loud."

Santiago kept his eyes on the hose. "I heard sirens, that's all."

"What did you watch?" Silvio said casually. He took out a notebook from his inside jacket pocket.

Santiago risked another look at the secretary. She continued her sour lemon act. "When?" he asked.

"When you were watching television the night of the El Tigre fire." Silvio walked over to the chauffeur and put his foot on the coil of hose.

The secretary stiffened and Emilia nearly snorted.

Santiago stared at Silvio's foot. "What night was that?"

"Saturday," Silvio said.

"*Lucha libre*," Santiago said. "The *libre* fights. They show it live from the Coliseo on Saturdays."

Silvio nodded. "What did you watch after that?"

"I went to sleep."

"With all the sirens and all the noise?"

"I went to sleep," the chauffeur repeated.

Silvio shook his head and put his notebook back into his pocket. "Thanks, that's all the questions I have." He stepped back from the hose and turned to Emilia. "You got anything for him, Cruz?"

"No, that's it," Emilia said. "Thanks for your help."

The secretary escorted them back through the law office building, casting nervous glances at Silvio as if he was going to steal a painting or break something valuable. Emilia wanted to laugh at the woman's expression of relief as they walked out.

Her phone cell rang just as they were back in the car and strapping on seat belts. Emilia put her back to Silvio before answering. "*Bueno*, Kurt."

"Hey, Em." Kurt's voice sounded normal again, not raspy or hoarse the way it had on Sunday. "How you doing?"

"I'm okay," Emilia said. They usually didn't speak during working hours. "How are you? Everything all right?"

Silvio started the car and pulled into traffic. At the corner, he turned right. He made another right, pulled the car over, and let the engine idle.

"Look, I know you're busy," Kurt said. "I just wanted to check that you're okay. How's the hand?"

"It's all right."

"We didn't get to finish our conversation Saturday night."

"Can I call you later?" Emilia asked, belatedly remembering she'd promised to go over to Berta's house for more information about the missing Lila.

"Look," Kurt said. "Check your schedule and see if you can make it out to the hotel Saturday night. I'm leaving for Belize on Sunday. A couple of days there and the following week in London."

"Um." Emilia looked out the window. "I don't know." They were parked a block south of the El Tigre, on a residential street interrupted by a run of small shops. A scratched metal sign touted snacks, gum, and discount minutes for pay-as-you-go phones in front of an *abarrotes* shop. White plastic tables and chairs from a tiny restaurant spilled over the sidewalk. Most of the clientele looked to be laborers.

Kurt didn't reply. The phone connection was a soft hum. She wanted to see Kurt, see for herself that he'd survived the fire unscathed, pull off his clothes and ride him until they were both wild with the feel of each other's bodies. But they'd end up talking about the job in Belize; it was unavoidable. She was afraid of that conversation, afraid she'd break down, throw away her pride and beg him to stay. And afraid that she wouldn't, too.

Silvio killed the engine.

"I might not be able to get away from the investigation," she said lamely.

"Let me know," Kurt said.

Silvio suddenly leaped out of the car, slamming the driver's door behind him.

"I have to go," Emilia gabbled into the phone. "Saturday's

fine. Seven. The hotel."

She broke the connection as Silvio came back to the car, Santiago shoved in front and the unwilling man's arm held in an iron grasp. The chauffeur had traded his rubber boots and apron for black shoes and a navy cotton zip-front jacket. Silvio tossed him into the backseat and slid in next to him. Emilia hit the automatic door lock.

"You ready to start telling the truth?" Silvio demanded.

"I told you," Santiago protested. He was sweating and the pockmarks on his face were ugly and pronounced.

"You were talking shit back there," Silvio barked. "You were up to something and didn't want that old *bruja* to know. What was it? Or do we take you in for setting that fire?"

The man's eyes bugged in fear. "I didn't light that fire! *Jesu Cristo*, I got no reason to do something like that."

"You weren't watching television, either." Silvio's bulk filled most of the rear of the car. Emilia got up on her knees to peer into the back.

"Look, I don't know anything," Santiago whined.

Silvio slapped the chauffeur. The crack of his hand was loud in the confines of the car. "You tell me what you were doing last Saturday night and I'll decide."

Santiago looked at his knees, face flushed with embarrassment and the sting of Silvio's hand. "I'll get fired."

"What's the sentence for arson, Cruz?" Silvio asked.

The chauffeur lifted his head and looked from one detective to the other. His breath came in a little gasp.

"With eight people dead?" Emilia scoffed. "That's arson and eight counts of murder."

"You heard her," Silvio said. He took out his handcuffs. "You're fucking screwed, *pendejo*."

"Maria," Santiago blurted. "She's a good girl, you know."

Silvio jingled the cuffs. "Go on."

"Maria Garcia Lira," the chauffeur said. "She's a *muchacha planta* for the Cisneros."

"A good girl?" Emilia repeated his line, her voice laced with suspicion. "How old is Maria?"

"Old enough," he said.

Emilia leaned over the front seat and grabbed him by his jacket collar. "How old?" she snapped.

"Fifteen," he mumbled.

Emilia shot Silvio a look as she let go. She got a *what-did-you-expect* shrug in return.

"Cisneros know she was with you?" Silvio asked.

"No," Santiago said. "I'll get fired if they find out."

He touched the door handle and Silvio smacked his hand away. "So you snuck her in?"

"Yeah." Santiago tried to wedge himself into the corner of the backseat, away from Silvio's volatile presence. "Just for some fun. That's all."

"So you two were in your room off the courtyard?" Emilia asked. "Inside? The whole night?"

"Not the whole night. We were outside for a while." Santiago considered. "After we… you know… afterwards." He gulped. "I didn't hurt her or anything."

"Okay," Silvio interrupted. "After you fucked her dry you went outside."

"In the courtyard. Maria wanted to dance. You can hear the music from the restaurant most nights."

Emilia remembered the music, the lilting guitar music from a stereo, not a live band. She'd swayed a little as the wine had relaxed her, feeling sexy in her black dress, enjoying the spark of lust in Kurt's eyes.

She pulled in a lungful of stale air. The air conditioning was off in the car, and the combination of sweaty bodies and the sun beating down on the roof was making the interior uncomfortably hot. "So you went outside to listen to the music," she said. "What time was this?"

The chauffeur shrugged. "I don't know. " He blinked nervously. "Maybe a little before 11:00 p.m. When we went back inside the movie hadn't started yet."

"Okay," Emilia said. "It's a little before 11:00 p.m. You're outside. Listening to music. Maria's dancing. Anything else going on?"

Santiago looked miserable. Beads of sweat collected around his hairline and one trickled past his left eye. "A truck came through the alley. I was sort of surprised because so few cars are ever in the alley at night. Sometimes Señor Serverio's car, but I know its sound. This was louder."

"How did you know it was a truck?" Silvio asked. "Did you see it?"

"Maria saw it." Santiago wiped at the sweat. "She was over by the gate, and if you look through the slats a certain way, you can see out. She said it was a real big truck, but kept dancing."

Emilia bit her lip, the image of the young girl in her head. Dizzy with what might have been her first sexual encounter, maybe thinking she was in love with this older man who offered some crude affection and an escape from the Cisneros household. Emilia wondered if the young girl looked anything like the missing Lila Jimenez Lata.

"Did she see who was in the truck?" Silvio pressed.

"She didn't say."

Silvio handled the cuffs. "What happened next?"

The chauffeur darted a glance from Emilia to Silvio, obviously hoping to appease them enough to be released from the car. "The truck idled for a little while and then drove off. We heard a couple of big bangs, and I guess that's when the fire started."

"Did you see the truck?"

"No, Maria just said there was a truck and I heard it."

"How long between the truck driving by and the fire starting?"

"I don't know." He wiped his face again. "Not long."

"A whole song?" Emilia asked.

"What?"

Still kneeling on the front seat to face the rear, Emilia poked him in the chest. "You said you were listening to music. Did a whole song go by between the time Maria saw the truck and when you heard the bangs?"

"No, not a whole song. It was fast."

Silvio leaned back as if to give Emilia the floor. "So the truck goes by and Maria keeps dancing," she reminded the chauffeur. "You heard a big bang."

"Yeah. Like that."

"What else did you hear?"

Santiago shrugged. "We went back inside."

"You didn't go outside to look? Call the *bomberos*?"

"No." For the first time he looked abashed. "I wanted to do it some more."

Emilia clenched her fists. "Did you know the restaurant was on fire?"

Santiago shrugged. "We never did. Maria wanted to watch the movie, so I kept the television on."

"What did Maria say about the truck?" Emilia pressed. "It's a pretty narrow alley. That truck must have been right by the back gate. Maybe she saw faces, haircuts. Watches."

"We didn't talk about it." Santiago eyed the door handle again. "We were busy . . . you know."

"Think about it, *pendejo*." Silvio gave Santiago's shoulder a rough shake.

"Look," Santiago said. "I'm supposed to get my lunch and go straight back. Matilda will have my ass if I take too long."

"The way she'd get you fired if she knew you had Maria there Saturday night," Silvio said.

"Yeah, she's like that."

"Did you use a condom with that little girl?" Silvio asked abruptly.

"Um . . . sure," the chauffeur stuttered. His eyes darted between Silvio and Emilia.

Silvio grabbed the front of Santiago's jacket. "You been to Franco's, right?" the detective snarled. "A couple of weeks ago. Lost money betting the spread on Cruz Azul."

Santiago's eyes widened in sudden recognition. "Fuck," he breathed. "You're Franco."

"That's right." Silvio shook him like a rag doll. "And in a couple of months, if I hear that little girl is pregnant, you'd better be doing right by her. You know I'll find you."

He let go of Santiago's jacket, reached out, and hit the unlock button on the driver's side door handle. Santiago scrambled out of the car and ran into the restaurant.

"*Madre de Dios*," Silvio said in disgust.

Emilia drew in a few breaths and turned back in her seat to

face the windshield. The aura of violence in the air settled to the floor erratically, like dust motes, as she scribbled the times Santiago had given them in her notebook.

"I thought you weren't making book anymore," Emilia said when Silvio was behind the wheel again.

"It's got nothing to do with you, Cruz."

"I got a partner who's an illegal bookie? It's my business."

"I'm not your partner."

"Rufino thinks you are," Emilia pointed out. "So does Chief Salazar."

"Shut up, Cruz."

"You get in trouble, I'm not covering for you," Emilia warned.

"Nobody asked you to."

They sat in silence for a few minutes. Emilia felt Silvio's eyes cut to her. "We going over to the lawyer's house?" he asked. "To find the maid?"

The question was the big detective's version of a peace offering. It wasn't much, but she'd take it. "Yes. The Cisneros place is right around the block," Emilia said. "This time, I do the shoving."

Santiago came out of the restaurant carrying a paper bag. Silvio started the car and revved the engine. The chauffeur threw a wild glance behind him and darted down the street.

Silvio guffawed and eased the car into the mid-afternoon traffic. "Was that Mr. Hollywood Hotel on the phone before?"

"Speaking of." Emilia put her head against the seat and closed her eyes. "Stop gossiping that I was with him. You sound like some old lady. He's got nothing to do with anything that concerns you or anybody else."

"He's the big hero of Saturday night."

"Jealous?"

"Just chatting up my partner," Silvio said. "So if her personal calls get me killed one day, at least I'll know she was getting a good fuck out of it."

"I'm not your partner," Emilia said.

Emilia saw Silvio's jaw harden as Maria came into the Cisneros's kitchen, summoned by the cook. Another maid had let them into the house, a sprawling affair with a dramatic view of water and cliffs. When they identified themselves and asked to see Maria, the maid's face had registered outright fear. She led them through a corridor to the back of the house and the modern kitchen. Once she murmured a few words to the cook, she'd been instructed to find Maria and bolted from the room.

The wait was brief. Maria looked to be about 12, a flat-chested waif with a thick black braid hanging down her back that made her look even younger. Her navy blue uniform dress, with its white apron, looked two sizes too big, as if she'd inherited it from someone else. But she was a pretty thing, with big eyes and a full mouth, and she didn't seem nervous when Emilia introduced herself and Silvio.

The cook edged out of the room after a pointed "Thank you" from Silvio. He remained in the doorway. Emilia took a seat at the counter-height stainless steel worktable in the middle of the room. After a moment's hesitation, Maria sat on one of the stools by the table as well.

"We understand that you were out last Saturday night," Emilia started.

Maria clasped her hands in her lap. "It was my weekend off," she said carefully. Her diction was good, but her voice sounded as young as she looked. Emilia wondered how much schooling she'd had.

"You know Santiago, don't you?" Emilia went on. "The chauffeur who lives at the law offices."

Maria just stared at her hands.

"He told us you were there last Saturday night," Emilia said gently.

"Are you going to tell Señora de Cisneros?" Maria whispered. "She'll fire me."

"Not if you answer all my questions." Emilia heard the steel in her own voice.

"What do you want to know?"

"He said when you were there, you were outside," Emilia

said leadingly. "Listening to music."

The girl's face brightened. "Santiago had some beer and we listened to the music coming from the restaurant down the street. Santiago said he can hear it most nights."

"It was guitar music," Emilia said.

"That's right." Maria looked wistful. "Someday I'm going to be a dancer. I showed Santiago."

Emilia gave her an encouraging smile, as if that was a real possibility. "Santiago said you heard a car drive by when you were outside showing him your dancing."

Maria smiled. "A truck went by."

"What kind of truck?" Silvio broke in.

Maria shrugged. "I don't know. Dark."

"A dark truck?" Silvio pressed. "You're sure?"

The girl nodded. "Maybe. It went right by the gate and through the light on the outside wall. It was really big."

Emilia pulled out her notebook and started writing. "A big dark truck," she repeated. "As big as a dump truck? The kind they use for construction?"

"No. A regular truck." The girl shrugged. "Just bigger. A big army truck."

"An army truck?" Silvio came to the counter and leaned over it. "Why did you think it was an army truck?"

Maria looked at Emilia. "There were army guys in the back."

Emilia nodded as if this made perfect sense. "How could you tell they were army guys?"

"They had on army clothes," Maria explained. "All spotted like in the movies."

"Camouflage," Emilia said. "Men wearing camouflage in the back of the truck?"

"How many?" Silvio interrupted.

Maria looked at Emilia, who nodded encouragingly. The girl sniffed. "Two. Standing up in the back of the truck. Wearing their spotted jackets."

"Which direction was it going?" Silvio asked. "Toward restaurant or the white house?"

Maria made a brushing-away movement with her hand. "To

the restaurant."

"Did it stop in the alley?" Silvio pressed.

The girl looked confused. "Maybe."

"You were right up against the gate and you didn't see if the truck stopped?"

"I… I…" Maria looked at Emilia.

"Just think for a moment," Emilia said softly.

Maria shook her head. "I don't know. Santiago and me, we went back inside." She blushed to her hairline.

"Did you hear the motor stop?" Silvio went on. "You were listening to the music. Was the truck louder than the music?"

Maria nodded, her hands now twisting in her lap.

"Did the truck sound get softer, then loud again?" Silvio pressed. "Or did it just die away?"

"I don't know," Maria said. "We went inside."

"Did you hear a bang after that?"

"No." The girl sniffed, frightened of Silvio's blunt manner. "I don't remember."

"Tell us again about the truck," Emilia said softly, wishing she could punch Silvio in the head. "You said it was dark. How dark?"

"Dark blue, maybe," Maria considered. "Or dark green. Just dark."

"Did it have fancy wheels?" Emilia went on. Silvio folded his arms and watched.

"No."

Emilia asked every question she could think of, trying to pin down any distinguishing feature of the truck the girl had seen only briefly through the metal slats of a security gate. Every question was met by a simple "No," until the last thing Emilia could think of to ask. "How many doors did it have?"

Maria's face scrunched in concentration. "Two on each side, I guess."

"Four doors?" Club cab trucks weren't that common, and they had a close idea of the color. Emilia felt a surge of hope; this was something they could trace.

Maria nodded. "It was big."

Chapter 7

It was nearly 8:00 p.m. by the time Emilia could leave what in less than 12 hours had changed from being a relatively organized detective squadroom into a shrill, panicky, pressure-filled madhouse. Carlota's staff had assigned at least five different people to be the liaison with city police and another half a dozen to bring the investigation to the attention of her political party. Meanwhile, Obregon's role had the union stepping over itself in an effort to get involved, and at one point Lt. Rufino had to come out of his office and broker a treaty between a mayoral staffer and a union flunky. Chief Salazar had been called, and then the whole lot of them left for the central police administration building.

Emilia took a pain pill just to help block out all the noise. The late afternoon had been a waste of wrangles with Carlota's office, the union, and the state of Guerrero party offices, all while trying to run a trace on trucks with four doors registered in Acapulco and nearby areas.

When the city people and the union minions left, she and Silvio collected Macias and Sandor, and the four crowded into one of the interrogation rooms to map out a strategy. Over the next few days, she and Silvio would run down the truck, interview the owner of the El Tigre, and find as many people as possible who'd been at the scene Saturday night. Macias and Sandor would work with Carlota's office to create a list of everyone who'd known the mayor was going to be at the El Tigre late Saturday night, plus try to formulate a list of anyone who'd ever threatened her or held a grudge against her.

Emilia called Sophia and told her that she wouldn't be there to eat *la cena* before climbing into the white Suburban that she'd been driving since it had been confiscated in a routine traffic violation case. The vehicle turned out to have been rigged for drug and money smuggling. It had been taken apart and put together a few too many times so that it clanked when she turned corners. But only detectives got assigned cars, and clanky wreck or not, the big vehicle was a symbol that she was at the top of her profession.

She showed her identification to the guard at the parking lot gate, and he raised the barrier. Fifteen minutes later, Emilia pulled to a stop in front of the little tailor shop on Calle Tulum.

Berta Campos Diaz greeted Emilia with the same stoic expression she'd worn on Sunday.

"I haven't found out anything yet, Berta," Emilia said. "But I told you I'd need to come by and look through her things. Get a list of her friends."

"I remember." Berta stepped back to let Emilia in.

The bottom floor of the small green house was taken up by the *sastrería*. What would have been the living room housed two sewing machines, a rack of clothes, and boxes and dressers labeled with handwritten words like "zippers," "patches," and "thread." Emilia followed Berta up a steep staircase, ducking her head to avoid hitting the laundry strung across the opening.

The space at the top of the stairs functioned as both living room and kitchen, with dishes stacked on a bookshelf and a two-burner electric hot plate substituting for a stove. Next to the stack of dishes, a small television sported a rabbit ear antenna. A wooden table and matching chairs occupied center stage. The bathroom door was open and a coffee maker was on the floor, connected to an outlet by means of a power cord that snaked around the doorway. The walls were plain beige and decorated with a large canvas reproduction of the Virgin of Guadalupe. The floral curtains were worn but clean.

Berta crossed the space and opened a door next to the bathroom. Emilia followed her into a bedroom with a neatly made twin bed. A large crucifix competed for wall space with magazine pictures of Mexican *telenovela* actresses and Latina Hollywood stars. The small desk angled into a corner was piled with magazines and school notebooks.

"This looks like a teenager's room," Emilia said with a smile.

"You can look." Berta gave a shrug as if to say Emilia would be better served looking for Lila on random streets than in her bedroom. "It's all here."

A pocket-sized closet revealed two navy blue skirts and two white polo shirts with a school logo, plus a couple of dresses and blouses hanging from a metal pipe next to a jacket with the same school crest and a navy cardigan. A box held shorts, underwear, and a pair of cotton pants. Black rubber-soled school shoes were lined up neatly next to two pairs of dressy sandals. Blankets were folded on a shelf above the pipe.

"Is this everything?" Emilia asked. "You said she took a dance class? Where are her dance clothes? Or her school backpack?"

"She had it all with her when she disappeared. When she didn't come home," Berta said from the doorway as Emilia rifled through the clothes to find anything in the pockets. "I didn't want her to take that class. All she did was learn how to show off. And now this."

Emilia backed out of the closet to see Berta with her arms crossed, her mouth drawn into a scowl reminiscent of Silvio on a hot day. "What about jeans?" Emilia pressed. "Tops? Makeup? Nail polish?"

"I told you," Berta said. "I don't allow Lila to be no *puta*. No makeup. No boys."

No fun. "Okay," Emilia said. "Can you find me a recent photo of Lila while I look through her desk?"

Berta sniffed and left.

The desk yielded little that would help. Glossy teen magazines, two with pages torn out and ostensibly now on the wall. A dictionary and a sheaf of small blank maps, the kind that every school in Mexico seemed to require. Notebooks, math worksheets, a blank permission slip for a school trip. Pens and pencils tangled with cheap rosary beads in the single desk drawer. There wasn't any makeup, notes from giggly friends, or those colorful rubber bracelets Emilia saw every other kid wearing. No mirror, either.

Emilia rifled through the papers again. A smudge of pink lacquer caught her eyes. Emilia rubbed at it. It was almost certainly nail polish.

She went through the closet a second time and looked under

the bed. The floor was clean and bare. Emilia ran her right hand between the bed and the walls and again between the mattress and the wooden platform it sat on. Her finger touched something.

She pulled out a small zippered pouch and a magazine. Tucking the magazine under her arm, she opened the pouch to find a tube of lipstick, pink nail polish, an eyeliner pencil, and an eye shadow compact with most of the colors used up. She put down the pouch, glanced at the magazine, and nearly dropped it in surprise.

The woman on the cover had melon-sized breasts and a black leather thong. The headline promised Real Ass and Easy Bitches. As Emilia rifled through the pages, wincing at the raw poses, a photo strip with four images slithered out.

Tucking the magazine under her arm again, Emilia studied the photo strip. It was the kind taken in an arcade photo booth for 20 pesos: four color images of a girl with short dark hair and a handsome boy—a young man, really—with their arms around each other. They were laughing into the camera. The boy had perfect white teeth and high cheekbones and the same coal-black hair as the girl. He wore a bright blue polo shirt and his arms were well-muscled. The girl was stunning in an exotic sort of way, the sort of beauty that the society pages captured at parties and on fashion runways. She had on jeans and a pink satiny halter top, and her smile was genuine in all four images.

Emilia heard Berta moving around in the other room. Instinctively, Emilia shoved the porn magazine inside one of the notebooks on the desk, in the process catching the bandage on her left hand in the spiral binding. The burn gave a momentary throb that spiraled up Emilia's arm.

Berta came in and gave Emilia a photo and a piece of paper with several names written on it. "Lila's school picture. And her friends."

Lila Jimenez Lata was even more striking than in the photo strip, with sleek black hair worn in a chin-length bob with bangs. Her eyes were big and slightly hooded, giving the girl a sultry Asian look despite her youth. "How old is this picture?" Emilia asked, breathing deep to counter the pain in her hand.

"Just a few weeks ago," Berta said.

Emilia held out the photo strip, which, if the length of Lila's hair was any indication, had been taken several months before the school picture. "Who is this in the picture with Lila?" Emilia asked.

Berta stared at the picture. Her lips twitched as if she couldn't control them, and in that moment Emilia knew the older woman was going to lie.

"I don't know," Berta said.

"Lila's boyfriend?" Emilia asked.

"He's no one important," Berta said.

Emilia sat down on the bed. It was late, people had been either lying or insanely stupid all day, and her hand hurt. "Do you really want my help, Berta?" she asked.

Berta looked confused. "Padre Ricardo said you'd help."

"Why should I help if you're going to lie to me?"

"He's not important," Berta insisted.

Emilia stood and dropped the school photo, list of names, and photo strip on the bed. "Well, good luck. I hope you find her. I really do."

Berta blinked. "You're done?"

"I have a job," Emilia said angrily. "I don't have time for games."

She let the silence draw out.

Berta's face tightened. "He's Yolanda's boy," she muttered.

"Who's Yolanda?" Emilia asked a little too loudly.

"Lila's mother," Berta said. "But the boy isn't the child of my Enrique. She never even knew his father. A bastard boy. Wild."

Emilia picked up the photo strip again. Only now did she see the resemblance between the boy in the photo strip and Lila. They were half-siblings. "What's his name?"

"Pedro Lata," Berta said scornfully. "He only ever had his mother's name. And what kind of a name is Lata?"

Mexicans traditionally took their father's name as their first surname and their mother's as their second. More progressive Mexicans were dropping the second surname, but if the boy only ever used his mother's surname of Lata, which meant *can*, his unknown paternity would be obvious to all.

"Where is he now?"

Berta shrugged. "She left when Enrique died. Took the boy with her. Pedro was grown. Lila was just a little thing, barely in school."

"Do you know where he lives?" Emilia asked.

Berta gave her head a stiff shake.

Emilia considered what Berta had said. "Does Lila see her mother, too?"

"No!" Berta nearly spat the word. "She's dead. Lila knows she's dead." The older woman exhaled sharply as she poked at the photo strip. "Maybe she saw him once. No more. He's dirt."

Hidden makeup, pink nail polish, porn magazines, visiting a wild half-brother. Lila Jimenez Lata was coming into sharper relief. But Emilia was fairly sure that the picture she was gaining of the teenager wasn't the one her grandmother would acknowledge.

She saw Berta's eyes go to the zippered makeup pouch on the bed. "That's mine," Emilia heard herself say. She tucked it into her bag along with the pictures and added the spiral notebook with the magazine hidden inside. "I'll be looking for her, Berta. But you call me if you think of anything else that will be useful."

Berta nodded and led the way down the stairs.

Emilia's bag felt heavier than it should, given the few things in it, as she followed Lila Jimenez Lata's grandmother down the dark stairway.

Emilia threw herself on her own bed and tried to quiet her thoughts. The day had been an exhausting whirl, and random images kept passing through her brain like a slideshow she couldn't control. Kurt covered in soot, hands on his knees, coughing his lungs out. Silvio threatening the chauffeur in the back of the car. The waif of a maid saying she was going to be a dancer. Berta lying, trying not to admit she knew the boy in the picture with her missing granddaughter. Fire licked toward

Emilia, clouding her vision and choking her with smoke and heat.

Suddenly there wasn't enough air in her room. Emilia drew herself into a sitting position with her head between her knees. She stared at her blanket, gulped big breaths, reminded herself that she was home, she was safe, and that she had things to do. Laughter floated up the stairs from where Ernesto and her mother were watching television.

The dizziness and panic subsided, and Emilia dug out the porn magazine from Lila's bedroom. It was two years old. Less than 40 pages of grainy images, some in color but most just in black and white. The pages felt like newsprint.

Emilia wondered if Lila had been experimenting with sex. Or if a friend of hers had posed for the magazine. Or if Lila had.

Most of the pictures were amateurish shots of naked women in erotic poses or close-ups of couples having sex. A few were graphic group sex scenes taken from odd angles, although the participants appeared to be aware that they were being photographed. Emilia scanned the pages, looking for Lila's face. It was a relief not to find it.

There was a gentle thump on the wall, followed by the creak of the bed in the next room. Other than that, the house was silent. The television was now off. The creaking continued, a rhythm of soft chirps that meant Ernesto Cruz was in her mother's bed again. Usually the knife grinder slept on the living room sofa. But occasionally he'd slip upstairs, Emilia would hear a few minutes of creaking bedsprings, and Sophia would be wreathed in smiles for a week afterwards.

On one hand, Ernesto was married to someone else, a woman whom he'd deserted. He owed that woman an explanation, a divorce, something. But on the other hand, Ernesto helped Sophia stay in the here and now better than Emilia could do alone.

And Sophia was happy.

The creaking intensified, making Emilia think of Kurt.

Stay. Could she tell him she wanted him to stay in Acapulco? Would he stay? For her?

Maybe he would stay, bored where he was and resenting the loss of a more lucrative job. Or he wouldn't stay, and his leaving would hurt all the more.

Emilia fell asleep listening to the creak of her mother's bed.

Chapter 8

The arson investigator was younger than Emilia expected. His name was Lieutenant Antonio Murillo Gomez, and he wore a navy blue polo with an official logo. He had a bottle of water with him as he stood behind the podium. A slideshow of the burned El Tigre building was projected on a giant screen in back of him.

"As we were able to quickly deduce," Murillo said, "The fire was caused by two explosive devices, which left a discernible burst pattern of destruction and caused secondary explosions of the propane tanks used for an indoor grill." A picture of the wrecked restaurant kitchen slid onto the screen. He used a laser pointer to indicate the orange paint splotches Emilia had seen yesterday. The glowing red dot traced an outward path along the splotches.

"Recovered fragments were sent to the crime laboratory in El Paso and the preliminary report is already in," Murillo went on. He paused and drank some water.

The auditorium could easily seat 800, Emilia figured. She'd last been there two years ago, when Chief Salazar had shaken her hand, given her a detective badge, and pressed his lips together in an unspoken message of disapproval.

The presentation in the central police building's auditorium had started a little after 11:00 a.m. It had been slated to start at 8:00 but had been delayed as they all got conflicting text messages about the location. Emilia assumed that the messages were an online argument between the police and fire department over who was going to be in charge. She also assumed that Chief Salazar had won.

Both Police Chief Salazar and Fire Chief Furtado were seated on the stage near the podium. Lt. Rufino was behind Salazar. Obregon was there, not on the stage, but seated in the second row. Emilia had a good view of him from her vantage point on the other side of the auditorium. One cheek was a crosshatch of red scratches.

Several dozen seats in the auditorium were filled with union types, party officials, and minions from Carlota's administration. Emilia's side was filled with cops. Besides the detectives, a number of uniformed units had been called in to attend the briefing.

Next to Emilia, Silvio shifted restlessly. Macias and Sandor both had their arms crossed, as if impatient to get to dealing with Carlota's people.

A new slide appeared on the screen: the image of a dull metal egg with a handle on top. Murillo trained the laser dot on the bottom edge, where some numbers had been pressed into the metal. "We believe the grenades used were similar to this one. If the estimation is correct, they were from a lot manufactured in the United States."

"An attack on the mayor by the *norteamericanos!*" someone squealed.

The ensuing babble was quieted by Murillo's raised hand. "A lot of several thousand was sold to the Mexican Army two years ago." He paused. "Although the army isn't subject to civilian law enforcement, we'll be following up to discern if any have been stolen. We'll also be using resources to investigate possible black market sources of grenades."

Murillo wrapped up his remarks with some technical details and sat next to Furtado. Lt. Rufino came to the podium. He was smaller than Murillo, and there were a few awkward moments as he tried to adjust the microphone, swinging the metal arm jerkily until Murillo came and adjusted it for him. Lt. Rufino nodded his thanks and cleared his throat.

"Acapulco detectives developed our most promising lead yesterday." He cleared his throat again. "We have a witness who claims a vehicle of this type was seen in the rear of the El Tigre building shortly before the fire." He fumbled with something on the top of the podium and looked hopefully at the blank screen in back of him. Painful seconds crept by.

"What the hell?" Macias muttered from Silvio's other side.

Emilia felt a stab of pity for *el teniente* standing up there, clearly uncomfortable speaking in such a large venue, the faulty projector making it worse. She glanced across the auditorium at Obregon. He was smiling.

Murillo got up again and the screen filled with the image of a black club cab truck. Lt. Rufino visibly collected himself. "According to the witness, at least two men in camouflage clothing were seen in the truck."

He covered the type of truck, the large number registered in Acapulco and surrounding areas, and the methodology being used to connect the truck to any known threats or criticisms of the mayor. A citizen hotline was being set up so concerned citizens could call in with any information about a black truck seen near the Plaza las Glorietas last Saturday night. He didn't once use the words "army uniform" instead of camouflage; everyone there knew how easy it was to buy fake uniforms in Mexico. But the question of army complicity hovered in the air and had those from Carlota's administration muttering nervously.

Chief Salazar gave a nod as Lt. Rufino went back to his seat. For the next 20 minutes, the chief of police discussed enhanced security for the mayor's office, gave assurances that all available assets were being used to make sure she was safe, and promised that the perpetrators would face arson, murder, and attempted murder charges. It was a masterful performance, targeted mostly to Carlota's staffers, whom everyone knew would be leaking information to the media as well as making official press statements.

When it was over, the detectives waited, letting the over-excited city administration, political party, and union officials file out of the auditorium first. Obregon hung back as well. Emilia positioned herself so that Silvio was between her and the union chief and watched as Obregon engaged Chief Salazar and Lt. Rufino at the base of the stage. Even at this distance, and with all the people between them, the body language of all three was clear to read. Obregon's black-clad body leaned forward aggressively. Chief Salazar kept tapping a forefinger against the clipboard he held in the other hand in an expression of impatience. Lt. Rufino stood partly behind the police chief, arms at his sides, fingers twitching.

"Excuse me."

Emilia turned to see Murillo, the arson investigator. "Hello."

"You're Detective Cruz, aren't you?" he asked. "The detective who was actually at the fire."

"Yes."

He put out a hand. "Antonio Murillo Gomez."

Emilia shook it, liking the fact that he'd introduced himself without his rank and didn't feel the need to express his manliness by crushing her hand. A lot of would-be colleagues had learned the hard way that Emilia had a very strong grip.

"I'd like to ask you a couple of questions," Murillo said. "Mind if I walk out with you?"

"Sure." She introduced Silvio, who said he'd meet her at the car.

"So you were there Saturday night?" Murillo asked Emilia.

"Yes. We'd just left," Emilia said. "Stopped to talk just outside the entrance."

"We?" Murillo asked.

"My date and I," Emilia said.

"So you weren't there with the mayor?"

"No. Just a private night out."

"Did you notice anything odd, any people in the area who didn't look as if they belonged?" Murillo asked. "Somebody a little too excited, maybe?"

"No." Emilia rubbed her hand below the bandage. "I've gone over it a dozen times in my head. We went out. We stopped walking to . . . to talk. I remember that a car drove through the intersection."

"A car, not a truck?" Murillo asked. "You're sure?"

Emilia nodded. "According to the witness, the truck would have been going in the other direction. This car was probably Jorge Serverio, the owner. He left when we did. To go to his other restaurant."

Murillo tipped his head as if he didn't quite understand her. His hair was military short and bristly. "We spoke to him already. He says he wasn't there at the time of the explosion."

Emilia leaned against the wall. "Technically, that's right. He left the same time we did." The timeline was laid out in her notebook.

"Do you think he knew the place was going to be attacked?" Murillo's stare was direct and unblinking.

Emilia stood up straight again. "Silvio and I are talking to him later today."

She waited for Murillo to insist it was his case, he'd follow up, and that she could give him whatever she had. But to her surprise, he nodded and handed her a card with his name and a cell phone number printed on it. "Your date was Rucker, right? Guy who got the mayor out."

"Yes." Emilia felt her face get warm.

"I'll be talking to him, too," Murillo explained. "Anything I should know?"

He's leaving. He's moving to Belize and leaving me. "He's former military," Emilia said. "A *norteamericano*. He fought in Iraq and Afghanistan."

"I hear you went in, too. That took guts." Murillo gestured to her bandaged hand. "Doing all right?"

"Yes," Emilia said. "It'll be fine in a couple of days."

Murillo seemed like a decent guy. He was her age. Handsome in a thick, square-jawed kind of way. Observant and employed.

Put 40 pounds on him and he'd be Rico.

Chapter 9

The Polo Club was less serious than El Tigre but much larger. It catered to an exclusive clientele that had to present identification at an entrance gate before being admitted. It was only open in the evening, and this early in the day the place was empty except for two bartenders prepping the bar and several waiters setting tables with heavy silver flatware and dark green napkins folded into fans.

The vast space was styled as an Argentine polo lounge, with pictures of horses and famous players from the past. Most of the photographs were sepia-toned, and the padded booths were upholstered in dark green leather. The tables were pale wood parquet and the walls were papered in maroon tartan. A mirrored bar was at least three times as long as the bar in El Tigre, and almost as long as the mosaic-clad oceanfront bar at Kurt's hotel.

Jorge Serverio was still dapper in a navy blazer and camel-colored trousers, but he appeared exhausted as he led them to a booth across from the gleaming mirrors. The Spaniard was unable to hide his surprise when Emilia asked if he remembered her from last Saturday night at the El Tigre and let him know she was an Acapulco city police detective investigating the fire.

Emilia saw herself pass in the mirror. She still had on the grey suit, cream top, and low sandals she'd worn to the briefing. Her hair was yanked back into its usual ponytail, her eyes needed some mascara, and she felt drab and out of place. Oddly enough, in his white tee, jeans and leather jacket, Silvio fit in just fine.

They slid into a booth near the bar and Silvio lost no time in getting to the point. "The El Tigre appears to have been set on fire by grenades possibly stolen from army stockpiles," he said. "We're investigating this as a deliberate attack of arson."

"The news reports are true?" Jorge Serverio looked from

Emilia to Silvio across the table, obviously referring to the media's continued bold news headlines and sensational stories. "Someone tried to kill the mayor by burning down my restaurant?"

"Yes," Silvio said.

"Are you sure?" Serverio asked. "A gas leak, I thought. The connection to the stove."

"The arson investigator from Mexico City confirmed that it was a grenade attack this morning," Silvio said.

Serverio looked as if he was going to burst into tears. Emilia looked away.

After the big auditorium briefing, they'd gone back to the station for a meeting with Lt. Rufino. There were over 300 club cab trucks registered in Acapulco and the surrounding towns. Lt. Rufino had talked knowingly about the methodology they would use, apparently unaware of the fact that due to the lack of integration between vehicle registration and identification card databases, his so-called methodology was little more than a labor-intensive comparison project.

One of the bartenders came with three cups of coffee. Serverio thanked him distractedly.

"Can you think of anyone on your staff who would want to harm the mayor?" Silvio asked.

"No," said Serverio, appalled. "She's very popular. It is always a pleasure to have her visit one of my restaurants." He stopped and dipped his head, trying to stay in control. "At the El Tigre, she was always thanking the servers and going into the kitchen to compliment the chef. He'd trained at the Cordon Bleu, you know."

Emilia nodded, feeling her throat tighten. That morning's newspaper had contained short biographies of all of the dead, including the five-star chef.

"Did you know she was coming to the restaurant that night?" Silvio asked.

"Her office called ahead," Serverio said. "Maybe an hour before she came. We immediately reserved the semi-private booth for her."

"You say she'd been to the restaurant before." Silvio stirred his coffee some more. "Had she sat in that booth before?"

"Yes." Serverio's anguished expression deepened as he understood the direction of the questions. "Every time she came."

"Was Señor Obregon with her every time?" Emilia asked.

"I don't recall," Serverio replied. "He was the last time. About two weeks ago."

"Did anyone ask about him, either that time or Saturday night?" Emilia sipped some coffee, looking at Silvio over the rim of the cup. She'd looked up Serverio's business profile. He still maintained Spanish citizenship but had been in Acapulco for more than 15 years and his wife was Mexican. In addition to El Tigre and the Polo Club, he owned a company which provided restaurant supplies for numerous restaurants and hotels in the local area; it was headquartered behind the Polo Lounge. Among the three enterprises, he employed over 200 people.

"No. I always emphasized to the staff that they needed to be discreet about our clientele." Serverio passed a shaky hand over his face. "I still can't believe this. I have five dead employees. Everyone is frightened. My wife and I . . . " He trailed off, swallowing hard while looking at nothing across the room.

The conversation was stalling out. If it was an inside job, Serverio wasn't involved. They'd talk to the surviving members of the El Tigre staff, but Emilia had the feeling that if one of the restaurant employees was responsible—maybe they'd opened the gate or made a phone call—they were probably now among the dead.

"One last thing," Silvio said. "We have a witness who saw men in camouflage uniforms in the area behind the restaurant shortly before the explosion." He slowly drank some coffee.

Serverio clasped his hands together. Emilia watched as his fingers dug into his flesh and the knuckles strained against his skin.

"We know how popular camouflage is." Silvio put down his coffee cup. "But we're not discounting army involvement."

"I don't know anything about that," Serverio said.

Silvio nodded. "As the owner, I think you're entitled to as much information as we have. Of course, we'll have to ask you to be discreet. This is an active investigation."

Serverio nodded. His knuckles were now white.

"Señor," Emilia started. Serverio mechanically turned his attention to her. "You left El Tigre before the fire. Where did you go?"

"Here." Serverio relaxed. "Saturday nights are the busiest for both restaurants, and I split my time at the height of the dinner hour."

"Can anybody substantiate that you came here?"

Serverio looked affronted. "Of course." He turned toward the bar. "Alejandro? Can you come here for a moment?"

The bartender who'd brought the coffee left off slicing limes and walked over to their table. He was a handsome young man with an alertness that was very appealing.

"Alejandro Hernandez," Serverio said by way of introduction. He stood and motioned the bartender into his seat. "I'll let you speak in private."

Emilia watched him walk over to the bar and finish slicing the limes. She liked Serverio, liked the way he'd do real work instead of just ordering people around. Kurt was like that; she'd seen him haul boxes around a storeroom, polish glasses, count sheets for the monthly hotel inventory, and clear dirty dishes from a table. Serverio spoke to the other bartender and they both smiled, obviously sharing some joke.

Silvio flashed his badge at the bartender at their table. "Have you worked here long?"

Alejandro nodded. "About two years."

"As a bartender?"

"I started as a busboy. One night the bartender didn't come in and I convinced el señor to give me a try. That was a year ago."

"Any problems?"

"What do you mean?"

"El señor have any problems with his business?"

"No. He pays everybody on time. Never cheats anybody for their pay."

"What about other people?" Silvio leaned back and toyed with his empty coffee mug. "Anybody doesn't like Señor Serverio?"

"I don't know."

Silvio nodded. "You were working here Saturday night?"

"Yes."

"What time did Señor Serverio come in?"

Alejandro shrugged. "Around 11:30 p.m., I guess."

"Anything special going on that night?"

"Here?" Alejandro gazed around the room. "His wife was waiting for him. Came in early, around 8:00 p.m. Looked real upset."

"Upset?" Silvio frowned. "Upset how?"

Alejandro pointed to a small booth at the back. "She sat over there and ordered two whiskeys, neat. I'd never seen her drink like that. Plus, she looked like she'd been crying. Eyes all red. We all figured they'd been fighting or something."

Emilia scribbled in her notebook, thinking furiously. At El Tigre, Serverio had given no indication that he was on his way to see an upset wife. "They fight a lot?"

"No." Alejandro seemed sad at the recollection of Serverio's wife sitting alone with her whiskey. "When he walked in around 11:30 p.m., she jumped up and hugged him. They sat back there for maybe 20 minutes and then went into his office."

"You sure about the times?"

"Yeah. I was just starting the late shift when the wife came in. And Tina was still here when he came in, and she got off at midnight."

"Does he usually come in around this time?"

"Yeah." Alejandro nodded. "He splits his time between the two places most nights."

Emilia jotted the word *normal* next to the time in her notebook timeline. "Do you know if he has any connection to the army?"

"The army?" Alejandro shook his head. "Some of the officers from the *campo militar* come in to have dinner here sometimes. General Hernandez was here once."

Emilia knew enough about the local army presence to know

that Hernandez was the general in charge of Mexico's 27th military district which included most of the state of Guerrero. His headquarters was the *campo militar* in Atoyac, 30 minutes west of Acapulco on highway 200. "When was the last time any army officers were here?" she asked.

"I don't know. Maybe a few weeks ago."

"Any arguments? Any of them go into Señor Serverio's office and talk to him in private?"

"No." Alejandro sounded bewildered. "They ate and paid and left. Maybe four of them with ladies, I think."

"How did you know they were army? Were they in uniform?"

"No, but they looked like it." Alejandro brushed a hand flat across the top of his head. "Military haircuts. And one of them kept saying *mi coronel* and the other one acted like he was a big shot."

Silvio looked at Emilia and it was her turn to shrug. The Polo Club was a high-end restaurant, and it would naturally attract senior officers from the *campo militar* as a place to take their wives or mistresses. She handed her card to Alejandro. "Thanks for talking to us. If you remember anything significant about Saturday night, please call."

They thanked Serverio and left the Polo Club. It was warm outside. Silvio tossed his leather jacket into the backseat before getting behind the wheel.

"Army?" Emilia asked as he turned the key in the ignition.

"Army," Silvio agreed. "Serverio was scared shitless as soon as he heard the word."

"You think he knew they were going to attack the restaurant to get at Carlota? Or Obregon?" Emilia replayed the scene with Serverio in her head, comparing today's clenched hands and shaky gaze with the effusive charm that had been on display Saturday night.

Silvio turned the car out of the parking lot. "Or him."

"Maybe Serverio knows something he shouldn't." Emilia started testing theories. "Overheard *mi coronel* plotting to do something."

"Attack on El Tigre was a threat?" Silvio took up the thread.

"Letting him know to stay silent."

"I've heard worse theories," Emilia said. It was as good as anything else they'd come up with in the last two days.

"The best lead is still the truck," Silvio said.

Emilia agreed and took out her notebook with the timeline as Silvio drove back to the station. Things fit a certain theory, but only vaguely.

"What if this isn't about Carlota?" Emilia thought out loud. "Or the army?"

"Obregon?"

"Yes." Emilia felt slightly sick. Like her, Silvio had been caught up in the drug smuggling investigation that had cost Rico his life. And like Emilia, the senior detective also believed in Obregon's complicity. The union boss was dirty, he played for high stakes, and going inside his game to uncover a killer could be a death sentence.

"*Rayos*, Cruz." Silvio gave a short, crude laugh. "Weren't you at that briefing? Even if we prove the cook committed suicide with two grenades he got at the Mercado Oriente, this whole fucking thing is going to be about Carlota."

Chapter 10

The rest of the day was spent at Acapulco hospitals, interviewing other restaurant employees and the families of the deceased, trying to find some connection to the mayor or the army and failing miserably. Even Silvio's normally gruff attitude was on a low simmer as they encountered yet another burn victim or grieving family confused by their questions and resentful at the intrusion into their personal hell.

The police radio crackled with updates on the situation in front of the *alcaldía,* the mayor's offices, where a pro-Carlota rally was taking place, apparently spurred by the press releases coming out of her office. Each time they got into the car and called in, they were advised as to new traffic patterns in the downtown area.

Back at the police station, Emilia and Silvio parted silently. She got in the Suburban, drove out of the police lot, and found herself meandering in the direction of home, her throat tight and her head crowded with disturbing scenes.

The sign for Mercedes Sandoval's studio loomed white and shiny in the twilight, and Emilia stopped the car. She looked around, surprised to find she was only a few blocks away from the church, in a small strip mall in the one of the better sections of the *barrio*.

A heavy security grille fronted a brown metal door. It matched the grilles over the windows. Curtains kept anyone from seeing in but showed that the lights were on. Emilia rang the doorbell and was rewarded with a metallic voice asking who was there.

"Emilia Cruz to see Mercedes Sandoval." Emilia had to bend to speak into the small speaker panel next to the door. The intercom had been an afterthought and was fitted into a gouge in the green concrete wall.

"Do I know you?" asked the voice.

"I'm a detective," Emilia said. "I need to ask you some

questions about Lila Jimenez Lata."

"Police?" Suspicion filtered through the speaker.

Emilia's neck twinged from her stooped position in front of the intercom panel. "Her grandmother asked me to help."

A buzzer sounded and Emilia was able to open the security grille. A key turned in a lock on the other side and the brown door swung open. Mercedes Sandoval moved to the side to let Emilia walk through.

The former ballroom dance champion was about 10 years older than Emilia, with thick brown hair plaited down her back and unruly wisps curling around her forehead. She wore a loose gray sleeveless tank, capri-length leggings and ballet slippers. Her bare arms were muscular. Despite the woman's innate grace, Emilia figured she'd be good backup in a fight.

Emilia gazed around the studio. It appeared to be just one big room, with a wall of mirrors and stereo equipment sitting on a chair in the corner. A stack of CDs sat on the floor underneath. The floor was pale wood strips, worn almost to smooth whiteness.

Mercedes held out her hand. "I'm Mercedes Sandoval," she said crisply.

"Detective Emilia Cruz Encinos," Emilia introduced herself. "I'd like to ask you a few questions about Lila. Her grandmother told me she disappeared after a dance lesson here."

Mercedes nodded. "Do you want some coffee? I just made some."

Emilia followed the other woman across the open studio area to a neat and comfortable office with a desk, a filing cabinet, a large sofa and a couple of mismatched upholstered chairs. Emilia sat down and accepted a cup of coffee. It was at least her sixth of the day. She'd lost count several hours ago, but knew it would be nearly impossible to sleep tonight. "What can you tell me about Lila?" she asked.

"Lila's been taking lessons for about two years." Mercedes settled into another chair and drew up her legs. "I don't think her grandmother likes it, but she always pays me on time."

"Tell me about the last day she came."

Mercedes shrugged. It was a fluid movement. "It seemed like a regular day. We had the class. The other girls got picked up. I walked Lila and Itzel to the corner and they got on the bus. Regular driver. He waved. And that was it."

"Itzel Martinez Ramos?" That was one of the names on Berta's list.

"Yes." Mercedes wrapped her hand around her coffee cup as if she needed the warmth. "Both Itzel and the bus driver say she got dropped off right in front of her house, and they saw her go in. But I know Berta says she never got inside the house."

"So someone's lying."

Emilia waited for the dancer to say who that might be, but Mercedes merely shrugged again.

"Is Itzel still coming to dance lessons?" Emilia asked. She got out her notebook and wrote *Itzel? Reliable?*

"Yes, although it's clear she's terribly upset," Mercedes said. "Lila and Itzel are close, although Lila can be a little devious, and I think Itzel is afraid of her." She resettled herself in her chair. "You know, the girl who wants to be as cool as the coolest girl but knows she never will? That's Itzel."

"And Lila's the cool girl?"

"Definitely," Mercedes said. "Very confident about her looks. That girl could own a room."

They sat in silence for a moment. Neither had finished their coffee. Emilia put her cup on the floor, fished the photo strip out of her bag, and handed it to the dancer. "Have you ever seen this boy? His name is Pedro Lata and he's her half-brother. Same mother, different fathers."

Mercedes held the strip up to the light, studied it, then handed it back. "No. I never heard her talk about any other family besides her grandmother. But maybe Itzel knows."

"This is going to sound odd," Emilia said as she replaced the photo strip in her bag. "But Lila had a very graphic porn magazine. Hidden from her grandmother, of course. Do you know anything about that? Maybe one of the girls posed for some pictures?"

"No." Mercedes wrinkled her nose in distaste. "If the girls

had ever talked about something like that, I would have remembered it. These are good Catholic girls, all going to private schools."

"Berta seems to have been very strict with her." Emilia picked up her cup again. The coffee was still warm. "Do you think Lila might have run away because she was unhappy living with Berta?"

Mercedes's face hardened. "I would have counted myself lucky at that age to have what these girls have. On my sixteenth birthday, I won second prize in a dance competition and gave it to my father. A thousand pesos. He beat me for not coming in first, then went out and drank it all."

"At Lila's age I was selling candy at the entrance to the Maxitunnel," Emilia offered. "Wondering if there was going to be enough money for me to keep going to school."

Mercedes leaned forward and held her cup out to Emilia. "Look how far we've come," she said.

Emilia touched her cup to that of the other woman. "To survival," she said.

"To us," Mercedes corrected her. "Smart women who have learned not to take anybody's crap."

Emilia grinned. She liked this feisty dancer. They shared similar backgrounds and attitudes. She wondered what Mercedes would think of Kurt.

"Why don't you come back on Thursday?" Mercedes asked. "You could talk to Itzel after class. She might be more honest here than if you talked to her at home."

"Good point." Emilia nodded. "I'll be here."

Suddenly the dancer's smooth face crumpled. "I hate this. I hate what's going on in the city. A young girl like this. And we all know she's not the only one."

"Fifty-one women missing in the last two years," Emilia heard herself say. "I keep a log."

Mercedes pressed a hand to her mouth. Even that gesture of distress was marked by grace. "*Madre de Dios*," she said softly around her fingers. "Just here in Acapulco?"

"Yes," Emilia said. "Padre Ricardo from San Pedro asked me to help Lila's grandmother because he knows I keep track of missing women cases. Maybe in time I can give their families some closure."

"Maybe Lila ran away to this brother," Mercedes said hopefully.

"And told a friend who just hasn't said anything yet," Emilia said.

Mercedes looked down and sighed. "That must be the best case scenario when you're looking for a missing girl," she said.

"Yes, it is," Emilia said.

Chapter 11

The video showed three men seated at a long rectangular table covered with a white cloth. Each man was fully clothed in black—black turtleneck, black face mask, black gloves. There was an unopened bottle of water on the white tablecloth in front of each man, as if the video was intended to look like a press conference. The backdrop was white as well. It looked like a sheet. A banner was strung across it with the words "LOS MATAS EJERCITO" handwritten in block letters. The banner was hung high enough to be clearly visible over the men's heads. The audio hummed with slight static.

Clustered around the computer screen, the detectives watched as the man in the middle began speaking. His voice was deep and he spoke slowly. The mask didn't have an opening for his mouth and Emilia realized that it was a military balaclava, the kind the army and navy wore in photos of cartel raids. It distorted the man's voice.

The one on the left played with his water bottle. He was the only one who moved at all. Emilia realized that even if the water bottles had been open, the men's masks prevented them from drinking.

"The army is terrorizing the city of Acapulco," the speaker said. "The army attempted to kill our beloved mayor, our beloved Carlota. We are dedicated to restoring order to the city and are declaring war on the army. We will kill any army personnel caught setting fires in the city."

Emilia decided he was reading an off-camera script.

The masked man's diatribe against the army went on for several minutes, the other two men silent on either side. They were all big, Emilia thought, as she compared the size of their hands and torsos against the water bottles. The black shirts they wore were all the same: a tight-fitting knit that showed off well-built, heavyset bodies. They were a black pyramid of vigilante menace.

The opening for the eyes in their masks was a slit rather than two eye holes. There was nothing distinctive about any of their eyes, and the openings were so narrow they didn't show brows above or smile lines at the corners. If she had to guess, Emilia would have said the men were all *mestizo*; their eyes were all dark brown and the skin around their eyes was caramel colored.

At the end of the video, the man simply stopped talking. The camera stayed on the strange tableau for a minute more as the men sat motionless. The video stopped at four minutes, 12 seconds.

"Looks like we've now got a vigilante problem," Lt. Rufino said.

"Only if they take action," Silvio countered.

It was less than 36 hours since the official statement that a truck and personnel in camouflage had been at the scene shortly before the fire at the El Tigre, which Acapulco's mayor had barely escaped. General Hernandez's office had blasted back with a strongly worded denial of army involvement. An archly worded response from Carlota's office about compromised safety and security for Acapulco citizens then sent the media into overdrive.

It got worse. Two hours after the detectives saw the Los Matas Ejercito video, the first funeral was held. Carlota attended, leaning on a cane and wearing a somber black dress and veil.

The whole thing went viral almost immediately. Social media whipped up a popular frenzy across Acapulco, and within hours everyone was talking about how citizens of the city had to protect the mayor. The Los Matas Ejercito video got a million hits and was replayed on television. Carlota's ratings skyrocketed, and pictures of her at the funeral appeared everywhere. The orderly demonstrations outside the *alcaldía* ballooned into crowds and tents for an extended Carlota lovefest. More uniformed cops and rapid reaction forces were detailed to the scene, as were Macias and Sandor. Flunkies from both Chief Salazar's office and the *alcaldía* were in and out of Lt. Rufino's office, and his interactions with the detectives were briefer than ever.

But even as the demonstrations ballooned, social media went nuts, and the video replayed on an endless local television news loop, by Thursday Emilia's world had shrunk to the computer on her desk and a list of over 300 club cab trucks registered in Acapulco and the neighboring areas. The soundtrack of her world was an endless stream of muttered curses from Silvio as he grappled with his half of the list.

The lack of compatibility between various databases meant that for each truck listed, they had to access not only the registration database, but also three or four others in order to find the owner's address and other personal information. At this rate, Emilia figured, as the internal police browser crashed yet again, overloaded by the number of windows she had to open, it would take about a week to run down all the truck owners.

The ring of her desk phone was a welcome diversion. The caller was Javier Salinas Arroliza, from the state attorney general's office. After an exchange of pleasantries, he asked when he could expect the first reports on the raid on the El Pharaoh casino.

Emilia leaned back in her desk chair as a little hourglass icon pulsed in the middle of her blank blue screen. "The arson at the El Tigre restaurant is going to cause a delay," she hedged. Castro and Gomez had refused her offer of a briefing and had hardly been in the squadroom since Monday. They weren't there now, either. "I've been reassigned to that case."

"I'm sorry to hear that, Detective," Salinas said. They'd never met in person, but Emilia imagined a harried middle-aged lawyer who needed to exercise more and eat fewer tortillas. "I know that everyone has priorities, but I'm expecting evidence to corroborate the initial investigation. The El Pharaoh has already lodged a protest, disputing the closure order. No evidence, no charge that will stick. They reopen and we'll all look like fools."

"I fully understand," Emilia said. She toyed with the buttons on her phone. "Let me refer you to Lieutenant Nelson Rufino Herrera. He's our new chief of detectives. He'll have more information for you."

Salinas sounded mollified and Emilia transferred the call to Lt. Rufino's office. Through his closed door, she heard his phone ring once. Silvio looked at her around their computer monitors and snorted, fully aware of what she'd done.

Five minutes later, Castro's phone rang. After five rings and no pickup, Gomez's phone rang.

Eventually Lt. Rufino came out of his office. "Where are Castro and Gomez?" he demanded as he approached Emilia's desk.

"No idea," Silvio said without looking up.

"Tell them to mark all the seized money from the El Pharaoh case and get the armored van to take it over to the state attorney general's office," Lt. Rufino told Emilia.

"They should verify all the accounting documentation as well, *teniente*," Emilia pointed out. "There's no reason to separate evidence." Marking seized money so it couldn't be stolen out of official police custody was fairly standard procedure, but she knew that half the money was going to disappear before it got marked, even if it was counterfeit, if he left it up to those idiots.

"Priorities, Cruz," Lt. Rufino said shortly and went back into his office.

Emilia stretched over her desk and rapped on the pile of papers by Silvio's computer mouse. "Hey," she said, trying to keep her voice low. "Did you hear *teniente* just now?"

Silvio kept looking at his computer screen. "He said shut the fuck up."

"This is a stupid way to handle the case," Emilia insisted. "I don't think he's thinking about anything besides the El Tigre fire and Carlota."

"Then I'll say shut the fuck up," Silvio growled.

Emilia settled back in her chair. Her computer screen was still blank except for the hourglass. "*Rayos*," she swore.

When life returned to the screen, her inbox icon was blinking. Emilia toggled through the messages, hardly believing the updates about the magnitude of the demonstrations going on downtown. An estimated 150,000 people were in front of the *alcaldía*, clogging all the nearby streets. Tensions were high as demonstrators chanted both support for Carlota and anti-army slogans.

"Look at this." Silvio snapped his fingers to get Emilia's attention. "This name mean anything to you?"

Emilia came around the side of both desks to look at his screen. It showed the national identity card, or *cédula*, database. The identity card of a man named Lester Torrez Delgadillo was displayed.

"No," Emilia said. "Should it?"

Silvio rubbed his jaw. "Torrez is former army with a funny address. Looks like a *hacienda* outside of town, but nothing comes up." He toggled to a map application to show that it had returned a null search.

"I know where else to look." Emilia scribbled down the address information and quickly logged on to the single computer in the squadroom that was connected to the outside Internet. She tried not to get too excited as she called up a search program, but this was why she wanted to be a detective: to put together bits of information, to find out things no one else could, to draw the threads together. To win.

"Fuck," Silvio breathed five minutes later as he read over her shoulder.

Emilia printed out the results and they knocked on Lt. Rufino's door.

"I think we've got a result," she said as soon as they were in the office.

Lt. Rufino squinted at both of the two detectives. "What?"

"A truck owned by Lester Torrez Delgadillo," Emilia said. "He's a former army sergeant, 48 years old, married, two children. The truck is six years old, bought here in Acapulco. His address is a big ranch east of the city. Maybe a two-hour drive."

"So?" Lt. Rufino made a *come on* gesture.

"Torrez Delgadillo is the foreman." Emilia struggled not to speak too rapidly. Silvio stayed behind her, feet apart, arms folded, forearm muscles bulging. "The ranch is owned by Fidel Macario Urbina. The housekeeper at the ranch says Torrez

Delgadillo lives on the property but was gone over the weekend. She doesn't know where."

Lt. Rufino looked at her blankly.

"Carlota defeated Macario Urbina in the election last year." Emilia couldn't quite keep a note of triumph out of her voice. "It was a slugfest."

Lt. Rufino finally held his hand out for the papers. He looked through the printouts, looked up, and nodded. "Old-fashioned police methodology."

His phone rang. After an initial exchange of greetings, he described the information on Torrez and Emilia realized *el teniente* was speaking to Chief Salazar. After a few minutes, Lt. Rufino hung up.

"Meeting at the *alcaldía* in two hours," he said.

Chapter 12

Emilia hadn't expected to see General Hernandez at the meeting in Carlota's office. He was a fit man in his early fifties with deep squint lines around the eyes and short hair brushed back from a smooth forehead and graying at the temples. He wore stiffly starched camouflage fatigues and a minimum of gold badges of rank. His flunkies numbered only two, four less than hovered behind the mayor's chair. Emilia recognized all of Carlota's staffers from the meeting in the police auditorium.

"This has become a media circus," he said and gestured at the demonstrators outside the window. Sounds of chanting were partially muffled by distance and swaths of sheer draperies. "Based only on the fact that a so-called expert arson investigator says that grenades were used to set fire to a local Acapulco restaurant. That sort of loose talk resulted in that atrocious video. Now you've come up with a very tenuous link between someone with the right type of truck who once served in the army."

"I was at that restaurant," Carlota retorted. "And I want answers."

At times Emilia could make out the chants from the throngs outside: *Can we give the army our Carlota? No! Do we want army criminals burning our city? No!* Cops in riot gear and Plexiglas shields were keeping open the back gates leading into the *alcaldía*. Emilia had felt uncomfortably hemmed in as their police car had passed through.

"The answer is that the army in this military district had absolutely nothing to do with that fire." General Hernandez folded his arms. "Regardless of who the police are guessing may be responsible."

Carlota got up and walked to the window, moving easily without the aid of the cane she'd taken with her to the funerals. She stood to one side so that she wasn't visible through the sheer drapery. The mayor was the same elegant woman as at the restaurant Saturday night. Today she wore a trim black suit with rhinestone buttons and a cream satin blouse. Black platform slingbacks revealed blood-red toenails that matched the polish on her fingertips. She appeared totally recovered from her ordeal.

Besides Carlota, her minions, and the army officers, the group in the mayor's spacious office included Emilia, Silvio, Lt. Rufino, Chief Salazar, and a uniformed police captain named Vega from the chief of police's executive staff. Obregon was there as well, wearing another black suit, and accompanied by two of his own minions. So far the union boss had said nothing but his eyes were often on Lt. Rufino.

"The people are calling for swift justice," Carlota said and turned to face the group. Her expression was a mix of saint and fox. "Listen to them out there. I need to make a statement about this."

Next to Emilia, Silvio's face wore a set expression but the rest of him radiated impatience.

"Any official statement needs to make the unfortunate point that grenades can be purchased in this country on the black market," Hernandez said. "There's no proof that any explosive used at this fire came from military stockpiles, much less this district. The *norteamericanos* could be sending them over the border by the case, for all we know."

Carlota flapped her hand in a gesture of either dismissal or annoyance.

"Your statement should be a call for these demonstrators to disperse," General Hernandez went on.

"The demonstration could also be a ruse for another attack on you, señora," Chief Salazar said and shifted uncomfortably in his seat. He always reminded Emilia of pictures of old Spanish dons: a narrow face, hawk-like nose, bald head like a shiny brown egg emerging from his ornate police uniform. "By Torrez or by an accomplice. We can't afford a statement until Torrez is in custody. The decision we need to make is whether or not to inform Macario Urbina before the arrest. Or arrest him at the same time. Either way, your office needs to be prepared for the political fallout."

Carlota flung herself back in her seat, crossed her legs, and dangled her foot. "What exactly is the army connection to your suspect?"

General Hernandez bristled but before he spoke Chief Salazar gestured at Lt. Rufino who cleared his throat. "Torrez is a former army sergeant. We can assume that Macario Urbina knows this and encouraged him to use his connections to obtain the grenades."

"Once again," General Hernandez said ominously. "Are you suggesting that this Torrez Delgadillo obtained grenades from my military district?"

"We all know that the Acapulco police have no jurisdiction at *campo militar*," Lt. Rufino said. "But if you opened your armory and its records to a thorough vetting it would allow us to close out that part of the investigation and help defuse the situation with the public."

"No," Chief Salazar said. "The Acapulco police don't need to investigate at *campo militar*. This should be a matter for Murillo, the arson investigator."

General Hernandez folded his arms. "He can make a request to see the records."

"That's fine," Chief Salazar said.

Obregon still said nothing, just watched Lt. Rufino and Chief Salazar with the same look of assessment he'd worn in the auditorium.

On one side of Emilia, Silvio breathed noisily while on her other side Lt. Rufino seemed to wilt. It was clear to Emilia that the stress of the situation was getting to *el teniente*. In the squadroom, his exchanges with the detectives had become more and more terse as they reviewed what would be discussed at the meeting. On the way to the *alcaldía*, Lt. Rufino had breathed in short noisy bursts as the police driver navigated the official vehicle.

Emilia pressed her lips together, chagrined at the power plays going on in the room as the burbles of noise from the chanting crowds outside rose and fell. Murillo's brief was to determine the cause of fires, not to go grubbing around in the military district's records. But by throwing the responsibility on to the visiting investigator, who had no jurisdiction and could be recalled to Mexico City at any time, Salazar kept his police department from getting into a tangle with the army. General Hernandez looked smart enough to see that for himself but probably couldn't care less what Salazar did as long as the army didn't get blamed for the fire without better proof than the use of grenades, which, as he'd rightly pointed out, were easily obtained on the black market.

Hernandez struck Emilia as a seasoned player who was out of patience with Carlota's posturing. He knew the army had a bad reputation but wasn't going to let it get worse without some solid evidence.

"May I speak for everyone here, *mi general*," Carlota said as she stood up. "When I say we appreciate your goodwill and spirit of cooperation during a difficult time."

A muscle in Silvio's jaw jumped.

General Hernandez stood, as did the two officers he'd brought with him, neither of whom had said anything during the meeting. The general held Carlota's hand for a moment, speaking in an earnest and low tone to her. When she smiled and let go he acknowledged Obregon and Chief Salazar. One of Carlota's minions opened the door and the three army officers left.

A little more air seemed to circulate in the room.

"Army cooperation," Carlota said with a sniff when the door closed behind the army officers. She snatched up a proffered glass of water from an aide and stalked back to the window to look at the demonstrations below, drama in every movement. The rest of the meeting participants were obviously her adoring audience. "No doubt it will be priceless. Now that Hernandez knows we have a suspect, anything could happen. I expect the police to be prepared."

Chief Salazar looked as if he had indigestion. "Before we take action, we all need to realize the severity of the accusations and be prepared to deal with what could become an even more tense situation. There is a delicate political balance here. Macario Urbina—"

"Possibly colluded with the army to kill me," Carlota said.

She pointed to Chief Salazar. "I won the election, my opponent turned to the army for help, and they gave him Torrez. Hernandez thinks no one will find out but he's a fool."

One of Carlota's staffers leaned forward. "It would look bad to rush to conclusions, señora," he murmured.

"Eight people are dead," Silvio snarled, speaking up for the first time. "We've got a suspect. Do we want to get this *pendejo* or not?"

Everyone turned to look at him. A corner of Obregon's mouth twitched.

The staffer, a manicured young man with coifed hair and a herringbone suit, pursed his lips as if Silvio had said he liked sex with dogs.

"We'll go into executive session, now," Chief Salazar said icily. "Rufino, I know you and your officers want to get back to the office."

"My officers want to make an arrest," Lt. Rufino said. The lieutenant raised his chin toward the window. "Before this situation gets out of hand."

"This is support from the people of Acapulco," Carlota purred as she settled back into her chair.

Emilia looked at the smug faces of Carlota's staff, all six discreetly ranged outside the main seating area. The demonstration had been going on for three days. Who was feeding the ever-growing number of people? Providing bathrooms? Water? What about the pro-Carlota and anti-army banners and signs that had appeared out of nowhere? Hernandez was no fool, surely he was asking himself the same questions.

"Thank you for coming, detectives," Carlota said.

"I'll speak to you tomorrow, Rufino," Chief Salazar said.

Rufino made a small sharp gesture and led Emilia and Silvio out of Carlota's office. Once in the hall, it was as if the lieutenant had read Emilia's mind. "Get your vests on," he said. "Find Macias and Sandor, work the crowd. See if any pieces connect."

They walked to the lobby without speaking. The driver stood up from the bench where he'd been waiting, led the way to the lot inside the gates of the *alcaldía*, and popped the trunk. Lt. Rufino watched as Emilia and Silvio strapped the heavy vests on under their jackets to hide the word *POLICIA* stenciled on the back.

"The mayor's using the situation to get at the army," Silvio said. "She's got some problem with them and this is her opportunity. We should be arresting this guy. The riot cops can worry about this demonstration."

Lt. Rufino made a small nervous gesture. "We'll wait for Chief Salazar to give us the go-ahead."

"Politics and police work are a bad mix, *teniente*," Silvio warned.

Lt. Rufino got into the car and the driver shut the door.

Chapter 13

Emilia moved uneasily through the chanting crowd, the bulletproof vest heavy and hot under her denim jacket. A small stage had been set up and spokesmen for the demonstrators took turns leading chants and booming through a bullhorn, keeping emotions high with questions and cheers. *Can Carlota save our city? Yes! Can we tell the army we've had enough? Yes!*

Her shoulder holster fit even more tightly with the vest on. The gun was a reassuring presence on her left side, but using it in this situation would likely cause a stampede. Her best protection was the discreet police radio clipped inside her jacket.

Do you want tanks on our beaches? No! Do you want our businesses up in flames? No!

All the demonstrators waved small Mexican flags, held up signs or brandished pictures of Carlota. Big pro-Carlota banners were everywhere, strung up on the iron fence surrounding the front of the *alcaldía* and stretched across the walls of other nearby buildings. A few big anti-army banners were mixed in. Other signs professed support for Los Matas Ejercito. Several people wore black scarves across their faces in imitation of the video's heroes.

Can they come to our city and burn it down? No! Can we let them have our Carlota? No!

Reporters tethered to television vans interviewed demonstrators, made noisy but earnest broadcasts, and made Emilia nervous about inadvertently being caught on camera. Uniformed cops with riot shields lined the streets, ostensibly protecting local businesses, most of which were closed.

Static crackled in her earpiece and she heard Silvio's voice. "Army convoy is heading toward the *alcaldía*. Maybe Hernandez is coming back."

A moment later, the bullhorn blared and volatility rippled

through the crowd like the surge of the ocean during a hurricane. Shouts of *The army! The army! They're coming for Carlota!* rose up and drowned out Silvio's voice in Emilia's ear.

The crowd charged forward, taking Emilia with it. She fought to stay on her feet, locked inside the mass of people, as the surge carried everyone closer to the *alcaldía*. Emilia stumbled across grass, over a curb, and onto pavement. Shouts turned to screams and then to battle cries.

Do we want martial law? No! Can they have our Carlota? No! NO!

Some of the demonstrators broke ranks and Emilia realized that they'd surrounded a car. A swarm of at least 40 demonstrators rocked it from side to side as she watched, helpless to do anything. The driver was dragged out but wasn't in uniform. He managed to break free and made it to the safety of the line of riot cops.

The crowd managed to dump the empty car onto its side. The vehicle hung suspended for a moment, the undercarriage exposed like the entrails of a metal monster. In the next moment it crashed down on its roof with the rending sounds of crumpling sheet metal. As it settled onto the pavement like a giant dying *cucaracha*, someone threw a bottle. Emilia barely had time to register the rag stuck in the mouth before glass shattered, the air filled with the scent of gasoline, and the car burst into flames.

The crowd had been close and the blast of heat knocked everyone back. Emilia fell to the pavement amid the crush of bodies. Bright fire stretched out to touch her.

Silvio's voice crackled in her ear, asking where she was. Emilia groped to her feet, hardly seeing who or what she was stepping on, coughing as the smoke blew into the crowd. Panic enveloped her, and once again she was stumbling through a maze of blinding smoke, full of things that shifted and snapped in the scorching heat.

The voice in her ear kept calling, but nothing mattered except survival. She was desperate to get out of the restaurant, to find Kurt, to see if he'd made it out, too. She used her elbows to break away from the jumble of panicked people closest to the burning vehicle. Battering a path for herself, the sound of explosions drove her on, over glass and china and pieces of brocade wallpaper.

Once she'd fought her way out of the immediate crush, Emilia started to run, slamming aside anything in her way. Uniformed cops in riot gear streamed by in the opposite direction, but they hardly registered. Her breath came in ragged heaves, her eyes seeing only the inside of the El Tigre. The doorway was obscured by roiling smoke and greedy flames.

Horns blared, too close, and Emilia jumped back. A fresh breeze made her gulp hard, almost biting the air around her, and she stood still.

Panic ebbed and she saw that she was at a familiar intersection. South of the *alcaldía*, close to the wide Avenida Casa Blanca and the touristy art market at Mercado Artesanias Tlacopanocha, and not far from the Playa Manzanilla beaches. Traffic was solid and unmoving in every direction. Drivers swore at each other, half leaning out of the car windows. Tourists in cargo shorts, light jackets and floppy hats, clutching their colored plastic bags from the *mercado*, looked confused at the commotion.

"Cruz!" The radio boomed in her ear. "Stay there!"

Emilia clapped a hand to her earpiece, surprised to find it still intact. She also still had her gun and her cell phone. She wanted to call Kurt, make sure he was all right. Before she could make the call, footsteps sounded on the sidewalk and Silvio was there, face streaming sweat.

"Fuck sakes, Cruz." He bent over and drew in air, just as Kurt had done Saturday night. "What are you, some sort of fucking Olympic runner?"

Emilia couldn't have replied if she'd wanted to. She started to shake, her body churning with adrenaline and the residue of incomprehensible fear. Silvio grabbed her by the upper arm, pulled her down the street to a small *lonchería*, and tossed her into an orange vinyl booth.

"What the fuck, Cruz," he said hotly. "I must have called you a dozen times. You forget radio protocol all of a sudden?"

Emilia blinked at him. Her teeth chattered like castanets.

"I turn around and there you go, like a fucking speed racer," Silvio said in disgust.

The waiter put down two glasses of water and a pad of paper with menu choices on it.

"The car turned into a big wall of fire," Emilia said, her voice shaking as much as the rest of her. "Always smart to run away from a fire. Not into it. Away."

Silvio mopped his sweaty face with a paper napkin from the table dispenser. "This is it, Cruz," he snarled. "I never wanted you in the squadroom. Sure as fuck never wanted you as a partner. You are living proof that women can't do this fucking job."

Emilia started to laugh. Silvio was lecturing her with the same old shit he always said, and her teeth were clacking together, and all she could do was laugh. It wasn't even funny. She didn't know why she was laughing but she couldn't stop, either. Maybe it was because her teeth were making so much noise inside her head: *clakkety-clakkety-clakkety—*

Silvio threw a glass of ice water into her face and Emilia stopped laughing.

The tourists at a table across the aisle gasped.

The cold water ran down her chin and soaked the front of her jacket. Silvio grabbed a bunch of paper napkins from the dispenser and thrust them at her. Emilia slowly wiped her face. The napkins came away damp and sooty.

She dropped the soggy paper, lunged across the table and slapped Silvio. He leaned back, but even so, she connected hard enough with his jawbone to send a jarring sting up her entire arm.

The tourists scrambled out of their chairs and herded themselves toward the door.

Silvio fingered the bright red mark that Emilia's hand had left, then snapped his fingers at the waiter and ordered two beers.

Emilia blew her nose on a napkin. It came away laden with black muck.

The waiter put two cold bottles on the table and darted

away.

Silvio upended his bottle and took a long guzzle. Emilia swallowed a mouthful of cold beer, grateful for the cooling sensation as it went down her throat.

"Just how bad was that fire at the El Tigre?" Silvio asked after a while.

"Worse than I thought," Emilia said.

Chapter 14

Emilia sat in Mercedes Sandoval's office and watched the dance class, glad for the chance to decompress after what had happened that afternoon. Silvio had called a car to get them back to the police station, and she'd gone home after that to a long shower and a decent meal.

The girls were all young teens. They practiced a jazz routine as Mercedes led them.

It would have been such a gift if she'd been able to do what these girls were doing, Emilia reflected, hands wrapped around a cup of Mercedes's coffee. Move with freedom and joy, have a break from worrying about food or school or their mother wandering away and never coming back because she'd forgotten where she lived.

As Mercedes changed the music and the girls giggled and pranced around, Emilia realized that she hadn't changed so very much in all the years since she was that age. She was still too serious, a worrier, ready to fight anything that got in her way, desperate to keep her small household afloat, always denying herself anything too nice. There was never any sense of freedom or spontaneity. She rarely did anything for the pleasure of it. No wonder Kurt was thinking of leaving Acapulco.

After the class, Emilia volunteered to take Itzel home, saying that she and Mercedes were going shopping near Itzel's house. Mercedes let Itzel get in the front and hopped into the backseat of the Suburban, and Emilia made small talk to Itzel about dancing and how she'd always wanted to learn how to dance but never had the chance. Itzel was a small thin girl with long wavy hair.

They stopped at a light and Emilia turned to Itzel. "I'm a police officer, Itzel, and I'm looking for your friend Lila Jimenez Lata."

Itzel's face tightened. "I don't know where she is."

"You said she went home," Emilia said. "Are you sure?"

"Yes."

"Nobody saw her go inside."

"She did," Itzel insisted.

"Someone else told me she got off the bus after one stop," Emilia bluffed.

"He's lying," Itzel said immediately.

"Who's lying?"

"The bus driver."

"I never said it was the bus driver who told me that," Emilia pointed out.

Itzel started to cry.

Emilia pulled into the parking lot of a paint store closed for the evening. Itzel tried to unlock the passenger door and Emilia hit the lock button on her side. Mercedes reached between the two seats and pressed down on Itzel's shoulder.

"Where did she go, Itzel?"

"No," Itzel said between sobs. She shrugged off her teacher's hand. "I can't tell you."

Emilia jerked Itzel around to face her. "You'll be blamed if you know something and don't tell. Your friend could end up dead."

"You'll tell her grandmother," Itzel whispered.

"I don't have to tell anybody," Emilia said. "Where did she go?"

Itzel gulped. "She went to find her mother."

"Her mother's dead," Emilia said.

"Lila said she's not." Tears coursed down Itzel's face. Mercedes passed her a tissue from the backseat and Itzel blew her nose. She wadded the soggy tissue in a small fist. "Her grandmother made it up because she hates her mother."

"Where does Lila think her mother is?" Mercedes scooted forward and wedged herself between the two front seats.

"She didn't say." Itzel drew her shoulders together and struggled not to cry again. "She said that her mother is a Spanish princess. Lila says Lata isn't her real name, but she used it because she was a spy once and had to change her identity. Her real name is much more grand, but she never could say what it was. Lila said Montealegre, maybe. Or Castillo."

Emilia was starting to have a very bad feeling about the search for Lila. "So where was she going to go to look for her mother?"

Itzel shook her head. "Downtown. She only said downtown and she had to go that day because her grandmother had a big sewing job and wouldn't be in the house until later." The girl gave up the struggle and new tears poured down her face. "She made it sound like she'd only be gone a little while. She never said she wasn't coming to school on Friday."

Emilia looked in the rearview mirror and met Mercedes's eye. *Downtown* could mean so many things.

Chapter 15

"We made an arrest," Emilia said. "All hush hush for now, but with any luck, this is all over."

Kurt's eyebrows went up as she told him how Silvio had chafed and muttered throughout the Friday morning meeting. As it wrapped up, Lt. Rufino got a call from Chief Salazar's office giving them the green light to arrest Torrez. He'd dispatched Macias and Sandor—pointedly not Emilia and Silvio—to the *hacienda* owned by Carlota's defeated political rival Fidel Macario Urbina.

They had apparently found the foreman, Torrez Delgadillo, and his truck without much trouble. Torrez was currently in one of the detention cells in the central police building. Chief Salazar's staff would handle the interrogation. In hopes of defusing the still volatile demonstrations which had spread to the gates of *campo militar* in Atoyac, an early press statement had gone out stating that the police had a suspect in custody and that Carlota and the people of Acapulco were once again safe.

Everyone was nervous because Macario Urbina was on vacation in Europe and unavailable for comment on the arrest of his employee. Emilia was surprised that his office hadn't tried to issue some sort of contradictory statement, blaming Carlota for twisting law enforcement to hurt her political opponents. Emilia figured they were either scared because Torrez had indeed been acting on Macario Urbina's orders, or they hadn't been able to get in touch with him.

"Did he confess?" Kurt asked.

"He hasn't said anything," Emilia said. She jiggled her straw down around the ice cubes and crushed mint leaves in the bottom of her *mojito*. "No confession, no alibi. Won't say where he was last Saturday night. Macario Urbina's office sent a lawyer, but he hasn't said anything either."

"I don't usually jump to conclusions, but that looks bad to

me." Kurt finished his own *mojito* and took a nut from the bowl on the table.

"If it wasn't him, where's his alibi?" Emilia raised her hands in pretended exasperation. "Maybe they need to put Silvio in with him for a couple of hours."

Kurt laughed. "That bad, eh?"

Emilia had to smile. "Well, only sometimes."

To her surprise, Silvio had not said anything to Lt. Rufino about her panic Thursday at the demonstration. Nor had he lectured her again. Silvio had actually been quiet on Friday after the morning meeting, as if he'd known he had pushed *el teniente* as far as the new lieutenant could go.

"The only bad part of this is that Carlota is going to start talking about her damned Olympics again," Kurt said.

Emilia laughed. The *mojito* was cold and sweet, but not cloying, the lime and mint adding just the right double shots of zest. It was as if the Palacio Réal's bartenders knew exactly what she'd needed.

The hotel was located on the far eastern side of Acapulco, on the tip of Punta Diamante, the spit of land that created the bay-within-a-bay called Puerto Marques. Emilia marveled every time she drove down the steep and winding cobblestone road that led from the Carretera Escénica down the side of the mountain that rose above the bay. The hotel hung like tiered jewels down the side of the cliff, the stunning architecture creating the ultimate in luxury and privacy.

The Palacio Réal was so secluded that few besides hotel guests were to be found in the five-star restaurant or the vast Pasodoble Bar with its two terraced levels, inlaid glass mosaic bar and white curtains that could be pulled to block out the rain. For Emilia, being anywhere in the hotel was like being on another planet, one where the bartender made the world's best *mojito*, the white piano spilled out tunes that Emilia didn't recognize, wealthy people floated by in expensive clothing, and the evening tide lapped at the sand beyond the terrace. She usually felt underdressed when she was there, even tonight when she had on a simple white tank, a skinny black skirt, and the turquoise necklace she'd bought when she made detective.

The bandage was off her hand, too, and the remaining small red streak across the heel of her hand was barely noticeable.

Kurt put his empty *mojito* glass on the table. He wore a white polo shirt with a little alligator on the chest, khaki pants and loafers without socks. His muscular arms still showed scratches from his rescue efforts at the El Tigre. "This was all due to what you and Silvio found," Kurt said. "Why don't you seem more excited?"

Because you're leaving tomorrow for Belize and I can't compete with all that money. The evening so far hadn't touched on Kurt's plans. The need to get things out in the open was there, however; in his careful welcoming kiss, the stilted conversation, the way neither reached for the other's hand as they usually did.

But now he'd given her the perfect opening.

Emilia took a deep breath.

"I've got another case," she said. "A missing girl. Just 16 years old."

Kurt raised his eyebrows and Emilia found herself babbling, her eyes looking everywhere but at his face, telling him about Berta, meeting Mercedes, the conversation with Itzel, and how Lila believed that her mother was alive despite what her grandmother had told her.

"I had a couple of minutes yesterday and looked up the mother," Emilia went on. "Found an arrest record for Yolanda Lata from four years ago. Someone paid her fee and got her out a couple of days later. No address for either Yolanda or whoever paid her out."

"So she was alive four years ago." Kurt signaled for another round of *mojitos*. "Are you going to go back to the grandmother and ask?"

Emilia sighed. "I don't trust Berta to tell me the truth. She either won't face it or doesn't know. I'd rather be able to ask the brother but I found zero on him." She fumbled in her bag for the photo strip and put in on the table in front of Kurt.

Kurt studied the images. "This is the girl and her brother?"

"Yes," Emilia said. She and Silvio had supposedly been hard at work researching the remaining club cab trucks on the list on Friday, but he'd worked the points spread for tomorrow's games on his cell phone while Emilia looked up not only Yolanda but the woman's son as well. Surprisingly, there'd been nothing in any database; Emilia hadn't even found Pedro Lata's *cédula*. As far as official records went, the boy didn't exist. "All I have on him is a name. Pedro Lata."

The waiter came by and put down two fresh *mojitos* and took away the old glasses. Kurt smiled and saluted him with the glass, and the waiter grinned back.

Kurt was always doing that with his employees, creating a moment of connection, of acknowledgment. It was never forced, just a natural extension of his confidence, of the quiet authority that he wore like a second skin. She liked that about him, liked to be around him, liked to watch and learn from him. Emilia thought again about him leaving Acapulco, wearing his confidence and understated authority in Belize, and the bottom of her evening fell away.

He put down the photo strip and ate another nut. "You know that he works at the CICI water park."

"What?"

"The water park," Kurt said. He put the tip of his index finger on the logo on the boy's polo. "He's wearing a uniform shirt. Dolphin logo."

"*Madre de Dios*," Emilia exclaimed. She couldn't remember the last time she'd been to the huge water park, the chief feature of which was the opportunity for tourists to swim with dolphins in one of the park's huge tanks. Occasionally one of the dolphins would die, and the newspapers would be full of outrage over cruelty to animals and Mexico's bad record in caring for marine mammals in captivity. The police and animal control would argue over who had to deal with the *norteamericano* animal rights activists until the issue blew over and the water park bought another dolphin. "Are you sure?" she asked.

"Took a group over there a few weeks ago," Kurt said.

"You're a genius," Emilia marveled and tasted her fresh *mojito*.

They sat in silence as the surf slid up on the beach and the sunset spread itself into a kaleidoscope of pinks and golds.

Kurt took her hand and traced a circle around the red scar. "I'll be gone for two weeks," he said. "Don't run off with anybody else, okay?"

Emilia felt her face get warm. "I won't."

Kurt gave her hand a jostle so she'd finally look at him. "Even if I take the job, it's not a problem," he said seriously. "There's a direct flight. We'd see each other about as much as we do now."

"Is that enough for you?" Emilia heard herself ask. She felt like a moth dancing toward a flame, knowing it would extinguish her yet unable to help herself.

"I want what you can give, Em." Kurt's voice was steady, matter-of-fact, as if there was no pressure implicit in his words.

Emilia knew this was the moment. The moment to say *Stay* and he'd stay.

She looked away. Her throat was tight. She wondered how she'd remember this night when she looked back on it. Thought about how once upon a time, she'd had something really special. And messed it up.

"Want to take a walk?" Kurt asked. His voice was strained.

"Sure," Emilia said.

He led her across the big open bar. A small group laughed and chatted near the piano, couples smiled at each other over the glow of the candles, and the bartenders juggled bottles and made drinks with sultry names. Kurt nodded at each person wearing a Palacio Réal uniform, and Emilia saw the immediate respect in their eyes as they smiled back at *el jefe*.

He kicked off his shoes and waited for Emilia to do the same. Together they stepped off the lower terrace and onto the hard-packed sand. They walked across the beach to the water's edge and Kurt turned right to keep them parallel to the softly lapping surf. The sun was nearly below the horizon, just the rim of a fiery orange ball visible as it sank into the dark ocean, the kaleidoscope reduced to flickering stripes woven through the water.

They kept walking, holding hands, leaving the hotel further and further behind. Emilia let her sandals dangle from her free hand, trying not to think about Belize or the future or how the sunset reminded her of smoke and fire.

The hotel's lights and music receded; the sand became more coarse and the ocean more angry and violent. The waves surged onto the beach and sucked at the sand, reaching higher each time, thirsty for something hidden underneath and angry when dragged away before the treasure was found.

Kurt slowed his steps, then stopped. Emilia looked behind them. In the distance, the hotel glittered down the whole length of the cliff. She could see the curve of the bay and the hotel's private marina. Lights hung in the sky, and she knew it was the even more distant Costa Esmeralda apartment building. The dark night had swallowed up cement and stone, and only the lights were left to compete with the stars.

"I feel like there's more to say, Em," Kurt said. "About this whole thing. About us."

Emilia swallowed hard. She wriggled her toes into the damp sand. "I know."

He waited for her to go on. When she stayed silent, Kurt drew in a breath. "I mean, do you care if I go?" he asked. "I'd really like to know."

The last flicker of the sun vanished below the horizon. There were no shadows on the beach, just opaque darkness and the smell of a wide and lonely ocean.

"There's so much money at stake for you," Emilia said. A noisy wave washed over her feet and she sank up to her arches in the wet sand. "I can't even imagine how much."

"Forget the money." Kurt dropped her hand but didn't move away. They stood shoulder to shoulder, facing the waves and the ocean and the darkness. "I'm saying I want to know if I matter a damn to you, Em. Or are we just having fun, no strings attached?"

"I can't tell you what to do," Emilia said, and knew that she was hurting him. But she couldn't think of what else to say, anything that wouldn't leave her open and vulnerable. "I can't take that kind of responsibility for your career."

"What about taking some kind of responsibility for us?" Kurt asked. "What are you willing to put into this relationship?"

Emilia turned to look at him then, provoked by the raw tone in his voice and her own anger at not being able to handle the conversation. For not being able to give Kurt what he wanted. Her moment of epiphany in Mercedes Sandoval's studio came back like bitter acid. Maybe she couldn't give Kurt what he wanted because she didn't have it to give.

"I don't know what you want me to say," Emilia said. She pulled a foot out of the sand and traced a line with her toe. A wave drove up the beach and gobbled up the indentation.

"Why the hell can't you answer a simple question?" Kurt demanded.

"Because it isn't simple," Emilia blurted.

"Because you're a cop and your mother is losing it and you've had to fight for everything you've ever gotten in life." Even if his face hadn't been turned away, it was too dark to see his expression. "And I'm a *gringo* so nobody you know will approve."

"Not true." Emilia pushed herself to sound lighthearted in order to get past the emotion, the way she always did with him. "I told you about my new friend. Mercedes Sandoval. I bet she'd think you're fantastic."

"Is she my type?"

"No," Emilia said with a nervous little laugh. "She's not a cop and her mother's dead and she knows what she wants and she's really nice to people. I don't think she's shot anyone in a while, either."

"Yeah." Kurt took Emilia's hand and started walking again. "Not my type at all."

The beach was deserted. It was narrow here, where rich people didn't come to play. Rocky patches and scrubby pines stretched toward the water, held back by sand and salt. Stars twinkled overhead, reflections streaking the ocean with silver.

"This would be simpler if you were more of a jerk," Emilia said.

Kurt laughed. "Give me time."

Just what we don't have. Emilia's eyes stung and she blinked until they didn't. Why did she have to make everything so hard? Why did she feel a pull toward him and a fear that pulled her away at the same time?

They just kept walking, picking their way slowly in the dark. Maybe they'd never stop, just keep walking along the shore of the world until they found the North Pole.

Kurt stopped. "We should head back," he said. "It gets pretty rocky further on."

"Okay," Emilia said.

He dropped his shoes and took her face in both hands and kissed her hard. When he pulled away Emilia clutched at him; the kiss had been urgent and bruising, and she didn't want it to be over.

They made love on the beach, on the damp cool sand, breathless and laughing a little as Kurt produced a condom and they got it on him in the inky darkness. Emilia held on tight as he pulsed deep inside her, a little roughly, his breath fast and ragged. She didn't know if this was a farewell or a claim he was staking, but either way she was right there with him, giving him everything she could and everything she'd ever held back.

The waves surged at them in the dark and Emilia came hard, shaking and crying, Kurt's skin salty on her tongue as she pressed her mouth into his neck to keep from screaming in utter surrender. A minute later he came like a pounding drum inside her. She gripped his body between her legs, her ankles crossed over his spine, letting the drum beat her into the wet sand.

They lay together afterwards, both winded, until the night air cooled their bodies. Their clothes were damp and sandy when they got dressed, fumbling and clumsy, both a little awed at the rush of emotion they'd experienced, more powerful than the rise and pull of the ocean. They walked back to the hotel with Kurt's arm around her shoulders. Emilia's knees were like rubber and the echo of the drum still pounded in her blood.

Chapter 16

It was a relief to reach the *privada* gate. The steeply pitched road up from the Palacio Réal was always a challenge to navigate in the big Suburban when it was dark.

The guard opened the gate and Emilia turned left onto the Carretera Escénica toward Acapulco. There was little traffic along the road, which wound around the mountain above Punta Diamante and along the outer edge of the entire bay of Acapulco. The ocean twinkled on her left, but she rarely looked down. Experienced drivers knew that without guardrails or a safety net, the road was best driven at night by keeping eyes on the painted middle lines.

After their wild interlude on the deserted beach, she'd collected her shoulder bag in his small fifth-floor apartment, refused the offer of a shower or drink, and picked up her vehicle from the valet. Their lovemaking had said it all, and she sensed that he was as emotionally exhausted as she was. He'd try to text her from Belize or London, and they'd parted with a last, lingering kiss under the hotel's portico.

The lights of the city grew brighter as the Suburban rumbled along the smooth highway. Emilia abruptly started to cry. The sobs came from nowhere, violent and uncontrollable, forcing Emilia to gasp for air and fight to keep her eyes open. Suddenly it was all she could do to control the heavy vehicle, and she instinctively braked and turned right at the first intersection. There was a car behind her, so she drove down whatever street it was, blubbering and wiping her nose with the back of her hand, afraid that she was crying so hard she was going to throw up. She turned again and again until by a miracle she saw an open parking space. It took a second miracle to parallel park.

Emilia turned off the engine and gave herself up to it then, crying in the darkness over Kurt and the uncertainty of what she was doing with him and why she had been unable to answer his questions. She cried over the burn victims in the hospital, swathed in bandages and delirious from the pain. She cried, too, for the daily grind with Silvio, the dislike that emanated from him and the constant need to show that she was impervious to his barbs. And for the embarrassment of how she'd behaved on Thursday and the fear that she was unraveling, that she wasn't a good cop anymore.

When her sobs subsided to a sad shakiness and a runny nose, she found a paper napkin left over from some *comida corrida* meal and wiped her nose. Her watch said it was a little after midnight and she realized she was in Playa Guitarrón, the popular nightclub area. If she got out of the vehicle, she'd see the pink neon glow from the famous spaceship-themed Palladium nightclub; the place was large enough for the lights to create a regional landmark. Even inside the car, she could hear the pulsing bass of music and dimly remembered a memo about uniforms working security at an outdoor beach concert that night.

The car rocked. A flash in the rearview mirror caught her eye. Emilia snatched her head around, sure that something had hit the car. But instead of another car, she saw fire.

Emilia strung her badge around her neck, snatched her gun and holster out of her shoulder bag, and slammed out of the SUV with her cell phone.

She ran straight at the flames spouting out of a building on the corner of the next block. The neon sign proclaiming the Luna Loca club was still brightly lit. Emilia called it in as she ran, shouting her badge information and location, while also managing to get her holster on.

The Luna Loca wasn't nearly as big as some of the clubs in the area, but it was packed with a good Saturday night crowd. Drunk patrons stumbled and screamed as they gushed out of a side door, the one Emilia got to first.

To Emilia's intense relief, the club had ample uniformed security, and they all appeared to have working radios. She found the guy who seemed to be in charge and showed her badge. "I'm Cruz." She had to holler to be heard over the din of people and fire. "I called it in. The *bomberos* should be here any minute. How many people inside?"

"Three hundred or so," he shouted back. His face was streaked with sweat and soot, but he looked like he knew his business. "Most out the front and rear."

"Where'd it start?"

"Behind the bar," he shouted back. He waved an arm toward the other side of the building. "The bar just blew out."

The Luna Loca was a corner property. Two sides were engulfed in flames. Black smoke billowed out of the crumbling wall and spread a pall over the street. The heat was too intense for Emilia to even stand on the opposite side of the street, so she yanked up the hem of her tank top to cover her mouth and ran through traffic again to the front of the building where more guards in Luna Loca uniforms were swiftly shepherding people away from the flames.

Traffic was a mess all around the area, even worse than at the El Tigre fire due to the many clubs and the *maldita* concert which must have just finished. Emilia was ready to place a second call to emergency services when she saw a club cab truck in the line of traffic. As it crept forward, a streetlight splashed light over it and Emilia saw that it was a dark maroon color.

"*Madre de Dios*," Emilia choked. She ran down the block toward the truck, cursing the sandals she wore that had been for a date, not for running. Her gun was a reassuring pressure against her side as she went.

The truck moved with the other vehicles, caught in stop-and-go traffic. People thronged the sidewalks and parking lots that lined the streets, the snap and sizzle of the fire mingling with the music that continued to pour out of the other clubs and restaurants as well as the burning Luna Loca. Emilia tried to block out the chaos and the noise and focus on the truck as she ran down the sidewalk. She dodged honking cars trying to exit parking lots and muscle their way into the snarl of traffic, as well as shouting drunks who blocked her way as they stopped to gape at the burning building.

It was too dark and there were too many vehicles behind the truck for her to see the *placa* numbers. Emilia cursed as she realized that the street intersected with the artery leading back to the highway. She darted into the street, hoping to be able to move faster and catch a better glimpse of the truck as it passed under streetlights. A car's bumper kissed her leg, spinning her around. The driver honked loudly, leaned out of his window, and grabbed her left arm.

"Let me teach you how to cross the street, *chica*!" The driver was in his early twenties, a rich party boy. She'd seen his type a million times. The alcohol on his breath rolled ahead of his words.

Emilia reached into the car with her free hand, snatched up a handful of hair, and banged his head into the steering wheel. The car horn blared and he let go of her arm.

The traffic lurched forward and picked up speed. Emilia hauled out her gun and started to run again. She was still two cars behind the dark maroon truck when it jinked around the car in front of it and jumped the curb. The right side tires bit into the concrete and the truck rumbled forward, right side elevated by the sidewalk, left side still in the street. Emilia saw a hand clutch the side of the truck bed; there was one, no, two people in the back.

Pedestrians scattered as the big truck accelerated, the sound of its engine competing with screams and the blaring of horns. The truck's left front bumper crumpled as it pummeled the line of cars, sending them careening into the incoming lane, the truck's size and weight allowing it to shove them out of its way.

Emilia bounced off the hood of a car tossed aside by the truck and somehow managed to land on her feet. She got onto the sidewalk again, dodging panicked people and debris thrown up by the truck's tires.

The truck careened down the street, still partly in the road and partly on the sidewalk, almost at the intersection.

"Get out of the way," Emilia hollered. She stopped running and aimed the gun at the tires, trying to slow her breathing, ignore the screaming around her, and keep the sights level. The automatic was both familiar and heavy in her hands as she fired over and over again at the moving truck.

Her ears rang with the sound of shots and breaking glass. The truck swayed violently. The right fender smashed into a metal trash can, one of Carlota's prized *Keep Acapulco Clean* bins affixed to metal stanchions that rotated for easy clean-up and were cemented into the sidewalk. The bin sailed through the dark night, spewing trash, a brightly colored metal monster aimed directly at Emilia. She barely had time to throw herself to the ground and roll towards the nearest building before the projectile hit the sidewalk, chewing up pavement, bouncing like a runaway train into grass and plants, and bending the wrought-iron grating around a tree.

Emilia sat up in time to see the truck slam back into the street. Bits of rubber trailed it like sparks. She realized that it had no license plates.

The dark maroon truck made the turn that would take it to the highway and disappeared.

"Cruz," Lt. Rufino shouted. "Maybe you're the firebug. You show up every time."

It was dawn. For the second time in a week, Emilia stank of smoke and wet ash. Plenty of people had been taken to the hospital and at least two were dead. The Luna Loca smoldered quietly behind them, the once vibrant blue stucco building smeared with soot. A hole gaped in the side. Shards of pottery and broken plants were strewn all around, making walking difficult.

Until last night, the Luna Loca had been a trendy club-style restaurant that advertised 50 different types of margaritas in colorful flyers that cute girls handed to tourists on the beach. The front of the building was known for its eye-popping mural of a huge grinning moon face. Now the artwork was stained gray.

The emergency services vehicles were gone. The *bomberos* had set up a plastic shelter. The police were using it as an emergency conference room.

One of the nearby restaurants was doing an early morning business selling coffee to all the cops and fire department personnel, and Emilia was grateful for the double latte that

Silvio had unceremoniously shoved at her. He'd taken down everything she could remember about the truck, what direction it had been going when she first saw it, the color, make and model, and the fact that it didn't have any license plates. The two people hiding in the back.

Both Emilia and Silvio had been surprised when Lt. Rufino showed up, steel travel mug in hand. Emilia had repeated her story to him. Ten minutes later, Chief Salazar's convoy shrilled up the street and halted in front of the restaurant. Lt. Rufino climbed into the back of the chief's SUV and conferred for five minutes. Whatever had been said inside Salazar's vehicle hadn't been good. Lt. Rufino was livid.

"*Teniente*," Emilia said. "I swear what I told you is true. I just happened—"

"You left the scene," Lt. Rufino said. "To chase a car like a dog. I don't expect my detectives to chase cars. Or don't they teach detectives how to do things properly here?"

"The truck had the same description as the one at the El Tigre, *teniente*," Emilia said, torn between anger and surprise at his reaction. "It went up on the sidewalk to get away from me. A car behind the truck honked and it must have gotten the truck's attention."

Murillo parted the panels of plastic that formed the enclosure's door and stepped into the shelter.

"So?" Lt. Rufino snapped at the arson investigator. "What have you got?"

"This looks like a copycat of the El Tigre," Murillo said. He had on a big baggy orange coverall with cargo pockets and was soot-streaked from the thighs down. "We're probably going to find that two grenades detonated against the side of the building, right where the bar was located. Might have been targeted because the arsonist knew where the bar was, or maybe the exposed side of the building made for an easy target. Either way, the initial explosion set all those bottles of alcohol on fire and it spread from there."

"A copycat or a second fire for the same person?" Silvio asked.

Lt. Rufino drank noisily from his travel mug.

"I won't know until we trace the fragments," Murillo said. "But it's the same burst pattern, the same signature. My guess is we've got a serial arsonist on our hands."

"A serial arsonist," Lt. Rufino said slowly. He swung around to stare at Emilia. "Impossible."

"Or a copycat," Murillo said reluctantly.

"And Cruz runs away from the scene," Lt. Rufino said acidly.

"I was running after a truck that matched the description given by a witness at the last fire," Emilia repeated.

"We've already arrested the owner of the truck," Lt. Rufino shouted at Emilia, spittle flying.

Silvio made an abrupt cutting gesture that caught Lt. Rufino's eye. "We haven't proven that Torrez was there, *teniente*," the senior detective said. "Just that he might have had motive and access to the weapons."

Lt. Rufino's eyes bulged.

"We'll connect later," Murillo said hastily to Silvio. The arson investigator's face was expressionless as he nodded at Emilia and stepped outside.

His hand shook as Lt. Rufino jabbed a finger in the air at Silvio. "Don't you dare presume to correct me, Detective." He swung to Emilia. "You wanted to play the little heroine, no? First at the other fire, now at this one. Are we going to find a special radio hookup to the *bomberos* dispatch in your car, Cruz?"

Emilia took a step back and felt the plastic panel flap behind her. "No, *teniente*."

Lt. Rufino barely heard her. "But this time you went too far. Numerous witnesses saw you discharge your weapon and destroy city property!"

"That truck was trying to get away so badly it went up on the sidewalk," Emilia explained yet again. "The truck hit that trash can. Shouldn't we be asking why?"

"Consider yourself suspended, Cruz," Lt. Rufino snapped. "Today and tomorrow. When you get back, you'll be in basic training again."

"Suspended?" Emilia exclaimed.

Lt. Rufino ignored her, stalked out, and made his way to his official car and waiting driver.

Emilia clutched her latte cup with both hands, suddenly needing the warmth of the last dregs of coffee. "I am not trying to be some hero," she insisted.

Silvio folded his arms and nodded. "He's scared shitless we arrested the wrong guy. If we did, Carlota's going to crucify Salazar and Salazar's pretty much his only champion here in Acapulco. Obregon will make sure both of their heads roll."

"So now what?" Emilia asked. "That truck matched Maria's description, same as Torrez's truck. This one had people in the back and they were lying down. Hiding."

"We'll get off with retraining and shit assignments for a year," Silvio said, his voice low and harsh. "But if Rufino and Salazar go down because of the Torrez arrest, they'll take Macias and Sandor with them because they made the actual arrest."

"*Madre de Dios*," Emilia murmured, knowing he was right.

"Macias and Sandor have friends, Cruz," Silvio went on. "You know the kinds of friends I mean. You ever wonder why Inocente always gave them the best assignments even when their arrest record is dirt? Why nothing bad ever happens to either of them? Why they're so fucking close, like fucking twins?"

"Payoffs." Emilia mouthed the word, almost afraid to say the truth out loud. Some cartel paid Macias and Sandor to protect their interests. The detectives, in turn, had always passed a cut to Lt. Inocente and others who mattered to a cop's career. "You think Lt. Rufino knows?"

"That's not the point, Cruz." Silvio rolled his eyes in disgust. "You think their friends won't know we did the research, that we were the ones who started things rolling that got their boys in the shitter? If I were you, I'd be praying hard that Torrez doesn't have an alibi, Murillo doesn't know a fuck about doing his job, and you just shot up a truck full of nothing."

Emilia swallowed back a lump of pure fear. "So what would you have done?" she asked quietly.

Silvio passed a hand over his face, kicked at the ground in frustration and exhaled. As before at the El Tigre fire, he'd been the first detective on the scene, and he'd rapidly created a semblance of order out of panic. The Luna Loca's uniformed guards had done a good job and he'd talked to them, made it known they'd done everything possible and had minimized casualties by responding rapidly and well.

"I would have killed as many as I could," Silvio said. "Including whoever was in the truck bed. They were the grenade throwers, same as at the El Tigre when they probably stood in the bed to get over the fence. If they were all dead, Rufino and Salazar could put it out that they'd been copycats. Salazar could still fry Torrez's ass for the El Tigre and Carlota gets her wish to burn Macario Urbina. Maybe the army, too. Nobody gets embarrassed."

"Torrez might be totally innocent," Emilia said.

"Why doesn't he have an alibi?" Silvio retorted.

When she didn't reply, he grabbed her by the upper arm and shoved her out of the shelter. "Go home, Cruz," he said. "Use tomorrow to clean up. See you on Tuesday."

Chapter 17

"There was another fire," Ernesto said from the table.

"I heard." Emilia buried her nose in her coffee mug. Behind her at the stove, her mother was humming.

Sunday had been a lost day. Emilia had spent it alternately sleeping, showering, mulling over Silvio's predictions, and wondering if Kurt's plane had taken off yet. Now it was Monday morning and the day stretched out before her, a day she should be in the office, going through the truck records again, combing through to find specific color descriptions. Maybe Silvio was doing that. Or maybe he was up to his eyeballs in shit.

Ernesto pushed a newspaper across the table. It was a local rag that captured attention with sensational headlines and lurid pictures. On humid days the newsprint came off on skin and regular readers would be seen holding it as if the paper was delicate china.

The picture on the front took up nearly the whole page. The picture of the burning restaurant, flames silhouetted against the night sky as a tired firefighter paused to wipe his face with a soot-darkened glove, had a certain macabre beauty to it. The headline read ARMY STRIKES AGAIN?

The brief article said nothing about a police detective chasing a suspect truck or shots being fired. Instead, the article was a hysterical rant that the army was lashing out at Carlota because she'd refused to pay political kickbacks to them. Emilia didn't know whether to laugh or cry. The charge could be a total fabrication or holy truth.

She put down the paper and fortified herself with some coffee.

Ernesto indicated the headline. "Is this your case?" he asked.

Probably not tomorrow. "Yes." Emilia pushed the paper back across the table to him.

"Is this true?" Ernesto slowly shook his head. "The army setting fires?"

Emilia shrugged. "It sounds odd, doesn't it?"

"Restaurants have money," Ernesto said pointedly.

"More than us, huh?" Emilia grinned at him.

"Who would want them to stop making money?" he asked as Sophia put a plate of fried eggs and potatoes in front of him.

"Whoever wasn't getting their fair share," Emilia said with a laugh as she got up to get her own plate.

Ernesto made a satisfied grunting noise, as if he'd had all the conversation he could manage but that it had pleased him. Emilia kissed her mother as Sophia scooped eggs and potatoes onto a plate. Ernesto was often as vague as her mother, but at other times there was a spark of a real person in there.

Sophia talked about some upcoming event at the church as they ate. Ernesto wolfed down his food and went outside. In a few minutes, Emilia heard the creak and whirr of the grinding wheel starting up and the whine of metal as he began to sharpen something. Still chattering happily, Sophia washed the dishes and joined Ernesto outside.

Emilia sat by herself in the kitchen and toyed with her food, her thoughts sluggish. She read through the newspaper article again, wishing desperately that she could text Rico. Instead, she found her notebook, made another pot of coffee, and sat at the table alone re-reading her notes from the fire at the El Tigre. They'd arrested Torrez because he had a possible motive, an army connection, and the right vehicle. His only connection to the El Tigre had been Carlota's presence there.

Torrez had been behind bars since midday on Friday. His truck was impounded. Emilia doubted they'd find any connection between him and the Luna Loca.

She redrew the timeline, trying to see past the focus on Carlota and the army that they'd all had since the fire at the El Tigre. Something was there, but it was elusive. Each time she thought she'd grasped a thread, it turned out to be nothing more than a wisp of smoke.

Eventually Emilia closed her notebook and went upstairs to change. There were other things she could be doing with her day.

☼

Her badge got her through the turnstile at the CICI water park, but Erick Aguilar Valle, the burly manager, looked harried and unimpressed. His office was a humid cell containing a desk, some cabinets, and a jumble of older computer equipment liberally strewn with paperwork, most of which appeared to be unpaid invoices. The place smelled like a recently opened can of tuna.

"What kind of name is Pedro Lata?" Aguilar asked dismissively. He wore a blue polo with a gray dolphin emblem on the chest. The shirt was tight enough to show that he didn't work out. "Are you making a joke?"

Emilia took out the photo strip and put it on the desk in front of Aguilar.

The manager picked it up and grinned. "That's Pedro Montealegre." He handed it back to Emilia. "What's the *lata* joke about?"

Lila said Montealegre, maybe. Or Castillo.

"I'm sorry." Emilia smiled broadly as she put the picture back in her bag. "It's a family joke. I forget sometimes."

"You're family?" Aguilar asked. "You just said you were a cop."

"I'm his stepsister," Emilia lied. "His grandmother isn't doing well and I hadn't seen him in a while. I didn't know if he was still working here…" She trailed off and looked tearful. Their grandmother was very, very sick.

"Sure," Aguilar said uncomfortably as Emilia sniffed. "Pedro's one of our best handlers." He glanced at a clock on the cement wall. The paint glistened with damp. "He's probably got a few minutes between shows. You'll find him in the big tank."

Emilia followed Aguilar's directions through the employee corridor and found herself in the park's dolphin tank. The huge indoor pool was surrounded by an undulating concrete deck. Wide shallow stairs led into the clear depths, where two dolphins glided side by side just under the surface. They might have been reading each other's minds as they dove and twisted as one.

Halfway between the water's edge and a tier of wooden benches for spectators, two young men in short-sleeved wetsuits posed with three little boys as the parents took pictures. Clad in swim trunks and life vests, the boys were clearly in awe of the experience they'd just had swimming with the sea creatures.

When the picture-taking wrapped up and the family was led to a changing room by a waiting attendant in a CICI polo shirt, Emilia approached the two CICI swimmers.

"Pedro Montealegre?" she asked.

The younger man lifted his chin and she recognized the face from the photo strip with Lila Jimenez Lata. He had the same pronounced cheekbones and sultry good looks as his sister and was the right age, if Berta's story had been correct. "How can I help you, señorita?" he asked with the smile of a man used to having women approach him.

His diction was clearly upper class, and if the picture hadn't been such an accurate likeness, Emilia would have thought she had the wrong person. Pedro Montealegre was fit, handsome and polished, hardly the product of a brief union between a tramp and a stranger.

"A family issue," Emilia said. "If I could have a minute of your time?"

Pedro Montealegre's smile didn't fade, just became more brittle. But there was curiosity in his eyes, too. "Give us 10 minutes, José?" he asked the other man. "Then I'll help you get ready for the next show."

The man called José nodded at Pedro Montealegre and walked past Emilia. He passed through a door, leaving Emilia and the younger man alone by the big pool with the dolphins.

Pedro picked up a towel from a bench at the bottom of the tier of bleachers and rubbed his wet hair. "My name is Pedro Montealegre," he said. "I dropped out of UNAM halfway through my degree in economics due to a dispute with my father. My family's in Monterrey and I haven't seen them since. I doubt you know them, señorita."

He delivered the words with that flawless diction, his smile still pasted on. It was a speech he'd given dozens of times, and it was very convincing.

Emilia took the photo strip out of her shoulder bag and held it out to him. "Your real name is Pedro Lata," she said. "Your sister is Lila Jimenez Lata. Her father was Enrique Jimenez. He wasn't your father, but you and Lila share the same mother, Yolanda Lata."

Pedro's smile faded and his eyes narrowed. "Where did you get those pictures, señorita?"

"I found them under Lila's bed." Emilia watched his expression tighten as she continued. "Lila's been missing for several weeks and her grandmother Berta asked me to help find her. I'm a police detective. Emilia Cruz Encinos."

"Lila's missing?" Pedro balled up the towel as fear etched across his handsome features. "Did somebody snatch her? Does Berta need ransom money?"

Emilia shook her head and sat down on the bench. For no reason at all, she'd half believed that he would say that Lila was with him. That his sister had run away from Berta and he'd given her a place to stay.

Instead, his face told Emilia everything she'd feared. Lila hadn't run away to her brother. He didn't know where she was.

She told him what Itzel had said, about Lila wanting to find her mother despite Berta's claims that Yolanda was dead. How Lila had planned to go "downtown" but never returned home. Halfway through, he slumped onto the bench next to her and buried his head in his hands.

"Your mother was arrested for prostitution four years ago," Emilia wound up. It was warm in the enclosed pool area and she could feel sweat trickle between her breasts. Her bra felt damp, and no doubt her ponytail looked like limp string. "Do you know who paid her out?"

Pedro sat up and wiped his face with the towel. "The last time I saw my mother was in a porn magazine."

Emilia took the magazine out of her shoulder bag. "This one? I found it under Lila's bed along with the photos of the two of you."

"I gave that to her," Pedro said. His voice cracked but he didn't lose his precise manner of speech. Emilia guessed he'd practiced long and hard to make himself into Pedro Montealegre from Monterrey. "So she could see who her mother really was. Page 19."

Emilia found the right page. He tapped the bottom photo as the magazine lay open on her knees.

"That's Yolanda," he said and got to his feet. He walked to the edge of the pool and slapped his hand against the surface of the water. The dolphins' sleek shapes broke the surface. They glided up onto the shallow step and he petted their heads as if they were puppies.

Emilia pulled her eyes back to the smut on her lap. She tried to imagine having a picture like this of Sophia and failed. In the grainy magazine image, Yolanda was naked and engaged in sex astride a man whose face was cropped out of the picture. The camera had captured Yolanda with her chin lifted, her mouth open, and her face turned partway toward the photographer, enough for Emilia to see the same sultry eyes and high cheekbones, the same exotic Asian cast to her features that the woman had passed to her children. It was hard to tell her age, given the angle and poor quality of the picture, but her body was still in fairly good shape.

"Hell of a thing, isn't it?" Pedro said from the side of the pool, the perfect pronunciation tinged with disgust. "To have that be the only picture of your mother that you have?"

"The magazine is two years old," Emilia pointed out. "Have you been in touch with Yolanda since then? Maybe gave Lila an address for her?"

"I ran across the picture by accident," Pedro said. He walked over to a box built into the wall, took out a pail of fish, and fed a snack to both dolphins. Each animal bumped its head under his hand afterward, as if thanking him for the fish. The humid air filled with the scent of sardine. As Pedro stood up, one of the dolphins did that peculiar backwards dance while chattering at him. Emilia laughed. Pedro gave a little bow before stowing the fish bucket and washing his hands in the pool.

He came back to the bench and Emilia was struck again by his exotic good looks and the way his body looked strong and fit in the wetsuit. "Wherever she is," he said as he sat down again, "the woman is still an addict and still a hooker. Making money on the side with pictures like these. She dumped me on the side of the road when I was 15 because I wouldn't pimp for her. Best thing that ever happened to me."

"How much does Lila know?" Emilia asked. She wanted to ask what he'd done in those intervening 11 years, how he'd come to be working at the CICI water park as a dolphin handler, but she sensed he didn't want to share his story. He was only a few years younger than she was, and while his looks were youthful, his demeanor was much older, as if his experiences had drained away too much of his soul too soon. She closed the magazine. "Besides this?"

"Lila knows she's a hooker," Pedro said. "Maybe once a year I get a money order. Just cash. No message, no address. I see Lila every six months or so, when she can sneak out, and I give the money to her."

"Does Berta know about the money?" Emilia asked.

"No. I told Lila to save it. Finish school and go to college. Grab the opportunity for a decent education that Berta is giving her." He gazed at the silently gliding dolphins. "Lila hates Berta, you know. Lots of rules. Catholic school. Has to keep her mouth shut when Berta says Yolanda is dead. The truth is that Berta always hated Yolanda, knew she was an addict the whole time she was married to her sainted Enrique. Happiest day of Berta's life was when Yolanda walked out of that house."

"I didn't know any of this, you know," Emilia said. "A priest asked me to help Berta and I found all this out by accident."

He nodded. "Thanks for coming and telling me."

There wasn't much else to say. Emilia stood up and held out a card with her name and cell number on it. "If Lila gets in touch, will you call me?"

He took the card. "I'll text you with my number," he said.

"If there's anything I can do, tell me."

"It was nice meeting you, Pedro Montealegre from Monterrey." Emilia shook his hand. "The manager thinks I'm your step-sister, just passing through to tell you about your grandmother, who isn't well. She'd like you to patch things up with your father. But he's a hardcase and I doubt he'll understand you're doing something you love."

Relief crossed the young man's face.

Emilia pulled the strap of her bag over her shoulder before realizing she'd forgotten one last question. "How much money have you given Lila from those money orders?" she asked.

"All together? About 5000 pesos."

Emilia took a deep breath of damp, fishy air. "Lila can keep searching for a long time with 5000 pesos in her pocket."

She watched the carefully cultivated Pedro Montealegre façade crumble. For a moment, just a moment, the young man was just some kid who was scared and lonely and lost on an unknown road. And then he squared his shoulders and became himself again.

Chapter 18

Emilia spent the rest of Monday afternoon and more than 200 pesos at an Internet café, trying to find some reference to the publisher of the porn magazine with Yolanda Lata's picture. All she got for her time and money was a sick appreciation of homemade porn sites and some lecherous looks from the café proprietor, who obviously monitored his patron's searches.

She eventually gave up and checked a news site, only to find a new video from Los Matas Ejercito on the front page. As before, the masked men sat in a row, with the tallest in the middle. He was the only one to speak. There was nothing on the table, no way to identify them, nothing distinctive except the bottles of water. The speaker blamed the latest fire on the army and vowed revenge. Emilia played it through twice, but there was nothing to suggest who was behind the self-proclaimed vigilante group or what they planned to do.

A few more clicks brought her to other top news stories. The area in front of the *alcaldía* was now a flower-heaped shrine to the dead from both fires. Acapulco uniformed police were there in large numbers to ensure calm. Demonstrators had occupied land near *campo militar* in Atoyac. Military police there were on alert but so far the protest was orderly.

As dusk settled, Emilia logged off, found a food stand on a street corner, and loaded up. If Lila Jimenez Lata had been looking for a hooker, Emilia had a few ideas about what "downtown" could mean.

Emilia parked the Suburban in the Hotel Parador's parking garage, crossed the lobby, and let herself out of the hotel through a side door. A dozen steps and she was in the warren of back streets behind the big downtown area hotels. As the sun set, the evening turned cool. She was glad she'd pulled on a sweatshirt from her gym bag before setting out. In the baggy garment, jeans, and sneakers, she was nothing special and unlikely to attract attention.

The waterfront area known to tourists as Hotel Row was a polished white wall hiding the best places to find a girl for 15 minutes or an hour. Or all night if you were a high roller. Sometimes young boys were on offer as well, but Acapulco was generally an old-fashioned city, clinging to its faded reputation as a 1950's Hollywood playground, and most men still came to find girls.

It was easiest to get a girl in the hotels where the fixers worked. They'd mark out a man who looked lonely and work out a deal. Some money would change hands, the fixer would go get a girl who'd been waiting for his call, and bring her up to the buyer's room.

There were other places besides the backstreets of Hotel Row to look for a girl who was trying to make her way on her back, like the gentlemen's clubs and escort services that provided "models." The better gentlemen's clubs advertised in *Que Paso Acapulco*, the monthly about-town glossy magazine that also carried bold advertisements for restaurants, tours, parasailing, helicopter rides, and shopping day trips.

For the less discriminating sex hunter, Acapulco also offered *haciendas de confianza* where men could have a quick afternoon sex fix and total anonymity. There, on a busy day, a girl might have to service 10 or 15 customers.

Emilia shifted her shoulder bag as she turned east. It wasn't yet fully dark, but the nightlife was already getting under way. Music spilled out of bars as she passed. Girls and their fixers eyed her from the front seats of cars parked parallel to the curb, or from the service entrances of the smaller hotels.

"Carla." Emilia walked up to a thin woman leaning against a wall set a few feet back from the curb. "Having a good night?"

The woman was Emilia's own age, with frizzy shoulder-length hair. She wore a denim miniskirt, a blue tube top that hugged small breasts, and leopard print booties designed to help her break an ankle on the uneven sidewalk.

Carla took a moment to place Emilia but broke into a smile when recognition dawned. "Hey, Emilia." Her voice had the rasp of a heavy smoker. "Been awhile."

"Yeah." Emilia embraced the other woman, catching a ripe perfume of bad teeth and nicotine. "Did you eat tonight?"

Carla shook her head. "Not yet."

Emilia pulled a foil-wrapped cylinder from the food stand out of her bag and held it out to the other woman. "Here."

"Thanks, Emilia." Carla peeled back the foil from the burrito filled with beans, rice, and cheese and took a huge mouthful. "Did your mother make it?" she asked as she chewed.

"Straight from Mama's kitchen." Emilia watched Carla wolf down the street vendor's food. They'd gone to school together, both struggling to pay the school fees and buy the required books and uniforms. Emilia had fought to the last peso to get through and graduate near the top of her class, but Carla had given up the fight long before completing secondary school, which wasn't mandatory, after all. She'd worked in a shop for a while and gotten pregnant. When the father took off she parked the baby with her mother and drifted to the streets. The baby was 12 now, still living with Carla's mother, while Carla lived with a man she called her husband. Emilia knew he was a fixer at one of the low-end hotels, working arrangements through one of the kitchen staff. Carla looked closer to 50 than 30.

Emilia pulled out the picture of Lila Jimenez Lata. "Have you seen this girl?" She angled the photo to catch the street light's glow.

Carla kept chewing, both hands locked possessively around the foil-wrapped burrito. "She's a looker."

"So you'd remember her, right?"

"Couple of weeks ago, I think." Carla shrugged and took another bite.

"Really?" Emilia couldn't believe her luck. "When? Recently?"

"Emilia." Carla rolled her eyes at all the quick questions. She took another bite. "Does somebody want her specifically?"

"Carla." Emilia nearly laughed. "I'm not pimping. I'm

trying to find this girl for her family."

"Oh." Carla regarded the picture with a little more interest. Sauce from the burrito dripped down her hand and she absently sucked it off. "Okay, yeah, I've seen her. Couple weeks, maybe. She was lost."

"Where was she trying to go?"

Carla frowned. "*Madre de Dios*, Emilia. This was weeks ago. I don't know. I can hardly remember how to fuck these days." She laughed at her own joke and took another bite.

Emilia managed a smile. "Okay, well, tell me where you were when you saw her."

Carla looked around. "I guess I was down there." She pointed the last bit of the burrito at the next street corner.

"Great." Emilia took Carla's elbow and gently steered her in that direction. "So you were down there. Did she pass by? How did you know she was lost?"

"She walked right past like I was invisible." Carla sniffed and gulped down the remainder of the burrito, folded the foil wrapping, and stuffed it into her bag. "I can use that, you know."

"Sure," Emilia agreed. For all she knew, Carla would use the piece of foil as a blanket. Or a condom. "What about the girl?"

"Yeah, I remember her good now. She had this *my shit don't stink* look as she went by."

They were at the corner now. "You were here or across the street?" Emilia asked.

"Over there," Carla said.

They went across the street. Emilia pulled a candy bar out of her bag and used it as a pointer. "Which direction did she go? Towards the Parador or away from it?"

Carla's eyes flickered away from the candy toward the next street. The quality of the neighborhood diminished the further east a person went. Working the next corner over might earn Carla 20 or 30 pesos for a hand job, slightly more if she got on her knees behind a building and opened her mouth. She probably didn't get much other business these days.

The blue tube top had a burrito sauce stain. Carla licked her thumb and rubbed at it before going on. "She asked Pica Pica how to get to Julieta Rubia's place." She looked up at Emilia. "You know Pica Pica? She works for Oscar Abrazo."

"Sure," Emilia said. She would agree with everything Carla said if it kept her old friend talking. "Pica Pica. Is she around tonight?"

"No." Carla sighed. "She got beat up real bad two nights ago. Haven't seen her since."

"What's her real name?"

"Pica Pica?" Carla shrugged. "I don't know."

"Okay." Emilia made a mental note to see what she could find out about the unfortunate Pica Pica. "Julieta Rubia's place. You're sure that's where the girl wanted to go?"

"Pica Pica told her how to find it and the girl kept going. Guess she was after a job."

Until a few weeks ago, Julieta Rubia had been the most powerful fixer in this part of Acapulco, running a lucrative string of girls and paying off enough of official Acapulco to operate undisturbed. It had been a shock when Julieta was arrested a few weeks ago for offering a 13-year-old girl to a visiting Canadian mayor in town for a conference with Carlota. Julieta had walked the girl into the hotel herself, apparently knocked on the wrong door, and smilingly told the Canadian in English that he would have to pay up front for a night of fantasy with his "model."

Carlota had been furious. Julieta's bail was set impossibly high, and she was in prison awaiting a trial that had yet to be scheduled and probably wouldn't be for some time. Under Mexican law, timing wasn't prescribed and trials were rarely swift. Trials were closed as well, a paperwork exercise between lawyers and the judge.

Emilia gave the candy bar to Carla and pulled up the zipper of her hoodie. Carla seemed oblivious to the cool night air as she unwrapped the candy bar, but her bare skin was pimpled with gooseflesh.

"So who's in charge now that Julieta's in jail?" Emilia asked.

"I hear it's Olga," Carla said "Olga la Fea. You know her?"

"No." *Olga the Ugly One*. Emilia would have remembered that.

"She's a real *puta*," Carla observed.

Emilia didn't point out the irony of calling the woman a whore. "Did you ever see the girl again?" she asked instead. "Heard anybody talk about a girl named Lila?"

Carla bit into the candy bar. "I can't remember every crap piece of gossip on this street," she said around the mouthful.

"Think, Carla," Emilia pleaded. "This is important."

"Emilia, don't be so pushy."

"I know, I'm sorry."

A car slowed and Carla took a step forward. Emilia moved in front of her and snapped her fingers at the car to keep moving. It continued down the street.

"You're pushy, Emilia," Carla complained again. She held the candy in one hand and wrestled a cigarette out of her bag with the other. She jammed the cigarette into her mouth, flicked a lighter, and sucked in smoke around the bite of chocolate.

"Just a couple more questions, Carla," Emilia said, trying to be patient. "Did you see the girl again? Say in the last two weeks."

"No." Carla alternated between the candy and the cigarette as they walked back to her original place on the street. "I'd remember. She was pretty enough to be an inside girl."

Inside girls never worked the streets, but drifted through the bars and clubs of the most upscale locations on Hotel Row, either working with a well-placed fixer or paying off key hotel staff such as the concierge to look the other way. Dressed in designer clothes and subtle makeup, an inside girl could command 5000 or even 6000 pesos a night. Inside girls always had the best clientele, too: nothing weird, no anal, no violence.

"Did Julieta have any inside girls?" Emilia asked.

Carla finished the candy bar and flicked both the wrapper and her cigarette butt into the gutter. "Julieta had everything. She kept everybody safe, you know?" The thin woman shivered, finally seeming to notice the cool night. "It's not like that now."

"You need to take better care of yourself, Carla," Emilia said, wondering if Carla had anything contagious.

"I'm good." Carla shook out a new cigarette and lit it. She drew in a lungful of smoke and looked critically at Emilia. "You know, with better clothes and heels, you could be an inside girl. Make enough money in one night to buy a cell phone."

"I already have a cell phone," Emilia said.

It was very dark by the time Emilia went into Mami's, the pool hall all the cops knew had been Julieta Rubia's place of business. Emilia had been in too many bars like this; first as a kid with her cousins, trying to hustle jobs selling things to tourists, and later as a cop trying to find out things from people who liked to play pool, drink heavily, and hide from the law. Her success rate in both instances was low.

Olga la Fea wasn't hard to find. In response to her question, a heavyset man behind the bar scanned her from head to toe, grinned, and jerked his head to the rear.

Emilia drifted through the place, which was packed with a local clientele that looked to be comprised of workers from the docks and *mercados* as well as the city's constant construction projects. The pulse of techno music competed with the clink of beer bottles and the din of conversation. The atmosphere was fairly friendly and Emilia got a few appreciative looks. She acknowledged them with shy smiles, not wanting to risk an altercation with a drunk who felt slighted, and made her way to the rear door labeled "Office."

A man by the door, who was a larger and more menacing version of the bartender, frisked her before letting her pass through. Grateful that she'd had the presence of mind to stash her bag, gun and badge in the Suburban, Emilia found herself in a large reception room. She could see an office through a wide doorway to the left.

The reception room looked like the waiting room over at the health clinic, except that all the patients were girls in high heels, dresses the size of bandages, and enough makeup to spackle over every beach in Acapulco. They sat on worn vinyl furniture and preened in front of hand mirrors. A few looked up as she came into the room and regarded her with expressions that ranged from boredom to dismissal. In her hoodie and jeans, Emilia obviously wasn't competition.

The room had plain white walls and a few travel posters tacked to the cement. Emilia wondered if it was sometimes used for private parties or other events. Two long rectangular tables, the kind the church set up for weddings and *quinciñera* celebrations, were pushed up against one wall. Metal folding chairs were stacked next to them. The tabletops were littered with bottles of water and liquor, a tray of plastic cups, paper plates and napkins, and dirty aluminum food containers. A trash bin held dirty paper plates and empty water bottles.

"You looking for a job?"

A woman stepped to the doorway of the office and Emilia tried not to react to her appearance. Olga la Fea's features had been rearranged by someone's fist at some point in her past, although it might have been a baseball bat. Her hairline was made irregular by a dramatic gouge that had been taken out of her forehead over her right eye, which drooped lower than the left by at least the width of Emilia's thumb. It wasn't just the eye, Emilia realized; the woman's right cheekbone had been crushed and never replaced, so that entire side of her face was flat and sagged downward. Olga apparently wasn't one to soften the effect of her appearance; she wore sparkly blue shadow that accentuated the uneven eyes, her hair was pulled back into a severe twist, and her stick-thin body was clad in black leggings and a too-youthful pink bustier.

"I'm looking for a girl," Emilia said. "She might have come here asking about her mother."

She reached in her pocket to find the picture of Lila and heard the unmistakable click of a gun. "It's just a picture," she said without turning around.

"Why do you think she came here?" Olga asked. The woman pushed herself past the office doorway, sauntered into the waiting room, and produced a snort of disgust at the mess on the tables. She had an expensive smartphone in one hand. Her fingernails were the same bright pink as the bustier. Emilia placed her age at about 40, although the disfigurement and unhealthy mottled skin made her look at least 20 years older.

"I heard she came to see Julieta." Emilia held out Lila's school picture.

Olga snatched it up with a guttural laugh. "Well, this is fresh bait. Come look at this."

The picture got handed around to the men by the door and two other women who came out of the office behind Olga. They were also hard older women who had seen their best days pass by, but could still make a living servicing the pool hall patrons in the alley behind the building four or five times a night.

"She came here a month ago, looking for Julieta," Emilia said quickly, unsure how far the crude humor generated by the picture would take her. "Her name is Lila Jimenez Lata. She was looking for her mother, a hooker named Yolanda Lata."

Olga flicked the picture to the floor at Emilia's feet. "Never heard of her, cop girl."

Emilia bent and picked up the picture, keeping her breathing even, forcing herself to appear unconcerned at the woman's taunt. "I'm only interested in finding the girl. Doesn't matter where she is or what she's doing. Or anything else happening around here."

Olga shrugged and looked around at her little empire. One of the older women smiled, showing a gap where a front tooth had been.

"Anybody else around when this girl talked to Julieta?" Emilia asked.

"Nobody here seen your little girl." Olga found a straw, put it into a plastic cup, and added something from one of the bottles. She sucked on the straw. The right side of her face didn't move at all. "If Julieta saw her, then Julieta saw her. She liked to keep things private."

"Julieta wasn't here alone when Lila came calling," Emilia gambled. "I'm just looking for the girl. Anything about the girl."

"I said Julieta kept her things private." Olga curled her free hand into a tight fist and held it to her heart. "You know Julieta? Like this. Small and hard."

The women in the room laughed dutifully.

"Looks like things aren't so private now," Emilia said. "New management?"

Olga unclenched her fist and waved her arm around. "These girls, they're all waiting for sewing lessons."

"Maybe I should hang around," Emilia heard herself say. "Pick up a few tips."

The left side of Olga's face smiled. The right maintained its perpetual sag. Olga stepped closer and Emilia smelled the acidic bite of cheap tequila. "You forgot your needle and thread, *puta*," Olga said softly.

"Next time," Emilia said. She nodded to the ugly woman, pushed past the man with the gun, and left.

Chapter 19

Lt. Rufino was the first person Emilia ran into as she came into the police station Tuesday morning. To her surprise, he nodded at her and asked, "How's the hand, Cruz?"

It took her two beats to realize he was asking about the now-healed burn from the El Tigre fire. She'd taken the bandage off days ago. "Fine, *teniente*," she managed. "Thank you for asking."

"Silvio said you were at the doctor again, so I'm glad to hear you're feeling better," he said. "You two have a lot to follow up on."

With that, he continued down the hall towards the restrooms, and Emilia made her befuddled way into the squadroom and to her desk. She unlocked it, dropped her shoulder bag into the bottom drawer, and looked around for Silvio.

He was sitting on the edge of Sandor's desk as the latter spoke on the phone, chair tipped back, free hand clutching his hair in exasperation. Macias leaned over his partner's desk, also trying to listen in on the conversation. Emilia walked over to the little group and Silvio gave her his usual welcoming scowl.

"I understand that, señor," Sandor said into the phone. "And we appreciate that the mayor is of the people and very interested in the success of Acapulco businesses." He started to go on, but squawks from the receiver cut him off. Sandor rolled his eyes in frustration before he was able to continue his end of the conversation.

"I fully understand what you are saying. The mayor had planned to visit the Luna Loca club last Saturday night. But the fire happened before she arrived."

More squawking indicated the caller's relief that Sandor had finally understood the point of the conversation.

"So who had access to the mayor's plans?" Sandor listened

as the squawking grew earnest. "Just her personal staff, you say?"

He rolled his eyes at the group gathered around his desk. "So one of them would have to be involved, don't you think? I mean, you've just said no one else knew she planned to go there." He stopped talking.

Silvio snorted and Emilia had to grin, although it was sad to think how easily Sandor had caught Carlota's staff in a lie.

The squawks eventually resumed, but they were brief. Sandor said, "I'll be waiting for your call," and hung up. He let his chair bang down on all four legs. "Fuck this. They're so desperate to make this all about Carlota, they called and insisted that she had planned to go to that club."

Silvio shook his head. "It's clean slate day. Let's forget Carlota, get some interviews done, and meet back here this afternoon."

Macias and Sandor both stood up and hauled on jackets.

"What about the morning meeting?" Emilia asked.

"Cancelled." Silvio went back to their desks and grabbed his leather jacket from the back of his chair. "Rufino's got to go over to the state attorney general's office and report on the El Pharaoh investigation. We've got an appointment to talk to the owner of the Luna Loca."

Emilia glanced at the desks occupied by Gomez and Castro. Neither detective was there. She had a bad feeling about what had happened to the El Pharaoh investigation and an even worse feeling about Lt. Rufino. Her hand trailed over Rico's desk as she left. Just a touch. For luck.

Ted Conway was the *norteamericano* owner of Luna Loca. He wore designer jeans and a designer V-neck tee shirt with a pin-striped designer blazer. He was younger than Emilia, a playboy surfer type with a shock of sun-streaked hair and a jittery manner that could be the result of too many energy drinks, stress from losing his business, or the death of two employees. Or a recent and healthy dose of cocaine.

Conway was flanked by his lawyer, Oscar Zeledón Rivera, and a man who'd been introduced as Agent Clark from Seguridad Plata Asociados. Clark was the ostensible host, given that the meeting was being held in an SPA conference room.

Emilia had been given business cards for both Zeledón and Clark. Zeledón was a well-known lawyer to the rich and famous. She didn't recognize Clark personally, but knew that SPA was one of the biggest private security companies in Mexico, providing everything from bodyguards for visiting movie stars to uniformed guards for shopping centers. As if to proclaim the company's impressive reach, a large crystal globe in the center of the long table sat on a broad wooden base emblazoned with a gold SPA logo.

Clark slid a small plastic zip-lock bag across the table to Emilia and Silvio. "This was passed to an employee of the Luna Loca approximately three weeks ago."

Inside the clear bag was half a piece of printer paper, a copy of a copy that had been printed crookedly. The word ATTENTION was repeated three times across the top. Underneath, slanted text announced an army protective tax of 5000 pesos, payable to the army collection team. There was no mention of how the tax was to be paid, or how often.

There was no direct threat, no notice that if the recipient didn't pay, their business would be the victim of a grenade attack.

"Passed?" Silvio frowned. "What do you mean, passed?"

Clark folded his hands together on the tabletop. As big as Silvio, he had the weathered look of a man who'd learned how to stay calm in bad parts of the world. His suit jacket strained to contain his biceps, and Emilia decided he was bald from choice rather than genetics. "One of Mr. Conway's employees was handed the paper by a man who came into the restaurant shortly before it opened one day. The employee gave it to Mr. Conway, who assumed it was a joke and put it in his pocket. Now, however, he feels it may be relevant to the fire at the Luna Loca."

"Can Mr. Conway tell us about the man who came into the

restaurant?" Emilia asked.

Conway's leg started to jingle hard enough to vibrate the table. Clark cleared his throat. "He didn't see the man. The only person who did was the bartender."

"Why aren't we talking to him?" Silvio growled.

"The Luna Loca bartender was a victim of the fire," Clark said.

"He'd only worked for me for a couple of weeks," Conway blurted. For a *gringo*, his Spanish wasn't bad, although it wasn't as good as Kurt's. He put a trembling hand to his head and Emilia saw that his hand was bandaged the same way hers had been. "I poached him from the Polo Club. He had style and I really pushed hard to get him to come work for me. If I hadn't, he'd still be alive."

Emilia slid her eyes to Silvio. He'd made the connection, same as she had.

"Between the time the message was passed to your bartender and the night of the fire," Emilia asked gently, "did anyone make an effort to collect this so-called tax?"

"No," Clark said.

"Mr. Conway?" Emilia prompted, ignoring Clark.

Conway shook his head.

"Are you sure?" Emilia pressed. "No one came up to you at the restaurant? Near your car? Ask you for money? Ask any of your employees?"

"If they did, no one told me," Conway said. Sweat now stained the neck of his expensive tee shirt. Emilia decided it was silk.

"Just to make sure I get this all down," Emilia said. She glanced at the timeline in her notebook as Silvio turned over the notice in its plastic bag. "You hired a new bartender who had previously worked at the Polo Club?"

Conway nodded and his leg pumped furiously again. "Hector Roque."

"About how long between Hector coming to work for you and getting the tax notice?"

Zeledón whispered something to Conway, who had to bend sideways to hear the shorter man. Conway whispered something back and Zeledón nodded.

"Maybe two weeks," Conway said.

"Why did you think the message was a joke?" Silvio leaned forward.

"Surely you can see what an amateur effort it is," Zeledón said, indicating the plastic bag.

"But he took it seriously enough to hire a lot of new security." Silvio rapped on the table for emphasis, his fist as big as the crystal globe. "Maybe there are a few details he's left out?"

"Anything about the person who left this message would be very helpful," Emilia added. "I'm sure Mr. Conway wants whoever set fire to the Luna Loca to be found."

Clark stood up. "That's all Mr. Conway has. We're sorry we can't be more helpful."

Both detectives stayed in their seats.

"We'll need a copy of this notice," Emilia said.

"That's all Mr. Conway has," Emilia repeated as Silvio started the car. "Oddly enough, I think it's true. Conway strikes me as a rich little boy who until Saturday night was having a pretty good time drinking and partying down here in Acapulco."

"*Rayos*," Silvio swore. "He probably had half a kilo of *coca* up his nose."

"What was so interesting on the back of the notice?" Emilia asked.

"The Luna Loca's address." Silvio put on his sunglasses and backed the car out of the space in front of the SPA building. "Small printing. Pencil."

"You think somebody printed off a bunch of these flyers and labeled them with the addresses of where they were supposed to go?"

"Places that could afford to pay an army tax," Silvio said.

"Think the Polo Club connection means anything?"

"I guess we'll find out."

Emilia let her head fall back against the seat as she mulled over this new development. An army tax, but as the lawyer had pointed out, done in such an amateurish way.

Yesterday's conversation with Ernesto came back to her. *Whoever wasn't getting their fair share.* "Simple extortion," she said out loud. "Everybody knows that most decent restaurants in Acapulco coin money, and the ones that don't launder cash for the drug cartels. Haven't heard Murillo say yet that *campo militar*'s armory is airtight. Maybe a couple of soldiers simply pocketed a couple of grenades and decided to set up a little extortion business."

"What's that got to do with Carlota?" Silvio asked. "Or Torrez?"

"Nothing," Emilia admitted.

"So you're saying we have a serial arson and extortion ring," Silvio grumbled.

"Maybe," Emilia said. "But think about this angle. Los Matas Ejercito. They haven't done anything besides make videos. But what if they know something we don't?"

"They are army types, too," Silvio suggested. "Pissed that their buddies didn't let them in for a cut."

"And get it on social media where all the kids live these days," Emilia said.

"They're better bad press than the usual," Silvio said thoughtfully. "You know, most of the time the army is being rightly accused of one atrocity or another. Rapes, drug deals, random shootings. A news story comes out and people scream. *Federales* say there will be an investigation. Nothing happens. This is different. These guys are making a big splash with their videos and those ninja costumes."

"Creating more pressure for action than usual." Emilia pulled out her notebook and scribbled down their ideas. "When I came in this morning, Lt. Rufino asked how I was feeling, said you'd told him I called in sick because of my hand."

Silvio braked for a red light and looked at her over the top of his sunglasses. "He didn't remember a thing about Saturday night. I don't think you have to worry about that suspension going on your record."

"Well." Emilia decided to see that as a positive development.

Five minutes later, Silvio turned into the road leading to the gates of the Polo Club and slowed as the guard held up a hand.

Chapter 20

"I gave them the money the first time," Jorge Serverio said, looking close to tears. "But when they came back, they asked for 20,000 pesos. We simply didn't have it. I said we could give it to them here."

Serverio and his wife had been eating their lunch when the two detectives came in to the Polo Club. The restauranteur looked as if he'd aged 10 years since they'd spoken to him last. Lines of pain and worry were etched into his face. His wife was a well-kept woman in a simple but expensive tan suit and heavy silver jewelry. Her hand shook as she set down her fork and knife. He'd introduced her to the two detectives as Vanessa de Serverio.

"That's why you were here in the Polo Club all evening," Emilia said to Vanessa.

The woman nodded. "But they never came," she said.

"Let's start at the beginning," Silvio said. "You got the same notice? How?"

The copy of the message Conway had received lay on the table. Serverio gingerly touched it with a fingertip as if it could hurt him. "One of the kitchen staff brought it to me. Said a man delivered it to the back gate."

"How long ago was this?"

"I'm not sure." Serverio curled his hand into a fist. "At first, I thought it was legitimate. After all, the army has been very much in evidence here in Acapulco over the past year. If you watch the news, you know how expensive it is to keep them deployed all the time, on guard in front of the hotels and public spaces. I was going to discuss it with Kurt. Maybe some of the others on the Acapulco hotel board knew about it. But things got busy. I had trouble with a supplier and some staff quit."

"What about Hector Roque?" Silvio asked. "He used to work here, didn't he?"

"We heard he died at Luna Loca," Serverio said.

"Why did he quit?"

"He got a better offer," Serverio hazarded. The look on his face said he didn't know why and didn't think it was important. "There were no hard feelings. Good bartenders and wait staff generally have a lot of options in Acapulco."

The bartender was a dead end, Emilia decided. She made a subtle rolling motion with her hand at Silvio.

"So you decided the tax was legit and that you'd pay," Silvio prompted.

"Maybe two, three days later." Serverio's mouth trembled. "Two big men, wearing army jackets, came in and asked for the tax money. They took it, thanked me, and left."

"This was at the El Tigre?"

"Yes." Serverio sipped some mineral water. Neither he nor his wife had finished their meal of seafood *paella*. Emilia felt her stomach rumble at the rich smell of saffron and shrimp. Maybe after they left here, she and Silvio could get some pizza.

"When did they ask for another tax payment?" Emilia asked.

"Two days before the fire." Serverio's wife laid a hand on her husband's arm and answered for him. "That's when we realized that it hadn't been a real tax."

"Did they say if you didn't pay they'd burn down the restaurant?"

"They talked about consequences," Serverio said. "We thought they meant kidnapping."

"But you declined to pay?"

Vanessa again took up the story. "We said we would, but we never kept much cash at the El Tigre, being so close to the plaza with all those pickpockets and all. Everyone always paid with a credit card." A tear ran down her face. "I had the money with me here, but they never came."

Emilia could well picture her sitting alone with a bag of money, terrified at the exchange she would have with the extortionists, drinking to calm her nerves. No wonder the bartender thought the Serverios had quarreled. She flipped to a fresh page in her notebook. "Tell us a bit more about who talked to you."

Serverio twisted his hands together as his wife dabbed at her eyes with a napkin. "Big types. Both of them."

"Bigger than me?" Silvio asked.

Serverio nodded. "About your size. Tall, heavyset. Clean shaven."

"*Mestizo*?"

"Yes."

"Were they wearing uniforms?"

"Military jackets. And hats. I remember thinking that they were so big their uniforms barely fit them." He wiped his eyes with his index finger.

"How did they get to the restaurant?" Silvio asked next. "Did you see a vehicle?"

"No. I was in my office and they just walked in."

Silvio pumped Serverio for every detail, from what time the men had come in to collect the money to insights as to their mode of speech. His wife sat next to him, crying silently until she suddenly slammed her hands on the table.

"Why didn't they just come and take the money?" she burst out. "We would have given it to them. Why did they have to kill so many people? Destroy such a beautiful place?"

Serverio put his arm around his wife. Emilia felt horribly sad. These were good people running a decent business in Acapulco.

"They couldn't risk coming through the gate here at the Polo Club," Silvio said matter-of-factly, completely without emotion. "That's why they torched the El Tigre. Thought you were setting a trap."

Both Serverio and his wife gazed open-mouthed at the stolid detective. They were shattered, and Emilia felt like slapping him on their behalf. What he'd said was almost certainly true, but he could have delivered the message in a less harsh manner.

"Why don't you take the rest of the day to think about things," she suggested, and their pained expressions turned to her. "But first thing tomorrow we'd like you to come to the station, look through some pictures, see if we can't build some sketches of what these men looked like."

"Of course," Serverio said.

Chapter 21

"Two well-known restaurants," Emilia started off. "Two Saturday nights."

"Fires about the same time," Sandor added. "The hour before midnight."

"How about Serverio and Conway in this together to collect insurance money?" Silvio interjected.

"Got tired of dishing up *ceviche* and decided to burn down their places?" Sandor asked.

"Hired some army types to do it for them?" Macias threw out.

Silvio started writing on a white board that had been used so many times it no longer came clean. His handwriting was hard to pick out from the faded blue and black print still clinging to the thing.

"No," Emilia said. "Don't even bother with that one. Conway is so scared he's living with his private security company, and the Serverios are in shock."

Maintenance was working on the air conditioning in the squadroom and nearly everybody had found somewhere else to be. The four detectives had decided to brainstorm in the largest interrogation room near the holding cells. Murillo and Lt. Rufino were there as well. *El teniente* sat silently at the table, his steel travel mug held close to his mouth.

Silvio had divided the board into two halves, one labeled *El Tigre* and the other *Luna Loca*, and was lining up the facts in each column. "Let's keep going. What else do we have?"

"Okay." Emilia flipped open her notebook. "Same employee once worked for both Serverio and Conway. Hector Roque. Bartender. Worked at the Polo Club, left a few months ago to work for Conway at the Luna Loca. One of the victims of the fire."

Silvio wrote it down and she went on. "Club cab truck seen at both locations either shortly before or shortly after the fire.

Army types seen in the truck."

"Don't know they're army," Silvio corrected her. "Only that they were wearing army camouflage."

"Okay." Emilia conceded the point. "The maroon truck at the second location didn't have plates and makes a suspicious getaway."

Rufino made a snorting sound. When Emilia looked at him, his eyes were closed. The mug, however, was still held close to his mouth.

"Did the truck at the first fire have plates?" Murillo asked.

"We don't know," Emilia said. With six people in the room, it was warm and stuffy. "The witness didn't see any, but she wasn't looking for them, either."

"So." Silvio wrote in a question mark after the word *placas* on the El Tigre side of the board. He looked incongruous with the slim marker in his big hand, shoulder holster keeping his automatic tight under his left arm, white tee shirt stained with sweat. "What else?"

"Same army tax message delivered to both," Emilia supplied. "One payment from the owners of the El Tigre. A bigger payment promised but never picked up."

"Same type of grenade used at both fires," Murillo added.

"Both grenades and camouflage support the army theory," Sandor said. "I say we shake *campo militar* and see what falls out."

Murillo shook his head. "Both grenades and uniforms can be bought on the black market."

"Was there ever a robbery at *campo militar*?" Emilia asked.

"I don't know," Murillo said. "The request to give me access to their records is tied up somewhere between Acapulco and Mexico City."

"Okay, so what do we have?" Silvio took charge of the conversation again. "Army or pretending to be army, we need a pattern to trace or a motivation that gets us close."

"I say an army type who got kicked out of both restaurants," Sandor said. "Maybe they overcharged him."

"Most soldiers can't afford to eat at those kinds of restaurants and they know it," Emilia said.

"Cruz should know," Macias quipped.

Emilia folded her arms. "It's extortion. These two restaurants are the ones that didn't pay. Or didn't pay enough. That should be our starting point."

"So the next question is how many other restaurants are paying some sort of protection money?" Sandor asked. "Excuse me. Army tax."

Silvio scribbled on the board.

"There's another issue here." Emilia was amazed that no one was getting it. "Businesses would rather pay protection money to these thugs than report them to the police."

"Come on, Cruz," Silvio scoffed. "Most of the places getting this army tax notice probably think it's the police asking for money and hiding behind the army's bad reputation to do it."

Rufino spoke up for the first time since they'd started the conversation. "In Mexico City, this would be a ridiculously simple case. I'm amazed how you have evaded the real facts." He sipped from his mug. "I had no idea that Acapulco would be full of amateurs."

Silvio's face darkened. Murillo looked embarrassed. Sandor and Macias tried to mask their shock. Emilia bit her tongue.

Rufino went on. "The major factor here is the connection between the two owners. It is obviously a feud over staff. Conway's bartender is poached and he attacks El Tigre over it. Serverio retaliates against Luna Loca. Both of them collaborated with Torrez Delgadillo, who had both means and motive to assist." He gazed at the others in the room, his small moustache twitching in triumph. "In return for being able to carry out his assassination attempt on the mayor."

"That's an interesting theory, *teniente*," Silvio said. He tapped the information about the truck. "But Torrez being behind bars for the second fire makes it difficult to sustain."

"You scratch Conway and Serverio and you're going to find your connection." Lt. Rufino planted his hands on the scratched tabletop. "Conway attacked El Tigre, and Serverio struck back."

"Hector Roque worked for Serverio at the Polo Club first,"

Silvio said. His tone was even, but the senior detective was nearly vermillion. "Then went over to the Luna Loca. Nothing connects Conway or Serverio to Torrez Delgadillo. None of them are behind the army tax notices."

Rufino bolted to his feet, his chair overturning in back of him. "Detective Silvio, are you disrespecting me?" he shouted.

Silvio didn't reply.

"I've solved this." Lt. Rufino looked around the room. "Go arrest Conway and Serverio and charge them both with murder. Press them a little bit and they'll implicate Torrez. Arrest the bartender, too. He started all this."

He snatched up his notebook, which he hadn't opened the entire time, shoved it under his arm, took his travel mug and marched to the door. There was a moment of juggling and he dropped the notebook. Bits of papers flew out and drifted under the table like dry leaves.

No one made a move to assist him. Emilia threw Silvio a questioning look. The man's face was perfectly blank.

Murillo got out of his chair, picked up Lt. Rufino's notebook, and handed it back. Lt. Rufino juggled the travel mug between his hands, finally taking the notebook with his left and tucking it under his right arm, only to switch it back to the left side. Murillo held the door open for him.

Ignoring the fire inspector, Lt. Rufino reached for the door and dropped the notebook again.

"Let me get that for you, *teniente*," Emilia said and grabbed the notebook.

Lt. Rufino plucked it out of her hand and paused in the doorway. "Good job the other night identifying the truck, Cruz. Pity you couldn't stop and apprehend."

As Emilia watched, he marched down the hall, listing to the right, his stride very deliberate, knees lifting high with every step. His shoulder brushed the wall and he tacked to the left, continuing past the holding cells.

The uniformed officer on guard duty by the holding cells walked into the hall as Lt. Rufino passed. There was a funny look on the guard's face as he looked at the open door and saw Emilia. She shot him with her thumb and forefinger, like she always did, as if to say *no worries*. He shot her back and went back to the holding desk. Emilia stepped inside the interview room and closed the door.

"Congratulations, Cruz," Sandor said. "He knows your name."

Emilia sagged into her chair. "So what do we do?"

"We can't arrest Conway or Serverio," Macias said. "There's no justification. We can check into the insurance angle, but it'll be a waste of time."

"I meant about the arsonists," Emilia said. "Extortionists. The tax collectors."

"What about Torrez?" This from Macias. "Are we saying that we got the wrong guy?"

Emilia remembered what Silvio had told her and suppressed a shiver. Of course she'd assumed that Macias and Sandor had something going on; most cops did. It was one of the reasons she'd liked working with Rico; he was one of the few cops she'd met who wasn't on the take, didn't have something shady on the side like Silvio's bookie thing. But she had never tried to find out who the other detectives might be aligned with and until now that policy had worked fairly well.

"He still hasn't come up with an alibi," Silvio reminded them.

"Well, he's not going to give it to us," Macias said. "Salazar's people hauled him out to the Cereso de Acapulco."

"*Rayos*," Silvio muttered.

Emilia closed her notebook. The Cereso was the federal prison outside Acapulco.

Everything about this case had a ragged edge. Torrez hadn't lit the second fire but still didn't have an alibi for the first. She wondered if Chief Salazar's office was keeping information from them, maybe to do a favor for Carlota. Or Obregon. At any rate, if Torrez was at the federal prison, it meant that it would be virtually impossible to have access to him without Chief Salazar's staff being notified.

"Emilia's extortion theory is your best bet," Murillo said. "The question is whether it's really army or somebody pretending to be army with black market explosives and cammo."

"Maybe Serverio will give us a face tomorrow," Emilia said.

"Even if he does, what do we do?" Sandor huffed. "Talk to every restaurant in Acapulco? See who's gotten one of those tax notices?"

Murillo nodded. "You'll need to do it before they hit someplace else next Saturday. We've seen it before. Arsonists who establish a pattern treat it like a ritual."

"Maybe folks are starting to pay up," Emilia said. "Maybe they won't have to set another fire."

"Or they've discovered that the fires let them demand more money," Silvio said.

"Wait a minute," Macias exclaimed. "There's no way we can interview every restaurant owner in Acapulco before Saturday."

"*Madre de Dios,*" Emilia murmured. There were hundreds of restaurants in Acapulco, and they couldn't just call. If the owners were as scared as Serverio, it would be very easy to deny it over the phone. "Can we get the beat cops to help? Get them to go into some of the places on their street and ask?"

"Worth a shot," Macias said.

"We'll tell *el teniente* later," Silvio said. He silently locked eyes with each detective in turn.

"I'm in," said Macias.

"Me, too," said Sandor.

"Right," Emilia said softly.

"Let me know how I can help," Murillo said, looking at Emilia.

It was around 9:00 p.m. and dark when Emilia finally left the squadroom. Silvio was the last one there, but he was closing down his computer as she unlocked her desk, got out her bag, and tiredly told him she'd see him tomorrow. After Lt. Rufino had left two hours earlier, they'd pulled together a huge list of restaurants from the online yellow pages. It put the truck list to shame, and they hadn't even finished that yet. They divided it up by neighborhood, but it was so vast Emilia knew they had little chance of completing the interviews before Saturday.

As she crossed the police parking lot and approached the Suburban, a slim figure materialized out of the shadows and approached her.

"Hi." The speaker was a wiry man about her age wearing jeans and a slouchy nylon jacket, his hair slicked back into a ponytail. Despite the late hour, he wore gradient-tinted sunglasses. A police badge dangled from a lanyard around his neck. "Are you Cruz?" he asked.

"Who are you?" Emilia responded.

"Castro," he said. "Vice."

It took Emilia a moment to realize that he'd extended his left hand, not his right, and in that single heartbeat of incomprehension, he grabbed her by the neck with his right hand and slammed her head against the side of the Suburban. "Word has it you were nosing around at Mami's last night," he snarled, his face close to hers.

"I was looking for a disappeared girl," Emilia managed. The inside of her head was ringing like a bell, her vision was blurry, and it was all she could do to keep her knees from buckling.

"You stay away from Mami's," the Vice cop said. "That's my meat wagon now and everybody on the street knows it. I'm not having some *puta* who thinks she's a detective trying to move in on me." He rapped her head against metal again, making Emilia see stars. "You're not looking for lost girls who might be at Mami's. Not talking to none of the girls from Mami's. You're not even walking on the same side of the street as Mami's. You got that?"

Emilia brought up both fists in a crosswise motion and broke his hold on her throat. The force of the break made Castro stumble back a step.

"Who's your friend, Cruz?"

Silvio came around the rear of the Suburban and stood next to her. Castro evidently recognized the senior detective because he raised both palms in a gesture of surrender. "Hey, Silvio, good to see you again."

"Castro," Silvio acknowledged the other man.

"Just talking to your girl here," Castro said affably. "Letting her know which streets might be a little dangerous these days. We gotta take care of our own, right?"

Silvio didn't move away from Emilia's side as they watched Castro walk through the parking lot. He saluted the guard, the big metal rolling gate slid open, and Castro strolled out as if he had all the time in the world. The gate clanged shut behind him.

"You want to tell me what that was all about?" Silvio asked.

Emilia slid down the side of the Suburban and landed on her rump. She hauled in air and the silver sparklers in front of her eyes slowly winked out. "You know that place Julieta Rubia used to run? Mami's?"

"Yeah." Silvio looked down at her, a frown creasing his forehead. "I heard there's new management now."

"Bitch named Olga who looks like somebody took a hatchet to her face." Emilia rubbed her throat where Castro's fingers had dug into her windpipe. "I was there yesterday. Looking for a girl from my neighborhood last seen asking for directions to the place."

"Let me guess," Silvio said. "Castro thought you were moving in on his action, and this was a gentle warning to stay clear."

"How do you know him?"

"He's our Castro's brother." Silvio reached down and pulled Emilia to her feet.

"Is he really Vice?" Emilia asked. Her head pounded but she was pretty sure she didn't have a concussion. "I thought they were deep undercover. How could he risk being seen walking into a police compound?"

"My guess is that every outfit in town that falls under Vice's jurisdiction is paying Castro or one of his buddies for the pleasure of staying in business. And they know damn well who he is."

"Fuck," Emilia said, suddenly close to tears. Everything was always so fucked up. "This girl's been gone over a month now. Mami's was my best lead."

"*Rayos*, Cruz," Silvio swore. "Try not to get yourself killed before we catch the firebug."

Chapter 22

Serverio never showed up Wednesday morning. By 10:00 a.m. Emilia and Silvio had learned that he and his wife had paid their housemaids a generous severance last night before getting into an airport limousine. They were probably in Spain by now. Getting an extradition order would take weeks; Acapulco would be an ash heap by the time they got him back.

Silvio cursed steadily as they left Serverio's home and headed out to the first restaurant on their list, copies of the army tax message in hand. By noon they'd asked six different restaurant managers if they'd seen the notice and received the same frightened denial each time.

"This isn't going to work," Emilia said as she paid for two coffees at an outdoor café near the eastern edge of the big Parque Altamirano and picked up that month's free edition of *Que Paso Acapulco*. "There are too many restaurants and all we're going to do is start a panic."

"*Hijo de puta*," Silvio swore. "I know."

It was cool and breezy as they took a break on a bench. The whole of Acapulco Bay stretched in front of them, and for a minute Emilia felt like an explorer, the first person to discover this sweeping curve of land and the jeweled waters swaying inside. If she looked south, toward the curved peninsula that protected the western side of the bay, she could see a huge white cruise ship, bigger than several of the nearby hotels. Its decks looked clean and deserted as it lay nestled against the relatively new terminal, safeguarded between the peninsula and the rugged Fuerte San Diego on the mainland. The other side of the bay stretched upwards; the mountains in the distance behind the ring of hotels and condos were tinged with blue as if reflecting the water they guarded. She couldn't see all the way to the Palacio Réal; its location on the tip of Punta Diamante was obscured by the closer and larger triangle of mountain that narrowed down to Punta Bruja.

The explorer feeling faded and reality set in. The reality of not knowing what to do next and being too tired to figure it out.

"It's not shit."

"What?"

"It's not shit." Silvio waved a hand at the sparkling view as a man pushed an ice cream cart past them, the bell on the handle tinkling faintly. "Up close you see too much of the dirt. But this isn't shit."

"*Madre de Dios*, Franco, you're a poet." Emilia drank some more coffee and mentally thanked the Virgin for inventing the stuff. She'd hardly slept the past few nights and needed to get her head together. First she'd panicked at the demonstration, then she'd let that *pendejo* of a Vice cop get the drop on her. This investigation was all over the place, there were too many stray bits and pieces, and until she found Lila Jimenez Lata, only half her attention was going to be in the squadroom.

But mostly she missed Kurt. Badly. How many times since they'd met had she discovered a new angle, a new approach to a difficult case after talking it over with him? Felt her batteries recharge as she lay with him? She was going to lose so much when he left Acapulco.

She reluctantly pulled her thoughts to the case at hand. They'd been disappointed but not terribly surprised at Serverio's flight; the man and his wife had been terrified by what had happened. Torrez still hadn't produced an alibi, but neither had he been released. His arrest had finally made the news with speculation that he had set the first fire and unnamed cohorts had lit the second. Macario Urbina had denied that he had anything to do with the arson attacks. Nonetheless, Emilia figured that Carlota's staff was working hard to dig up something that would tie the big landowner and opposition politician to at least the El Tigre fire.

None of that, however, was as sensational as the videos from Los Matas Ejercito. They had become the top news story, buoyed by the ongoing demonstrations at the *alcaldía* and *campo militar* and repeated media references to men in camouflage at the first fire. General Hernandez was taking the threat of retaliation seriously, and so the local army presence was now constantly in riot gear, including Plexiglas shields and helmets. As if to keep Hernandez on the defense, Carlota had declared publicly that the army was scaring away tourists and crippling the city's economy. Emilia was waiting to see if Carlota would go to the funeral for Hector Roque and the other man who'd died at the Luna Loca the same way she'd gone to the El Tigre funerals. Somehow she doubted that Carlota would fit it into her busy schedule.

She flipped idly through *Que Paso Acapulco* while Silvio slurped noisily at his hot coffee. There was an article about the cruise ship docking and another about how to pick the perfect bikini and matching *pareo*. Women who stayed at the Palacio Réal read stuff like that.

Silvio's phone rang. He answered with his usual gruff "*Bueno*?" He listened, said, "On our way," broke the connection, and stood up.

"What's going on?" Emilia stuffed the magazine into her bag.

"They got a video of the extortionists."

The quality was grainy and there was no sound. Obviously intended to watch employees and make sure they weren't stealing out of the till, the camera was angled to show the cash register rather than the patrons behind the bar. All that could be seen of the two men in camouflage jackets were their hands and the middle parts of their torsos.

But just from the size of their hands on the counter next to a row of glasses, it was clear they were both big, as Serverio had said.

"What's he holding?" Silvio squinted at the screen.

The clip was from Casa Casa, a trendy restaurant a few blocks away from Planet Hollywood's red awning and giant globe entrance. Emilia had been to Casa Casa once with Kurt and knew that it attracted the same well-heeled crowd but offered a quieter, less touristy atmosphere.

They were watching the clip, which the manager had

transferred onto a CD for Macias and Sandor, on the open Internet computer in the front of the squadroom. It was the only machine with drives for portable media.

Macias stopped the video and tapped the screen. "What's in his hand?"

"It's a copy of *Que Paso Acapulco*," Emilia said immediately. The hand on the screen sported a thin wedding band and carried a rolled-up glossy magazine. It was the same magazine she'd been looking at less than an hour ago. "This month's edition."

"Planning how to spend the army tax?" Sandor quipped.

"It's full of advertising." Emilia wanted to dance like a *loca*. She rushed back to her desk, fetched the magazine, and showed it to the others. "Both the El Tigre and Luna Loca are just the sort of high-end places that advertise in it. So is Casa Casa."

"You think they're picking restaurants out of there?" Silvio asked.

Emilia heard Lt. Rufino's phone ring through his closed office door as she flipped to the index of advertisers. Luna Loca's ad was on page 3, a big splashy graphic featuring a girl holding a margarita glass. The ad for the El Tigre was more elegant, with a picture that was a sad reminder of what the place had once been. "They're both in here," she said. "It would have been printed before the fires started."

"That would really narrow the list," Sandor observed.

Macias got the video rolling again. The man who wasn't holding the magazine pushed a copy of the army tax message across the bar. The person behind the bar didn't touch it. The magazine holder leaned over the bar as if to intimidate, and more of his camouflage jacket came into the shot.

"Stop it again," Silvio ordered. Macias hit the button. Silvio bent toward the screen. "Look at his jacket. There's a name."

"He's wearing an ID tag," Emilia exclaimed. "Guetta." She spelled it out.

The camouflage-clad men backed out of view and the video ended. The detectives looked at each other.

"This has got nothing to do with the mayor," Emilia declared.

"Carlota," Macias intoned. "We've got some good news and some bad news."

"All that wasted time," Sandor said disgustedly.

Silvio smiled grimly. "Okay. We're moving on. We're getting someplace. Two big soldiers picking places out of a magazine, telling them to pay a tax and using grenades to punish the ones that don't pay."

"You think they're real army?" Emilia asked.

"Doesn't matter. We don't need to work it from that angle," Silvio said. "We work it from the victims' side. All the advertisers in the magazine need to be contacted. See if they've gotten a visit from Guetta and friend. Find out if they have security cameras. Get their footage and have them refocus the cameras so we see who is coming in, instead of looking at the cash register. We'll go over the truck list again, too. Check for the name Guetta. Buyers plus anyone who has brought in a damaged truck to be repaired."

Lt. Rufino's office door opened and he walked into the squadroom. If he was surprised to see a group huddled around the computer, he didn't show it.

"Cruz," he said without preamble. "I'm assigning you to the El Pharaoh case for the rest of the week. Castro and Gomez need to handle a body down by the docks."

"*Teniente?*" Emilia had a hard time changing gears. The connection to *Que Paso Acapulco*, the fact that they had a name.

"You heard me." Lt. Rufino drank from his travel mug. "Silvio hardly needs you to help arrest Conway and Serverio." He jerked his chin at Silvio. "Take some uniforms and let's make this quick. Torrez still hasn't confessed, and the mayor needs to see some action now. I want both of those restaurant owners in an interrogation room within two hours, implicating him and his truck. And where's my report on the copycat at the second fire? I asked for that days ago."

He made a big looping gesture with his travel mug. It wasn't clear if he was expressing frustration or telling them to get to work.

Teniente, there have been some developments in the case.

Emilia knew something needed to be said. She widened her eyes at Silvio.

The senior detective rubbed his jaw. "*Teniente*," Silvio said. "We just got a real break in the arson case and it looks like we'll be going in a different direction. A security video from one of the restaurants that received the extortion notice."

Lt. Rufino sighed noisily. "Detective Silvio, is this another of your delaying techniques?"

"It's a major lead," Silvio said flatly. "We've now got a name and a probable list of places being targeted. Solidifies the army connection as well."

"You will arrest those restaurant owners," Lt. Rufino sad. "And they will confess to complicity with Torrez Delgadillo."

Silvio stepped close to Rufino. "We're not in the business of politics here, *teniente*."

Lt. Rufino blinked, then turned on his heel and went into his office.

"Very smooth, Franco," Macias said.

Franco. It was catching on. Emilia wondered how long Silvio would let her live.

Chapter 23

From the arrest record Emilia knew that Julieta Rubia's real name was Julieta Arana Vela and that she was 47 years old.

Her arrest file made more entertaining reading than the mess that Castro and Gomez had made of the El Pharaoh files. Emilia found most of the original boxes they'd pulled out of the place, but they seemed lighter than she remembered. As she pawed through the contents, trying to match things up with the evidence spreadsheets, a few things quickly became clear.

All the euros were missing, as were the crucial accounting ledgers.

In contrast, all the counterfeit pesos and dollars were neatly catalogued, marked and bundled.

No euro bills had been catalogued and there was no paperwork verifying that any euro bills had been marked. Emilia knew that they'd confiscated euros along with pesos and dollars, although she didn't know the exact amount of any currency. Silvio would remember all three of the currencies, she was sure, but he hadn't had time to count it or scan for counterfeits, either.

"Neither Castro nor Gomez have mentioned anything about missing euros," Lt. Rufino told her as Emilia stood in his office with a pile of spreadsheets in her hand.

"I think that might be the problem, *teniente*," Emilia tried to keep outright accusation out of her voice.

"Call the state attorney general's office and see what they've got." Lt. Rufino took a sip from his mug as it sat on his desk amid the piles of papers.

Emilia waited for him to realize his error. As far as the El Pharaoh case went, the state attorney general's office was wholly reliant on information from the Acapulco police. More specifically, from the detective unit.

Lt. Rufino narrowed his eyes at her. "What are you waiting for, Cruz?"

Emilia looked down at the spreadsheets, ready to shout at him in frustration. This had been Rico's case, his last case, and now she'd probably find that the remaining evidence was useless. Castro and Gomez had taken the euros, possibly because they were the only real currency, and had probably sold the ledgers back to the owners of the El Pharaoh. "I'll do better than that, *teniente,*" she said. "I'll go right over."

Lt. Rufino nodded. "Good, you do that." He raised his mug to his lips again.

Emilia realized that she'd seen him drinking from the mug all day, but not once had he filled it from the coffee maker in the squadroom. "Would you like me to make some coffee before I go?" she asked.

Lt. Rufino looked at her coldly. "No, thank you, Cruz."

She knew he was going to say that.

He waved her out of the office. Emilia closed up the El Pharaoh boxes, found Julieta's arrest file, left the office, and drove to the Cereso de Acapulco, the massive concrete bastion that was the federal prison.

In person, Julieta Rubia looked half her age. She was on the heavy side, but it suited her, making her look lush and voluptuous. Her hair was nearly platinum blonde and worn long and straight. Her eyes didn't have any crow's feet, there were no creases between her softly feathered eyebrows, and her neck and jawline were firm. Her skin was flawless, with that lit-from-within luminosity touted in ads for French makeup brands that Emilia never bought, sold at department stores like Palacio de Hierro where Emilia never shopped.

In fact, if Julieta hadn't been wearing a cotton prison dress and plastic flip-flops, Emilia would have thought she was ready to have her picture taken for a magazine.

They were in the women's section of the prison. The visitor yard was a courtyard with backless wooden benches ringed around three walls. The fourth wall was chain-link fencing. The green-painted cinder block was the material of choice for the entire prison complex, which had been built years ago without regard to color, air conditioning, or sanitary conditions.

A door with a small window was set into the middle of the end wall, and a male guard with a long gun stood in front of it. Emilia hadn't been able to convince the prison staff that she needed privacy; the guard had been adamant that the women's section had no private interview rooms and gave every indication that he wasn't going to be more helpful unless she paid him to do so. Emilia had ended up in the visitor yard as she'd waited for Julieta to be brought to her. Four other inmates had visitors, including a crying child clinging to an inmate who was obviously the mother.

The yard was hot and smelled like sweat and vomit.

Julieta was led into the yard by a female guard. The two women exchanged a word, and Emilia saw the guard nod before Julieta stepped away from the doorway and into the yard. She looked down at the dirty concrete in disgust, and Emilia decided Julieta didn't spend much time there.

"Detective Cruz." Emilia introduced herself by holding up her badge on its lanyard.

"A girlie cop," said Julieta and sat on the bench. "This is new."

"Do you recognize this girl?" Emilia laid the much-handled picture of Lila between them.

She'd had to surrender her bag and gun at the outer prison perimeter guard post; they'd been stowed in a locker and she'd been given the key, attached to a large wooden disk that was now in her jeans pocket. In the guard room inside the women's section, just on the other side of the door, the guards had another elaborate check-in procedure that included photocopying Emilia's identification and making her fill out a two-sided form, which also had to be laboriously copied before she could be given a visitor pass. The picture and her badge were the only things she'd carried into the yard with her.

"What if I do?" Julieta asked.

"Maybe you'll keep her from getting dead," Emilia replied.

Julieta smiled. Only her lower lip moved; the rest of her face stayed perfectly in place. "What do I care?"

"Her name is Lila," Emilia pressed. "She came to see you at Mami's. Would have been a Thursday night. Said she was looking for a woman named Yolanda Lata."

Julieta's lip pouted. "You think Mami's is some lost souls agency?"

Emilia felt sweat trickle down her neck. The woman's air of amusement was infuriating, and the sobs of the child and mother on the adjacent bench were almost unendurable. "Lila," Emilia prompted. "Lila Jimenez Lata. She was pretty enough to be an inside girl."

Julieta glanced at the picture and back at Emilia. "So if I talk to you, you'll get me out of here?"

"Sure," Emilia lied. "I'll see what I can do." Even if she wanted to help Julieta, this wasn't a sanctioned investigation and she couldn't do much, maybe just find Julieta's lawyer when the trial was finally scheduled and pass along the information that the woman had been helpful in an unrelated case.

"You got nothing for me, *puta*." Julieta's coarse manner of speech didn't match the beautiful face and crystal hair.

Emilia's head began to pound. The desire to get out of the stifling visitor yard was overwhelming. She felt an intense dislike for the woman next to her on the bench. The beautiful façade hid something rotten and diseased, a woman who'd used and abused other women for years, probably keeping them beaten and frightened and so loaded with debt they were afraid to leave her tightly controlled world.

She put the picture of Lila in her jeans pocket. "Olga's running things at Mami's now," she said, trying to find some way to break through. "She said you'd tell me if you'd talked to Lila."

"Olga set me up." Julieta looked around the yard, at the chain-link fence and the dirty concrete walls and the other inmates. She glared hard at them and they shrank away.

It didn't take a genius to see that Julieta was the queen of the women's block. Emilia compared her prison dress with that of the other inmates; Julieta's was fitted and of a finer cotton weave. And clean. Pressed. The other women's prison dresses fit like flour sacks and were rough, dirty, and wrinkled.

Not only was Julieta's prison dress decent quality, but her hands were also perfectly manicured. One finger bore a thin tattoo like a wedding ring; it was a delicate line, not a crude prison tat. She wore the same dark red nail polish that Carlota had worn during the meeting in the mayor's office. No chips or scuffs, which meant that Julieta wasn't working at any of the menial labor jobs all inmates were supposed to perform. Emilia wondered what she'd find if she saw Julieta's cell. Probably a maid and a flat screen television.

The child across the yard cried even more loudly, red-faced now and close to hysteria. Julieta stood up and snapped her fingers at the door to the guard post. A minute later, the female guard opened the door to the cell block, detached the child from its mother, and dragged the woman inside. The child wailed even louder and was led out. Once the child's screams faded the other inmates and their visitors resumed their whispered conversations.

"You swing some weight around here," Emilia observed.

"See, *puta*?" Julieta said and made a flicking motion. "I got everything I need. You can't do nothing for me. So you go home. Say a rosary for your little girl."

Emilia wiped sweat off her forehead. "I can mess up Olga for you," she heard herself say.

Julieta cut her eyes to Emilia, suddenly interested. "You're one little *chica* with a badge. Olga knows lots of bigger people with badges."

"Tell me what you know about Lila Jimenez Lata and her mother and I'll see what I can do."

As soon as Emilia said the last part of the sentence, the blonde woman snorted. "Again, you got nothing."

Emilia knew it was a losing battle. Julieta was simply toying with her, using the conversation to relieve the tedium of another dull prison day. There was one last card to play and it wasn't a strong one. "You're in jail for prostitution," she said. "There will be a trial at some point, but at the end of the day it's not that serious a charge. Murder is different. If this girl turns up dead, and you had the chance to tell me what you know . . ." Emilia let her voice trail off. The stink in the yard was making her nauseous.

Julieta didn't buy it. She crossed her legs as if she was wearing spike heels and bobbed her foot while staring at the opposite wall.

Emilia crossed the yard and pounded on the guard's door.

Chapter 24

Emilia collected her gun and her bag at the prison's outer perimeter. There was a bottle of water in her bag; it was tepid, but she sloshed down half anyway as the guard gave her a stony *get out* look. She recapped the bottle and looked around the room. It was little more than a narrow counter shielded by a wall of bulletproof glass. Maybe she could make this trip a two-for-one.

She dumped her bag and gun on the counter again. "I'd like to see Lester Torrez Delgadillo," she said.

The sign-in routine was repeated all over again on the men's side of the prison, but with a great deal more scrutiny and security procedures. The contrast between how Julieta Rubia and Torrez Delgadillo were treated was like night and day. Emilia attributed it to the difference in their crimes. Julieta had been caught peddling a young girl. Torrez was charged with arson and murder and even more dire political motivations.

It took an hour for her identification to be scrutinized and for Torrez to finally be led into the small interview room with a one-way mirror set into the wall. He was a well-built man in his forties, with wavy hair, a firm jaw, and intelligent brown eyes. He wore an orange prison jumpsuit with the word *DETENIDO* stenciled in black block letters across the chest, and his hands and feet were shackled, with a chain running between them. He was unshaven and his face was lined with fatigue, but otherwise he didn't look too bad. Emilia pointed wordlessly at the shackles, and the guard released the chain running from hands to feet but didn't take off the steel bracelets around either wrists or ankles before shoving Torrez into one of the metal chairs flanking the plain wooden table.

The door closed and Torrez raised his eyebrows at her.

"I'm Detective Cruz from the Acapulco Municipal Police," Emilia said, sitting in the chair across from him. "I know you're not responsible for the fire at the El Tigre."

Torrez blinked but didn't speak.

"It's an extortion ring," she went on. "They're army or they want us to believe that they are. Asking high-end restaurants for cash and calling it an army tax."

"So why am I still here?" Torrez asked. He had a deep voice, like Silvio.

"Because you don't have an alibi and your truck matched a description," Emilia said. "You've been in the army and might have contacts there with access to *campo militar*'s armory. Plus you work for Carlota's political rival."

"You came out here to tell me that?"

"I came here to get your alibi." Emilia leaned forward and lowered her voice. "You know damn well that Carlota isn't going to pass up this chance to get back at Macario Urbina for all the mud he threw at her during the election campaign, and she'll use you to do it. I don't know why she's ready to take on the army as well, but I'm not going to deal with that right now."

Torrez looked away.

Emilia wondered how much time she'd have before someone from Chief Salazar's office was told Torrez was talking to a female cop and came to break things up. No more than 45 minutes, she decided. She clenched her fists on the table. "I want to catch an arsonist. As long as you don't have an alibi you're still at the top of Carlota's list. You're making it easy for them to sacrifice you so she doesn't look bad. It also means that while the attention stays on you, we can't get any traction on the real case."

Torrez put his manacled hands on the tabletop not too far from Emilia's fists. She waited for the door to open and a guard to come in, but no one did.

"I was the one who connected you and your truck with Macario Urbina," Emilia went on desperately. "You don't have any reason to trust me any more than you can trust the *pendejos* from Chief Salazar's offices who have been trying to get something out of you. But I'll be honest. I don't want it on my conscience that I put away an innocent man for arson and murder."

Torrez gave a short laugh. "Is that the way women detectives operate?" he asked. "You going to cry next?"

"I might," Emilia replied. "How's your wife holding up?"

"She and the kids are still on the *hacienda*."

Torrez wasn't some scared teen and he'd held up well, but the mention of his family had caused a little crack in his armor. Emilia saw his mouth tighten.

"How come nobody on that *hacienda* is coming forward to say that you were with them that Saturday night?" Emilia asked. "It's been over a week. You know Salazar's people are going to haul in your wife next. And the kids. I've seen it before."

"It's a big place, that *hacienda*," Torrez said.

"They can't hide." Emilia glanced at her watch.

"Listen." Torrez said the word softly but distinctly. "I meant that the problem is that the *hacienda* is so big. We get workers up from Guatemala and Honduras, migrants hoping to make it up to El Norte. Got a lot of locals, too. There are always jobs in the fields and with the cattle. Some of the ranch houses are in pretty lonely spots. Near the fields but nothing else."

Torrez had practically been whispering. He stopped and swallowed hard. Emilia waited.

"We got the Sinaloa cartel poaching the workers. They come at night, round up 20, 30 at a time out of our bunkhouses. Force them into hauling bales of weed up to El Norte."

"Most make it a hundred miles or so before they can't go any further," Emilia said in the same low tone. "Cartel kills them, dumps the bodies." The practice was common knowledge.

She thought she heard a noise outside the room, but the door handle didn't turn. The room didn't have any obvious microphones, but the one-way mirror meant that somebody was watching and almost certainly trying to overhear the conversation.

Torrez looked relieved that she understood. "Exactly. At the next waypoint, the cartel grabs more workers from another *hacienda* or a busload of locals headed for San Diego. They're just looking for mules to keep passing the stuff north." He exhaled shakily. "Three times now I've driven into the desert, met up with a representative, and paid them not to poach our workers."

Emilia felt her stomach clench. "You know that they are Sinaloa?"

Torrez nodded. "The last payment was the weekend of the El Tigre fire. The meeting place was a full day's drive north, up in the Sierra Santa Rita de Casta hills. Every time they blindfold me, dump me in the back of a truck, and take me to their camp. I pay, we share some *mezcal*, they boast about El Chapo."

"You pay with Macario Urbina's money?" Emilia asked. "He knows?"

"Yes," Torrez admitted. "We talked about it, decided we'd take the risk."

"They'll crucify him if this gets out," Emilia reasoned. Carlota would do anything to see her political opponent aligned in the press with the notorious Sinaloa cartel. "That's why you haven't talked."

"He's been good to me," Torrez said. "Good to my family."

"*Madre de Dios*." Emilia slumped back against the hard metal chair. She felt sick.

"It isn't right," Torrez said. "We know that. But what else can we do to keep our workers alive? I'm trying to grow corn and feed cattle. That's all."

The door banged open and two uniformed cops strode into the interview room along with the guard who'd brought Torrez in to see Emilia.

"You're Cruz?" the taller cop asked.

Emilia recognized him from the meetings in Carlota's office, although they hadn't been introduced. His name was Vega. The chief of police's adjutant. Assistant. Top flunky. Whatever. She stood up. "I'm Cruz."

"What are you doing here?"

Emilia shrugged and stood up. "Wasting my time."

The guard quickly shackled Torrez's hands and feet together again. The prisoner was smart enough not to look at Emilia as they led him out of the room, his feet shuffling slowly.

Emilia drove back to the police station, trying to sort out the threads from the two very different conversations she'd had at the prison. Julieta Rubia had toyed with her, and Torrez Delgadillo had given her information she didn't know how to use.

She parked, cut the engine, and forced herself to think. Julieta was living high. Someone was helping her. Someone inside the prison. Probably the guards, with a few payoffs to the warden to look the other way. Maybe Julieta was trading sex for favors. A lot of sex. Or maybe a courier brought in cash and nail polish.

Emilia considered who else might be visiting the former madam. Would they have also had to fill out a form for someone to type into a prison visitor database? Emilia wouldn't have access to the federal prison records through the Acapulco police intranet. But some people knew how to work the system better than she did.

Her cousin Alvaro answered his cell phone on the second ring. "How's Daysi?" Emilia asked, trying to sound happy.

"Two weeks to go," Alvaro answered.

Emilia prayed the baby wouldn't decide to arrive early. "So you're going to be in the office tomorrow?"

"What do you need, *prima*?" Alvaro asked.

"I need to know who's been visiting Julieta Rubia at the Cereso."

"Julieta Rubia?" Alvaro clicked his tongue. "The hooker who used to run Mami's?"

Alvaro knew everything. He was a walking encyclopedia of insider information. "Her real name is Julieta Arana Vela." Emilia paused. "And it would be good if nobody knew I was looking for her records."

"Mami's has friends," Alvaro said.

"I know." Emilia heard the hesitation in his voice. Alvaro was always careful where he stepped, making few enemies, trading favors as he moved upwards in one of the most successful bartering careers she'd seen yet.

"Julieta might have been the last person to talk to Lila Jimenez Lata, the girl Padre Ricardo asked me to find," Emilia said.

There was another long pause. Alvaro's sigh filtered through the connection.

"Come by the office tomorrow around 6:00 p.m.," he said. "Don't call me on the office phone, just come by."

Chapter 25

As promised, Alvaro was in his office late on Friday. His two assistants had gone home for the night and the evidence locker was dark and deserted except for Emilia's cousin sitting at his desk in front of the wire enclosure. The windowless evidence locker took up a large portion of the basement of the central police administration building. The lamp on Alvaro's desk threw a circle of light over the surface; otherwise the room was dim.

It had been a long day, Emilia reflected as she took in the scene. The two teams of detectives plus Murillo, who rode with Emilia and Silvio, had talked to the manager or owner of every restaurant advertised in *Que Paso Acapulco*. Twenty out of 105 admitted to having received the army tax message. Nine had paid. The others said they'd planned to after the El Tigre fire, but the men hadn't come back.

They got the same basic description in every case. They were looking for two men at least as big as Silvio. Both had regular features and wore camouflage ball caps. Yes, one had the name Guetta on his camouflage jacket. But no one saw them get in or out of any vehicle or provided more concrete information about them.

Lt. Rufino called both Emilia and Silvio several times during the day; Emilia told him she was tracking down missing information from the El Pharaoh case. Silvio said he was searching for Conway and Serverio. She didn't know what Macias and Sandor had said.

Alvaro looked up as Emilia approached, gym bag in one hand and an aluminum container full of her mother's homemade *empanadas* in the other. "Chicken," she said. "Mama's best."

"Nice, *prima*," Alvaro took the container, partially unrolled the foil on top, and inhaled. "Tell Tía Sophia that I love her and her stove."

"I will."

Alvaro put the container on his desk and handed her a slip of paper. "Who came and when," he said simply.

Two names were written on it with dates next to each: Alfredo Soares Peña had visited Julieta Rubia twice, the first time about two weeks after she'd been arrested, and again two weeks after that. Dr. Felipe Ramirez Palmas visited Julieta every Tuesday.

Emilia held up the slip of paper. "Do you know—?" she started but Alvaro cut her off.

"That's all I got, *prima*," he said.

"Right." Emilia gave him a wry grin and nodded at the container of *empanadas*. "Are we even?"

Alvaro shook his head. "Find the girl," he said.

Emilia kissed his forehead. "Tell Daysi I said hi and good luck."

The slip of paper went into Emilia's pocket as she left the evidence locker and headed for the big gym down the hall. She worked out there when she could; it was the biggest gym she had access to and it had new equipment and heavy bags to practice kickboxing.

She changed in the woman's locker room, stretched on the mats, and pulled on her leather workout gloves. There were a half a dozen other night owls there, cops who had just come off a shift or were getting themselves psyched to go on a shift or those who hadn't anywhere else to go and weren't ready to start their weekend drinking just yet.

Emilia pounded on the 100-lb. bag, alternately jabbing and punching, imagining she was teaching Castro from Vice a lesson. The bag was suspended from the ceiling by a heavy metal chain, and when she heard the chain jingle she knew she was hitting hard. The bag swung and jumped as Emilia vented herself on it, feeling her muscles get warm and loose and powerful as the chain squealed.

The sweat poured off her face as she hit the bag again, a powerful jab that should have sent the bag kicking backwards, but this time it didn't absorb the force. Emilia did instead. The jar went all the way up her arm and her teeth rattled.

"Nice work, Cruz," Obregon said from the other side of the bag.

He leaned to one side and she realized he had held the bag still. "Hello," she said, panting a little.

Obregon was dressed to work out himself, in black basketball shorts, expensive cross-trainers, and a gray sleeveless tee shirt. He was thick with muscle and his forearms were covered in fine black hair.

"Taking out all your frustrations, Cruz?" he asked, his voice sardonic. "I hear things are in the shitter in the squadroom."

Emilia aimed a fist at the bag and followed up with a roundhouse kick. Obregon stepped back when the force of her kick shoved the bag against him.

"Or maybe you figure your days are numbered," his mocking voice went on. "Silvio runs through partners pretty fast, doesn't he? Fuentes wasn't even around a year. And the one before that. What was his name?" Obregon snapped his fingers. "I remember now. Garcia. A lot of folks still think it was Silvio did him in."

"Before my time." Emilia pummeled the bag, as if she could wipe the smirk off Obregon's face. Fuentes had been the dirty cop who'd killed Rico. In one nightmarish hour, Fuentes had killed Rico, then been fatally shot himself by another dirty cop named Villahermosa, who at the time had been Obregon's deputy at union headquarters. Emilia had killed Villahermosa. Only a handful of people knew the truth about that night, including Silvio and Chief Salazar. Obregon wasn't one of them, although she knew he suspected.

But as far as Emilia knew, Garcia had been an honest cop killed in a drug bust gone bad nearly three years ago. Silvio had his enemies and they'd tried to pin Garcia's death on him. They hadn't been able to make it stick although the senior detective had ended up suspended for six months nonetheless. The rumors still swirled.

"Still, I'd be watching the calendar if I was you," Obregon said as the bag jumped on its chain.

"Why does Carlota want the fires to be the army's fault?" Emilia asked, her voice ragged from the workout. "I know her office organized those demonstrations. All those banners and the megaphones."

To her surprise, Obregon roared with laughter and shook his head as if to clear it. "You're right. It was a Carlota lovefest until things got out of hand and they started burning cars and Salazar sent in the riot boys. But she learned her lesson."

"What's her problem with the army?" Emilia pressed. She kicked the bag and the chain rattled. "Besides the usual."

"General Hernandez is from the past," Obregon said lightly. "Thinks women like you and Carlota should be at home pumping out babies. Hernandez was stupid enough to tell her."

Emilia would have laughed if she'd had the breath. "That was stupid."

Obregon steadied the bag again. "So I hear your arrest isn't talking. Torrez Delgadillo."

Emilia delivered two punches to the bag, shoulder height. *Jab, jab.* Her punches didn't have as much force as her kicks, and the bag stayed steady in Obregon's hands. "He's innocent."

"He's got no alibi, according to Salazar's office."

"He doesn't need one," Emilia said.

"He looks good for it."

"We've traced both fires to an extortion ring. Might be army or pretending to be. We're following up."

"He could still be involved. Torrez needs an alibi that holds up." Emilia ran a forearm across her forehead, pushing the sweat out of her eyes. Obregon looked at her with definite interest, but she didn't know if it was from the things she was saying or if he liked sweaty women.

As the head of the police union for the entire state of Guerrero, Obregon had assets and resources she could only guess at. Plus he obviously had a direct line to Carlota. Could he help? Or was the risk too great?

"Well," he prompted.

"Torrez has an alibi." Emilia drove her fist into the tough, unyielding leather of the bag. "You need to tell Carlota, get her to take the heat off Chief Salazar. We can't blame Torrez."

"No good enough, Cruz." Obregon made a come-on motion. It was a gamble, but the only idea she had. Emilia dropped her fists. "He was paying off the Sinaloa cartel the night of the El Tigre fire," she said. "So they'd stop press-ganging the workers off Macario Urbina's place."

Obregon looked interested. "How do you know this?"

"He told me," Emilia said. "Yesterday. At the prison. He's loyal to Macario Urbina. Doesn't want it to get out."

"Why did he tell you? Why hasn't he told Salazar's people?"

"If you were Torrez, who would you trust?"

"The pretty girl detective." Obregon gave a low chuckle and gave her the look she remembered from their interactions several months ago. The look of a predator assessing his prey. It left her with a cold, gnawing feeling of unease.

Obregon walked over to the weight bench and pulled on a pair of bag gloves, the kind like Emilia's that looked like thick leather mittens. His looked new, however, and she guessed that he mostly lifted weights. As he stood with his back to her, she found herself frankly assessing his physique. He was heavier than Kurt, with a thicker middle and less definition to his arms and legs. Once upon a time, she'd thought he was handsome, sexy even. Now he looked like just another *macho* in basketball shorts, dark and dumpy in comparison to Kurt, but with a tension in his body that made her wary.

"Señor Torrez would appear to be facing the end of his days," Obregon observed as he came back to the heavy bag. "Probably Macario Urbina, too. As soon as Torrez gets out of jail, Sinaloa *sicarios* are going to come after him for squealing. If they don't get him in jail first. Doesn't matter if he keeps his mouth shut or not. They'll assume he told everything."

Emilia backed away as he hunched low and punched hard, sending the bag rocking on its chain. "He's got a family. A life," she said.

Obregon danced a little from side to side, then pounded the bag again with a quick left and two rights. "Life is hard these days, Cruz."

"You can do something about it."

"Why me?" Obregon looked at her around the side of the bag. He was already breathing hard. "Tell Rufino, let him figure out a way to protect Torrez."

"Torrez met them up north in the Sierra San Rita hills. It's out of Acapulco's jurisdiction."

"Okay." Obregon hit the bag again. "Why would Carlota want to do something for Macario Urbina? The man bloodied her nose in the election."

"He'll owe her a favor."

"Are you calling in your marker? Or rather, Rucker's marker for getting me and Carlota out of the El Tigre?"

"If that's what it takes," Emilia said.

"Very nice, Cruz. I like the way you think." Obregon put his gloved fists down and grinned, the pleased predator. "But aren't you really trying to tell me that Rufino can't help?"

Emilia hesitated and his grin widened.

"Tell me," Obregon said. He punched the bag again, easy this time. Playing, not fighting. "How is he managing the pressure? Thinking clearly? Giving cool, crisp directions?"

Emilia didn't answer.

Obregon pulled off one glove, pushed his hair back from his forehead, and replaced the glove. "Rufino was a good cop once upon a time," he said, attacking the bag again. "Undercover counternarcotics. But he made the mistake of getting married, having a kid. They stayed in Mexico City while he worked the Cuernavaca *plaza*. Fake name, fake identity, everything." He kept crouching, weaving and jabbing the bag as if it was an opponent. "Even so, he got fingered. They killed the wife and daughter and dumped the bodies in front of his door. Don't know how he got out of Cuernavaca alive, but he's been blind drunk ever since. Salazar took a chance, thinks he can save him. But he can't."

Emilia's throat was tight. "I'm putting down the marker. Will you talk to Carlota? Help Torrez?"

"I think you just declared your allegiance, Cruz," Obregon said. He steadied the heavy bag as it swung gently from the force of his last punch, winded from his workout.

"I don't want to see an innocent man go down for something he didn't do," Emilia said stubbornly.

"No one ever does."

Emilia gave him an abrupt nod, stripped off her sweaty gloves, and went into the locker room. As she changed back into her street clothes, she wondered what exactly Obregon was to Carlota. Lover? Confessor? Confidante?

Spy?

Chapter 26

By noon on Saturday, Emilia was ready for whatever the next 12 hours would bring. She had a complete list of all the restaurants that had been listed in *Que Paso Acapulco* and a camera with a long-range lens from the detectives' inventory. Her phone was fully charged, her gun was fully loaded, and the police radio was tuned to the emergency frequency. Silvio's car smelled like fried grease from a take-out bag of burgers. A shrink-wrapped six-pack of water and two tall coffees in thermal cups rounded out their supplies.

If the grenade throwers kept to their pattern and attacked another restaurant around 11:00 p.m., the detectives had plenty of time to figure out the entrances and exits for each restaurant and to map out the most useful route between them. It was a long shot, but maybe they'd catch these *pendejos*.

Emilia and Silvio would patrol 48 places on their half of the *Que Paso Acapulco* list. Their half kept them on the east side of the city, while Macias and Sandor's half was on the west side. Both teams would just keep prowling around the restaurants, paying special attention to the ones they knew had received the notice but hadn't yet made a payment.

The Saturday party and beach crowds meant a lot of stop-and-go driving. Silvio didn't seem to mind, however, and the afternoon slid into night as he drove. Emilia navigated, kept in touch with Macias and Sandor, and photographed the most vulnerable locations.

They stopped twice for bathroom breaks and to grab more fast food. As it grew darker and nothing seemed amiss, Emilia found herself increasingly nervous. The *Que Paso Acapulco* lead felt right. The pieces fit. It had been her idea. But nothing was certain.

"It would have been too easy," Silvio said, breaking the silence of the last half hour or so.

"What?"

"Finding a truck registered to somebody named Guetta."

"Or finding one in a repair shop." They'd called at least 30 garages asking about club cab trucks coming in for repairs. Nothing.

Silvio shrugged. He wasn't wearing his jacket in the car; just his usual grim expression, white tee, and scuffed leather shoulder holster. "That makes it easier for us tonight. We see some shot-up truck, *oye*, there's our friend."

"Rico used to say that," Emilia said.

"What?"

"*Oye*," Emilia said. The time would have passed so much more quickly if it had been Rico in the car instead of Silvio. Rico would have talked about the last woman he'd dated, what his mother had cooked the other night, if he had enough money to buy some new electronic gadget. Told her jokes, played some music. In contrast, Silvio was just a heavy, brooding presence, emanating waves of disapproval. She'd never be entirely comfortable around him.

"Yeah." Silvio shot her a sideways glance as the car slogged through the traffic in front of the iconic white Torre Pacific condominiums. "So what's the deal with you going over to Mami's?"

"I told you," Emilia said. "There's a girl missing from my neighborhood."

"That's not my question, Cruz."

Just the way he said it, with an edge that didn't need to be there, irritated the hell out of Emilia. "It's pretty late in the day for games, Franco," she snapped. "Just spit it out."

"You got an investigation going on the side?" he asked. "Something you don't want to tell me about?"

It was on the tip of her tongue to lash out, ask him why she'd have to tell him anything. He wasn't her partner. But they had to spend at least another two hours cooped up in the car together.

"She's a Missing Persons that Rufino sent to the *federales* in Mexico City," Emilia said, keeping herself in check. "A girl named Lila Jimenez Lata. The priest in my neighborhood asked me to help. But don't worry, I'm doing it on my own time. It doesn't affect you."

"You go to Mami's and end up dead, I got a problem," Silvio warned.

"You get arrested for your illegal bookmaking, and everybody's going to say I was involved," Emilia countered.

"You need to relax, Cruz. Like Isabel."

"Your wife is a saint." Emilia had met Silvio's wife once and knew that they'd been married for more than 20 years. In her own way, Isabel was as tough as her husband.

Silvio snorted and didn't reply. They passed the Mesa Italia restaurant, turned and drove slowly by the back. Traffic was light. No club cab truck in any direction. Emilia checked it off the spreadsheet.

"So why Mami's?" Silvio asked.

Emilia glanced at him in surprise; she'd thought the conversation was over. "According to Lila's brother, their mother is a hooker someplace," she said. "Lila went to see Julieta Rubia. Guess she'd heard of Julieta and thought she'd find her mother there."

"*Rayos*, Cruz," Silvio grumbled. "Julieta Rubia's not at Mami's now."

"I met Mami's new management," Emilia said. "A hatchet-faced *puta* named Olga."

Silvio gave a dry chuckle.

"So I went to see Julieta in prison," Emilia went on. "She acted like she owns the place and wouldn't talk."

Silvio braked for a red light and both detectives scanned their respective sides of the car, looking for signs of trouble, taking in the people on the street, other cars. "You really thought Julieta Rubia was going to talk to you?" Silvio scoffed. "What else you got?"

"A doctor visits her every week," Emilia said. "If we catch the grenade throwers tonight, I'll go see him on Monday."

"On your own time," Silvio warned.

"I just said that."

Once again, the exchange with Silvio had hit a sour note. The day was lasting forever. Emilia checked her watch. Only 10:00 p.m.

Silvio cleared his throat. "You got another problem," he said.

"You don't like working with women." Emilia smirked at her own wit.

"And why do you think that is?" Silvio growled. "Half the time I have to babysit you, make sure you don't run off. The rest of the time I gotta keep the moths away."

"What are you talking about?" Emilia asked.

"Murillo."

"What about Murillo?"

The arson investigator had somehow convinced his superiors in Mexico City to let him stay in Acapulco another week. Between helping the detectives piece together the *Que Paso Acapulco* leads and sifting through the two fire locations, he'd been around a lot. He had the same sense of humor as Rico and was a pleasant coworker.

They turned north toward the next restaurant on the route. Vespa's ad on page 6 of *Que Paso Acapulco* featured a bright red vintage scooter. "Murillo's acting like a lovesick cow," Silvio said in disgust. "Apparently he went to talk to Rucker again and found out Hollywood's not there." The big detective cut his eyes to Emilia. "Asked me if he could take you out. Like I'm your keeper or something."

Emilia bristled. "What did you tell him?"

"I fucking told him that I'm not some grade school kid, and I'm not carrying notes for him."

"Well." Emilia had been prepared to wax indignant, but Silvio's words deflated her ire. "Thank you."

"So?" Silvio slowed the car and they cruised past Vespa. Like the El Tigre, it had a bar in front, but this one was open to the street. Fairy lights were strung across the courtyard, and the restaurant's signature vintage red scooter was parked in front where people could pose for pictures with it. Silvio followed traffic and they made the block. No club cab truck, nothing unusual for a Saturday night.

"So what?" Emilia asked as she checked Vespa off the spreadsheet.

"You and Rucker still on or what?"

Emilia sniffed. "That's none of your business."

Silvio blew out a mouthful of air. "So what's the deal with Murillo?"

"There's no deal with Murillo," Emilia exclaimed in exasperation. "He's a nice guy. Reminds me of Rico."

The radio crackled with a call for all units. *Meet the bomberos at the Toby Jones Beach Club. Reports of an explosion and fire.* An address on the west side of town was given.

"*Madre de Dios,*" Emilia swore. She grabbed the magnetic strobe light from its niche in the center console, switched it on, and clapped it to the roof of the vehicle. Silvio simultaneously hit the siren and swung the car into a U-turn, sending oncoming traffic spraying in all directions.

"Fuck!" raged Silvio. "Is it on the list?"

The car picked up speed and Emilia was pressed into her seat by the safety belt. As the car sped under a streetlight, she scanned the alphabetized list. "No," she shouted above the siren. "It's not here. It's not on the list."

"We fucked up." Silvio hit the steering wheel in fury.

Emilia rubbed the red weal on her hand from the burn at El Tigre as her heart started to hammer. She'd be walking into it all again. Scorching heat. Choking smoke. Paralyzing fear. Bodies.

Without slowing, the car hit a *tope* speed bump, sailed into the air, and came down with a crunch of rearranged metal. The words to the Hail Mary ran through Emilia's brain.

Chapter 27

"Hey, Em."

"Kurt!" Emilia struggled to a sitting position on her bed with her cell phone pressed to her ear. She glanced at her watch to discover that it was 8:00 a.m. Sunlight poured through her bedroom window, brightening the gray blanket, the white wall, and the cross above the bed.

She must have fallen asleep in her clothes, shoes, jeans, gun and all. "Where are you?" she asked.

"I'm in London." Kurt's voice was as clear as if he was calling from the Palacio Réal. "I thought you'd be up by now."

"I am, I am." Emilia kicked off her shoes and wriggled herself out of her shoulder holster without putting down the phone. "Tell me all about London."

"Just got here," he said. "London in November is cold and rainy. I'll walk around a little, check out what's near the hotel. Meetings start tomorrow."

"Have you seen the queen yet?"

He laughed, and Emilia closed her eyes and drank in the sound.

"Don't worry," Kurt said. "As soon as I see her, I'll let her know you've been asking after her."

"How was Belize?" Emilia asked.

Her mother's bedroom door opened and shut. Footsteps went down the stairs. The bathroom toilet flushed at the same time. Ernesto had apparently spent another night in Sophia's room.

"Belize was nice," Kurt said. His tone was neutral.

Emilia coughed. Her hair smelled like a barbecue. "Go on," she said.

"Big place," Kurt said after a pause. "New development. Very exclusive, very secluded."

"As nice as the Palacio Réal?" The acrid smoke smell was making her eyes water. Emilia pressed the fingers of her free hand against her eyelids.

"I could make it as nice," he said.

"Do you want to?" Emilia couldn't help asking. Her throat tightened as she waited for his answer. Every pinch of air that got by tasted of smoke and soot.

Her clothes stank worse than her hair. Emilia held the phone with one hand and whipped off her tee shirt with the other.

"I told you, this was just to look," Kurt said. "Nobody made any promises."

"Okay." Emilia coughed again, stood up, and shoved off her sooty jeans. On the other side of her closed bedroom door, footsteps again crossed the hall and started down the stairs.

"Are you all right?" Kurt asked.

Emilia curled up against her pillow again, wearing just her bra and panties. "There was another fire," she said. "The third."

"And you were there," Kurt said, concern sharpening his voice.

"We had a good lead," Emilia said. "I was so sure. An extortion ring targeting the places advertising in *Que Paso Acapulco*. But the place they hit wasn't on the list."

"So where does that leave you?"

"Back at zero," Emilia said. "No witnesses, of course, and the manager too panicked to say much of anything."

Last night had been another nightmarish scene of fire and fear. Emilia tried to keep her voice calm as she gave Kurt the bare minimum, skipping over the panic attack that had gripped her throughout the night.

Macias and Sandor had been first on the scene. She and Silvio had arrived 15 minutes later, about the same time the fire and rescue trucks showed up. Emilia had shaken like a shock victim as soon as she saw the flames and smoke. Her teeth clattered for hours as she forced herself to do what needed to be done.

The damage wasn't as extensive this time and there were no deaths. No one had seen a club cab truck or army camouflage. The owner said he'd never gotten a tax notice. They all knew he was lying.

By 3:00 a.m. Murillo had been able to ascertain that the fire had been started by one explosive device. Unlike the first two fires, this time the explosion did more damage to the cars in the restaurant parking lot than to the building itself.

They were trying to assess the type of explosive device—which everyone knew would turn out to be an army grenade—when Lt. Rufino showed up and the night went from bad to worse. *El teniente* berated all four detectives as well as the arson investigator for everything: for depending on a worthless list from the *Que Paso Acapulco* magazine, for never arresting Conway and Serverio, for the fictional club cab truck no one had ever seen. Emilia in particular was singled out for driving around in search of firebugs when she'd been reassigned to the El Pharaoh case.

Having all the *bomberos* witness *el teniente*'s tirade had been humiliating and all the detectives were furious by the time Rufino left.

"I wish I was there, Em," Kurt said seriously. "Wish there was some way I could help."

"With any luck, Lt. Rufino won't even remember." Emilia rubbed at a crick in her neck, feeling grubby and miserable and lonely. "After the last fire, he suspended me and didn't remember. Silvio had to tell him I'd called in sick. I think he's losing it." *Even worse than me*.

The smell of coffee wafted in, a welcome mask over some of the smoke stink.

"I tell you what," Kurt said. "Go over to the hotel for dinner. Have a decent meal, unwind. Charge it to my account. I'll send them a text to say you're coming."

"I can't do that," Emilia said.

"I can hear how wound up you are all the way from here," Kurt chided her. "A good meal will help."

"You're in the right line of business, you know," Emilia said. "You always want people to eat and relax."

"It always works."

Emilia didn't want to get into a wrangle about owing him for a dinner, or how odd it would feel to walk into the Palacio Réal on her own. "When are you coming back?" she asked instead.

"Next weekend." He paused. "It's good to hear your voice, Em. I miss you."

Her eyes were stinging again. Emilia took a deep breath.

Come home. Don't leave Acapulco. I need you.

Stay.

"Bet you say that to all the girls," Emilia said.

"Take as long as you need," Mercedes said. She led the way across the dance studio to her busy and colorful office. "Print whatever you need. The paper is right by the printer."

"I really appreciate this," Emilia said.

Mercedes had been surprised but pleasant when Emilia had called her in the early afternoon to ask if she could use the dancer's computer. In church Emilia had mechanically followed the Mass as her brain picked apart Lt. Rufino's actions at the fire. It was a crime scene, but he'd been careless in what he touched and where he walked. By the time she was following her mother out of the church, Emilia had been forced to admit to herself that *el teniente* had been drunk at Toby Jones's. To be honest, he'd probably been drunk at the Luna Loca fire, too. And that day when he couldn't get out of the interrogation room. Certainly on Thursday, when she'd tried to talk to him about the missing euros. Obregon's words in the gym now seemed prophetic and Emilia wanted to know the truth.

If Lt. Rufino's family had been killed, no doubt it would have been reported. A couple of Internet searches would let her know if Obregon had played her or not. But her computer at work didn't have external access, and if she used the single Internet-enabled machine in the office, her search would be tracked and logged. Alvaro had a computer at home, but he'd want to know what she was doing, and she wasn't sure what he'd do with the information. Another trip to an Internet café would not only be expensive, but her search would be tracked there, too, as her last experience had showed.

Besides, Mercedes was . . . well, a friend.

"Do you want some coffee?" Mercedes asked. The dancer wore capri-length teal leggings, a gauzy white tunic, and flat sandals. Emilia felt heavy and clumsy in jeans and an old tee shirt from a long-ago Maná concert.

"Thanks," Emilia said as she sat down at the small desk. The laptop screensaver was a picture of a line of ballet dancers in feathery white costumes. A swath of fabric hung on the wall behind the desk onto which Mercedes had pinned a scrapbook of sorts. Most of the images were from magazine cut-outs or cards that her students had made.

The hanging collage was a sad reminder of Lila's bedroom, with its own wall of magazine pictures. Emilia swiveled the chair. "I haven't told you yet, but I found Lila's brother."

Mercedes looked around from the coffee maker, her mouth a perfect O. "You really found him?"

"Long story, but yes." Emilia nodded. "He goes by a new name now. Pedro Montealegre. Works at the CICI water park."

"Did he help?" Mercedes wore a hopeful expression.

"Not really," Emilia admitted. "He says their mother is still alive, but he doesn't know where she is. She's a hooker and sends him money now and then. He gives it to Lila."

Mercedes looked confused. "So Lila really ran away to find her mother?"

"I think so." Emilia told Mercedes about finding Carla and going first to Mami's and later to the prison to talk to Julieta Rubia.

Mercedes's eyes grew wide as she listened, breaking away only to pour the coffee. "*Por Dios*," the dancer said as Emilia finished. "You are so brave. I can barely face Berta. She's so mad at me. She's been saying that Lila's disappearance is all my fault. Two of my students have quit because of what she's been saying."

"Berta is only now finding out who her granddaughter is," Emilia observed.

They finished their coffee and Mercedes gestured to the laptop computer. "I'll let you get on," she said. "I've got some cleaning to do."

Emilia swiveled the chair back around, navigated to a

search engine page, and typed in keywords like "Cuernavaca" and "murder victims." It took her the better part of an hour to narrow the searches and focus the date, but eventually she found what she was looking for on a newspaper website.

Matilda Vargas de Rufino had been 36 years old and a teacher at a private elementary school. Her daughter Paola was eight and a student at the same school. They were the victims of a carjacking.

The news story was fairly comprehensive. Vargas de Rufino was reportedly divorced, and she and her daughter lived in Mexico City's Santa Fe suburb, in a gated *privada* neighborhood. The carjacking had occurred as the mother and daughter returned home in the evening. As Vargas de Rufino drove up to the slowly opening *privada* gate, two vehicles closed in. An armed gunman smashed the side window of Vargas de Rufino's car, jumped in, and drove away with both victims still in it. The *privada* guards said it happened so fast they were unable to react. Besides, it had happened outside the gate. They were only authorized to take action inside the *privada* itself.

The naked bodies of mother and daughter were found a day later in a small apartment building in the city of Cuernavaca, located about an hour away from central Mexico City. Both had been mutilated. Their deaths were attributed to a random act of violence. Drug cartel violence was no longer limited to surrounding areas, but was making dangerous inroads against the relative stability of Mexico's capital.

The keyboard blurred. It was impossible to imagine what Lt. Rufino felt when he found the bodies. Horror? Anguish? Guilt? Reading between the lines, Emilia could see how he'd tried to protect his wife and daughter. The fake divorce. Setting them up in an ostensibly safe upscale *privada* neighborhood. Maintaining a separate residence while no doubt using a fake name for himself.

Emilia kept hunting, looking for any mention of the residents of the apartment building where the two bodies were found, or of Vargas de Rufino's supposedly estranged husband. After another hour, she'd found nothing and was too emotionally exhausted to continue. Her stomach growled.

"All done?" Mercedes asked, coming back into the office. She put a stack of magazines on the floor by the window.

Emilia blinked. The magazine on the top of the stack was *Que Paso Acapulco*. The cover featured a photo of a statue dedicated to author and poet Carlos Fuentes. Emilia bolted out of the desk chair and scooped it up. "This is last month's edition," she gulped.

Mercedes raised her eyebrows. "You can have it if you want. They're free, you know. I collect them for the girls to cut up and make collages with when they need a break."

"Last month." Emilia could have slapped herself. They'd been in such a rush to track down the places in the current month's edition of the magazine that no one had thought beyond it. Emilia hurriedly flipped to the index of advertisers.

There it was. Page 24. An eye-popping ad for the Toby Jones Beach Club. Two for one drinks every Wednesday night. Live steel drum band every Saturday in October.

Emilia wanted to jump up and down, jig across the room, howl in triumph. She closed the magazine and grinned at the perplexed dancer. "Do you have dinner plans?" Emilia asked. "I have a tab at this place with great *mojitos*."

Chapter 28

On Monday morning Emilia felt recharged and ready to go. Of course, Kurt had been right. The *mojitos* had been cold, the food spectacular, and the conversation easy and relaxed.

Dinner at the Palacio Réal last night with Mercedes had been a much-needed break from work and the situation at home. The chef at the restaurant, whom she'd met before, was a Frenchman. He came out of the kitchen just to greet her and say how glad he was that she'd dropped by even though Kurt wasn't there. The exchange meant that Emilia had to tell Mercedes a bit about Kurt, but it was nice to finally be able to tell someone. Mercedes was quite impressed, which made the telling all that much sweeter.

The dancer had also agreed to take on a new student. Emilia told Mercedes about little Maria Garcia Lira, maid to the Cisneros family who dreamed of being a dancer some day. If Maria wanted to take lessons on her days off, Mercedes would only charge half the usual rate for a beginner class. Emilia would pay part of the cost.

Emilia trotted happily into the squadroom, last month's *Que Paso Acapulco* in hand. Although she now had greater sympathy for Lt. Rufino's erratic behavior, it was going to be nice to show him how wrong he'd been at the fire. She skidded to a stop as she saw four men in suits, none of whom she recognized, boxing up the files on her desk.

"Hey," she exclaimed. "Just what the—"

"Cruz!" Lt. Rufino pointed at her from his office doorway. "My office."

The men continued to pack as she passed her desk. "*Teniente*," Emilia began as soon as she was inside Lt. Rufino's office with the door closed behind her. "What is going—"

"The El Pharaoh case is being handed off to the state attorney general's office," Lt. Rufino said. He sat behind his desk and waved a hand to indicate she should sit down.

"There's been some sort of legal something. They say they can't give us any more time."

"*Teniente,* this is not good."

Lt. Rufino leaned forward. "What's the problem, Cruz?"

"Someone has taken a lot of the key evidence," she said.

"Are you sure?" Lt. Rufino was clear-eyed and calm, the complete opposite of the angry inebriate she'd seen late Saturday night. The steel travel mug wasn't on the desk, and he looked starched and professional in his usual dark suit and narrow tie.

"The euros are gone," she said leadingly.

Lt. Rufino frowned. It was clear he didn't remember their previous exchange about the missing euros. Emilia wondered if he had also forgotten his tirade at the fire. She nervously rolled the magazine into a tube. "They were probably the only currency that wasn't fake."

"Are you saying we had a break in the chain of evidence?" Lt. Rufino asked.

Emilia wanted to shout *Yes! Gomez and Castro!* "It would appear so, *teniente,*" she said.

He passed a hand over his face and sighed. "We'll have to leave it up to the state attorney general's office. It's their case now."

Emilia scooted forward on the chair. She couldn't just let Rico's case evaporate like this. Couldn't let Castro and Gomez get away with whatever they'd done. "Send me over there for a week, *teniente,*" she suggested. "Just a week. I'll help them make the case, make it stick."

Lt. Rufino fingered his moustache, seeming to give the idea some thought. Emilia waited, willing him to agree.

He reached for the place on his desk where the mug usually sat. It wasn't there. He blinked, straightened up, and shook his head. "This unit has higher priority cases and we haven't delivered. We're under a lot of pressure from Chief Salazar's office. So this decision stands."

"*Teniente,* please." If she had to beg she would. "This was Portillo's case."

Lt. Rufino opened a desk drawer and looked through it as he

spoke. "From all that I hear, Portillo was a good man, and I understand your need for closure, Cruz. But things change. We move on to the next thing. See you at the morning meeting." He closed the drawer and began to rifle through the papers on his desk.

Emilia moved to the door, searching for a way to say that they had both experienced loss. He'd lost a family, she'd lost a partner. This case had been her little bit of vengeance, her tribute to Rico. Surely he'd understand that.

But there was nothing about the man behind the desk that invited familiarity.

She walked into the squadroom. Silvio was at his desk with a cup of coffee. "Getting a little more love from *el teniente*?" he asked.

The rest of the detectives were already over by the coffee maker. The men from the state attorney general's office were gone, as was everything from the El Pharaoh case. Emilia threw the copy of *Que Paso Acapulco* onto his desk. "Toby Jones advertised in the October edition," she said. "There are probably others. We need to add those advertisers to the list. Maybe go back another month as well to be sure."

"Shit." Silvio gulped down more coffee, opened the magazine, and found the ad. "Can't believe we didn't think of this before. You showed this to *el teniente*? What did he say?"

Emilia shook her head. "We discussed the El Pharaoh case. The state attorney general's office just came and took all the files. You must have seen them leaving as you came in."

Silvio swung his eyes to Castro and Gomez. The two younger detectives were at their desks, talking to each other about the weekend's *fútbol* games as they surfed their inboxes.

"The case is gone," Emilia whispered furiously. "Who knows what those two have done."

Silvio finished his coffee.

Emilia locked up her shoulder bag and banged on her keyboard until her computer came to life, so angry she was nearly seeing double. She skimmed her inbox, trying to simmer down. When Macias and Sandor came in, she and Silvio showed them the previous month's *Que Paso Acapulco* and decided how to follow up. Emilia would expand the list they'd used Saturday night while Silvio kept on the hunt for the club cab truck, calling more repair garages and car dealerships. Macias and Sandor would make the rounds of the additional restaurants to see which had been contacted by Guetta and his associate. Next, the detectives would again interview everyone who'd been at Toby Jones. See if Murillo had finally gotten permission to discuss the origin of the grenades with the army at *campo militar*. If he had, they could add Guetta and friend to the discussion.

At least they had a plan, Emilia thought, as Lt. Rufino came out of his office for the morning meeting, steel travel mug in hand. They were onto Guetta and his friend. They had a simple motive, a clear pattern, and a better list of locations where the two extortionists could potentially show up. They could end this craziness this week.

"Listen up. We're going to be doing some housecleaning," Lt. Rufino announced. "Closing out some inconclusive cases and taking on some new ones. Notably, there has been another Los Matas Ejercito video, and the demonstrators are collecting in force again around *campo militar* as well as in front of the *alcaldía*."

He went to the stand-alone computer and clicked to play a video.

It was the same as the others. Three men in black seated at a long rectangular table covered with a white cloth. The homemade "LOS MATAS EJERCITO" banner strung on a white wall in back of them. The man in the middle delivered a statement virtually identical to the other videos, accusing the army of terrorizing the citizens of Acapulco and endangering the life of the city's beloved mayor.

"Like Carlota was going to Toby Jones's Saturday night," Macias snickered. He got a baleful glance from Lt. Rufino.

Emilia jiggled her knee with impatience. The Los Matas Ejercito bunch was a distraction, nothing more, except that social media turned every video they made into a rallying cry for demonstrators who had nothing else to do. At least she wouldn't be going back to police any of the demonstrations;

with the plan they'd just drawn up, all the detectives would be too busy.

Silvio got up and poured himself more coffee. He remained standing.

The video ended and Lt. Rufino glanced at the senior detective before continuing. "Before we deal with the new video, the El Pharaoh money laundering case has been transferred to the state attorney general's office. They may have a few questions for us, but we won't be taking any new action. Second, for those who haven't heard, there was another fire last Saturday. Chief Salazar's office will take over the arson investigation. The extortion theory is still in play. However, no one is abandoning the assassination angle just yet. But Torrez Delgadillo's death will make that a difficult avenue to pursue."

Emilia half-rose out of her desk chair. "What did you say, *teniente*?"

"Torrez is dead," he affirmed. He looked at Emilia, Sandor and Macias, but avoided eye contact with Silvio. "Killed in prison early Sunday morning. Chief Salazar's top assistant, Captain Vega, will take over the case. He wants statements from all of you who were at the Toby Jones fire. I don't have to tell you that Chief Salazar's office has not been impressed with your progress on the case. Captain Vega will get every assistance. Is that understood?"

Emilia stopped listening, only able to hear the blood pounding in her head. *Madre de Dios*, what had she done? Torrez Delgadillo had been a good man, someone caught in a pincer between Carlota's ambition and the Sinaloa cartel. Obregon's words came back to her. *I think you just declared your allegiance, Cruz.*

Obregon had solved the problem by having Torrez killed. If he was dead, the political issue evaporated. Carlota could still ride the popularity wave as the would-be victim of an assassination attempt. Nobody had to ask her for a favor. Maybe the Sinaloa cartel had gotten to Torrez first with a *sicario* inside the prison, but the timing pointed to Obregon.

She'd been a fool to trust Obregon. She'd known who and what the man was, and she'd actually trusted him. All that talk about calling in a marker and liking the way she thought. Emilia had swallowed it like a fish swallowing a steel hook.

"They haven't committed any crime," Silvio boomed out, and Emilia was suddenly pulled back into the meeting.

"Chief Salazar wants these videos stopped," Lt. Rufino said testily. "They're inciting violence. Demonstrations."

"They haven't committed any crime," Silvio repeated, more loudly this time. "Some jokers want to dress up in masks and black shirts and say that the army is corrupt. It's not a matter for the police. A lot more important things are coming through from the dispatch desk. Loyola and Ibarra can't keep taking all the rota assignments. There are just too many and the bodies are piling up at the morgue. Cruz and I can take the new cases."

Lt. Rufino took a step backwards. "You and Cruz are assigned to Los Matas Ejercito," he said. "Start by finding everyone who rabidly supports the mayor and check if they have a video camera. Macias and Sandor should have a list of her supporters from the El Tigre investigation."

"If we're serious, we start with video forensics," Silvio said.

"I expect you know all about video forensics, Detective Silvio?" Lt. Rufino asked. He drank from his mug.

"There are a dozen video companies in this city," Silvio said. "There's going to be some expert that can read those videos and give us a better starting point."

The tension in the room was heavy and dense.

"You and Cruz are assigned to Los Matas Ejercito," Lt. Rufino repeated, his voice shrill. "The rest of you have your assignments as well. Dismissed." He scuttled into his office. The door banged behind him.

Emilia pushed her way out of the squadroom, needing to get outside, find some place where she could breathe. Silvio caught up with her before she got to the rear door near the holding cells.

"Hey!" He swung her around by her upper arm. "Don't walk away when I'm talking to you."

"Let go!" Emilia jerked away, blundered her way to the door, and shoved it open.

It was crisp and sunny outside. Emilia found a piece of

shadow and leaned against the wall, gulping air to keep from crying.

Silvio loomed over her, one hand against the wall by her head. "What's the matter with you? This better not be about Murillo and your man problems."

"Torrez," Emilia managed. She pulled in air but couldn't catch her breath.

Silvio stared at her.

"It's my fault he's dead." Emilia bent over and felt the emptiness rattle in her chest.

"You're losing it, Cruz," Silvio said. He pulled her around the corner, away from the curious eyes of the uniforms guarding the impound yard and the glaring sunlight glinting off the roofs of the confiscated vehicles. "What the fuck are you talking about?"

"Torrez." Emilia dashed a hand across her eyes. "I talked to him. At the prison."

"When did you talk to him?"

"Thursday," Emilia said. "I talked to him on Thursday. Less than a week—"

"When were you going to tell me?" Silvio snarled.

"Listen to me," Emilia shouted and Silvio flinched in surprise. Emilia lowered her voice. "He gave me his alibi. He was up in the hills paying off the Sinaloa cartel so they'd stop snagging the workers off Macario Urbina's place."

"Ah, shit," Silvio breathed. "Sinaloa got to him in prison."

Emilia shook her head. "Obregon. I told Obregon."

"What the fuck?" Shock seared across Silvio's face.

"I asked him to get Torrez out of prison. Torrez hasn't been handing army tax notices to restaurants. The whole Carlota assassination thing was a public relations stunt and Obregon knows it."

"Why Obregon?"

"I saw him at the gym Friday night and he asked about the investigation." Emilia leaned back against the cool concrete wall, desperately wishing she could turn back time. "One thing led to another and I told him that Torrez had an alibi. That he'd been paying off Sinaloa but would never admit it because that would implicate Macario Urbina. And he's loyal to his boss."

Silvio passed a hand over his face. "You told Obregon that Macario Urbina is paying off Sinaloa and didn't think he'd use that somehow?"

"I asked Obregon to talk to Carlota," Emilia said. Her explanation now sounded like a child's logic. "Get her to get Salazar to back off. They're so invested in the whole Carlota assassination thing that she's the only one who could get them to back off on Torrez and put the attention onto the extortion ring. Macario Urbina would owe her a favor if she did."

"But instead, Obregon simply got rid of the problem," Silvio said bitterly. "You know who Obregon is. What he's capable of. *Rayos,* Cruz!"

"I killed him," Emilia said. She pressed both hands to her temples, her breath still forced. Torrez was dead, just like Lt. Rufino's family, and it was all her fault. "He had a family and he didn't want to talk because he was protecting Macario Urbina. He was a decent man."

"And you got him killed," Silvio said.

"Don't you think I know that?"

"Fuck, Cruz, I don't know what you know and what you don't. Another surprise just like that Missing Persons case." Silvio slapped the wall next to her. "First, you might have wanted to share the fact that you'd been to the prison and talked to Torrez. Second, you might have wanted to share with your partner some shit idea about asking Obregon for a favor."

"Suddenly you're my partner?" Emilia exclaimed.

Silvio threw out his hands in exasperation. "We ride together every fucking day, Cruz. You should have told me."

"Did it ever occur to you." Emilia doubled up her fists. "That maybe I would have said something if every conversation with you wasn't such a fucking battle?"

A muscle in Silvio's jaw jumped. "I never wanted to work with you and this is why."

"You never wanted to work with me because you don't want to work with anybody." All of her resentment at his constant grating attitude tumbled out in a furious rant, unlocked by anger at both herself and Obregon. "You're a bully. A good detective, the best we've got. But you knock down everybody. Me. Lt. Rufino. He hits back by taking things away from us. That's why we lost Rico's case and the arsons. Because you can't show anybody a little decency."

"I can't show any decency?" Silvio shot back. "Do you know what it's like every fucking day? You, me and Portillo's ghost. Rico was a good guy, but he wasn't the best cop that ever lived and he wasn't a fucking saint."

"You *pendejo!*" Emilia raged. "Don't you dare talk about Rico to me."

"You're not the only one who ever had a partner die," Silvio said harshly. "But if you're a real cop, you let them sleep."

"No, you don't." Emilia was beyond livid. "You take it out on some poor lieutenant whose wife and daughter were murdered. You didn't know that, did you? They were murdered and left on his doorstep, and that's why he drinks. Because there's a nightmare in that poor man's head that he'll never get rid of!"

Silvio folded his arms and they glared at each other.

"You got any other surprises to share?" Silvio asked softly. "Anything that puts me in somebody's sights?"

Emilia shook her head, too angry to say anything else.

"Well." Silvio looked around as if just now realizing where he was. "I got some personal stuff to do."

Emilia didn't answer him.

"Good luck with whatever disaster you create today," Silvio said. He turned on his heel, and Emilia watched him walk around the side of the building toward the lot where the detectives left their personal vehicles and undercover Vice cops paraded as if they owned the place.

"This lady is from the police," the receptionist said from behind her glass and chrome desk. She pronounced *police* in the same way she might have said *sewer*.

"Dr. Ramirez, I'm Detective Emilia Cruz Encinos." Emilia held up her police credential and badge.

Dr. Felipe Ramirez Palmas was a sleekly groomed man with pale brown eyes behind gold-rimmed spectacles. He wore a starched white lab coat monogrammed with his name over a pink striped shirt and rose-colored tie with a tight knot. High-quality gold and amber cufflinks showed inside the lab coat sleeves as he crossed his arms instead of making any move to shake Emilia's hand. His pants were dark gray, his shoes were nearly reflective with polish, and he looked faintly amused to have a representative from the police in his office.

"And what can I do for you, Detective Cruz?"

"Perhaps we might speak somewhere privately?" Emilia suggested.

"I don't have a lot of time, Detective." Ramirez smiled, showing teeth so white and even they might have been *chicle* gum tablets.

Emilia looked around the expensively decorated reception area, taking in the black and chrome chairs, glass cocktail table, silvery window shades, and display of pamphlets advertising miracle skin products and treatments. Two middle-aged women, whose faces looked like inflexible masks, alternated between watching Emilia and the flat screen television.

"I need to ask you some questions about Julieta Rubia," Emilia said, loud enough to ensure that everyone in the office heard her.

After the argument with Silvio, she'd gone back to the squadroom, updated the arson list, stuffed a copy into her bag, and left. She'd found the doctor's office easily. But Silvio's words still stung and Emilia wasn't inclined to treat Julieta Rubia's doctor delicately. She didn't care if she created a disaster in that snobby office.

"The hooker queen who was arrested a while ago," she went on as if he hadn't understood her. "She looks really great for her age."

Ramirez's left eye twitched slightly. "Would you care to step into my office?"

Emilia walked around the reception desk and followed him down a stark white hallway into a stark white office. She stayed standing, ignoring his gesture for her to sit as Ramirez closed the door and settled into a black swivel chair behind another glass and chrome desk.

The white walls were minimally decorated with framed diplomas and certificates. A low black bookcase was topped with an open binder. Emilia flicked through *before* and *after* pictures of middle-aged women. Most of the *after* pictures looked as if their faces were molded from plastic.

"You visit Julieta Rubia every week in prison," Emilia said. She turned away from the binder to face Ramirez. "Why is that?"

"Doctor-patient confidentiality," Ramirez said, showing his amused look again.

Emilia clicked her tongue. "Of course. I'll just have to come back with a technical team to look through your records." She lifted her chin at the silver laptop on the desk. "Looks like all your records are digital. We'll try not to mess up your files as we go." She sighed. "But you know how incompetent we are. Can't even catch somebody throwing grenades. I'm sure you read the papers this morning."

"Shouldn't you be looking for that arsonist, Detective?"

"We got a crack arson investigator in from Mexico City," Emilia said blithely. "New lieutenant from the big city, too. They're on it."

"Sounds like they could use a little more help."

Emilia took down a diploma mounted on a wooden plaque. "I've got lots of time to figure out why you're visiting Julieta Rubia, a woman who has been selling little girls for years. Are you a regular client? She must be pretty good for you to go all the way out to the Cereso for a fuck."

"Julieta is a patient," Ramirez said stiffly.

"Who needs weekly attention." Emilia tossed the diploma onto the desk and it landed with a clatter. She was in a mood to fight. With this doctor, with Julieta Rubia, with anybody. "What's she got? Leprosy?"

Ramirez's eye twitched again. "What exactly are you looking for, Detective?"

"We'll start with why you go to the prison every week."

Ramirez tapped a key and his laptop came to life. As Emilia

walked behind the desk to watch, Ramirez navigated through several menus to a client list. He clicked on Julieta's true name and a file came up.

He scrolled through. "Señora Arana has been my patient for a number of years," he said uncomfortably. "We have a weekly depilatory session, a pulsed laser treatment and a pectin mask, followed by injections of Botox, vitamin B and human growth hormone."

Emilia gave a short laugh. "Julieta must be paying you a fortune."

"Fifty thousand pesos a week."

Emilia nearly toppled over. It took a detective almost four months to earn that much. "You do all this in the prison visitor yard?" she asked. "With everybody else having their visitors at the same time?"

"Of course not," Ramirez huffed. "I use the private clinic on the prison grounds. It is my understanding that it is reserved for privileged detainees."

"Do you pay the prison for the use of the clinic, or does Julieta?" Emilia asked.

Ramirez closed out of Julieta's file. "I have no contact with prison officials and certainly do not pay them for the use of their facilities."

"So Julieta pays for everything." Emilia paced the office. Fifty thousand pesos a week for the doctor. Plus more for Julieta's prison privileges, her manicures, and designer prison clothing. Who knew where the list ended? Despite her tough talk, Olga la Fea had to be printing money for Julieta to pay for all of it.

"When is your next appointment?"

"Tomorrow morning."

"You'll have a new assistant for that visit," Emilia said.

Ramirez pursed his lips. "Am I to assume that it will be the last visit?"

"That depends," Emilia said.

Chapter 29

Emilia and Silvio sat stonily through the morning meeting on Tuesday. When Lt. Rufino asked if they were making progress on finding Los Matas Ejercito, Silvio just said, "Yes."

The senior detective left the squadroom without speaking as soon as the meeting was over. Lt. Rufino looked relieved as he went inside his office, hand wrapped protectively around the steel travel mug. He hadn't been near the coffee maker.

Emilia told Macias and Sandor she'd help with the phone calls and interviews later in the day. She collected her bag and left the squadroom, letting her hand touch Rico's desk as she went. For luck.

But the luck didn't take. Castro fell into step with her as Emilia walked down the hall toward the holding cells. He was tall and spare with a straggly goatee, ponytail and denim jacket over a faded rock band tee and jeans. "Heard you met my big brother last week, Cruz."

"What of it?" Emilia didn't break stride, but her heart stuttered.

"I never figured you for a thrill seeker," he said. "You and Rico always played the straight and narrow. Branching out now that he's gone?"

"I don't know what you're talking about." Emilia shot the holding cell guards with her thumb and forefinger like she always did. They shot her back.

"When Diego said some hot girl cop was prowling around Mami's, I knew it had to be you." Castro moved in closer, trying to pin her into the corner by the exit.

Emilia shoved him away with both hands on his chest and he stumbled against the opposite wall. "I was looking for a missing girl," she spat. "I don't care about Mami's. You can let him know."

Castro peeled himself off the wall and held up his hands in mock surrender. "You and me had our moment," he said.

"We're all right now. That's why I'm doing you this favor."

"What favor is that?"

"Letting you know that if you try to move in on my brother's territory, you're going to lose."

"That's a favor?"

Castro winked at her. "You want better, we got it. The Castro brothers can give you a three-way you'll never forget." He straightened his jacket and pushed open the door. "See you round, Cruz."

Emilia waited until a reasonable amount of time had gone by, enough time for Castro to get in his car and drive away. Besides, she couldn't have rushed out if she'd wanted to. Her legs could barely keep her upright as she realized how close she'd come to mouthing off and revealing what she knew about the missing evidence from the El Pharaoh case.

If she'd done that, Emilia knew that the proffered three-way would be neither optional nor survivable.

Dr. Ramirez had a driver. Emilia sat next to the doctor in the backseat of his late-model sedan as they drove up to the prison complex. The driver showed some sort of identification and the guard checked a roster. They were waved in, and the driver took a side road to the back of the main building and parked in a visitor spot. Dr. Ramirez had a leather satchel that no one asked him to open or otherwise checked. He signed in on the women's side, just like Emilia had done, and was directed to the main prison. He was obviously well known to the guards, and they accepted his statement at face value that Emilia was his assistant. She'd put on one of his real assistant's starched white lab coats, and no one asked for her identification.

Emilia followed the doctor through the entrance the guard indicated. They didn't go through the metal detector. Emilia wouldn't have left her gun behind if she'd known.

The clinic was more modern than the rest of the prison, with pale blue stucco walls and locking cabinets for supplies. The walls were bare except for a few posters that used simple diagrams to demonstrate the importance of frequent hand washing and the use of disposable tissues, not towels or clothing, to blow the nose.

A male orderly in the reception area was playing a virtual building block game on a computer but looked up as Ramirez approached. The orderly stood as if receiving royalty. "Dr. Ramirez," he said. "Number Two exam room. I'll call for the patient."

Ramirez went into one of the exam rooms, Emilia on his heels.

She looked around the space. It looked like a typical medical examination room with a padded examination table, big adjustable overhead lamp, another floor lamp with a long gooseneck, and a rolling stool for the doctor. A sink was set into a clean white counter and waste cans were marked with the biohazard symbol.

"Go ahead and sit down," Emilia said to Ramirez.

He sat down on the stool and she made him wheel it into the far corner before leaning on the wall next to the door.

They waited only a few minutes before the orderly ushered in Julieta Rubia. The blonde woman was dressed as before in a tailored cotton shift and flip-flops. Her fingernails were a glossy black and her blonde hair was held off her face by a matching fabric headband.

At first Julieta saw only the doctor sitting forlornly on his stool, leather satchel on his lap and both hands on the handle as if it was a lifeline. "Why aren't you ready?" she asked him.

Emilia latched the door. Julieta spun around.

"Good to see you again, Julieta," Emilia said.

"The girlie cop." Julieta acknowledged Emilia with a dark glance at Dr. Ramirez.

"That's right," Emilia said. "Detective Cruz. I asked you some questions about a girl. Lila Jimenez Lata. She came to you to ask about her mother. A woman named Yolanda Lata."

Julieta moved past Emilia and hopped up on the examination table. "You need to make your own appointment, *puta*. This is my time."

Emilia stepped away from the door. "Doctor Ramirez can't

see you until after we've talked." She nodded at him and Ramirez walked out, taking his satchel with him. Emilia latched the door again.

Julieta shook her finger at Emilia. "I paid good money for that doctor to come here."

"I know," Emilia said. "Fifty thousand to him every week. Plus something to the prison staff to get him in without anyone looking inside his bag or checking to see what's in those needles he brings. A little something for the orderly to make sure no one else uses this room every Tuesday morning. Bet your cell has a color television, too. A lot of girls are still out there hustling for you."

Julieta crossed her legs and swung her foot. "So what's your deal? You want part of it, too? A little something to keep quiet?"

"I want you to tell me about Lila Jimenez Lata."

"What's with this girl?" Julieta exclaimed. "She was a pretty nobody."

"You talked to her." Emilia leaned over and grabbed the neck of Julieta's cotton prison shift. "She came to you looking for her mother. Then disappeared. What did you do with her?"

Julieta reached around Emilia's grasp and smacked the side of her head. Emilia let go of the dress and punched Julieta in the face. It was a tight hard jab, the kind that always set the heavy bag bouncing on the chain, and it propelled Julieta to the edge of the examination table with her legs spread wide to reveal black underwear. Emilia lunged over the table and grabbed her dress before the woman toppled over the side.

As Julieta flailed for a handhold, Emilia dragged her sideways across the table and caught her in a headlock that had the blonde woman staring at the ceiling with her butt balanced on the edge. The woman kicked at the wall and Emilia bounced her hard against the table. Julieta continued to fight and Emilia tightened her hold until the kicking stopped. Julieta made an involuntary choking sound.

"You want to tell me about Lila now?" Emilia barked.

Julieta gasped and reached over her head to claw at Emilia's face. Emilia flipped the woman face down on the table with her hands pulled behind her. Julieta squirmed and only succeeded in getting herself turned sideways again. Emilia climbed up and sat astride Julieta. The woman's hands were pinned behind her back, and her head hung off the side of the table.

"Start telling me about Lila Jimenez Lata," Emilia ordered.

"You're ruining my face," Julieta panted as she turned red.

"She came to see you just before you got arrested. What happened?"

"I told her I didn't know any *puta* named Yolanda."

"And then what?"

"Sergio," Julieta gurgled.

"Sergio who?"

"Sergio Diaz Centeno."

Emilia gave Julieta's arm a shove. "Go on."

"He likes the young ones."

"Did you let him do her that night? Test her out?"

"He paid good," Julieta said, gasping in between each word.

Emilia pulled the woman up but kept one arm twisted up behind her. "So she came to you looking for her mother," Emilia said, sick at heart. "And you turned her out."

"I put her in a white dress," Julieta said and coughed. "Lit a candle. She looked like a real virgin."

"You let this Sergio rape her," Emilia accused.

"She said she'd do it and I paid her decent." Julieta was limp in Emilia's grasp. "Showed her the kind of money she could make working regular."

Emilia fought to keep her anger in check. "And what happened afterwards?"

"They went upstairs and I didn't see them again," Julieta said. "It was the same night I was arrested. I took a girl out and haven't been back to Mami's since."

"So what about this Sergio?" Emilia tossed Julieta onto the stool vacated by Dr. Ramirez. "Who is he? Where does he live?"

"He's a *lucha libre* fighter," Julieta said. "He comes sometimes to Mami's for pool and the girls. They like him. He's big. Good looking."

"A *luchador*?"

"He's part of the team with Alfredo."

"Alfredo Soares Peña," Emilia said, recalling the other name that Alvaro had given her. "He's visited here."

"Of course he has."

The woman's hands went up to the blonde hair and smoothed it back under the headband. Emilia caught sight of the thin tattoo encircling one finger. "You're married to him?"

Julieta tucked more hair in place and straightened her dress. "You keep away from Alfredo, *puta*."

Emilia didn't care about the skank relationships between well-preserved hookers and their *lucha libre* swains. "Where do I find Sergio?" she asked, standing in front of the stool with her arms crossed.

"There's a gym in Colonia Santa Cruz," Julieta said, naming a neighborhood on the west side of the city. "I think on Calle Zaragoza."

"What's the same of the place?"

Julieta shook her head. "I don't know. Alfredo talks about old Tinoco. I guess he runs it. A lot of *luchadores* train there."

"What about home?" Emilia asked. "Where does Sergio live?"

"I don't know."

"Where does Alfredo live?"

"Above Mami's."

Emilia gritted her teeth. She wasn't going back there. Before she found Alfredo and got him to tell her where Sergio lived, she'd be dead in the gutter behind the place.

She tried another angle. "You said that Alfredo and Sergio are part of a team?" Emilia had never been particularly interested in *lucha libre* fights, with their capes and theatrics, but it was hugely popular. The most popular fighters—the ones that made it to the national level—often kept their identities secret. They used stage names and masked costumes. Three-man tag teams known as *trios* were especially popular. "Who are they when they fight?"

"Alfredo is El Rey Demonio," Julieta said proudly. "Sergio is Puro Sangre and Pepe is El Hijo de Satán."

The Demon King, Pure Blood and the Son of Satan. "Let me

guess," Emilia said. "They wear red masks and tights."

"El Rey Demonio is the greatest *luchador* of them all." Now that she was free from Emilia's grasp and her hair was in place, Julieta's fight was coming back. "He's going to beat your ass for what you did to me, *puta*."

Emilia resisted an urge to punch Julieta until the chemicals in her face oozed out. "You'd better come up with something else about this Sergio, or Dr. Ramirez isn't coming back," she snapped. "Who else knows him? He didn't just come out of nothing. Does he have family in Acapulco? Does he have a job?"

"He's Alfredo's friend and he pays in cash when he takes a girl." Julieta shrugged. "You want to talk to him so bad, go to Tinoco's gym. Or the fights on Saturday night. At the Coliseo Acapulco."

"Okay." Emilia suddenly couldn't deal with Julieta any more. She moved to the door, intending to call Dr. Ramirez, but turned back. "What do you know about a vice cop named Castro? Does he collect protection money from Mami's?"

Julieta cocked her head and regarded Emilia. Her left eye was beginning to close. "He's a prick. How do you think Olga got to look like that?"

"Who collects for him?" Emilia asked. "Do they have a schedule?"

Julieta stepped to the small mirror hanging over the sink. "You think you can move in on him?"

"Maybe I just want to do Olga a favor," Emilia replied.

"Olga and Castro deserve each other. Nobody takes on Castro. Nobody."

"Not even Alfredo?" Emilia asked.

Julieta turned around. "That's who you are, *puta*. Nobody."

Emilia was done. She let Doctor Ramirez come in and smiled grimly at his reaction when he saw the rapidly swelling bruises on Julieta's face. He glared at Emilia, as if she'd defiled his most prized painting.

Chapter 30

For once, the cathedral of Nuestra Señora de la Soledad wasn't full of tourists gawking at the soaring blue vaults. Even so, Emilia was sure she was the only person there wearing a gun. She fastened the middle button of her tan linen jacket as she slid into one of the hard wooden pews at the back.

With only the occasional rustle as someone walked up the main aisle, the big church was cool and quiet. It was a better place to think than the squadroom, or home where Sophia and Ernesto were always moving about. Besides her tiny bedroom, there was no privacy anywhere in her life. Nowhere to breath deep and let thoughts fall into place.

She hadn't been in the cathedral in a long time and it looked a bit more worn than she remembered. The arched altar with its inlaid cobalt blue mosaic background anchored the vast space, looking more Byzantine than Mexican. The theme was echoed in the wide curved niches on either side that were roofed with mosaics of golden rays of sunshine against more of the church's vibrant blue. Mimicking the religious motifs, the late afternoon sun streamed in, illuminating a smaller blue niche holding the cathedral's prized statue of the Virgin.

Emilia closed her eyes and fragments of prayers floated through her head. *Our Father, who art in Heaven, hallowed be thy name . . . Nuestra Señora, tell me that Torrez didn't suffer. Please help Lt. Rufino. Ease his pain. Help Berta, too, because she doesn't understand who Lila was . . . is. Find me a partner who isn't Silvio. Please don't let my mother get pregnant.*

She'd made too many mistakes. The whole Carlota assassination thing had sidetracked the arson investigation; they should have pressed Serverio and found out about Guetta and the army tax scheme immediately after the El Tigre fire. Torrez would still be alive and keeping his workers safe.

Lt. Rufino wouldn't be crumbling under the pressure and the El Pharaoh case would have dealt a big blow to money laundering in Acapulco. But it was probably gone. Months of work turned over, as if Rico's death meant nothing.

Silvio's remark about living with Rico's ghost had stung, mostly because he was right. Rico had been her partner, but also her friend and mentor. Without him, Emilia had to fly solo. Silvio would never take his place; the senior detective was neither mentor nor protector. In an odd way, Silvio demanded that she be an equal more than Rico had ever done.

A couple of tourists in shorts and nylon jackets came in, their flip flops slapping against the tile floor. The sound made Emilia jump, and she glared at them as they talked loudly, but all they saw was some local girl with a surly expression. They drifted up the center aisle with cameras, not genuflecting or otherwise behaving properly in a place of worship. She hoped they'd put something in the donations box in the back of the church.

At least she had a thread to follow for Lila. Emilia wondered about the night Julieta had led Sergio the *luchador* to the room where Lila waited in a white dress. Julieta probably hadn't been entirely truthful when she said Lila had agreed. There had been pressure at Mami's, Emilia was sure, because a girl like Lila could command a hefty price from an eager man like Sergio. No doubt most of what he'd paid had ended up in Julieta's pocket. Had Lila been too immature, too used to being popular to resist the pressure of a glamorous-looking and wily woman like Julieta Rubia? Was Lila still at Mami's being tricked out by Olga? Emilia dreaded telling the girl's grandmother what she'd found out so far.

She thought briefly of asking Pedro Montealegre to go over to Mami's. But if he did, so soon after Emilia had been there asking about the girl named Lila, Olga would surely link Pedro with the girl cop and Castro from Vice would find out. Not only would he come to teach Emilia another lesson but he'd go after Pedro, as well. Pedro might be Lila's half-brother but he didn't deserve to die for it.

When the tourists left, Emilia went over to the side chapel where a tiered iron rack of candles flickered below the statue of the Virgin. Emilia stuffed 100 pesos into the donation slot and lit four candles using a long sliver of wood kept in a pot of sand.

One candle for Rico. One for Torrez, one for Lt. Rufino's family, and the last for those who'd died in the arson attacks. Emilia felt all of their souls reaching out to her, silently asking for peace. For a sleep she could not give them.

The afternoon sun hit her like a spotlight as she left the cathedral, its two blue mosaic domes glittering like giant blue suns against the clear sky. Her phone rang as she crossed the plaza in front of the church. She pulled it out of her shoulder bag and checked the display. The caller was Javier Salinas Arroliza, her contact on the El Pharaoh case at the state attorney general's office. She sat on a section of the low wall that surrounded the round pavilion in the middle of the plaza.

"*Bueno?*"

"Detective Cruz?"

"Hello, *Licenciado.*" His degree entitled him to the honorific.

"Detective, I received some files from your office yesterday, and they appear incomplete." Salinas sounded fatigued and harried. "I was expecting data that would corroborate all the preliminary material. But what came in, frankly, is all but useless."

Emilia rubbed her forehead. On the one hand, she wanted to point fingers and cry out her suspicions. On the other hand, it was an unspoken code within the police department not to report corruption or incompetence to outsiders; one never knew the allegiance of those outside the circle or what they'd do with the information that would make it rebound negatively to the source. And the penalty for being that source could be very, very high.

"It was disappointing," she said cautiously.

"That's not what you told me right after the raid." Salinas had gone from tired to angry. "I don't like being fooled, Detective."

The tourist group from the church passed by in their annoying flip-flops, and Emilia watched as one of the women hopped awkwardly as she reached down to brush grit off her foot. "I'm not on the case anymore," Emilia said. "Why aren't you calling Lt. Rufino? He briefed your office, he should be your point of contact."

There was a long pause. Salinas knew the code, too. He wasn't about to badmouth Lt. Rufino.

"Just listen for a moment," Salinas said, his voice more persuasive. "Those evidence boxes were full of basic business records. You told me about handwritten ledgers, multiple bank account records. Counterfeit cash."

"I'm not on the case anymore," Emilia said again. "I don't know what was in the boxes when they got to you."

"There's no point in holding back unless you're working the wrong side of this with the El Pharaoh people," Salinas said. "My office issued the closure order because we thought the police would deliver. Now I find that didn't happen. What do you think my next step is going to be?"

For a moment, Emilia was speechless. Was he really accusing her of complicity with the casino owners and their money laundering operations?

She stood and walked to the far side of the plaza, where she could see the full sweep of the bay.

"Detective?"

"I'm here," Emilia said. "Just finding a more private place to talk."

Silvio had looked at the bay and said that everything wasn't shit, but the shit was always there, spoiling the drama of sky and boats and ocean.

Emilia was sick of it. Sick of the shit and the endless minefields, always having to protect herself from other cops who sought to use each other for power or money, the same way Julieta had used Lila. The way Castro's brother from Vice used the women at Mami's.

"Detective?" Salinas asked again.

"We had a break in the chain of evidence," Emilia admitted. "Material got lifted out of the evidence boxes. It happened after Franco Silvio and I got reassigned to the arson investigation."

"That's pretty thin, Detective," Salinas scoffed. "Either you or Silvio could have lifted it."

"If Silvio or I wanted to get something out of this case, we could have gone directly to the El Pharaoh," Emilia countered. "Taken a payoff for whitewashing the preliminary investigation. Never bothered with trying to close them down in the first place. That would have been a lot easier and less dangerous than trying to make evidence disappear after we'd gotten your office involved."

"All right," Salinas said after a pause. "But based on what's in these boxes, there's no case to support money laundering. Some counterfeit, but they can say they didn't know it was fake. We can drag it out, but there's nothing here that won't have them back in business in a week."

"There were euros," Emilia said. "A lot of cash. Probably real. You know, not all flat and new. It looked like the casino took them in from tourists but didn't have time to do anything with them before the raid. Whoever took the euros will exchange them."

"A lot of people exchange euros for pesos every day in Acapulco, Detective."

"Tourists do. How many private Mexican citizens come in to exchange them?" Emilia realized she was standing hunched over with her free hand clenched into a fist so tight she was hurting herself. "What if you circulated names and asked to be alerted if they attempted to cash euros?"

"You're talking hundreds of cash exchange places."

"It would be a lot of euros. They'd only have to be on the lookout for a big amount."

"Anybody trying to exchange stolen euros would know to do it in only small amounts."

"They're not that smart," Emilia said.

There was silence on the other end of the connection as Salinas apparently digested what Emilia had suggested.

"Putting out an alert is a lot of work," Salinas finally said. "And what's the payoff? We snag somebody with euros. Will that let us put the El Pharaoh case back together? No one is keeping the missing evidence under their pillow. We both know how things work."

Emilia thought of Castro and Gomez in the squadroom;

playing cards, fooling with their chairs, sneaking stuff out of the evidence boxes and trying to doctor the spreadsheets.

"Maybe whoever took the evidence is dumb enough to think they can keep asking El Pharaoh for money as long as they've got the ledgers." She stood where she could see the bay, feet apart, as tourists and vendors and locals out for a late afternoon stroll in the warm sun swirled by her. She was a fixed point on the map, stuck, immobile, something for others to trip over or push aside, but this time she was going to stand her ground and salvage something. She owed Rico that much.

"You sound like you know the way they think."

"I do."

"Care to give me any names, Detective?"

"Will you put out an alert?"

"Names, Detective."

Emilia looked around. Far out on the water, boats rode gentle swells. The tall white towers of the hotels ringing the shoreline were like sentinels. Or guards. Beacons.

Just a few meters from her, a family was getting ice cream from a vendor wearing a white shirt with an Helado logo on it. He grinned as he presented each of the kids with something swirly on a stick. The parents laughed. A couple passed holding hands; they were dressed as if they'd just gotten out of work. Maybe they were going out to dinner. Two weeks ago, that could have been her and Kurt.

It wasn't shit.

"There are two," she said. "Rubén Castro Altaverde and Luis Gomez Pellas."

It was too late and Emilia was too wrung out to go back to the station, so she simply went home. Ernesto waved to her from his seat by the grinding wheel in the courtyard as she got out of the Suburban. She lifted a hand in reply and went inside.

Sophia was in the kitchen in her usual floral dress and an apron. Emilia gave her mother a kiss on the cheek, mumbled a greeting, and went upstairs to shower and change. The sun was just starting to dip by the time she came back to the kitchen in a tee and shorts and sat at the kitchen table with a beer.

"How nice that you're home early," Sophia said. "You can help me. I went to the fish market this morning. I'm going to make *albondigas de camarónes.*"

Her mother's recipe for shrimp meatballs in a spicy tomato broth was one of Emilia's favorites, but she could only summon a weak smile as she looked at what Sophia had set out on the counter. Boiled shrimp in their shells were heaped in a bowl of ice, and an array of chilies and spices waited for the chopping board.

"That's nice, Mama." Emilia slumped at the table and wrapped her hand around the cool beer bottle. She was out of energy. The situation with Kurt, the fires, Lila, the El Pharaoh disaster, Lt. Rufino, Torrez.

Her problem was trust. She kept trusting people. Like Mercedes and her late husband, Emilia would dance with a partner, thinking it was going to last forever. And then the other person would give her a savage twirl with a pitch about caring for her or wanting to do the right thing or that they owed her a favor—calling in a marker—and Emilia could spin and crash.

Belatedly, she realized she'd done it again with the conversation with Salinas. Now that he had names, would he try to make a deal with Castro and Gomez for a cut of the euros? Would Salinas give her up as the person who'd squealed?

Maybe she was simply too stupid, too naive to be a detective.

Emilia drank some beer, and only when she got a mouthful of foam did she realize that her hand was shaking.

"Come here and stir the tomatoes," Sophia said.

Emilia managed to pull in some real beer before going to the stove. The chopped tomatoes and onions sizzling in an iron frying pan would become the base of the *caldillo* broth for the meatballs. The smell was rich, and as Emilia stirred the mixture she felt a sense of normalcy that had been missing since the night at the El Tigre.

Sophia kissed her daughter's cheek as she tied an apron

behind Emilia's back. "You never cook with me, Emilia," Sophia said. "This is nice."

Emilia poked at the mixture in the pan with a wooden spoon as Sophia poured hot water from a saucepan into a bowl of dried *ancho* chilies. Fragrant steam rose as the chilies absorbed the moisture. "Mama," Emilia said. "What if I had a boyfriend?"

Sophia put the saucepan of hot water back on the stove. "Of course you have a boyfriend, Emilia." She smiled broadly. "All those nights you go out all dressed up and so happy. I know you'll tell me about him when you're ready."

"He's a *gringo*, Mama," Emilia said. The sound of the grinding wheel and Ernesto's whistling filtered through the window.

Sophia selected several stalks of cilantro from the small pot by the windowsill. "Did you meet him at school?"

"I work now, Mama. You know that," Emilia snapped. She retrieved her beer from the table, wincing at her tone. Sophia often slid between today and yesterday, and just as often cried when Emilia got angry at her inability to tell the two apart. Emilia softened her voice. "He manages a hotel. He won't be around much longer, but I just wanted to know what you thought about the idea."

Sophia started mincing the cilantro. "Is that why you're not happy today?"

"I'm happy, Mama," Emilia said automatically.

"Not like me and your father." Sophia put down the knife and tapped Emilia's arm. "Don't let the tomatoes burn."

Emilia shoved the spoon around the tomato mixture again. "Speaking of Ernesto," she said. "Does he use a condom?"

"Emilia!" Sophia clapped a hand to her mouth. "What are you talking about?"

"He's in your room more and more, Mama." Emilia stopped stirring to look at her mother. "I want to know if he's using a condom."

Sophia dropped her hand and carefully scraped the minced cilantro into a bowl. "I can't get pregnant," she murmured. "After you, the doctor said I couldn't ever have any more babies."

Emilia turned off the stove, surprised at her mother's clarity. "You never told me that, Mama."

"It's not something to talk about."

"Did you want more children?" It was a rare event to talk to her mother as one adult to another.

"No." Sophia gave Emilia an embarrassed smile. "I had my wonderful smart girl. And now I have Ernesto back, too."

"Mama," Emilia said. "I'm glad you're happy but we need to talk about Ernesto."

Red-faced, Sophia wiped her hands on her apron and pulled an envelope from her apron pocket. "This came today."

Emilia took the envelope and opened it to find 300 pesos in well-fingered bills and a short note written on lined school paper. It was brief, just saying that Ernesto should come back to Mexico City and that the money was bus fare. There was no expression of love or missing him, just three sentences of instruction and a printed signature. *Beatriz Lopez de Cruz.*

"She's his real wife, Mama," Emilia said sadly. "She wants him to come home."

Sophia shook her head. "I'm his wife now."

"Mama, stop."

"I want him to stay," Sophia insisted. "He feels good here. Like he belongs."

"Is that why you keep introducing him at church?" Emilia asked.

Sophia busied herself at the counter, pulling cloves of garlic off a fresh bulb, checking to see if the *ancho* chilies had softened in their bath of hot water. "I shouldn't have showed it to you."

"Mama, it has to be his decision," Emilia said. "You can't just say 'stay' and trap him here because he feels sorry for you."

"I want to stay with Sophia." Ernesto's voice was plaintive.

Emilia hadn't paid attention to the halt of the grinding wheel or heard Ernesto come in. He stood at the entrance to the kitchen wiping his hands on a rag.

"With Sophia," Ernesto repeated.

Sophia crossed in front of her daughter, eyes straight ahead as she got Ernesto a beer out of the refrigerator. He sat at the table with it. Emilia grabbed her own beer and sat across from him.

"You are married to Beatriz," Emilia said. "She sent you money to come home."

"I'm married to Sophia now," Ernesto said, more firmly than usual.

"You're not really married to my mother." Emilia rubbed her eyes as Sophia started to mince the garlic with exaggerated force, thumping the knife on the chopping board. "You can't be married to two women at the same time."

"Sophia?" he asked.

Emilia's mother scooped the garlic into the bowl with the cilantro. "You're my husband now. You should stay here."

Emilia closed her eyes and drank some beer. *Life isn't that simple, Mama*, she wanted to say.

Ernesto dug into a pocket and put a handful of wrinkled peso bills on the table. He pushed them across to Emilia. "Send her this to pay for a divorce. Plus what she sent."

Emilia turned to look at her mother. Sophia smiled and started deveining the shrimp with a small knife.

"That's it?" Emilia asked into the silence. "Ernesto wants to stay and that's the end of this?"

Her phone rang. Emilia plucked it out of the back pocket of her shorts. *Silvio.* Possibly the last person in the world she wanted to talk to right now.

She walked out of the house before she hit the connect button on the phone. "*Bueno?*"

"Macias says you never showed up in the office this afternoon," Silvio said by way of a greeting. "Where the fuck were you?"

"You're the one who keeps disappearing," Emilia tossed back at him. "Where were you?"

"Answer my question, Cruz."

"Well, Franco," Emilia said, in as snide a voice as she could manage. "I took personal time. You know, just like you."

"I've been working the Los Matas Ejercito videos."

Emilia clicked her tongue as if impressed. "Tracking down everybody in town with a video camera?"

"No." Silvio's voice was tight. "All shot with a cell phone. Whoever uploaded to YouTube isn't very tech savvy, either. Plus they uploaded a test video. A couple of seconds of a street scene. Couple of cars going by. Hard to know where that is."

"Oh." Emilia fought a wave of guilt. He'd actually been doing real work, despite the fact that he thought the assignment was a waste of time.

"I talked to Murillo, too," Silvio went on. "Only needs one more approval to get inside *campo militar.* We can go with him, ask some questions, see if Los Matas Ejercito has made any direct threats."

"Okay." Emilia leaned against the fender of the Suburban. "I talked to Salinas at the state attorney general's office. He says the evidence they received isn't enough to do anything except give the El Pharaoh people a lecture for receiving counterfeit."

"We knew that was going to happen," Silvio said. "Leave that shit at home and get your ass into the office tomorrow morning. We got to talk to Vega after the morning meeting."

The line went dead.

"You *pendejo*," Emilia said to the phone.

They'd get through the immediate crisis and when things were calm she'd talk to Lt. Rufino about getting a new partner. If he wouldn't let her and Silvio go their separate ways, maybe she'd talk to Alvaro, see what opportunities there would be if she went back in uniform. She'd suffer a big pay cut, but it would be worth it not to deal with Silvio again.

She pocketed the phone and went back into the house. Ernesto was still at the table drinking his beer. The money was on the counter. Emilia pulled open the refrigerator door and got another bottle of beer. Maybe tonight was a good night to get drunk. After all, how much worse could things get?

Sophia had mixed the spices and the chopped shrimp. She dropped balls of the mixture into a pan of sizzling oil, and once again Emilia was struck by the smell of home and normality: tomatoes, garlic, rice, seafood. Ernesto got up and put the pickled vegetables that went so well with *albondigas de camarónes* into a small earthenware bowl. Silverware and napkins were already on the table.

Emilia slowly put the beer back in the refrigerator. A second beer wouldn't make her drunk like Lt. Rufino, but it wouldn't fix any of her problems, either.

"Are you jealous of your mother's happiness?" the priest asked.

They were in the rectory kitchen with cups of *manzanilla* tea that he'd prepared. As the ladies of the parish continually brought Padre Ricardo food, Emilia was pretty sure tea was the only thing the priest knew how to make. But his recipe was based on frugality. The tea bag had obviously been used before. He'd dunked it briefly into both cups and set it in a saucer for the next time.

"I just think it's odd that he left this Beatriz with no warning." Emilia warmed her hands over the hot cup. "But Mama thinks he'll stay with her just because she asks him. What if he leaves her, too?"

"She'll have known love for a while at least," Padre Ricardo said.

"She's not strong," Emilia countered. "Mentally. You know that. She barely survived my father's death and half the time she thinks I'm still in school."

"It's her coping mechanism, Emilia," Padre Ricardo said.

Emilia sipped the pale yellow liquid in her cup. It was really just hot water with a grassy aftertaste. "I thought priests were against divorce," she grumbled.

"He's trying to do the right thing, Emilia," Padre Ricardo said. "Give me the address and the money and I'll wire it to his wife."

She gave it all to the priest and couldn't suppress a shiver of relief. If Padre Ricardo was able to accept Sophia's relationship with Ernesto, maybe she should, too.

But his question about jealousy had struck home. It wasn't

that Emilia was jealous of her mother's happiness, it was that she was resentful of the way Sophia could so easily say what she wanted, like a child who wasn't aware of consequences.

Padre Ricardo put his own cup down on its saucer. He'd evidently enjoyed his tea. "Berta asked about you the other day."

Emilia shook her head. "I don't have good news for her."

"Lila is dead." It was a statement rather than a question.

"I don't know." Emilia told the priest everything she'd turned up so far about Lila, the whole sad story of Yolanda, Pedro, the girl's trip to Mami's, and Sergio the virgin-chasing *luchador*. "I'll try to find him, too," Emilia said. "Either at this gym or at the fights on Saturday."

"You let me know when you're ready to talk to Berta," Padre Ricardo said. "I'll come with you."

"That's the first good news I've had all day," Emilia said.

Chapter 31

"They're still talking about the fire at the El Tigre being an assassination attempt on Carlota," Emilia said.

"Yeah." Silvio started the car. "Vega made it sound as if he was more concerned about the demonstrations in front of the *alcaldía* and out at *campo militar* than some extortion story."

"I told him he should have teams staking out all the restaurant advertisers from the magazine," Emilia said. "That we'd pinned down a pattern with the notes and timing. Plus how they'd gotten a first payment from Serverio at the El Tigre, then tried to get a lot more out of him a second time. Guetta and his buddy either decided he was an easy mark, or they suddenly needed a lot more money."

It was midday on Wednesday, and each detective had had an interview with Captain Vega about the arson investigation as part of the turnover of the case to Chief Salazar's staff. Emilia had been amazed by the way Vega treated the whole thing. He'd barely listened to what she had to say and wrapped up with a lecture on how his staff had to start from the ground up because the detective unit had been so slow to develop any meaningful information.

"I told him the same thing." Silvio backed the car out of the parking space at the central administration building and waved a hand to the guard, who rolled back the gate for them to pass through. "My guess is that after three fires, Guetta can pretty much name his price now."

"So maybe there won't be another fire on Saturday," Emilia reasoned. "Everybody's scared and paying whatever the asking price is today. Vega is going to have to catch them in the act as they get paid off by one of the restaurants."

"Vega can't find his own dick without his wife's help."

Dressed in plain black pants, a white blouse, and her reliable tan linen blazer for her interview at the central administration building, Emilia had stopped and bought a dozen designer doughnuts before appearing in the squadroom. Kurt always recommended food as a way of smoothing the way and his advice had worked before. It worked fairly well that morning, too. Macias and Sandor didn't ask why she hadn't come in when she said she would, and Silvio ate two after giving her a grunt which, if she was charitable, could be interpreted as *I acknowledge you are alive*. They'd been silent on the drive over to the central administration building. Now that the interviews were over, the tension had slackened to the point where they could be civil to each other.

"Murillo has got a good theory about the fire at Toby Jones," Silvio went on. "They'd been able to throw the grenades out of the bed of the truck for the first two fires. Stand up in the bed, pull the pin, throw hard from a distance. Accuracy and force resulted in big damage. When you shot up the truck they probably stashed it somewhere. Hit Toby Jones in a car. Best they could do was roll the grenade out the door and drive off."

"Makes sense."

"Murillo's coming in to talk to us around 3:00 p.m.," Silvio said. "Before he heads back to Mexico City. Says he's been recalled but he can pass on his permission to talk to somebody inside *campo militar* to us."

"You think Chief Salazar would be okay with that?"

"We won't be talking about arson and grenades. We'll be talking about Los Matas Ejercito," Silvio observed. "You heard *el teniente*. Chief Salazar wants the videos stopped."

"Fine line," Emilia said.

Silvio shrugged.

"Drop me off on the corner," Emilia said. "I'll catch a taxi back to the station in time to talk to Murillo."

"Personal time?" Silvio asked without slowing down.

"I got a lead on the Lila Jimenez Lata missing person case." Emilia pointed to the next corner.

"*Hijo de puta*, Cruz," Silvio swore. "Did you go to Mami's again?"

"No. Julieta decided to talk to me." Emilia waited for him to lose his temper, but the big detective just kept his eyes on the road.

"What's the deal?" he asked.

"Lila hooked up with a *luchador* at Mami's." Emilia dropped her hands to her lap as the car kept going. "Julieta Rubia tarted her out to him. Apparently he pays big if he gets to break in the girls."

"Nice," Silvio growled.

"All I know is that he works out at a gym on Calle Zaragoza."

"Tinoco's place," Silvio said.

"That's right." Emilia turned to him in surprise. "How did you know?"

"Boxers work out there, too," he said. "Once upon a time I trained with Tinoco. What's this *luchador's* name?"

"He fights as Puro Sangre," Emilia said.

"With El Rey Demonio," Silvio added. "I've heard of him. You got a real name?"

"Sergio Diaz Centeno." Emilia had checked the *cédula* database for the man. Julieta had been right; even in a grainy identification picture, Diaz Centeno was a handsome man. "His address is the same as the gym's."

Fifteen minutes later the car dropped neatly into a space parallel to the street in front of a strip of shops that had seen better days. The places had once been colorful, but now the cement fronts were faded and peeling except where new advertising for instant coffee and packaged pastries had been painted directly onto the walls. Silvio pressed a buzzer next to a door bracketed with heavy iron bars and identified himself into a small speaker set in the wall, similar to the setup at Mercedes's dance studio. A solenoid hummed, the door popped open, and Emilia followed him down a short hallway to the snapping rhythm of a speed bag.

Silvio shoved open an inner door and they entered the gym. The place was worn and old-fashioned looking, and the canvas of the raised boxing ring that took up at least a quarter of the space was stained brown with age and blood. Three heavy bags hung from the ceiling across from the ring. A young man intently slapped one of two speed bags bolted to a rack. There weren't any shiny weight machines like in the police gym, just a couple of benches and racks of rusty iron barbells. Heavy round free weights lay on the floor, waiting to be racked together for deadlifts and bench presses or held to the body for killer sit-ups. Doors at the far end of the gym probably led to a changing room and bathroom.

"Franco Silvio!" An old man wearing a stained white singlet undershirt, threadbare khaki pants, and big white sneakers made his way around the side of the ring.

"Hey, Tinoco." Silvio actually smiled and embraced the old man. For a moment, the big detective shed years and was a hungry young boxer again. "Brought somebody to meet you. Emilia Cruz Encinos."

Tinoco looked Emilia over and smiled, revealing three missing lower teeth and a gold cap on top. His hair was still dark. "Franco, you got good taste."

Emilia grinned. Tinoco's look wasn't prurient, and she held out her hand. "Nice to meet you, Tinoco, and no, Franco and I aren't like that. He's still married to Isabel."

Tinoco's smile broadened as he shook Emilia's hand, testing her strength. His knuckles were outsized knobs, the product of many broken bones, and his fingers were gnarled with arthritis.

But Emilia didn't let him get away with testing her and he nodded in satisfaction. "You a fighter, then, *chica*? I'll put you in the ring. You'll do good and look good at the same time. Maybe almost as good as Franco here."

"How good was Franco?" Emilia asked.

"Ah." Tinoco lifted both hands, palms out. "Franco was the best fighter I ever trained. The kind that could take a beating and still come back with a knockout. No fear." He thumped his chest. "All heart and legs and a right hook like murder. A champion. Look at him, he's still got it. I could put him in the ring today and he'd still go the distance for me."

Silvio looked as if he'd swallowed a fly. Tinoco pulled Emilia over to a corner with a paper-strewn desk, a big bottled water dispenser, and baskets full of strips of cloth to wind around a fighter's hands. Posters, some yellowed with age and curling away from the wall, announced both boxing matches and *libre* fights at the Coliseo. A plain set of shelves was laden with trophies and plaques. Tinoco pointed to the middle shelf and Emilia saw a bronze pair of miniature boxing gloves and the name FRANCO SILVIO engraved on a dusty plaque.

"*Rayos*, Tinoco." Silvio cleared his throat and avoided Emilia's eye. "That was 15 years ago."

"There aren't fighters like you around now, Franco," Tinoco said.

"You still got enough to keep you busy," Silvio said, elbowing Emilia away from the trophy shelves. "I hear you're training *luchadores* now."

Tinoco shrugged. "They're all show. But I gotta make a living."

"You know a *luchador* goes by the name of Puro Sangre?"

"Sergio?" The old man cocked his head at Emilia. "Is that what the girl's about? The boy get her in trouble?"

Silvio shook his head. "Not this one. Another girl. Over at Mami's. Need to ask him a question about her."

It was clear that Tinoco knew that Silvio was now a cop. Emilia tried to look reassuring. "The girl ran away from home," she said. "But she met up with Sergio a couple of weeks ago at Mami's."

Tinoco sniffed and wiped his nose with the back of a big-knuckled hand. "The girls like him. He's a good *luchador*. Big. Showy. You know what I mean?"

"Do you know where we can find him?" Silvio asked. He took a 200-peso bill out of his pocket and laid it on the desk. "He lists your place as his address."

"A lot of the boys do that," Tinoco said. "They live a couple days with this girl. A couple days later it's another girl. Or the back of a bar. Hard to keep up with them."

Emilia blew out her breath in frustration. "It's important. Is he coming in later?"

Tinoco looked thoughtful as he eyed the money.

"Just looking for a little girl he met, Tinoco," Silvio said. "That's all."

Tinoco shook his head. "You keep your money, Franco. I haven't seen him in a week or so. Him and El Rey Demonio, they're big names now. They don't come in as much as they used to."

"What about a job?" Silvio pressed but didn't take back the pesos. "He's got a job somewhere?"

"That *trio* got too big for jobs," Tinoco said. "They won a lot of prizes. Cash money and El Rey got a set of fancy wheels. You want to find them, go over to the Coliseo on Saturday night."

Silvio glanced at Emilia. She lifted a shoulder in a half-hearted shrug.

"Are they worth betting on?" Silvio asked.

Tinoco smiled, showing his gold tooth. "Not like you, Franco. But they put on a good show."

Silvio cocked his head at the 200 pesos on the desk. "Lay down a bet with me the next time you have a good fighter."

They stayed a little longer, mostly because Tinoco seemed lonely in the nearly empty gym. It was nearly 2:00 p.m. when they finally walked down the hall to the barred door. Silvio shook a thick finger at Emilia. "You're not going over to the Coliseo on Saturday night."

"I'll find somebody to go with," Emilia said. They both knew that a single woman at the Coliseo was a woman who ended up in a Missing Persons file.

"*Rayos*, Cruz," Silvio swore as he shoved open the door and walked out ahead of her. "No. The Coliseo can be a rough place on fight nights."

"I've run down a lot of leads on this girl," Emilia said. "I'm not stopping now."

Silvio pulled out keys and bleeped open the car doors. "Get in the car, Cruz."

Emilia slid into the passenger seat and decided to change the subject rather than get into another argument with Silvio. "Why did you quit boxing?"

"It was time." Silvio started the car.

"Sounded like you had a big career going."

Silvio leaned back. The engine was running and his hands were on the steering wheel, but he didn't put the car in gear. "Tinoco wanted me to throw a fight. The other fighter had the same sort of friends that Macias and Sandor have. They offered Tinoco big money to make sure their boy won. Bigger money than the cut he'd have gotten if I'd won."

Emilia swallowed hard. "And did you? Throw the fight, I mean."

"Wasn't up to me." Silvio unclipped his sunglasses from his shirt collar and put them on.

"He accepted the deal before asking you," Emilia guessed.

"Tinoco always looks out for himself," Silvio said, and shoved the car into reverse.

Emilia sighed and found her own sunglasses. "You don't need to come with me. I'll find somebody else. I'll talk to this Sergio on Saturday before the fights start."

"I'm coming with you," Silvio insisted. "But when this is over, I'm talking to Rufino. You and me. This isn't working out."

He backed the car out of the tight parking space and changed gears with a jolt.

"For once we agree," Emilia replied.

They both stared straight ahead, hidden behind sunglasses, as the car turned south toward the police station.

Chapter 32

"It would seem that we are talking at cross purposes here," General Becerra said nastily. "I want you to find this *cabrón* making threatening and accusatory videos, and you're telling me that the army is responsible for an arson and extortion scheme. If I didn't know better, I'd say that you were making a joke."

"It's a fair question, *mi general*," Silvio said from across the table. "Could it be that the group calling itself Los Matas Ejercito knows something about the army's involvement that the police don't?"

"Very possible, as it seems the police know next to nothing." Becerra looked around in triumph and got a patter of dutiful laughter from the military officers ringing the table.

Silvio went on. "It's been in the news that the fires could be the work of an extortion scheme, but this group is still making videos blaming the army."

"Well, it's convenient to blame the army, isn't it?" Becerra bared his teeth in a strange expression of disgust. "Especially when your mayor whips up public opinion and encourages demonstrators in front of our gates."

"We have to rule out all possibilities," Silvio said.

"You have the gall to make this accusation to my face?" Becerra snarled. "To accuse army personnel of arson and extortion?"

It was all bluster. The Mexican Army had been accused of everything from rape to blackmail to murder over the past few years. The army had never had a sterling reputation, and its supposed role as the country's savior against the drug cartels had merely given it more opportunities.

General Becerra was General Hernandez's deputy. Hernandez had been called to Mexico City for consultations, Emilia and Silvio had been informed by Murillo when he'd stopped by to say goodbye. The rumor was that Hernandez would be reassigned or forced to retire. His superiors in Mexico City had been less than impressed with his exchange of press statements with Carlota, lack of explanation over the origin of the grenades used in the arson attacks, and failure to stem the ongoing demonstrations in front of the military facility's gates.

Becerra was in his early forties, with a long aristocratic nose, a bristly crew cut and an attitude of smug superiority. He had stamped into the conference room followed by an entourage that put Carlota's baggage to shame. His aide was a flushed lieutenant with a nametag that read Aguilar who'd pulled out the general's chair for him. All of the military minions who'd previously ushered Emilia and Silvio into the room rose to their feet, swivel chairs and booted feet making loud noises. They all wore pressed fatigues in the same camouflage pattern that Guetta and his friend had worn in the Casa Casa restaurant security video.

Counting the general, his aide Lt. Aguilar, and the two detectives, there were about 20 people in the room. Emilia was the only woman.

The general didn't extend to either Silvio or Emilia the simple courtesy of introducing themselves. He didn't shake hands, either, just launched into a 20-minute lecture on the Los Matas Ejercito videos, railing against the police incompetence that had led to citizens to believe that they had to be protected from the army. He accused them of mishandling the press and wanted to know the status of the investigation, not against the arsonists, but against Los Matas Ejercito. The three-man video team was depicted as a bigger threat than the Los Zetas cartel. He stabbed the air with his forefinger, making sure his underlings were paying attention.

As he went on, Emilia was reminded of Olga la Fea and her command of the room at Mami's. The way her words were veiled threats and her minions laughed on cue.

Emilia kept her face composed, trying to let Becerra's words flow over her without touching. Compared to Hernandez, Becerra was a joke.

But Silvio pushed back, outlining what public sentiment via

social media was saying about the army's likely involvement. He recounted the evidence they had that implicated the army in the extortion scheme: sightings of men in camouflage in the truck at the El Tigre, the Casa Casa restaurant's security video showing camouflaged men asking for payment of an "army tax," the use of grenades possibly attributed to army stockpiles. After all, neither the police nor the visiting arson investigator had been given access to the armory records at *campo militar*.

Before a red-faced Becerra could start yelling again or had a stroke, Emilia cleared her throat and both combatants glanced at her.

"Perhaps your staff would be willing to watch the videos, *mi general*," Emilia interjected. "A few questions afterwards and we can be on our way."

Becerra was sharp enough to know Emilia had just given him a way out of the meeting. He waved his hand idly in assent. Silvio folded his arms and leaned back in his chair.

Emilia's disc with four short videos on it had been turned over to their hosts before Becerra came into the room. Now someone dimmed the lights, a large screen television mounted on the far wall flickered, and the three masked men came to life.

Once again, Emilia mentally compared the size of the men to the water bottles in front of them. Each member of Los Matas Ejercito was as big as Silvio, with the one in the middle the largest.

The security video from Casa Casa played last. The video company Silvio had engaged proved itself useful. Some of the shots had been blown up, and in one view the name tag and the word *Guetta* was more clearly seen, as was the wedding band and the print of the army tax notice.

The videos ended and the lights came up. Silvio leaned forward. "All of the restaurants that have so far been contacted and asked to pay an army tax are turning over their security camera feeds to us. We'll use facial recognition software to compare the extortionists to the *cédula* database and make a positive identification."

He delivered the line perfectly, as if they had the technology to do that without the police intranet imploding, and Emilia scanned the table for reaction. Becerra looked as if he hadn't heard a thing. His lieutenant, Aguilar, appeared not to understand what all the tech talk meant. The others waited for Becerra to give them a cue.

Emilia cleared her throat. "Would you be aware of any former army personnel who perhaps left service under certain circumstances and could be making videos in revenge?"

Becerra looked at his aide. Aguilar shook his head. The general looked at Emilia triumphantly. "No. We have no troubled current or former personnel."

Of course not. Emilia smiled. "Has anyone received grudge messages?"

Becerra snorted. "Only threats as a result of the videos. Look at all the demonstrators!" Again, he got a polite round of duty laughter.

The rest of her questions got blunt and pointless answers.

Emilia closed her notebook. "Thank you, *mi general*. That's all. But before we go, we'd like to look at the personnel records for soldiers named Guetta who are assigned here."

Becerra waved a hand at his aide. "Check the records. We can show the good detectives here that we are cooperating fully."

Emilia could almost see the press release forming in Becerra's eyes. Of course the army would get some political traction out of the visit; she and Silvio had known that would happen. It was the only reason Silvio had held onto his temper.

Aguilar and three others quietly left the conference room. The general went to the far end where there was a small desk and several phones. No one said a word as the general called his secretary and in a loud voice postponed his next appointment.

The next 20 minutes were torture, everyone sitting around the table silently while the general barked over the phone at his secretary about various administrative issues.

The aide came back, carrying a slim folder. Becerra came back to the table.

"We do have a Sergeant Guetta assigned to our region, *mi*

general," Aguilar said. He glanced uneasily at Emilia and Silvio. "I brought his personnel file and asked for him to be sent for. He should be here in a few minutes."

Becerra looked through the file, nodding thoughtfully as he slowly turned pages. When he was done, Aguilar brought the file to the other side of the table and gave it to Silvio. He slid it to the side so that Emilia could read it at the same time.

The file was slim. Guetta was young, maybe in his mid-twenties, with a thin face and sharp, *indio* features. Guetta had joined the military ten years ago, when he was 16. He was originally from San Luis Potosi, a good-sized town in the middle of the country. He didn't work in the armory, but was a motor pool driver.

Another long time passed before there was a tap on the door. The other two officers who'd left with Aguilar now headed a small parade of soldiers in camouflage fatigues. One matched the picture in the file.

Becerra snapped his fingers and Aguilar marched the soldier identified as Sergeant Guetta to stand in front of the general.

"Have you asked any Acapulco businesses to pay an army protective tax?" Becerra barked.

"No, *mi general*." Guetta stood at attention.

Becerra nodded. "Have you stolen grenades from the warehouse?"

"No, *mi general*."

"Do you know anyone who has stolen grenades?"

"No, *mi general*."

The soldier didn't react to any of the questions. Becerra might have been asking him if he liked to eat fish or go to the movies.

The general dismissed the soldier, and the group that had come in with him all left.

Becerra tapped the table in front of him. Aguilar retrieved the slim personnel file and laid it on the table in front of his superior.

"You see," Becerra said. "Full cooperation. You are wasting your time here."

"We appreciate that cooperation, *mi general*," Emilia said as

Silvio passed out pictures of three charred buildings and Murillo's glossies identifying the grenade fragments. They'd planned out this part of the meeting and knew it might prove the most controversial. "There is just one last thing."

"As you are well aware, the grenades used in all three attacks were military-use explosives," Silvio said.

"Permission was only given for the arson investigator to look at military records," Aguilar interrupted. For a military man, he had a surprising tendency to look down, as if speaking into his chin. Emilia guessed that anyone who worked very long for Becerra adopted that habit. "He was from the federal firefighting school and carried federal authority. You are only from a municipal police department."

"We understand that distinction," Silvio acknowledged. "But as our investigation is focusing on Los Matas Ejercito and the attention they are bringing to the grenade—"

"Frankly, this seems to be more of a continuation of the mayor's vendetta against the army than a legitimate police investigation." Becerra stood up. "You can send us a written statement of the events you'd like us to look into and the army will carry out an internal investigation. Now get out."

"You think someone in that room was the arsonist?" Despite the sunshine and the heated tarmac of the police station parking lot, Emilia shivered. The meeting in *campo militar* hadn't helped any investigation, just raised and confused her suspicions. She might have been sitting in a room with someone who'd killed eight people and wounded numerous others or she might have been sitting with rude but hardworking army officers trying to get on with the business of protecting the country.

Silvio stared at her. "There's something we're not catching here."

"Like the whole sham with Guetta?" Emilia drank some of the cola they'd stopped to get after being hustled out of the building and given an escort back to the gates of *campo militar*, where nearly 100 protestors were still camped out. "The file was barely five pages long."

"For a ten-year career?" Silvio crushed his own soda can in one hand and threw it into the trash can near the door. "I think they put that whole show together in a panic. Wanted to make sure they had a Guetta who was nothing like the person wearing the nametag."

"But why?" The logic to this case had long ago ceased to be linear. "What are we missing?"

"Somebody in that room knows the real Guetta," Silvio surmised. "Or at least the person stupid enough to wear a uniform jacket with a name tag on it."

"Okay." Emilia nodded. "Let's go with the theory that one of them is in on it. What do we do?"

Silvio shrugged and opened the door to the station. "It's Vega's case now," he reminded her. "You want to call and tell him you think something smells bad up at *campo militar*?"

What do you think Vega would do, Emilia started to say, but Silvio walked ahead of her past the holding cells, and she was left alone in the hallway.

Chapter 33

The Coliseo was a big arena. Not big enough for a really wild Maná concert, but big enough to handle the crowds that came to see the *lucha libre* battles held almost every Saturday night. There were two tiers of seating: on the ground floor surrounding the main ring, and up on the second tier under the ceiling's lofty web of metal rafters. The second-floor seats gave the best views of the fights and the big Corona beer logo in the middle of the ring's blue canvas floor. But Emilia knew that the ground-floor seats nearest the ring were the most coveted. The action sometimes spilled beyond the ropes, and everyone wanted to be up close and personal with a *luchador* when that happened.

Plastered to bulletin boards near the entrance, posters of that Saturday night's lineup featured drawings of El Rey Demonio and the leaders of two other *trio* teams. All the fighters were in costume, with latex masks that totally disguised their faces. Most of the *luchadores* that made it to the Coliseo had managers and even product endorsements. Their nicknames were evocative of evil, mayhem, or outer space. Only a few used their actual names.

"The fighters will be in the locker rooms," Silvio said. "Let's go see if we can find your guy."

They were on the ground floor of the arena about 45 minutes before the fights were due to start. Emilia followed Silvio past the posters in the wide lobby, past the concession windows, and into the main part of the arena. The ring dominated the center of the floor and was surrounded by rows of seating. It was on a platform raised nearly to the level of Emilia's shoulder. As she walked by, her eye was drawn to the thick stripe of beige tape bordering the blue canvas.

The place was rapidly filling up, mostly with men ready to holler, bet, and drink. A few women who looked like rougher versions of the girls at Mami's were mixed in. Emilia was grateful for Silvio's presence. Not only could the big detective push his way through the crowd with ease, but he'd been recognized by the guards working the entrance. Emilia assumed it was because of his former boxing career or his current bookie status; either way, no one had said anything when he and Emilia walked around the metal detector instead of through it. Her gun was still in its shoulder holster under her denim jacket, no questions asked.

Silvio walked up the rearmost aisle, passed a second set of concession windows, and pushed open a door marked STAFF ONLY. A uniformed security guard stepped in their way. Silvio gave a slow, easy grin. "Looking for El Rey Demonio and his *trio*."

The guard jerked his chin at Emilia. "Who's she?"

"They know she's coming," Silvio said with a wink. Some money changed hands and the guard pointed to the right.

"Did you have to let him think I'm here to give the guys a pre-fight lap dance?" Emilia whispered furiously.

"You want to talk to this guy without a big fuss or not?" Silvio asked. "Puro Sangre and El Rey Demonio are big names. Keep your badge in your pocket and don't even think about pulling a gun in this crowd. There are probably arrest warrants out for half of the people in this arena tonight. All you want is some information about that little girl."

"Fine," Emilia grumbled. They were still on only the barest of civil terms with each other and hadn't really discussed strategy on the way over.

It was the end of their so-called partnership, she reminded herself. Someday, when she didn't loathe Silvio so much, she'd see their few months together as a great learning experience. And he was doing her a favor; the Lila Jimenez Lata Missing Persons case wasn't officially theirs, and he didn't have to help her out by coming tonight. Nonetheless, she'd talk to Lt. Rufino on Monday and knew Silvio would as well.

They passed through another set of doors into a wide hallway and found a kid with towels willing to accept Silvio's money in return for telling Puro Sangre that someone needed to speak with him outside the locker room.

The hallway seemed to function as an anteroom for the various acts. A big exit door was propped open, keeping the space cool with a fresh night breeze, as men who looked like they could be managers or promoters came and went. Half a dozen scantily clad women with unbelievably taut breasts flirted as they carried various banners and placards, likely for the parade that kicked off each Saturday night extravaganza. Technicians with headphones around their necks passed through after evidently resolving a bit of business about the timing of the acts or the lighting for the events. A couple of fighters, already in costume, talked to the business types.

The kid did what he'd been paid to do, and three big *luchadores*, all in striking red costumes, came up to Emilia and Silvio, accompanied by two men in rumpled suits. Old Tinoco shuffled in back of them.

The *trio* was imposing, Emilia had to admit. Each was as broad as Silvio but more meaty looking. All three men were bare-chested, their heavily muscled chests outlined by tattoos which ran the complete length of both arms from shoulder to wrist. Their traditional *luchador* tights were red with silver insets at the knees, and their boxing footgear was silver as well.

Only their masks set them apart. Emilia recognized El Rey Demonio from the posters; his mask was red with black borders around the openings for mouth, nose and eyes. It had red vinyl triangles that stuck up on the sides of his head, giving him a look somewhere between the devil and Batman. In that getup, he certainly didn't look like anyone simply named Alberto Soares Peña.

"Kid says you're looking for Puro Sangre," El Rey said. The other two *luchadores* flanked him, one on either side. El Rey was the tallest and obviously the leader.

"I'm Silvio and this is Cruz," Silvio said. "We're looking for a girl. Heard he might know something about her."

"Lila Jimenez Lata," Emilia added. "Met her over at Mami's."

"He doesn't know nothing about a girl," El Rey drawled.

"Hey, Silvio's all right," Tinoco said from the side. "This is Franco Silvio. Used to be a boxer. Runs a clean book now."

"Franco Silvio?" One of the other *luchadores* stretched an arm across his chest, shoving the elbow up until his shoulder cracked. The words Puro Sangre rippled amidst the other tattoos as his bicep swelled and his pectorals bulged. "I've heard of you."

Silvio held out his hand and they shook. "Heard of you, too," Silvio said. "Tinoco tells me you put on a good show."

"More than a show," Puro Sangre said. His mask was solid red except for silver drops of blood that formed a zigzag design across the forehead. "You watch. We're like killing machines in that ring."

"Maybe we'll stay for the show," Silvio said. "Put some money down, you know?"

"Tinoco says you're a cop." This from El Rey Demonio. He indicated Emilia. "Her too?"

Silvio didn't acknowledge the question as he kept his eyes focused on Puro Sangre. "We're looking for a girl named Lila. Heard you knew her."

The big *luchador* shook his head. "Nah. I don't know a girl named Lila."

"You met her at Mami's nearly two months ago," Emilia said, trying not to sound nervous. She felt encircled by none-too-friendly men, with only Silvio as a barrier. The three *luchadores* alone were like a pyramid blocking her view to the other side of the wide hallway. The two men in suits looked to be promoters, with little interest in the conversation.

"We're here to fight, not talk to cops about cheap girls at Mami's," El Rey Demonio rumbled. He clenched his fists and Emilia's eye was drawn to a mark on one finger. It was the same ring-style tattoo that Julieta Rubia had.

"Lila came to Mami's looking for her mother," Emilia said. She tried to stand a little taller but still felt trapped and uneasy. "And ended up staying for Puro Sangre here. White dress. Short dark hair. You took her upstairs."

"The night Julieta got arrested." Puro Sangre pointed a finger at Emilia. "I remember her. She was like a fresh *jitomate*."

"It's time to go," El Rey said and mimicked punching an

opponent.

"Two minutes," Emilia stalled, still focused on Puro Sangre. "Just tell me what happened that night with Lila. When did you see her last?"

"She told me her name was Yolanda," he said. "Not Lila."

"Out of time," El Rey boomed. "They're starting the show."

"Later," Puro Sangre said to Emilia. He pressed forward and tipped up her chin. "You and me, we'll talk after. I'll tell you what you want and then it will be my turn."

Even through the mask, the man made it clear that his eyes were undressing her. Emilia pulled away from his hand, annoyed to feel herself flush with embarrassment at being handled by a half-naked giant. She could see why he was so popular with the girls at Mami's; he was well-built, not afraid to show it off, and made it clear that he liked women and liked sex with them.

A distorted voice came over a loudspeaker. El Rey swung his arms over the shoulders of his teammates, and they turned as one. Emilia watched them go and again was reminded of a pyramid: El Rey in the middle, an equally broad but slightly shorter man on either side of him.

"*Madre de Dios*," she murmured.

"If we gotta stay here all night," Silvio said. "I want to lay down some bets."

"Wait a minute," Emilia said. The hallway was gradually emptying out and she pulled Silvio back down the way they'd come in.

"Nobody's forcing you to make a bet, Cruz," he said, irritation thickening his voice.

"Forget the betting for a minute." Emilia pulled him to a stop before they turned the corner and ran into the guard. "The three *luchadores*. Didn't they remind you of anything you've seen lately? Maybe something on a video?"

It only took him a moment. "Los Matas Ejercito," Silvio said.

Emilia nodded excitedly. "The way El Rey was the tallest and in the middle." She pressed her fingertips together to make a pitched roof of her hands. "His voice sounded a little familiar, too."

"Could be," Silvio said.

"Should we call it in?" Emilia asked.

"They still haven't done anything," Silvio said. He leaned against the wall, his face wearing its usual grim expression. "You want to arrest them on suspicion of making videos? Right here in the Coliseo during a full house?"

Emilia folded her arms as she considered the mayhem that would ensue if they tried to arrest three *luchadores* on suspicion of making videos. "I guess not."

Silvio gave her a curt nod of agreement. "We'll tell Lt. Rufino on Monday. He can do what he wants with it."

"All right," Emilia said.

Silvio heaved himself off the wall. "If they got the balls to take on the army with those videos, maybe they'll make me a little money tonight. You gonna put down a few pesos on your boy Puro Sangre? Bet that he's livelier than Rucker?"

"Just shut up and go place your bet," Emilia snapped. Every time they had a halfway decent exchange, Silvio could always be counted on to screw it up with something totally offensive.

"Don't be wandering around," Silvio said, ignoring her tone. "Get in your seat and stay in it. I'll be along in a couple of minutes."

They'd bought tickets in order to get in and had ended up with some of the worst seats, on the ground but all the way in the back near the entrance. The seats gave them a partial view of the raised ring, but a better view of the backs of heads in the seats ahead of them or of the people traipsing up and down the aisle.

Once inside the main part of the arena, they split up. Silvio headed for wherever the bookies congregated, and Emilia plunked herself into her seat after buying a drink at the concession stand. The place was packed and the crowds were raucous as the loudspeaker blasted music, getting everyone spun up for the kickoff spectacle. It was a far cry from an evening at a nice restaurant with Kurt. Or a night on the beach with him.

The loudspeaker boomed again, this time with the

announcer's voice asking the crowd if they were ready, if they wanted to see El Rey Demonio and the other headliners. The place erupted into cheers and screams, and Emilia couldn't help getting caught up in the excitement. She yelled with the crowd.

More music swelled as the announcer kept talking and the parade started. The crowd rose to its feet, and Emilia stood on tiptoe to see a blaze of color and glitter resolve itself into four women in sequined bikinis and long capes carrying tall torches at the head of the parade. The announcer called out the names of the *luchadores* who followed the women out a set of wide double doors and down a carpeted walkway to the ring. Each of the *luchadores* gestured, beat their chests, or raised their arms over their heads to get the crowd to cheer for them. El Rey clasped his hands over his head and shook them in the classic champion's gesture while Puro Sangre spread his arms as if on a cross. The third man in their trio, El Hijo de Satán, pointed at the audience as if choosing his evil minions.

More scantily clad women pranced alongside as the roll of at least 30 *luchadores* went on, and Emilia realized just how long a night it was going to be. The parade circled the area in front of the ring and started back to the double doors.

Capes fluttering, the bikini-clad torchbearers fitted their torches into the tops of tall pillars on either side of the wide doorway, creating four man-sized birthday candles topped by gas-fed billowing flames. Colored spotlights circled around the doorway, turning the flames into a Technicolor light show. The crowd whooped and applauded. All but two of the *luchadores* marched between the pillars and disappeared back into the bowels of the arena. The two remaining *luchadores* climbed into the ring with the referee. The announcer introduced them with dramatic language.

That's when Emilia saw Aguilar, General Becerra's aide from *campo militar*. She didn't know why her eye was drawn to him; it might have been the pop of red from the sports drink in his hand, or it might have been a sixth sense, but there he was, standing in the aisle not two meters from her, surveying the place. He wore jeans and a yellow plaid shirt instead of his army uniform, but it was the same man.

Emilia found herself holding her breath. It could not be a coincidence. Aguilar had to know the three *luchadores* were Los Matas Ejercito.

She didn't move, hoping that her black jeans, denim jacket and old sneakers let her blend into the crowd. He moved on down the aisle, then backtracked a step and entered a row several seats ahead of hers. Emilia watched the ripple of movement that indicated he was climbing over people's knees. When the ripple stopped, she could see the shoulder of his yellow shirt through the crowd. No one appeared to be with him.

Emilia dug her phone out of her hip pocket and texted Silvio. She kept an eye on Aguilar as she waited for a reply. Three minutes later, it popped up on her screen: *Meet at rear concession in 5.*

The first fight started and the roar of the crowd swelled. Emilia watched the two men charge at each other, one in blue tights and mask, the other in black. They grappled, bare torsos gleaming, and one of them was flung into the ropes. The voice over the loudspeaker competed with the cheers, and Emilia wondered if she'd be deaf by the time the night was over.

She found Silvio at the concession stand. People were still milling about and she had to shout so he could hear her. He said something back, but the place was too noisy.

Emilia gestured to her ear. He nodded, and as the noise from the arena blasted in response to a particularly exciting *lucha* move, he led her around the side of the concessions back toward the area where they'd talked to the *luchadores*. This time, however, instead of heading for the STAFF ONLY door, he turned the other way and took them down a narrow hallway running in back of the concession windows to an unmarked exit.

Silvio pushed open the door and they were in a loading area next to a dumpster and piles of empty boxes that had probably once held frozen French fries or tubs of processed cheese for nachos.

A chain-link fence encircled the area which was dimly lit by a mercury lamp mounted on the wall over the door. Most big businesses that needed a trash area had a setup like this with a tall fence to keep out vagrants and drug addicts who otherwise would pick through the trash on a regular basis, leading to robberies, fights over the pickings, or even a nearby shantytown.

Beyond the perimeter of the blue-tinged light, Emilia made out a few cars parked inside the fence. Silvio found a piece of brick and wedged it so the door could not fully close.

"How'd you know about this doorway?" she asked. A pile of cigarette butts on the uneven pavement suggested that this was where the concession workers stepped out for a smoke.

"Not much changes," he said. "Are you sure it's Aguilar?"

"Yes, I'm sure. He stood next to me in the aisle as if he wasn't sure where to go and then sat in a seat three rows ahead of ours."

"By himself?"

"All alone," Emilia confirmed.

"You think he's here for Los Matas?"

"Maybe to warn them because we came sniffing around?"

It was still noisy by the door. They moved away from the doorway, out of the immediate circle of light from the overhead mercury lamp.

"But what's Aguilar's dog in the fight?" Silvio asked. "If your buddy Puro Sangre and his friends are making Los Matas videos, how is Aguilar getting anything out of it?"

Emilia peered into the gloom. This side of the arena was poorly lit, a prime spot for rapes and robberies. The chain-link fence reminded her of the lot at the police station and the scary encounter with Castro's brother. *Madre de Dios*, but she'd been spending a lot of time in parking lots lately. No wonder her life was such a mess.

"I don't know," she said. "Could it be some joke Aguilar is playing on his army buddies? Getting these guys to dress up, sound scary?"

Every investigation she'd ever encountered in more than two years as a detective had money at its core. But Emilia couldn't figure out how Los Matas Ejercito's videos involved money. Or how, if Aguilar was involved, he was making any money off them.

She turned back to Silvio, but he was staring past her, into the darkness. "What if they're more than Los Matas," he said softly.

"What are you talking about?"

Silvio didn't answer but walked ahead, nearly getting swallowed up by the night. Against her better judgment, Emilia followed him to the short row of cars at the far side of the fenced-in area.

A moment later, Silvio whipped a tarp off the back of a large vehicle, exposing a battered club cab truck.

"*Madre de Dios*," Emilia sputtered. In the dark, she could just make out a big panel of plastic stretched over the space where the rear window should have been.

Silvio squatted down, took out a clasp knife, and scratched at the truck's tailgate. Big flecks snowed off the metal. "They filled in the holes with bonding compound and painted over them," he said as he counted the holes. "You hammered it. Too bad you didn't take out a tire."

"What's it doing here?"

"Whoever the extortionists are, they have a friend who works here," Silvio said.

Emilia could barely breathe as suddenly the pieces fell into place. "El Rey," she murmured. "Tinoco said he'd won a set of wheels."

Silvio stood up, face softened by moonlight. "You think the truck belongs to El Rey Demonio?"

"If he won it, how long would it take the paperwork to transfer to his name?" Emilia asked.

Silvio nodded his understanding. "Not a standard process. Six months at least. Nobody will know how to get it registered. Take a couple of trips to city offices, maybe a little money changes hands. In the meantime, he's driving a vehicle that doesn't come up in any of our searches."

"Wearing a wedding ring," Emilia said, her thoughts tumbling over each other, competing with visions of Julieta in the prison clinic with her tailored shift, flawless skin, and ring tattoo.

"What?" Silvio reached into the truck bed and felt around. "Stay on topic, Cruz."

"Guetta had on a wedding band in the video." Emilia's words raced to keep up with her thoughts. "But the video quality wasn't good, so we thought it was real. But it's a tattoo. Julieta has the same thing."

"Nothing in the back," Silvio said. "Who the fuck is Julieta?"

"El Rey Demonio," Emilia said impatiently. "I told you. Alberto Soares Peña. He fights as El Rey Demonio, but at home he's Julieta Rubia's husband."

"How does Julieta Rubia figure into this?" Silvio asked impatiently.

Emilia wanted to scream at his thick-headedness. "Think about it, Franco. Julieta and Alberto got a good thing going. She's running girls out of Mami's and he's the big *luchador*. Then Olga makes her power play, probably backed by Castro's *pendejo* brother, Diego. Suddenly Julieta's in jail and everybody knows she isn't getting out any time soon. Olga la Fea takes over Mami's and Castro kicks out Alberto. Now Alberto needs money, because he's too important to have a job. He has to find someplace to live and pay for Julieta to live in style in prison. The woman gets Botox from her doctor. Fifty thousand pesos a week."

"So he comes up with this extortion scheme," Silvio said, picking up the thread. "The other two on his team are in it with him. After all, Julieta set them up with some fine girls when she was running Mami's. So they pretend to be army, print up some notes, and pick places out of a magazine. Saturday nights after the fights, they hit the places that don't pay. El Rey drives. The other two hide in the truck bed and throw grenades."

"*Madre de Dios*," Emilia swore again. The connections now seemed so obvious. "Aguilar sold him the grenades. Or he gets a cut of whatever Alberto collects."

"But why the Los Matas videos? And pretending to be army? Wouldn't that pinch Aguilar?"

"I don't know," Emilia admitted. "But everything else

makes sense."

The arena door suddenly opened, bathing the fenced-in area with light. Emilia and Silvio shrank back against the truck to avoid being seen. A man wearing a Coliseo concession worker's uniform kept the door propped open, threw a big bag of trash into the dumpster, leaned against the wall, and lit a cigarette.

He was obviously in no hurry to get back to work. Time actually stood still as he took long, thoughtful drags. Emilia's legs started to cramp as she remained frozen against Silvio. The big detective was like a statue. She could barely hear him breathe.

The concession worker finally threw down his cigarette butt, kicked the brick aside, and slammed the door behind him.

Emilia stepped away from Silvio and they went to the door. It was locked. Silvio swore as they looked around.

"So now what?" Emilia asked. The fenced-in area was like a miniature impound yard. The gate was wide enough to get a car or the dumpster out, but it was chained and padlocked. "Wait for somebody to push open the door from the inside? Or hot-wire a car and bust the gate?"

"Funny, Cruz." Silvio looked up and Emilia followed his gaze. The fence was maybe nine feet tall, but it wasn't topped by barbed wire. "Liked to climb things when you were a kid?"

"You think you can get over that fence?" Emilia asked doubtfully. She was confident she could climb over. But Silvio was weighed down by a heavy leather jacket and weighed easily twice what she did. While she was sure it was all muscle, his physique didn't exactly suggest that he was agile.

"Yeah, I think I can get over that fence." Silvio pulled out his cell phone. "First we'll get some backup. Once we know we got help coming, we can get over this fence and go around to the front. Once we're back inside, you stick with Aguilar. See what he does. I'll stay by the locker rooms, keep an eye on El Rey and his buddies if they try to leave."

"I still need to talk to Puro Sangre about Lila," Emilia reminded him.

"Right after we arrest them." Silvio dialed dispatch on his

phone.

Emilia hugged herself while Silvio talked. It wasn't their lucky night, and the dispatch cop on duty asked half a dozen inane questions before Silvio was convinced the kid understood the situation and was sending uniformed backup. He called Macias after that, and Emilia was relieved to hear that the other two detectives would head up the backup effort. They worked out a plan that had the backup coming in quietly, connecting with Silvio and Emilia via text message so they could find each other in the arena, and only then confronting the *luchadores* and Aguilar.

"Okay." Silvio pocketed his phone and grabbed hold of the fence. "Get on over and make for the front. Stick to Aguilar and text me anything funky."

Emilia reached high, wrapped her fingers through the wire fencing, and found a toehold as well. The fence wasn't stable and she found herself wobbling. She flattened herself against the wire mesh. The buttons of her denim jacket caught against the wires as she pulled herself up, alternating toeholds and handholds, swearing to herself under her breath. She was almost to the top when the fence sagged, the wire jangled against the support poles, and she lost her footing.

"What the fuck are you doing, Cruz!" Silvio whispered furiously.

"Come here," Emilia gasped as she dangled by her hands in the dark, feet scrabbling against the chain link in an effort to regain a toehold. "Let me kick you in the head."

The fence shivered as she slowly made her way to the top and gingerly got a leg over. Going down was easier than going up, and a moment later she was breathing heavily on the other side of the fence. She gestured for Silvio to start his climb.

"Go," he said. "Keep an eye on Aguilar."

Emilia headed through the parking lot but stopped as she heard the chain link rattle loudly against the fence's metal support poles. She turned, and in the dark could just make out a figure clinging precariously to the fence about halfway up. The fence swung away from the support pole and the figure plummeted to the ground.

Silvio's leather jacket still hung halfway up the fence on his side, no doubt hooked by a button. He slowly got to his feet, his white tee shirt noticeable in the dark. The shoulder holster was outlined against it.

Emilia ran back to the fence. "Are you all right?" she asked.

"I'm okay," he said, looking up at the jacket. "But my jacket is caught and the fence is busted."

"I'll unhook the jacket from this side," Emilia said. "Drop it down. You throw it over the fence to me. It'll be easier for you to climb over without it."

She could tell that he didn't like the idea, but Silvio agreed. Emilia climbed up her side of the fence. She didn't have to go far before she was even with the heavy leather jacket. As she thought, the jacket had been caught by its top button. Clinging to the fence with one hand and with both sets of toes, she used her other hand to work the button free. Silvio caught the jacket as it dropped.

Emilia eased herself back down the fence as Silvio tied the jacket into a ball and heaved it over the tall fence. Emilia caught it and was surprised to see him smile, teeth briefly showing white in the darkness.

It took two more tries before the big detective could get over the fence, and then only because Emilia braced herself against the loose metal support that was causing the fence to wobble. The wire bit into her hands and slapped her face as the fence shuddered under Silvio's weight. She heard him grunt as he levered himself over the top and jumped down, landing easily on his feet. Without his weight, the fence pulled away from Emilia's hands, the wire running painfully over the still-sensitive spot where she'd burned her hand at the El Tigre fire. Emilia gave a soft gasp but held the fence to minimize the rattling noise it made as it settled back into place.

"Why didn't you think I could make it over?" Silvio challenged as he put his jacket on.

"Now?" Emilia asked incredulously. "Now is a good time for an argument?"

The arena was larger on the outside than it seemed on the inside as they wound through the parking lot surrounding the place. They passed others as they got closer to the main entrance: a couple kissing passionately against the hood of a car, two men having an argument, a bunch of youths likely making a drug deal.

They had to present their tickets to get back inside. Emilia found her seat again and watched Silvio make his way around the outer aisle toward the opposite end of the arena. She glanced at her watch; they'd been outside for no more than 20 minutes, and the action in the ring was still lively. The *trio* matches had started and the crowd was screaming for blood. Two *luchadores* circled each other while teammates waited on their respective sides of the ring. The loudspeaker roared and the crowd's frenzy mounted as the team members rolled in and out of combat. Emilia was too far away to really figure out which team was winning, but she knew enough about *lucha libre's* few rules to know that a *trio* could win by pinning either the captain or the other two members of a team.

One of the *luchadores* swung himself into the air, twisted his body sideways, and stomped his opponent's bare chest. The crowd rose to its collective feet, screaming with excitement, and Emilia jumped to her feet as well, trying to keep an eye on Aguilar's yellow plaid shirt. But when people slowly subsided into their seats again, he was gone.

Emilia half stood and scanned the crowd but didn't see him. Maybe Aguilar had gone to the toilet or to buy something to eat, but the ease with which he'd slipped away made her stomach tighten. Emilia left her seat and headed for the entrance and the main concession stands.

She saw him at the same time he saw her. He was out in the open in front of the concession stands holding a cell phone. His face registered instant recognition. Aguilar pocketed the cell phone and walked toward her, weaving his way through the people in line for food or milling around talking and laughing. More than one held a beer bottle.

Emilia fixed a smile on her face. She was going to dance with him the way everybody else had danced with her.

"Detective Cruz, isn't it?" Aguilar held out his hand.

Emilia shook it. "Lieutenant Aguilar?" she asked. "From the

meeting with General Becerra, right?"

"That's right." Aguilar held her hand a little longer than was necessary. "I confess to being surprised to find you here, Detective."

"Call me Emilia. I'm off duty."

"You're a *lucha libre* fan?"

"No," Emilia said truthfully. "But my date is."

"Ah." Aguilar grinned and looked around. "Where is this date of yours?"

Emilia realized Aguilar was around her age. With his cropped hair and regular features, he wasn't bad looking. It helped that he wasn't talking into his chin the way he'd done with General Becerra around. "In the restroom," she said.

"So just a night out at the Coliseo with Detective Silvio," Aguilar said. He spoke in the same easy manner, but there was an undertone to his words. "You two work and play together, eh?"

Emilia realized he must have seen Silvio on his way to the rear entrance. "You know how it is," she said, keeping her voice neutral.

"I don't think it's a coincidence that you're here tonight," Aguilar said, glancing around. The concession area was doing a lively business. People moved to the windows with cash in hand and left with greasy paper baskets of chicken strips, hot dogs or quesadillas. An old man swiped ineffectually at the litter piling up in corners with a broom. "And I doubt a woman who looks like you is dating some old soldier like Silvio. You and Silvio are here to talk to the boys for a cut of the action."

Emilia played along. "We must have really surprised you with that security video," she said. "Your fake Guetta wasn't very convincing."

To her surprise, Aguilar snorted. "That show wasn't for you. I knew what you were fishing for. We can come to an arrangement."

A huge roar rose up from the main area of the arena. The announcer said something. The name Galexio was met with applause.

"Who was it for?" Emilia asked, edging closer to the wall

near the concession windows. "Becerra?"

"Very good, Emilia." Aguilar waggled a finger as he followed her. "Los Matas Ejercito. The army tax notice. The camouflage jackets. Don't you think it's been a masterful strategy? And the mayor jumped right in to help! It all worked perfectly."

Strategy? People were killed and dozens more injured. He wasn't making sense. "But you sold the grenades to the *luchadores*," Emilia said. "Why create a situation that pointed back to the army?"

Aguilar shook his head. "You and Silvio want money. El Rey wants money. I want money," he said. "Money is the great leveler, right? Becerra and Hernandez need to be taught a lesson about that."

"This is some sort of punishment for them?" Emilia wondered if he was unhinged.

"You could call it that," Aguilar said.

"Look," Emilia said and moved a step closer. She bent her head and spoke in a low voice. "If we're going to be partners here, I need to know the whole story."

"How do I know I can trust you?"

Emilia ran a finger over the line of his jaw. "Because I'm a sure thing," she said.

Aguilar looked around and dropped his head to hers. "Hernandez and Becerra need to learn a lesson about pockets," he said with a wink. "In some, share some."

A simple conversation with a simple man replayed in the back of Emilia's head. *Who would want them to stop making money? Whoever wasn't getting their fair share.*

"Sinaloa," Emilia said as her heart raced. "They're taking payoffs from Sinaloa and not sharing."

Of course the local head of the army was in the Sinaloa cartel's pocket. Paid to look the other way when the cartel raided places like Macario Urbina's *hacienda*. Paid to keep the soldiers at *campo militar* as cartel *sicarios* partied in the Sierra San Rita hills.

Aguilar narrowed his eyes. "You knew all the time?"

"A dead man told me," Emilia said.

"I like a woman who talks to dead men," Aguilar said with a grin.

Emilia swallowed with difficulty and managed a ghastly grin back. "So this whole thing was set up to discredit them?" she asked. "Get them fired and out of Guerrero?"

"Easier than setting up a hit," Aguilar said, stuffed full of pride. "Mayor Carlota was an unexpected help. She really hates Hernandez. Made him look like an even bigger fool than he actually is. They'll pull him out of Guerrero, and where he goes, Becerra will go, too."

Aguilar was taking revenge because his superiors hadn't shared their payoff. Maybe he was trying to replace them in the cartel's accounting department. Or maybe another cartel had offered him more to make sure that *campo militar* switched allegiances.

"When they go, who gets to play in Sinaloa's pocket?" Emilia asked.

"That's not your problem, Emilia." Aguilar moved closer. To anyone walking by the concession area, they might be a couple flirting intensely, heads close together, his hand itching to caress her. "You and Silvio just get rid of that security video and any other ones that are out there. Buy yourself a new dress with what you get for it, and I'll show you an Acapulco you've never seen before."

"But the *luchadores*?"

"El Rey needed cash." Aguilar licked his lips. "He's got plenty now. He'll know that cutting you and Silvio in will be good insurance, you know what I mean?"

"How did you meet them?"

"I took some boxing lessons at a gym in town."

"Tinoco's place."

Aguilar smiled again. "You and Silvio get around."

"Does Tinoco get a cut, too?"

"That's between him and El Rey."

"Sure." Emilia held up her hands, palms out. She was nearly touching his chest. "Let me text Silvio. I think he must have fallen in the toilet or something."

Aguilar swiped at his nose and gave a chuckle. "You two

really do everything together?"

"Not everything," Emilia said, hoping it sounded flirtatious. She grabbed her phone and furiously typed out a message to Silvio to come to the concession area. As the screen winked, telling her that the message had been sent successfully, an irritated male voice cut through both the casual conversations around them and the muffled din of the loudspeaker from inside the main part of the arena.

"Cruz! Cruz!" Lt. Rufino, wearing a wrinkled suit, charged past the lines at the concession windows. He skidded through a puddle of beer and a candy wrapper stuck to his shoe. His police badge dangled from a lanyard around his neck, his handgun was held loosely against his right side, and his face was flushed with the same look of enraged annoyance he'd worn at the Toby Jones fire.

"Where's Silvio?" he snapped. "Where are these *luchadores*? Are they planning on setting any more fires? I'm here to make an arrest, not get some cheap entertainment."

His breath was 100 proof.

Aguilar looked from Lt. Rufino to Emilia. "You bitch," he said.

He shoved her hard toward Lt. Rufino, but Emilia already had her foot hooked around his leg and carried him with her. All three crashed to the floor. Someone screamed. Emilia rolled as she fought to get Aguilar in a hold.

A shot reverberated off the walls and she realized that Lt. Rufino, flat on his back on the ground, had fired into the ceiling. "Stop it!" he shouted.

Aguilar slithered over Emilia and grabbed Lt. Rufino's arm. Suddenly the two men were wrestling awkwardly for control of the gun. A man tripped over Emilia as she got to one knee, sending her sprawling again. A trash can overturned as people ran past and greasy paper baskets, wax paper liners, and soggy paper cups spilled across the combatants. People scattered in all directions amid screams of panic.

Emilia managed to stand upright. Lt. Rufino and Aguilar grappled against the wall under the concession windows in a tangle of arms, legs, and trash. She couldn't see their faces, only the back of Aguilar's yellow plaid shirt on top of the dark suit.

Two shots rang out. Aguilar pulled away and lurched to his feet. Emilia saw blood spread across Lt. Rufino's chest.

Aguilar bolted out of the concession area, Lt. Rufino's gun still in his hand.

Emilia slid to her knees next to Lt. Rufino. He was still conscious, his bloodshot eyes darting around in confusion.

A burly man pushed Emilia aside. "I'm a paramedic," he said.

"Two shots to the chest." Emilia's voice sounded unnaturally calm. "He's very drunk."

As the paramedic tore open Lt. Rufino's bloody shirt, Emilia pushed her way out of the crowd that had rapidly formed around the prone body. Some people held cell phones high in order to take pictures over the shoulders of those closest to the man lying in the pool of blood.

Chapter 34

The main event had finally convinced most of the audience to stay in their seats, and the aisles were mostly clear. Up on the raised ring, two bulky bare-chested men, one in red tights and one in black, entertained the crowd with an extravagant display of bare-handed brawling. Emilia recognized the distinctive ears of El Rey Demonio's devil mask. His powerful tattooed arms flexed as he picked up his opponent and threw him bodily into the ropes.

The crowd roared with equal parts approval and dismay, and Emilia figured that El Rey's opponent was the other team's captain. The fighter shook himself off the ropes and thrust a meaty arm at El Rey, who made a two-handed *bring-it-on* gesture and lowered his head like a bull about to charge. The air pulsed with more roars of excitement and a rhythmic chanting started. *El Rey! El Rey!*

On one side of the ring, the eye-catching figures of Puro Sangre and El Hijo de Satán waited their turns in the tag team battle by shaking their fists, yelling taunts, and whipping up the crowd with the same gestures they'd used during the parade.

The two *luchadores* in the ring collided again. Both went down as a ripple went through the crowd to Emilia's left. She caught a glimpse of Aguilar's yellow shirt and set off after him, swinging around the rear section of seating.

Aguilar walked rapidly ahead of her, gun still in his hand, making for the main aisle. A few people noticed the gun, screamed and shrank back. The crowd's yells for the *luchadores* drowned out the reaction to the gun.

Emilia drew her own gun but kept it close to her side as she took off after him. It was hard to know what Aguilar would do next or where he was headed. She rounded the rear set of seats, skidding as she turned to follow Aguilar, and a heavyset uniformed security guard stepped into her path.

Emilia found herself looking into the barrel of a handgun.

"Drop your weapon," the guard demanded. His face was sweaty and the gun wobbled dangerously. Emilia was close enough to see that the safety was off. A radio clipped to his belt emitted a stream of excited static.

"I'm a cop," Emilia said rapidly. "Your shooter from the concession area is in a yellow plaid shirt just ahead of me."

"Drop your weapon," the guard shouted at her, his voice cracking with fear.

In another second, Emilia knew, he was going to pee his pants. Then he'd shoot her out of sheer embarrassment.

"*Rayos,*" Emilia swore. She gently placed her gun on the floor by her feet and stood with her hands by her shoulders, palms out. "What's come over your radio?" she asked. "Did anyone call in the shooting?"

"If you're a cop, where's your badge?" the guard asked suspiciously. He scooped up her gun while keeping his weapon pointed at Emilia.

Emilia pointed to her neckline. "I'm going to pull out my badge," she said. "That's all."

The guard gave a start as she pulled at the lanyard. Emilia nearly dropped to the ground, but he didn't move again as she worked the lanyard out from under the tee shirt and held the badge out for him to see. "My name is Cruz. Acapulco Municipal Police. Detective unit. Call it in. Your shooter's name is Aguilar. He's wearing a yellow plaid shirt."

The guard frowned at something behind Emilia. She turned to see Aguilar dart into a row of seats, shoving his way over people's feet and yelps of distress as the people in the seats realized he carried a gun.

"Call it in," Emilia ordered the bewildered guard and ran into the nearest row of seating herself. Aguilar was evidently heading for the main aisle on the other side of the section. She would emerge behind him. Without her gun, she didn't know what she'd do, but she wasn't letting him go.

"Sorry. Excuse me." There was little room to maneuver as Emilia crawled over knees, feet, and accumulated food leftovers.

"Get the fuck out of the way," a man bellowed and shoved

Emilia forward into the lap of the next person over.

The neighbor was blind drunk and flung Emilia aside as if she was a toy.

She landed on an empty seat in time to see Aguilar point Lt. Rufino's little revolver at her.

He fired three times, emptying the chamber, his shots wild as he fought to stay on his feet as people scrambled madly to get away from him. The gun clicked repeatedly as Aguilar continued to pull the trigger. As people in the rows between him and Emilia screamed and struggled to move away, he threw down the empty gun, vaulted over the last few terrified people in the row, and sprinted up the main aisle toward the ring, shouting, "Get out, get out!"

Emilia got herself untangled and half-fought, half-fell into the main aisle. Two security guards approached, but they were slow to understand the situation and even slower on their feet. She blew by them, straining into the sprint. Five steps and she launched herself at Aguilar, bringing him down in a flying tackle, arms wrapped around his waist. Aguilar pitched forward, landing face first, arms flung up in an abortive effort to break his fall.

The wind must have been knocked out of him because Aguilar didn't immediately put up a fight. Emilia felt hands grab at her, trying to drag her off him.

"He's the shooter," she yelled.

Her words were all but lost in the din. More than a dozen people surged around them, blocking her ability to move, deafening Emilia with shouts into her ears as confused drunks tried to pry her and Aguilar apart.

Emilia got one arm hooked around Aguilar's throat and pinned his legs with her own. Her free hand found her handcuffs. In a blur of noise, twisting muscles, and her own hammering heartbeat, she managed to get the cuffs fastened around his wrists with his hands behind his back.

One of the uniformed security guards broke through the mob and together they got Aguilar to his feet. "He's your shooter from the concession area," she panted. "I'm a cop. Acapulco Police."

A cry of excitement went up from the stands on either side of them. Feet stamped and rustling filled the air.

The *trio* fight had evidently been halted. All three *luchadores* in red tights were in the ring, gripping the ropes and staring down at the group surrounding Aguilar. The raised platform allowed the action in the ring to be seen from the stands, but it also gave those inside the ropes a bird's-eye view of the floor below.

As Emilia looked up, El Rey's eyes connected with hers. The distance between them wasn't much, just a few meters, and his stare slid down to her chest and connected with the badge dangling from the lanyard. Emilia stuffed it back inside her tee, but it was too late.

She didn't know if they said anything to each other, but the three *luchadores* hurled themselves out of the opposite side of ring, sending the audience on that side of the arena to its feet. Those in the seats nearest the torchlit walkway surged forward, eager for this unexpected chance to connect with their *lucha libre* idols.

Emilia thrust her way past the security guard and fought her way to the base of the ring.

She saw Silvio on the move on the other side, pitching people out of his way, and she knew by the intensity of his movements that he'd seen everything that had happened.

El Rey was on the walkway. He uprooted one of the gas-fueled torches burning on either side of the doorway leading backstage and the shadow of a flame swung overhead. Emilia watched in horror as he heaved it toward the raised ring. And her.

It landed at the base of the ring, forcing Emilia to take refuge in the nearest row of seats. Flames spurted up and licked the fabric bunting that skirted the raised platform.

Another torch hit the front row of seats on Silvio's side of the main aisle. The arena erupted into pandemonium.

The third torch ignited big fabric banners that decorated the walls, immediately flaring up the fabric to the second row of seating. The smell of charcoal and burning plastic filled the air.

People stampeded toward the main entrance and Emilia was

nearly swept off her feet by the tide of panicked spectators.

Clinging to a seat by the ring, she saw El Rey pick up the last torch. His mask with its pointed ears was shiny and metallic in the reflection of the flames. Puro Sangre made a grab for the torch as well, and it became a flamethrower as the two men struggled for control. The third *luchador* in red, El Hijo de Satán, disappeared through the double doors.

Puro Sangre lost his grip on the torch and El Rey heaved it after the others. It flew as far as the ring, bounced against the elastic ropes and catapulted back towards the walkway, igniting the carpet that ran like a stripe down the center.

El Rey turned to follow El Hijo de Satán through the double doors, but Puro Sangre grabbed him. The two men wrestled violently. Flames sprouted in front of them, forcing Emilia to look away, and when she looked again, the larger *luchador* twisted his opponent's head around as if his neck was a corkscrew driving into a bottle of wine. Puro Sangre slumped to the ground and El Rey passed through the double doors.

The canvas floor of the ring blazed up, blowing heat like a furnace across Emilia's left side. The rush of frightened, drunken *lucha libre* fans turned into a blundering stampede. Emilia felt panic engulf her, battle into her heart, replace her thoughts with animal fear. The arena filled with blinding smoke and things that shifted and snapped in the scorching heat.

"Cruz!" Silvio yelled in her ear.

Emilia stared at him. He shook her hard and she blinked. "El Rey," she managed. She clutched at his jacket front. Silvio was the only point of stability in the fire, in the chaos around her. "He's heading for the rear exit."

Silvio grabbed her by the arm. They both pulled their jackets over their mouths and somehow made it up the walkway, skirting the smoldering carpet. As flames licked over the rows of seating by the walkway, the burning plastic made Emilia gag. They stepped over the lifeless body of Puro Sangre. The *luchador*'s masked head was canted at an impossible angle.

Smoke followed them into the performers' area. The place was a madhouse of people who'd worked the secondary concession area as well as those rushing down a service stairway from the upper tier of seating.

With Silvio leading the way, the two detectives battled through the teeming mass of hysteria. The exit door was logjammed with people, and they were caught up in the crush. The smoke was suffocating, and Emilia fought outright terror as the stampede threatened to crush her. But once more, Silvio's size and strength got them through.

The rear parking lot was more pandemonium as stunned arena workers and *lucha libre* spectators stumbled, sobbed, or threw up on the pavement. But at least they were outside.

"I lost my gun," Emilia croaked. Her eyes stung from the acrid smoke and she couldn't breathe, couldn't pull in any air around the all-consuming panic.

Silvio swung Emilia to face him. His face was streaked with soot and sweat. "I saw what happened," he said. "Don't quit on me now, Cruz."

"He'll go for the truck," Emilia gasped. "Drive it through the fence."

"Or whoever has been hiding the truck will unlock it for him." He reached inside his jacket and hauled out his gun. "Can you make it?"

Emilia coughed, spat out phlegm, and nodded. Silvio led the way through the back lot, weaving around cars and people. The arena popped and crackled as it burned. Ash began to rain down as the two detectives broke into a run.

There were fewer people on that side of the arena, but the heat was more intense. No doubt the fires had spread to the concession kitchens. The rear door that led into the enclosure was open, and thick, oily smoke billowed out.

In the distance, a tall figure lumbered toward the fenced-in enclosure.

"Acapulco Police!" Silvio shouted, and fired.

El Rey hadn't taken off his mask and for a moment, before the smoke roiled up, the ridiculous ears were silhouetted against the dim blue haze of the mercury lamp above the door. Emilia heard a sizzling as the wiring melted or a fuse blew. The lamp winked out and the big figure was lost in the darkness.

He doesn't know how to get in, Emilia thought. *Or maybe he has a key to the enclosure sewn into his tights.* They couldn't see him and any sound of footsteps was swallowed by the mingled roars of fire and screaming. She ran blindly, choking on ash, waiting to hear the crackling of the building turn into the roar of collapse. The only sure thing was Silvio's solid presence in the nightmare.

And then she and Silvio cannoned into the big *luchador.*

Momentum carried them all into the chain-link fence. Emilia felt the slick fabric of his tights under her hands. A support post gave way, the fence plummeted to the tarmac, and they were all carried to the ground on top of the protesting mesh of chain link. Emilia's face pressed into the wire, but her arms stayed locked around the *luchador*'s knees. El Rey let out a bellow of anger, and Silvio responded with a grunt, and Emilia felt the big *luchador* heave beneath the two detectives.

It was like wrestling an angry elephant against a metal hammock. Emilia's lungs sucked in soot as the *luchador* flailed and she felt herself tossed up as if she weighed nothing. She had a sense of a tremendous rushing and a dull, chunky sound cut through the continuing jangle of the chain-link fence. The *luchador* flopped down, suddenly a dead weight.

"Get up," Silvio rasped. "I think I broke my hand."

Emilia crawled to her feet, surprised to find that she was unhurt. Silvio was bent over, his right hand held to his chest and wrapped around his handgun, as he tried to get handcuffs on the unconscious *luchador.* The big detective's face was white with pain.

"You punched him out with your gun?" Emilia managed.

"Cuff him to the fence before he comes to."

Emilia snapped one cuff around the *luchador*'s thick wrist and the other cuff to part of the fence nearest a still upright support post. If El Rey came to and ran, either the fence would hold or he'd take the entire enclosure, dumpster and all, with him.

Silvio leaned against the hood of a nearby car. Emilia carefully eased his hand away from the gun, feeling the bones grate together as his fingers straightened. She clicked the safety back on and put the gun into his shoulder holster. Silvio's mouth compressed into a tight line against the pain.

Emilia found her cell phone. She had two missed calls. One from Kurt and one from Macias. She hit redial and got Macias. It was a relief to hear him shout where the hell she and Silvio had gone, saying he and Sandor were in the front of the arena, and that some uniformed security guard had given him a gun that purportedly belonged to a lady cop.

"We're by the dumpster in back of the arena," Emilia told him. "We caught one of the *luchadores*. Another is dead. Look for the third one. He's got on red tights and has tattoos all over his arms."

She explained about Lt. Rufino, heard that they had Aguilar in custody, and gave him directions to find the trash enclosure. A minute after she broke the connection, sirens sounded and a flashing light could be seen around the side of the blazing building.

"You okay, Cruz?" Silvio asked.

"I'm okay." Emilia leaned on the car next to him. "How about you?"

"My hand is fucked," Silvio said. "But I'll live."

"How many people do you think died here tonight?" Emilia's teeth started to chatter.

"Not us," Silvio said.

Chapter 35

Dressed in a navy polo untucked over khaki pants and loafers, Kurt was waiting for her in the lobby of the Palacio Réal. It had been just over two weeks, but it seemed like so much longer since that night on the beach. He smiled, and his ocean-colored eyes lit up as she got out of the Suburban and handed the keys to the valet.

For a moment Emilia didn't know what to do; she was still sore and tired from last night's drama and unsure where things stood with the man in front of her. She'd longed for Kurt to get back and talk to her about the job offer in Belize, but her brain was having a hard time shaking off images of the fire at the Coliseo. Lt. Rufino's drunken expression and the crumpled body of a man who called himself Puro Sangre. El Rey and Aguilar both defiant and then deflated as Emilia and Silvio pitted them against each other in their separate interrogation rooms and taped their confessions. Vega's smug expression as he came into the police station and announced that he was in charge.

So she just stood there like an idiot in her simple gray jersey tank dress and flat sandals, clutching her shoulder bag. She'd added a skinny yellow belt and now regretted it. The thing was a stupid pop of color, just the thing some forgettable Mexican *chica* would wear. Hotel employees were there, attending to cars and guests, but eyeing her surreptitiously.

Kurt swiveled his eyes at the activity around them, letting her know he'd read her mind. Emilia gave him half a smile and he held out his hand. She took it and he tugged her close for a quick kiss.

"Good to see you again, Em," he said quietly. "How about a *mojito*?"

"I'd love one," Emilia confessed.

"Good." Kurt didn't let go of her hand as he led her across the wide lobby, down the steps by the white grand piano, and into the luxurious Pasodoble Bar with its blue mosaic-clad bar. A spectacular pink and bronze sunset was just beginning. The sinking sun spread a rosy glow over the ocean on the other side of the steps leading from the open bar to the beach.

Emilia sank into a chair facing the ocean as a waiter came around and lit the candle on the table. Kurt let the waiter know their order and once again made a brief connection with the other man like he always did with his people. The waiter grinned as he made his way back to the long bar. The bartender looked at their table and touched his hand to his head in an informal salute to Kurt before reaching for two tall glasses.

"You look nice tonight," Kurt said. "I don't remember you wearing that dress before."

"I guess I haven't worn it much," Emilia said, deciding not to give into temptation and press him for information about Belize right away.

Kurt reached across the table and took her hand.

Emilia squeezed his fingers. "Did you meet the queen?"

"No." Kurt chuckled. "I was so busy I missed our lunch date."

"No doubt she'll call to reschedule."

The *mojitos* came. Emilia swirled her straw around the rum and crushed mint and took a long drink. The alcohol helped ease the soreness from her muscles, and she relaxed enough to remember the mantra she'd repeated to herself over and over while driving to the hotel. *No matter what his decision, it will be the right one for him. And that's all that matters.*

A steel drum band began to play on the beach. The staff had lit torches, marking out a large area where an outdoor kitchen and a *tapas* bar were set up. Bar patrons began walking down to the torchlit area to sample the food and dance. The men wore expensively casual clothes like Kurt. Most of the women wore flowing maxi dresses and heavy necklaces or bikini tops and long pareo skirts. Of course, Emilia had chosen to wear a mini that night. She never got it right.

"Feel better?" Kurt asked.

"Why?" Emilia put down her glass. "Do I look sick?"

"Tired," Kurt said. "Tell me why your hair smells like

smoke."

"We caught them last night," she said simply. "The arsonists. A *lucha libre* team with a little help from an army officer handing out the contents of *campo militar*'s inventory."

"A *lucha libre* team?" Kurt's eyes opened wide in astonishment.

"A *luchador* named El Rey Demonio needed big money when his wife got arrested." Between sips of her *mojito*, Emilia told him what had happened while he'd been gone: the *Que Paso Acapulco* advertising theory, how the hunt for Lila Jimenez Lata had led her to Julieta Rubia in prison, the meeting at *campo militar*, and how she and Silvio had ended up trying to talk to the *luchadores* at the Saturday fights at the Coliseo. She even told him about the link to the Sinaloa cartel, Aguilar, her talk with Obregon, Torrez's death, and the bitter argument with Silvio over their partnership. And about Lt. Rufino.

The first *mojito* turned into two, along with small plates of *tapas* appetizers.

Kurt asked a few questions, but for the most part let Emilia tell her story. It was like therapy and the words tumbled out. She wound down as the sun sank into the water to the accompaniment of the steel drums. Kurt again reached across the table and took her hand as they watched the ocean turn into liquid bronze. "The dead *luchador*," he said. "Was he the end of Lila's trail?"

"Yes." Emilia sighed. "I don't have anything else. The priest at my church said he'll help me break the news to her grandmother."

"I'm sorry you didn't find her, Em," Kurt said. "And that so many innocent people got tangled up in the whole mess."

"Me, too." Emilia looked at their clasped hands. Talking to him always made her feel better, as if she hadn't made so many mistakes and was smarter than she knew. "Thanks for listening." *I'll miss this when you go.*

He stood and pulled her to her feet. "Let me take your mind off this," he said. "I need to show you something."

"All right." Emilia was surprised at his quick shift but followed him out of the bar, through the lobby and to the bank of elevators that led to the guest rooms as well as his efficiency apartment on the fifth floor.

The middle elevator swooshed open. It was empty and they got in. Kurt took a key card out of his pocket and waved it in front of a sensor. The top button on the display lit up. It wasn't numbered but instead bore the letter "P."

The elevator started to rise.

"Don't you want the fifth floor?" Emilia asked.

Instead of pressing the button for his floor, Kurt hit the large Stop button on the panel below the numbers. The elevator juddered to a halt. An alarm began to emit a regular low beeping.

"Do you remember that night on the beach?" Kurt asked. "The night before I left."

"Of course I remember it," Emilia said. "But shouldn't we—"

"We hadn't been together like that before, Em," Kurt interrupted, ignoring the alarm. "You know it and so do I. What were you telling me? Goodbye forever? Or something else?"

"Telling you?" Emilia faltered, unprepared for the question. The buzz of the alarm was insistent and the "P" button blinked furiously. She took a step back and gripped the handrail. "I was just . . . I don't know. I didn't think about it. I guess it was the way I wanted to be with you. All of you and all of me. You know . . . completely."

She felt the color rise in her cheeks, both at the memory of them naked on the beach and at her absolute inarticulateness.

Kurt stared at her.

Emilia tried a nervous smile. "That wasn't the answer you were looking for, was it?"

"It'll do," Kurt said, but he didn't smile back.

He popped a button, the alarm stopped, and the elevator began to rise again. He opened a panel, took out a telephone, and told whoever was on the other end that there was no need to worry.

The elevator rose past the fifth floor and continued to climb past the sixth before finally stopping at "P." The doors slid open and they stepped out into a vestibule decorated with a mosaic on the wall done in the same tiny blue glass tiles as the big one in the bar they'd just left. Tall aluminum pots of blood-red geraniums gleamed on either side.

They walked into a large living room decorated with white leather sofas, dark mahogany accent tables, and brushed nickel lamps. The far wall was all glass, divided in the center by a double sliding glass door bordered with black iron. None of the lights were turned on, but the big room was illuminated by a magnificent view of the moonlit bay. Emilia walked toward the glass doors. There was a covered balcony, wide enough to accommodate several sets of matching wrought-iron tables and chairs. Seven stories below, the torches on the beach were dots of flame, the steel drums were silver disks, and the dancers were happy colors in slow motion. The ocean was a deep cerulean, the leading edges of the waves striped with froth as they rolled towards the shore.

"Corporate office in London matched the offer in Belize," Kurt said.

Emilia spun around. "*Madre de Dios*," she exclaimed.

Kurt nodded. "A 25 percent salary increase and this penthouse."

"Well. An eco-lodge in Belize or this." Emilia clenched her fists, suddenly feeling tight all over. The glow from the *mojitos* evaporated. "That's a pretty hard decision, isn't it?"

"I took Corporate's offer and signed a new two-year contract," Kurt said.

"Just like that?" Emilia's nails bit into her palms. "Don't you need to think about it?"

"This is a great space," Kurt said. "Double the size of my place on the fifth floor. Two bedrooms. Three bathrooms. Lots of closets." He moved closer to where Emilia stood by the window and spread his arms in an expansive gesture as if he was a realtor on one of those home shows that Sophia liked to watch in the morning. "This place is big enough for two, Em."

"Let's get back to the contract—" Emilia still wasn't sure she understood the situation. They were supposed to talk this out.

Kurt dropped his arms. "I'd like you to consider staying

here with me. Just like it was your own place."

Emilia felt her jaw drop.

"I know the hotel is all the way across town from the station," Kurt continued. "It would be a pain for you to drive to work every day. But you could at least live here on the weekends."

"You're asking—" Emilia's voice cracked and she coughed. She pressed a hand to her forehead and started again. "Are you asking me to move in with you? Live here? In this penthouse?"

"Yes." Kurt grinned at her discomfort. "That's what I'm saying. Live. Move in. Stay here. At least on the weekends."

Emilia sank onto one of the white sofas.

"After what you just said in the elevator, I didn't think it would be that hard," Kurt said, the grin fading. "All I'm asking is for you to stay the weekends."

Stay.

He thought he did, but Kurt didn't really know what he was asking. Emilia imagined the gossip that would fly around the police station, the way Silvio wouldn't be able to resist rubbing her face in it. There might even be an internal investigation to see where her seeming sudden wealth came from. A hundred bad scenes ran through her head, but they all paled in comparison with what would happen when Kurt inevitably met Sophia and Ernesto.

Emilia looked around, feeling overwhelmed and disoriented. For a moment, the elegant room flickered as if she was back in the midst of fire and smoke. Things snapped and shifted or maybe it was the sound of her own heartbeat.

Stay.

She took a deep breath.

Chapter 36

"I cannot believe I'm going to work looking like this," Emilia said as she looked at herself in the mirror.

"You look very trendy," Kurt commented, and handed her a glass of orange juice.

They were in his fifth-floor apartment, and the reflection that looked back at Emilia was no one she recognized. She hadn't planned on spending the night at the hotel and hadn't brought clothes for work on Monday. But her gym bag, which Kurt had retrieved from the Suburban, yielded black capri leggings, and his closet held a black linen *guayabera* shirt he'd never worn. She started with the capris and one of Kurt's white sleeveless undershirts, added her shoulder holster, and covered up with the *guayabera*, cinching it with her yellow belt from last night's outfit. Coming to mid-thigh, the *guayabera* was nearly a mini-dress, and if she fastened the middle buttons, her gun could not be seen. The flat black sandals she'd worn the previous night completed the look.

It was a far cry from her usual work outfit of jeans, tee shirt, and cotton jacket. The other detectives, and probably the holding cell guards as well, would undoubtedly notice that she was wearing a man's shirt. Emilia decided to cross that bridge when she came to it.

Juice in hand, she followed Kurt to the small bar by the galley kitchen, where he served her *norteamericano*-style scrambled eggs and bacon. Emilia settled onto a stool with her plate and enjoyed the unique experience of having strange food for breakfast in a man's home. She supposed she'd have to get used to waking up with him and eating new things.

Her life had changed forever with one decision, one sentence. Emilia had cried a little and confessed how scared she was. But at some point during the night she'd opened her hand and let go of whatever it was that had been so frightening. In the morning, when she'd looked at Kurt asleep next to her, the decision seemed so simple, so obvious.

It wouldn't be easy to implement the decision, but she would do it. Moving in together, even just for the weekends, meant sharing more about herself than she'd ever done. Sharing where she came from: her *barrio* and the church and the places in Acapulco that had made her into the person she was. Sophia's vacant happiness and Ernesto's fatherly status. The sharing would go the other way as well. Living with Kurt would mean making more of an effort to navigate his world and fit in at the hotel. She'd have to polish her high school English. Maybe ask Mercedes to take her shopping for some suitable clothes.

When they finished breakfast, Kurt walked her down to the lobby, carrying her sports bag. He put his free arm around her as they waited for the valet to bring the Suburban to the front, obviously not caring if hotel employees saw them together like that. Emilia did not pull away.

"Will you be all moved into the penthouse by Friday?" she asked.

"Yes." Kurt grinned. "I'll leave the second closet empty for you."

The big white vehicle rumbled into the drive.

Emilia reached up to kiss Kurt. "Thank you," she said.

Kurt touched her cheek. "What are you thanking me for, señorita?"

"Waiting for me, I guess," Emilia said. "For being the light when everything else is shit. Having shampoo that gets the smoke stink out of a girl's hair."

"I'll take that as a compliment."

"It is."

"I'll have a key made for you," Kurt said.

A motorcycle engine growled in back of the Suburban as Emilia pulled into the police station lot. She didn't recognize either the bike or the rider in a black leather jacket, but he was apparently another cop because as she looked in her rearview, he showed a badge and the gate guard let him pass through without stopping. The bike kept with her through the lot and pulled up beside her when she parked.

"Detective Cruz?" The rider flipped up the Plexiglas visor of the helmet. He was young, probably just a few years out of high school. "Courier message for you."

Emilia looked around. It was 8:00 a.m. There were a lot of people in the lot, cops coming to work as well as those getting off the night shift. She was standing in the open and felt relatively safe. "All right," she said "I'm Cruz."

"I'm to pass along to you that your union dues are paid in full for the year." The rider held out a large flat envelope.

"Thanks." Emilia dimly remembered Lt. Rufino mentioning something about union dues at a morning meeting. Dues were deducted automatically from paychecks, and she'd never given his comment another thought.

"Have a good day, Detective." The rider flipped down his visor and gunned the bike. He sped through the lot and out the gate.

The squadroom was quiet when Emilia walked in. Macias and Sandor were taking down the wall of photos and notes that represented the arson investigation. Loyola and Ibarra were at their desks, and as Emilia nodded good morning, she could smell the first cigarette of the day on Ibarra's clothes.

She left the envelope on her desk, stashed her bag, made a pot of coffee, and traded a few grim jokes with Macias and Sandor about taking out subscriptions to *Que Paso Acapulco*. Logging on with a mug by her elbow, Emilia was pleasantly surprised to see that her inbox contained fewer messages than usual. A few stood out. Captain Vega would be holding a news conference at 11:00 a.m. Lt. Rufino's condition was stable.

Reading between the lines of the message from Chief Salazar's office about Lt. Rufino, Emilia knew he would not be returning to the squadroom. Maybe they could find him an innocuous desk job. Or maybe he had enough years to simply retire. Hopefully he wouldn't drink away what was left of his life, but he certainly didn't belong in police work anymore.

Before she could wonder if Silvio would be appointed

acting lieutenant, or even if he'd get a permanent appointment as chief of detectives, he came into the squadroom, cell phone clapped to his ear with his left hand. Two fingers of his right hand were bandaged and a purple bruise stretched from knuckles to wrist. "I can't help you, *amigo*," he said to whomever was on the other end. "Rufino's still in the hospital as far as I know. Call Loyola. I just got a text that he'll be the acting."

There was a screech of metal wheels as Loyola shoved back his desk chair and bolted up, a look of shock on his bespectacled face. A former teacher, he was a good and methodical detective, but was still junior to Silvio. Moreover, he usually avoided tasks that required that he take a leadership role.

Silvio pointed to Loyola's cell phone on his desk. Loyola snatched it up. Ibarra moved around his partner's desk to look at the phone's screen as well.

As Emilia watched, Loyola's face tightened. "No," he groaned.

"No," Ibarra echoed. "Nice way to get told."

Silvio broke the connection on his own phone, and a second later, Loyola's phone started to ring.

"That'll be Castro," Silvio said. "Brother is in trouble and he wants help."

"What am I supposed to do for his brother?" Loyola exclaimed as his phone continued to ring.

Silvio shrugged. "You're the boss."

Loyola muttered something under his breath as he punched the button to answer his phone. He listened for a moment, rolled his eyes, and walked out of the squadroom.

"What was that all about?" Emilia asked.

Silvio dumped his leather jacket on the back of his chair, picked up his mug, and peered inside. Apparently deciding it wasn't too dirty, he went over to the coffee maker and poured with his left hand. "Salazar's office says that Loyola's in charge," he said after a swallow. "He can deal with Castro and his *pendejo* of a brother."

"His brother the Vice cop?" Emilia asked.

"Yeah." Silvio sat down in his desk chair and leaned back. The swiveling mechanism creaked. "Castro and Gomez are at some bank. Castro's brother was arrested two minutes after trying to exchange a big pile of euros. Apparently more than some new limit."

Emilia tried not to react. Salinas had come through! But Castro must have been so worried that his evidence-tampering had been noticed that he sent his brother to make the currency exchange, never considering that their names were so similar as to trigger any alert. "You're sure that's what he said?" Emilia verified. "His brother the Vice cop has been arrested? He doesn't have another brother?"

"Diego Castro Altaverde," Silvio said. "Your friend in the parking lot. Vice has already suspended him. Must have been on somebody's shit list over there and this was the last straw."

Emilia tried to suck in a yelp of laughter, but part of it escaped in a snort.

Silvio eyed Emilia over the rim of his mug. "You know anything about that?"

Emilia shrugged "Sounds like a question for the state attorney general's office," she said. She waved a hand at his bandaged right hand. He'd broken two knuckles but had refused to go to the hospital Saturday night until both Aguilar and El Rey Demonio had confessed. "How's the hand?"

"Nothing worse than anything I ever got boxing," Silvio said.

Loyola came back into the squadroom, muttering angrily.

Emilia finished her own coffee. She got out the binder of *las perdidas* and typed up everything she could think of about the search for Lila Jimenez Lata. She printed it off and combined it with copies of the original Missing Persons report and all the pictures of Lila to make a new entry in the binder. She had less to work with for Yolanda Lata, but she made an entry for her, too.

When the entries were done and she'd annotated their information in the binder's master index, she called a frequently used number for the local newspaper and placed an ad to run with a picture of Lila. The headline would read

DISAPPEARED and the contact number would be Emilia's cell phone. She charged 400 pesos to her debit card and promised to bring the picture to the newspaper office in the afternoon.

"Last resort?" Silvio asked when she hung up.

"Maybe something will turn up," Emilia sighed. She took out Lila's school picture and replaced the binder in her desk drawer.

"What's that?" Silvio gestured with his coffee mug to the envelope from the courier, previously hidden under the binder.

"Some union dues receipt," Emilia said. "Did you get one?"

"No."

She ripped open the envelope. There was no receipt in it, just a large glossy photograph of a family.

The husband and wife were about as old as Silvio. The boy and girl standing in front of them were maybe 10 or 12 years old. Puzzled, Emilia flipped the photo over. On the back was written "Oaxaca" and last Saturday's date. The notation meant nothing to her, and Emilia wondered if the courier had given her the wrong envelope.

She studied the image again. The photograph looked like an unsuccessful attempt to pose the family formally, but only the husband was looking directly into the camera. The others were smiling and talking to each other.

"*Madre de Dios*," Emilia gasped. She glanced around the room.

No one but Silvio had noticed her outburst.

Emilia handed him the photograph. "Torrez," she whispered.

Silvio's eyes narrowed as he examined the picture and read the inscription on the back. A corner of his mouth twitched. He gave a single nod and handed it back.

Emilia hastily shoved the photograph back in the envelope and tucked it under the binder in the deep file drawer of her desk.

Obregon had kept his word. Torrez was now officially dead and probably living under an assumed name with his family in Oaxaca, hopefully well hidden from the Sinaloa cartel.

She would never acknowledge that he was alive and knew that Silvio would keep the secret as well. There was a shredder in Lt. Rufino's office. She'd stay late, and when no one else was in the office, she'd destroy the picture.

A shadow blocked the overhead light as Emilia locked the drawer. Silvio stood by her desk.

He had his jacket over his shoulder and his bandaged hand in his pocket. "Want to go find a beer?" he asked.

Her watch read 9:30 a.m.

"Sure," Emilia said.

She logged off her computer and grabbed her shoulder bag.

When she stood up, Silvio stared at the capri leggings. "Forgot your pants today, Cruz?"

"Fashion advice from Franco," Emilia intoned as if she was a television reporter. "This morning we're talking about the ever-versatile white tee shirt."

The other detectives laughed as Silvio scowled.

As Emilia followed him out of the squadroom, she let her hand touch the edge of Rico's desk.

This time it wasn't for luck.

This time it was for good night.

Fin

About the Author

In addition to political thriller *The Hidden Light of Mexico City*, Carmen Amato is the author of the Emilia Cruz mystery novels set in Acapulco, including *Cliff Diver, Hat Dance* and the collection of short stories *Made in Acapulco*. Originally from New York, her books draw on her experiences living in Mexico and Central America. A cultural observer and occasional nomad, she currently divides her time between the United States and Central America. Visit her website at http://carmenamato.net and follow her on Twitter @CarmenConnects.

CPSIA information can be obtained
at www.ICGtesting.com
Printed in the USA
LVOW08s1931281116
514774LV00003BA/761/P